Acclaim for *Retribution*

"A sophisticated plot with nonstop action . . . For lovers of [the thriller genre] *Retribution* is picture perfect. . . . A certain hit."

—*Chicago Star*

"Grant keeps the pace rolling."

—*Orlando Sentinel*

"Grant has poured his entire imagination into this story. . . . The characters are vivid, the story is brisk."

—*Ocala Star-Banner*

"Reminiscent of Tom Clancy and Joseph Wambaugh. His ability to create riveting plot lines makes his books nearly impossible to put down. *Retribution* will undoubtedly establish Michael Grant as one of the country's finest mainstream thriller writers."

—*News* (Stuart, FL)

"Will likely find a lasting place among super-thrillers in the genre of Tom Clancy."

—*Daily News* (Naples, FL)

Books by Michael Grant

Line of Duty
Officer Down
Retribution

Michael Grant

HarperPaperbacks
A Division of HarperCollinsPublishers

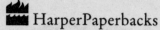 **HarperPaperbacks**
A Division of HarperCollins*Publishers*
10 East 53rd Street, New York, N.Y. 10022-5299

This is a work of fiction. The characters, incidents, and
dialogues are products of the author's imagination and are not to
be construed as real. Any resemblance to actual events or
persons, living or dead, is entirely coincidental.

A hardcover edition of this book was published in 1995 by
HarperCollins*Publishers.*

ISBN 0-06-109377-7

HarperCollins®, 🔥®, and HarperPaperbacks™
are trademarks of HarperCollins*Publishers* Inc.

Cover photograph by FPG/Telephone Colour Library

First HarperPaperbacks printing: September 1996

Printed in the United States of America

Visit HarperPaperbacks on the World Wide Web at
http://www.harpercollins.com/paperbacks

❖ 10 9 8 7 6 5 4 3 2 1

To Dorothy
From long ago and far away

ACKNOWLEDGMENTS

Thanks to Hank Harvey for showing me the innards of a modern office building and giving me a sense of its awesome complexities. Thanks to Tony Palmer for his information on state-of-the-art security devices. If there are any factual errors in this book, they are all mine, not theirs. Thanks to Rick Horgan for his terrific ideas and guidance. And, as always, a special thanks to Kathy Robbins for her support and guidance.

DR. JEAN MALROUX PUSHED through the highly polished revolving doors of the Downtown Athletic Club and quickly buttoned up his cashmere overcoat. His custom-fitted tuxedo offered scant protection against the blast of bitter January winds coming off the nearby Hudson River. Three men, similarly attired, huddled at the foot of the steps waiting for their car. One of them turned, smiled in recognition, and came up the steps with his hand outstretched. "Dr. Malroux, Dr. Walter Mankin. I just wanted to congratulate you on a brilliant talk."

Malroux shook the man's cold hand. "Thank you."

While the well-wisher rambled on about his own research with leukemia, a bored Malroux gazed over the man's shoulder at a poster board promoting the annual meeting of the Hematology Society. As he studied the glossy photograph of himself, which showed a handsome man with chiseled features and straight, slicked-back hair, he reminded himself to have a new one taken. Since his latest go-round with the plastic surgeon, he looked younger. *Still*, he thought, admiring the photograph, *even in that picture I look ten years younger.*

A gleaming black Lincoln Continental pulled up to the entrance and a young Hispanic, wearing a ripped ski jacket and a Mets baseball cap turned sideways, jumped out from behind the wheel.

The man who'd introduced himself started back down the steps. "Dr. Malroux, can we give you a lift?"

"Thank you, no. I have my own car."

As the Lincoln pulled away, the young man in the ski jacket turned to Malroux. "Your ticket?"

Malroux waved him away. "My car's parked around the corner."

As Malroux pivoted on his heel, the attendant gave him the finger. Just another cheap rich white guy who'd rather risk getting his car stolen than pay for garage parking and a tip, he figured. But the young man was wrong. The truth was that Jean Malroux refused to park in a public garage because he abhorred the thought of grungy parking attendants behind the wheel of his car. A Lamborghini was a temperamental precision instrument that required the kind of soft touch and finesse that few people—especially lead-footed car jockeys—possessed. He trusted only himself to drive it.

Colleagues and friends who were used to his eccentricities nevertheless cautioned him about parking such an expensive automobile on the streets of New York. But Malroux wasn't concerned. The car was insured, and as for his own safety, he pressed his elbow against his side and felt the reassuring bulge of his 9mm Beretta.

The truth was that Malroux enjoyed walking the

dark, mean streets of New York. On the two occasions when someone had attempted to rob him, all he'd had to do was display his weapon and it had been enough to send the cowardly would-be thieves scurrying back into the night.

Hot air billowing up from the manhole covers met the cold air and created swirling clouds of heated smoke. As he strode through the wispy steam clouds, the clicking of his Italian patent-leather shoes reverberated off the brick and concrete buildings. At the far end of the block, the sight of the apple-red sports car, looking purple under the mercury-vapor street lamps, gave him a rush of pleasure.

He quickened his pace, not out of fear but because the bone-chilling cold, which he loathed, was going right through him. Smiling, he comforted himself with the thought that this time tomorrow night he'd be sitting on the balcony of his condo in Cancun, savoring warm, humid breezes.

Malroux was so distracted by thoughts of Mexico that he didn't see the figure standing in the dark doorway across the street. The shadowy figure was a muscular man with the thick neck of an athlete, but his most unusual feature was his eyes. The large charcoal-brown irises blended with the black pupils, giving him the unnerving, blank-eyed look of a reptile.

From the moment Malroux turned the corner, the man had been following his every move. Without taking his eyes off the doctor, he pried a peanut from its husk with strong, thick fingers and popped the nut into his mouth, dropping the husk among a growing mound of shells at his feet.

Malroux climbed into his car and turned the key. The engine cranked, but it didn't catch. On the third try, the man, picking at his teeth with his tongue, stepped out of the doorway and casually walked toward the car.

He tapped the window. "Having a problem?" he asked.

Malroux angrily rolled the window down. "The goddamn car won't start. I can't believe this."

The man nodded sympathetically. "I used to fix sports cars. Temperamental as hell. Pop the hood. I'll take a look."

Normally Malroux would have been more cautious, but he was shivering and wanted to be on his way. The man raised the hood, leaned down into the engine compartment, and quickly reattached the two wires he'd disconnected earlier. "Try it now," he said, straightening up.

The doctor turned the key and the rumble of the powerful engine reverberated off the surrounding buildings. A relieved Malroux came out of the car. "Thanks. What was wrong?"

"Let me show you. It might happen again."

Malroux walked around to the front of the car and the man leaned over the engine. "See that vacuum hose?"

Malroux, being careful not to soil his cashmere overcoat, bent over and peered into the dark engine compartment. "No. I don't see it."

"Under the air filter. Lean forward so you can get a better look."

Malroux bent lower and squinted. "I still don't see it. Is it—"

Suddenly Malroux's left arm was whipped behind him and forced upward. The excruciating pain caused him to double over reflexively. A strong hand gripped the back of his neck and began forcing his face down into the racing engine. Through a numbing haze of surprise and terror, he noticed that the protective fan cowling was missing. His eyes widened as his face was forced nearer and nearer to the blur of whirling blades.

Snorting, he struggled to pull back from the churning engine, but the man had the advantage of leverage and superior strength. He felt his assailant's hot breath on his neck and smelled, inexplicably, the aroma of peanuts. Then the man whispered in his ear, "My name is Elgin."

Malroux stiffened. "*No*," he shouted above the roar of the engine, "I can explain. Please . . . "

"Too late for explanations."

As Malroux's face came closer and closer to the blades, the sound of the superbly tuned engine revving at 3000 RPMs grew louder and louder until it became his entire world. For one exhilarating, terrifying moment he and the engine were one. Then the spinning fan blades began to gnaw at his cheekbone and his agonizing shriek was drowned out by the high-pitched whine of the engine.

Elgin jerked his head back as a crimson spray of blood, tissue, and bone splattered across the underside of the hood. He felt the body shudder and go limp. Careful not to get caught in the whirling blades, Elgin lowered Malroux's limp arm toward the exposed fan. The blades caught the cashmere sleeve and yanked Malroux's arm into the engine compartment, wedging his head between the radiator and the hot engine block. The acrid smell of singed hair and seared skin filled the air.

Elgin took a towel out of his pocket and carefully

wiped the blood from his face and jacket. Then he went back to the doorway where he'd been standing and retrieved the car's fan cowling.

He walked the short distance to the Hudson River and tossed the part into the dark, oily water. While he waited for it to sink from sight, he popped a peanut into his mouth. Then he brushed the husk from his hands, ran his tongue around his teeth, and walked off into the frigid night.

WITH HIS BACK BRACED AGAINST the wall, Mike Devlin quickly ran through the checklist of everything he needed to do in the next fifteen seconds. The last item was the safety. His eyes flicked to the K&P submachine gun to visually make sure it was off. Then he glanced at the two men poised at the other side of the door. Clothed in tiger fatigues, with only their eyes showing through pullover black masks, they looked menacing and lethal. And that, of course, was the whole point. The sudden appearance of men in bizarre clothing, face masks, and jump boots created a much-needed psychological advantage for a SWAT team. That split second of surprise and confusion in the mind of the target could mean the difference between who lived and who died.

Devlin nodded imperceptibly to the men and held up one finger, then two. As he held up his third finger, one of the men, shouldering a stubby shotgun designed to take a door down, aimed it at the hinges and fired. The second man, kicking in the falling door, dove in, sweeping the left side of the room with his 9mm Colt automatic. Directly behind him came the first man, who covered the right sector. Devlin, the designated shooter, piled in behind them.

The room was small and dimly lit and the smoke from the shotgun blast further obscured visibility. Suddenly a closet door swung open. Devlin spun to meet the threat, but one of his team members was in his line of fire. He put his boot in the man's back and shoved. As the man sprawled to the floor, Devlin fired a quick burst.

"Jesus Christ! Mike." The man came off the floor and pulled his face mask off. "What the fuck's with you? Look. I got powder burns on the back of the mask."

Devlin snapped the safety on the submachine gun and popped the clip. "Nick, you're supposed to be in a combat stance, not standing around like a goddamn tourist."

"That doesn't mean—"

"All right, all right," a voice from a loudspeaker interrupted. The three men looked up at the tower overlooking the ceilingless room. "Report to the debriefing room. We'll discuss it there."

Devlin grinned up at the man in the tower. "Hey, Harry," he shouted. "We need to get different ammo for the shotgun. Way too much smoke."

Captain Harry Tedesco, the commanding officer of the New York City Police Department's Firearms and Tactics Section, punched the stop button on the VCR and turned to the ten fatigue-clad men seated in the small classroom at the police range at Rodman's Neck. "Okay, what went wrong with this exercise?"

Devlin, standing in the back of the room next to the coffee urn, said, "Nick was out of position."

Nick Mangi, still smarting from the kick and shaken by the close call with live bullets, snapped, "That's bullshit, Mike. I was—"

"Nick, you were standing up. You saw the tape."

Lt. Mike Devlin, just under six feet and one hundred seventy-five pounds of mostly muscle, walked to the front of the room, and all eyes followed him. He was not only the commanding officer of the TAC team but the best shooter in a room filled with the ten best marksmen in the entire police department.

"Guys," he said softly, "the average cop can expect to do his twenty years and never fire a shot in anger. That can't be said for you. When you volunteered for this unit you were told there was a very good chance you'd be shot at. So we gotta take this seriously. If this had been the real thing, Nick could have gotten himself, me, and probably Scotty killed." His eyes swept the seated men. "Am I right or wrong?"

All eyes were averted from his. Every man in the room knew he was right, but even these highly trained cops were reluctant to criticize one of their own. Devlin looked down at Mangi. The twenty-eight-year-old cop was one of his best men and he seldom made mistakes. But that was the whole point of this live-fire exercise: Make the mistakes here, not in a crowded apartment going up against a psycho with an assault weapon.

"Nick, am I right?"

Mangi squirmed in his chair. "Yeah, you're right," he said softly.

"I don't think so" came a forceful voice from the back of the room.

All eyes turned to Deputy Chief Charles Lynne, who'd been listening to the discussion with his habitual scowl. As the commanding officer of the Special Operations Division, Lynne was responsible for a variety of units ranging from the Emergency Service units to Scuba teams. A professional "headquarters man," he was uncomfortable commanding men in the field, and he was especially unhappy about this new TAC unit. Even though it was to be activated only when needed and the members had full-time assignments in other parts of the police department, he wanted nothing to do with these ten gung-ho, macho lunatics. Lynne was close to getting a promotion to assistant chief and it was no secret that he didn't want anything, or anyone, getting in the way of that promotion, especially some hotshot insubordinate lieutenant.

The stocky deputy chief stood up. "Lieutenant Devlin, I watched the exercise. You shouldn't have fired."

Devlin studied the chief with a confused smile. "Why not, Chief?"

"Because you almost shot one of your own men."

"No, I didn't."

"You fired too fast," Lynne snapped. "You didn't know what you were shooting at in that closet."

Devlin stopped smiling and fixed the chief with gun-metal-gray eyes that had turned hard. "I knew exactly what I was shooting at. The target was pointing a weapon at me and holding a child hostage. There was a kill zone between the hostage and the target and I took the shot."

Lynne, infuriated by Devlin's self-possessed certainty, snapped, "You couldn't know that. You only saw the target for a split second."

Just then the door opened and a range officer came in carrying the target that Devlin had shot. The chest of the cardboard figure pointing a gun was shredded. The child hadn't been hit. The other cops in the room whistled softly. They knew what it took to do that kind of shooting.

Lynne looked at the target and turned away, unimpressed. "Devlin, I let you talk me into a live-fire exercise, but effective forthwith, there will be no more."

Devlin faced the chief from across the room. "We need live-fire exercises," he said evenly.

Lynne's blotchy face turned crimson. "Goddamn it, *I* will decide what's best."

"For you or for us?"

Lynne, who'd started for the door, stopped and spun around. "What's that supposed to mean?"

"It means you're more concerned with your career than the lives of the men in this room."

An anxious Captain Tedesco stood up. "Mike, you're out of line. . . . "

"No," Chief Lynne said with a half smile. "Let the lieutenant say what's on his mind."

Nick Mangi, aware of Lynne's animosity toward Devlin, tugged at his lieutenant's sleeve. "Mike," he whispered out of the side of his mouth, "shut the fuck up."

Devlin pulled away. "Chief, ever since this unit started you've done everything you could to see that it failed. You wrote a report to the PC suggesting that the unit be abolished for legal reasons. When

that failed, you tried to get us assigned to another
division. The work of this team and the men in it are
too important to be entrusted to a headquarters hack
like you. You have no guts and you have no right to
make decisions for a unit like this."

The veins in Lynne's neck bulged. "Is there anything else, Lieutenant?"

"No. I'm finished."

"You certainly are," Lynne sputtered. "You're a
loose cannon, Devlin. As soon as I can draw up the
papers, you're out of this unit, and I'm going to do
everything in my power to see that you're put out of
the job."

After Lynne slammed the door there was an omi-
nous silence. Then Nick Mangi started to clap and
the others joined in. "Mike," Mangi said admiringly,
"you've got brass balls."

"And a brass brain," Captain Tedesco muttered.

Looking somber, Harry Tedesco walked with Devlin
out to the parking lot. He and Devlin had come into
the department together—almost twenty-two years
ago—and had been friends ever since. Devlin had
always been an outspoken hard-charger, even as a
dumb-ass recruit in the police academy. But five
years ago, soon after his divorce, that had all
changed. He became a man of mercurial moods,
shifting from maddening indifference to a stubborn
aggressiveness that bordered on self-destructive.
These wide emotional swings had put him at odds
with a lot of bosses and had ultimately cost him his
detective shield. In the last couple of years, he'd
settled into a pattern of indifference, registering

emotion only when the safety of his men was concerned. Knowing this, Tedesco understood the underlying reason behind Devlin's blowup with Lynne, but that didn't mean he liked it.

The two men stopped by Devlin's battered '89 Honda. "That was some shooting, Mike. Did you really see the target?"

Devlin grinned. "I wouldn't have shot otherwise."

Tedesco grunted. He'd personally timed the speed of the closet door opening to achieve the shortest window of recognition. He doubted that anyone except Mike Devlin, who had the quickest reflexes he'd ever seen, could have recognized the target and taken it out.

Tedesco kicked at the gravel with the tip of his shoe. "What Lynne said before was no idle threat. You're as good as out of the unit."

Devlin opened the truck and tossed his gear on top of a bald spare tire. "If Lynne is calling the shots, I don't want to be there."

"Goddamn it, Mike. That's no attitude. You—"

Devlin slammed the trunk down violently. "What *is* the proper attitude? It's all a big joke, Harry. Don't take it so seriously."

Tedesco ran his fingers through his hair in exasperation. "Your fucked-up attitude is screwing up any chance at a career in this department. Do you know that?"

Devlin grinned. "What career?"

Tedesco shot Devlin a look that was an equal mixture of bafflement and exasperation. "Don't you care?"

Devlin shrugged. "Not particularly."

Tedesco paused to wave to a carload of instructors

going to City Island for lunch. "You ever think of getting out?"

Devlin's gaze drifted toward the firing range across from the parking lot, where range officers were setting up new targets for tomorrow's exercise. Automatically, he estimated the distance and calculated where his point of aim would be to hit the center of the target. "Who doesn't?" he said finally. "But what would I do?"

Tedesco detected the uncertainty in Devlin's voice. "There *is* life after the job, you know. Maybe you need a change."

Devlin scowled as he climbed into his car. "Nothing stays the same," he said bitterly, and drove off.

Harry Tedesco stood in the parking lot and watched the Honda disappear in a cloud of gravel dust, not sure what worried him the most: the future of the TAC unit without Devlin or the future of Devlin without the TAC unit.

When Devlin got back to his office at the Dignitary Protection Unit of the Intelligence Division, a civilian aide handed him a telephone message. "Guy called this morning. Said it's important. Wants you to call him ASAP."

It was a message from a man named Kurt Floyd of Taggert Industries. Devlin didn't recognize the name, but he knew about Taggert Industries. The multinational conglomerate was mentioned at least once a week in the business section of the *New York Times*. He assumed Floyd was the security director. Devlin and other members of the unit got calls all the time from security directors asking for advice about executive protection.

A minute later Floyd was on the line. "Lieutenant Devlin, thanks for returning my call."

"No problem. What can I do for you?"

"I'm the personnel director for Taggert Industries. We have a possible opening for a security director and I was wondering if you'd like to come in and interview for the position."

Devlin laughed. "Who is this? Did Harry Tedesco put you up to this?"

"Excuse me . . . I'm sorry, Mr. Devlin. The name doesn't ring a bell."

Devlin was puzzled. "Then you have the wrong guy."

"I really think you should come in and see what we have to offer."

"How'd you find out about me?"

"We look for suitable candidates from various sources: headhunters, referrals, that sort of thing. I don't have your file in front of me at the moment, so I'm not sure exactly how we got your name."

Devlin found it hard to believe that a personnel director wouldn't know how he'd gotten his name, but he shrugged off his suspicions. What the hell, what did he have to lose? Maybe Harry Tedesco was right. Besides, after his clash with Lynne it might not be a bad idea to start looking for another job. "Okay, when do you want to see me?"

"Is tomorrow morning convenient? Say ten A.M.?"

The aide who'd given him the earlier message rushed up to Devlin's desk and dropped a copy of a department telephone message in front of him. He shrugged and mouthed the word "Why?"

Devlin read the message: *Effective 0800 hrs. Lieutenant Michael T. Devlin is transferred to the Manhattan Traffic Area.*

Traffic? Devlin crumpled the paper and tossed it in a wastebasket. "Ten A.M. will be very convenient, Mr. Floyd."

MIKE DEVLIN STOOD IN THE MIDDLE of the expansive terrazzo-tiled plaza and squinted up at the forty-story Taggert Tower, a tinted-glass-and-steel monolith that was the New York City headquarters of Taggert Industries. Yesterday, after he'd left the office, he'd gone to the library and spent several hours reading newspaper and magazine articles about the company. He'd even found a piece about the building in *Architectural Review* in which the author gushed that Shigeru Umemura, the award-winning Japanese architect, had succeeded in capturing the essence of the building's owner, Jason Taggert. Like the controversial CEO of Taggert Industries, the soaring, futuristic skyscraper overlooking Park Avenue was "bigger than life, aggressive in style, and rough around the edges." But most of all it "exuded naked power."

Taggert Industries, Devlin learned from more reading, was made possible by Jason Taggert's financial wheeling and dealing. Like so many others, he'd made millions in the "decade of greed," perfecting

the art of corporate takeovers and leveraged buyouts.
But unlike many of his contemporaries, he hadn't
succumbed to the siren call of more and more expan-
sion financed by mountains of shaky bond issues.

By the close of the eighties the boom had gone
bust and his fellow corporate raiders had seen their
paper empires crumble. But not Jason Taggert. He'd
been quietly jettisoning his unprofitable holdings
and consolidating his empire into an efficient conglomerate with wide-ranging interests in fast-food
restaurants, health-care products, pharmaceuticals,
computer software, and telecommunications. As a
result of his shrewd business acumen, Taggert
Industries emerged triumphantly in the nineties as
one of the top Fortune 500 companies.

Devlin took the elevator to the personnel department on the fifteenth floor. After a brief interview
with Charlie Floyd, who gave him a cursory overview
of the company and the duties of a security director,
the personnel director escorted Devlin to the fortieth
floor to meet Jason Taggert.

Devlin followed Floyd into a corner office that
was the size of a small auditorium. Two walls of floor-
to-ceiling windows looked south and west at a spectacular, if hazy, view of the Manhattan skyline.
Another entire wall contained a customized cherry-
wood wall unit complete with three TVs and VCRs
and a well-stocked bar. The remaining wall was filled
with commercially produced photographs and
posters flaunting the vast and varied line of products
produced by Taggert Industries.

Jason Taggert was sitting behind a massive glass
and ebony desk on which was prominently displayed
a brass plaque stating: CORPORATE RAIDERS ARE

PEOPLE TOO. With his square-jawed Hollywood good looks the CEO still looked very much like his 1984 *Time* cover photograph. He was in his late fifties, but trim and with a good tan that he spent a good deal of time working on at exclusive resorts in the Caribbean and the Mediterranean.

"Mr. Taggert, this is Mike Devlin," the personnel director said timidly.

Taggert, sitting in a tufted-backed spice leather chair, barely looked up from a report and pressed the intercom button. "Sylvia, ask Gloria Salazar to step in, would you?"

He stood up, and Devlin was surprised that he was a lot shorter than he appeared in his photographs. Devlin decided that it was his full-flowing mane of steel-gray hair that made him appear taller in photographs.

Taggert swept his hand toward an enormous conference table. "I think we can be more comfortable over there," he said in a tone that made the suggestion sound like an order.

It wasn't until Devlin sat down that he realized that the personnel director had disappeared.

Taggert glanced at his watch impatiently. "Coffee?"

"No, thanks. I just had some."

At a distance Taggert's face gave the impression of youth and vigor, but up close the CEO's face was covered with tiny networks of wrinkles. Clearly, all those hours in the sun had taken their toll. Drumming his manicured fingernails on the mirror-finished tabletop, the CEO seemed ill at ease. High-powered executives didn't spend a lot of time with job applicants. And that made Devlin wonder: Why *was* he spending this time with him?

Taggert clasped his hands in front of him, hands that betrayed his humble origins. They were big and rough, and not even the trappings of a daily manicure, English custom-tailored suits, and an expensive haircut could conceal that he'd once earned his money by the hard, physical labor required of a metal scrap dealer.

He fixed Devlin with pale blue eyes that had the intensity of twin lasers. "So," he said, "I understand you've been a police officer for twenty-two years."

"Yes."

"Doing what?"

"Various patrol precincts, then the Firearms unit, then the Detective Bureau. Now I'm in the Intelligence Division."

"I'm told you went to New York University."

Devlin nodded, impressed and curious. Without benefit of notes, Taggert seemed to know a lot about him.

"I presume Floyd filled you in on what we do here at Taggert Industries?"

"Briefly. I also did some research on the company."

Taggert's thick black eyebrows raised slightly, but Devlin couldn't tell if the CEO thought that was a good idea or a bad one. "Did you uncover anything in your research that you'd like to ask me about?"

Clearly, his tone said he thought it was a bad idea. Devlin was about to ask him why they'd sought him out when the door opened and a stunning woman, dressed in a smart black suit dress with a surprisingly provocative low V-neckline, strode in. She was wearing little makeup, but her finely featured face and delicate nose didn't need much help.

Devlin was mildly surprised by her sexy appearance.

From what he'd been reading, women in the workplace were supposed to dress down. But her manner and bearing seemed to blend well with her sexuality, enabling her to carry it off.

She ran her hand through her long auburn hair. "Sorry I'm late, JT. I couldn't get Birmingham off the phone."

Taggert scowled at the mention of the contentious board member. "Next time hang up on the son of a bitch. *That's* how you get him off the phone."

Salazar's laugh was open and deep-throated. "Easy for you, JT, you're the boss."

Taggert grunted. "Sometimes I wonder."

He looked over at Devlin as though he'd forgotten he was in the room. "Oh, Mike—it is Mike, isn't it?— meet Gloria Salazar, president of our health-care Division and my right-hand man."

"*Woman*, JT," she corrected, fixing Devlin with eyes the color of emeralds. "Right-hand *woman*. Pleasure to meet you, Mike."

As she leaned forward to shake his hand, her top came away slightly, revealing the soft curve of her breasts above a lacy black bra. Devlin's eyes flicked back to hers. She was watching him, but her smile gave no indication of approval or disapproval. She took a seat halfway down the table. Devlin didn't know if it was intentional, but with this arrangement he couldn't look at both of them at the same time. It was awkward for him, but he recognized it as a good interrogation technique.

"So," Taggert said, continuing the interview, "you were assigned to the Firearms unit. What did you do there?"

Devlin slouched in his chair. The body language,

which was intentional, said: *I don't give a shit if I get
this job or not.* "I was an instructor and member of
the department's pistol team."

Taggert regarded Devlin with one eye half closed
as though he were taking aim at him. "You a good
shot?"

"A very good shot."

Salazar, amused by his bold response, said,
"Apparently, modesty is not your strong suit."

Devlin shrugged. "It's not bragging if you can do it."

She studied him in silence, as though trying to
make up her mind about something. Then she said,
"You're absolutely right. I understand you also provide protection for visiting dignitaries?"

"Yeah, that's what I do now. Of course, the president and other big wheels have their own protection, but we know the city better than their security
people. Besides, the way things are today, a little
extra firepower couldn't hurt."

"Now you *are* being modest," Salazar said. "Five
years ago, you personally saved the life of the
Ugandan ambassador outside the Waldorf."

Devlin was surprised that she knew about that.
"No big deal," he mumbled. "Some ex-Ugandan who
didn't take kindly to the government over there tried
to make his point with a bullet."

"You threw yourself in the line of fire and dis-
armed the man," she persisted.

"It was an old, rusty automatic. We found out later
that it wasn't capable of being fired."

"But you didn't know that at the time."

"No, I didn't." Devlin turned away from her look of
admiration. It wasn't deserved. That year, the year that
Christine left him, he hadn't cared if he lived or died.

"Do you know anything about security hardware for buildings like this one—card access, alarms, that sort of thing?"

Taggert's question snapped Devlin out of his somber thoughts. "Oh, sure."

He was lying. Everything he knew about security hardware, which wasn't much, he'd learned from talking to the guys in Intel's tech services. But he'd decided that if he got the job he could always read up on it. How hard could it be?

While Taggert asked more questions that allowed Devlin to expand on his background, Salazar sat silently on the other side of the table listening. At times, Devlin saw each of them nod almost imperceptibly at his responses, as though they already knew what his answers would be.

Taggert sat back and brushed a speck of lint off his chalk pinstriped suit. "Mike, it's apparent that you've had a very interesting career in the police department." His white teeth flashed. It wasn't a warm smile, Devlin decided, more like the appraising look of a predator. "But you haven't told us anything about the TAC unit."

Devlin stiffened. Except for a handful of people in the department, no one knew of its existence. Back in the sixties, as terrorist and underground groups began to flourish, police departments large and small began to create SWAT teams to deal with the threat. But a string of New York City mayors and police commissioners, sensitive to pressures from the city's legions of special-interest groups, refused to follow suit. Instead, they turned the job over to the police department's Emergency Service Division. It was only after the bombing of the World Trade Center that a decision was made to form a specialized SWAT team. As part of the nervous mayor's plausible deniability plan, he'd insisted that the team be activated only when there was a real threat. At other times, members of this secretive, low-profile unit were to be scattered throughout the rest of the department.

During the progress of the interview, Devlin had been getting the odd feeling that both Taggert and Salazar already knew a lot about him. And now, with the question about the TAC unit, he realized that they must have had him investigated. He was irritated but at the same time intrigued. Why would this big company go to all that trouble?

"Why did you have me investigated?" he asked.

The blunt question caught Taggert off-guard, but an unperturbed Salazar stepped in. "It's quite simple, Mr. Devlin. This is a big company with a lot of valuable assets and we want the best security man that money can buy. We placed ads in the *Times*, but frankly, none of the candidates were suitable. So we went to a headhunter. He identified several promising candidates and we had their backgrounds checked. You"—she gave him a warm smile—"came out on top."

"Will you take the job?" Taggert tried to sound casual, but the impatience in his voice was unmistakable.

"I have a few more questions." Devlin saw the flash of annoyance cross Taggert's face. Obviously he didn't like wasting his time talking to job applicants. *Well, fuck 'em,* Devlin said to himself. *They asked me to come in.* "Mr. Taggert, why am I being interviewed by the top man in the company and"—he looked at Salazar—"his . . . right-hand *woman*?" He looked for a reaction in those big emerald eyes, but they revealed nothing. She must be one hell of a poker player, he decided.

Taggert sat back and made a bridge with his fingers. "I'm a hands-on guy. It drives my subordinates crazy, but that's the way I work. I like to get into the middle of things. Always have."

"The bottom line," Salazar interrupted, "is that we are a very large company and, as you can well imagine, we have a great deal of proprietary interests to protect."

"Simply put," Taggert said, regaining the floor, "if we can't protect our corporate assets, we're out of business. I have involved myself in the interview process because I think it's that important."

"I see," Devlin said. But he didn't.

During the interview he'd been trying to figure out Taggert and Salazar and what their relationship was to each other. Taggert wasn't hard to understand. The profiles he'd read in the business and trade magazines painted a pretty clear picture. Like many self-made men, he tried too hard to prove that he deserved his success, that he was an equal to all the Ivy League good-old-boy-network CEOs he rubbed shoulders with daily. He bolstered his perceived deficiencies by being tough, always in a hurry, and always getting his own way. No doubt he'd be a pain in the ass to work for; little abrasive guys with big egos always were. But Devlin could handle him. If not, he could always find another job.

Gloria Salazar, on the other hand, wasn't as easy to figure out. Why was she in on this interview? *Taggert's right-hand woman.* Clearly, he was the boss, but she acted like an equal and Taggert seemed to accept that. At first Devlin had assumed the two had something going, but after seeing how she held her own in the discussions, he dismissed that possibility. Jason Taggert didn't seem like the kind of guy capable of dealing with a mistress who'd tell him to go fuck himself.

His thoughts turned to himself. One thing was sure. This job was going to be a goof; big bucks and little stress. A real no-brainer. What more could he ask for?

The night before, while sitting on a bar stool in Toomey's, his favorite watering hole, he'd conducted a painful, in-depth assessment of his future with the New York City Police Department. And it had taken an astonishing number of martinis to finally confront, head-on, his bleak future.

Using olives to tally the score, he noted that he'd lost a good job in the Dignitary Protection unit. *One olive.* He knew he had a big mouth and his outspokenness had gotten him into more trouble than he would have wished. *Another olive.* He knew he should study for the captain's exam, but he'd lost interest in that. Besides, after his blowup with Lynne, his future in the department was pretty grim—as a lieutenant or a captain. *Another olive.* And finally, the prospect of working in the Traffic Division, the police department's version of Siberia, was really depressing. He added two olives for that. He carefully lined up the five olives on the bar.

On the plus side, the salary the personnel director quoted was a hell of a lot more than a lieutenant's; more than he ever dreamed he could make. *One olive.* He could work in a pristine environment with a reasonable expectation that no one would call him a four-letter word. That, he decided, was worth two olives. He placed the three olives in a separate row and, resting his chin in his hands, studied the results.

Tammy, a buxom, platinum-blond barmaid, came over. "Michael, what're you doing?"

"Deciding my future."

She poked an olive with a daggerlike fingernail the color of dried blood. "So what's what?"

"I'm trying to decide if I should leave the department—take a civilian job. Five olives says I shouldn't stay in the department and three olives says I should take the other job."

"What's the better score? High or low?"

Devlin regarded the olives with bleary eyes. "Damned if I know."

She picked up an olive and ran it across her voluptuous lips. "Seems simple enough to me." She leaned over the bar. "I'd sleep easier knowing your life wasn't in danger."

A transfixed Devlin watched her suck in the olive. "Tammy, what time do you get off?"

"Four. Same as always. Can you wait?"

"Yeah."

For the rest of the night that old devil, ambivalence, kept Devlin in a state of confusion. But sometime around five that morning, as he and Tammy were untangling themselves from the sheets, he announced, "I've made up my mind. I'm packing in the job."

Tammy's response was to slide her naked body on top of his and stick her tongue down his throat. "I'm glad," she whispered. "Now I won't have to worry about you getting killed."

"Are there any more questions?"

Taggert's voice brought Devlin back to the present. He wanted the job, but it was time to clear the air. As Devlin's eyes locked on the CEO, a little voice in his head said: *Don't say it. Don't blow this opportunity.* But it didn't do any good. For too long he'd been ignoring that voice of reason.

"Mr. Taggert," he said, "I think you're full of shit."

Salazar stifled a laugh while Taggert, who was not used to being spoken to in that manner, flushed. "Now wait a minute—"

"No, you wait a minute. None of this adds up. You want me to take a job I didn't ask for. Why? There are a lot of law enforcement people in this city who're just as qualified."

Taggert started to sputter a reply, but Salazar stopped him with a wave of her hand. "Mike, there *is* more to it than we've told you." She opened a folder and slid a piece of paper across the table. "This was sent to Jason."

Devlin looked down at the hand-printed note.

THE WAGES OF SIN ARE DEATH
JASON TAGGERT PREPARE TO DIE VERY SOON

"When did you get this?"

"A couple of weeks ago."

"Where's the envelope?"

She shrugged. "I guess we threw it away."

"Did you call the police?"

"No."

Devlin gave Gloria a sharp look. "Why not?"

"Taggert Industries has a corporate image to

maintain," she responded. "It's called goodwill, and, believe me, it's a very important and tangible asset."

"I understand that, but this is a death threat. If you think good PR is more important than finding out who sent this, you've got your priorities ass backwards."

Gloria leaned forward. "Tell me, what would the police do with this note?"

She had him there. She'd already figured out that the police would dust for prints and probably find nothing usable. With nothing further to go on, the squad would close it out. "Not a hell of a lot," he conceded. He looked back at the note. "Any idea who sent this?"

"No."

From what he'd read about in-your-face Jason Taggert, it was safe to assume that half the employees in the building were prime suspects. He looked at the CEO. "Do you take this seriously?"

Taggert made a face as if to imply that he had more important things to worry about, but Gloria said, "Yes, we do. We take this threat very seriously."

A pugnacious Taggert yanked opened his suit jacket. "I don't need a lot of protection. I can take care of myself."

Devlin groaned inwardly when he saw the automatic tucked into Taggert's shoulder holster. An armed and cocky bantam like Taggert was more dangerous to himself than any imagined assailant. As a range instructor, he'd trained a lot of corporate executives who'd convinced themselves that they needed to carry a firearm, but he'd met very few who could shoot worth a damn. If he took this job, his first order of business would be to get that gun away from Taggert—or at least take the bullets out of it.

Taggert got up and went to stand by the windows. Over his shoulder, Devlin could see the Statue of Liberty, which from this distance looked small and insignificant in the wide expanse of New York harbor. "This note got me and Gloria thinking about the level of security around here," Taggert said, gazing out at the panorama with his hands clasped behind his back. "We organized a task force to look into our security program and discovered that we need some serious tightening up."

"And that's why we want you to come aboard," Salazar said. "You've demonstrated your ability to protect lives, and with your extensive experience in security, we feel you're the right man for the job."

Taggert turned away from the window. "So, are there any more questions?"

Devlin heard the impatience in Taggert's tone and knew that if he kept breaking balls he wouldn't get the job. He wasn't sure how he felt about that. In spite of what he'd told Tammy last night, he was still struggling with the residue of ambivalence. "Just a couple more," he said.

Taggert's eyes narrowed. "Yes?"

"What would my job be?"

Salazar scooped up the note and put it back in the folder. "Threefold: provide personal protection for Mr. Taggert and tighten up the security in the building. Money is no object."

"What's the third part?"

She fixed him with her large green eyes. "Find out who wrote the note."

Devlin laughed. "How? There are no prints and you threw away the envelope."

The eyes turned cool. "You're resourceful. I'm sure you'll find a way."

Taggert buttoned his jacket, signaling that the meeting was about to be over. "What's your other question?"

"Who do I report to?"

"Me." Gloria Salazar fingered a string of pearls, her only adornment. "Is that a problem?"

Devlin met her unblinking gaze. He'd never worked for a woman, let alone one as attractive as Gloria Salazar.

"Nope," he said. "No problem."

Her eyes remained locked on his. "Anything else?"

"When do I start?"

"As soon as you can."

"I gotta give the department two weeks' notice."

"I'd like it to be sooner," Gloria said, "but very well."

AT EXACTLY 8:45 A.M. MIKE DEVLIN stepped off the elevator on the tenth floor and, following the directions of the receptionist, walked the length of the long corridor to room 1045. As he paused to study the sign on the door, which stated in small gold lettering SECURITY DEPARTMENT, the argument that had been keeping him awake every night for the last two weeks started up again. *It's not too late,* the little voice in his head said. *You can always pull your retirement papers and go back to the department. You wouldn't be the first—or the last—to change your mind.*

While he was considering his options, the door opened and a hefty woman holding an empty coffeepot rushed out, almost colliding with him.

"Oops, sorry," she said in a deep voice, gravelly from too many cigarettes. "You looking for someone?"

"I'm Mike Devlin," he blurted out. "I think I'm the new security director."

She peered at him over her wire-rimmed glasses with a bemused smile. "You're not sure?"

"What I meant was, I think this is where my office is. The receptionist said—"

"You've come to the right place, Mr. Devlin." She shifted the empty pot to her left hand and stuck her right hand out. "Carla Abbey. I'm your secretary. Welcome aboard."

"Thanks."

They both stared at the empty coffeepot. Carla broke the awkward moment of silence. "I was going to make the coffee."

"Okay."

"No, let me get you settled in first."

"No, go make the coffee."

"You sure?"

"Yeah." He wanted a few minutes alone. There was still time to leave, and if he did, he didn't want anyone witnessing his escape.

"Okay." She stepped aside and pointed at an office door. "That's yours. I'll be right back with the coffee."

Devlin was surprised at the size of his office. At Intel he'd shared less space with five other cops. And the view was a real change, too. Instead of the brick-wall side of a warehouse, he had a spectacular panorama of Park Avenue.

He spun around in the soft leather chair and slid open a desk drawer. It was empty except for a couple of paper clips, a crumpled telephone message, and a few pennies. Looking at the archeological remains of his predecessor, he wondered what had become of him and made a mental note to ask Carla.

The desktop contained the usual office equipment—pen and pencil holder, blotter, and tape dispenser. He smiled, fingering a shiny new staple gun. At Intel he'd shared one with seven other cops. Now he had his very own. Then he thought of Gloria Salazar's words: *Money is no object.* The well-appointed office was certainly a big change from the shabby, make-do atmosphere of the police department.

"I think I'll stay," he said aloud. Then he looked down at his hands. They were trembling slightly. *An anxiety attack or the residue of last night's excesses?*

The guys from the TAC unit had insisted on giving him a party at Toomey's and he'd had way too much to drink. Fortunately, even in his advanced state of inebriation, he'd had the presence of mind to refuse Tammy's offer to stay at her place. Had he gone, he knew he'd still be there. Daybreak was when Tammy reached the zenith of her sexual energy.

Carla came into the office with a full coffeepot and a Styrofoam cup. "Coffee, Mr. Devlin?"

"Yeah," he said, snapping out of his reverie, "I could use some."

After she poured the coffee, she sat down and peered at him over a huge mug that proclaimed in large black letters: DON'T TELL ME TO HAVE A NICE DAY, ASSHOLE! "I type, take dictation, and answer telephones," she said in a matter-of-fact tone. "I don't buy presents for wives and/or girlfriends and I don't balance your checkbook. I make the coffee, but I don't serve it."

Devlin held his cup up questioningly.

"This morning I made an exception. It's your first day on the job." She took a long, thin blue cigarette out of a pack and lit it up. "Do I call you Mike, Michael, or Mr. Devlin?"

Already Devlin liked this no-nonsense, late-fiftysomething woman. She reminded him of his first squad commander. He'd been a little rough around the edges, too, but when the chips were down, you could rely on him. "No one, not even the bank, can balance my checkbook," he said. "I'm not married, I don't buy presents for girlfriends, and Mike will do just fine."

She pushed her gray bangs out of her eyes. "Just so we understand each other. Is there anything I can get you now?"

That simple question stumped him. He wasn't sure what to do next. "How many people are there in the security department?" he asked.

"Fourteen guards and one supervisor."

"Do we have folders on them?"

"Yep."

"Okay. Bring them in. I guess I'll start there."

An hour later, a perplexed Devlin looked up at the guard supervisor sitting in front of him. As Devlin expected, the burly fifty-eight-year-old Tommy Nolen was a retired detective. What he hadn't expected was that few of the other guards had any law enforcement experience. According to their personnel folders they were mostly ex–mailroom clerks, ex–maintenance men, and ex-messengers.

"Tommy, how did this happen?"

Nolen scratched his snow-white hair. "The security department has always been a dumping ground for the misfits in the company. We're known as Department X."

"If they're misfits, why aren't they fired?"

Nolen shrugged. "I guess the company's afraid of lawsuits."

Devlin chuckled at the absurdity of it. "How can you run a security department with people who don't know anything about security?"

"Boss," Nolen said out of the side of his mouth, "I've been here for eight years, and let me tell ya, security has never been a high priority around here."

Devlin thought of Salazar's words: *Tighten up the security in the building.* She had some balls! It was like telling the captain of the *Titanic* to "tighten up" the hull.

"Are any of these guards worth spit?"

"A few. The rest are just putting in their time."

"You know any good retired cops looking for a job?"

"Yeah, a couple."

"Give 'em a call. If they're interested, tell them to call Carla and set up an interview. As I get new bodies in here, I'll get rid of the deadbeats."

Nolen scratched his chin. "Personnel isn't going to like that."

Devlin shrugged. "Fuck 'em. By the way, who was the last security director?"

"Some guy from corporate administration."

"A cop?"

"Nope."

"Law enforcement background?"

"I think he was an MP in Korea. He didn't know shit about security."

"What happened to him?"

"He was fired a couple of weeks ago."

Devlin looked at his desk calendar. That would have been around the time he'd agreed to take the job. Neither Taggert nor Salazar had mentioned that he was replacing a security director and he'd forgotten to ask. He stood up. "Come on, give me a grand tour of the building."

Nolen ran his hand across his beefy face. "I wanna warn you in advance. You're not gonna like what you see."

Nolen was right. Devlin stood at the entrance to the garage, which was open for public parking, and incredulously watched a steady flow of cars coming and going. "How come there are no security guards at this entrance?" he asked Nolen.

"We were told it's not our responsibility. The parking concession is a franchise. They're responsible for maintaining security."

"I guess no one around here ever heard of the World Trade Center," Devlin muttered as they headed for the elevator.

They went up to the lobby and Nolen took him behind the security guard station, where there was an impressive bank of TV monitors and blinking lights. Devlin watched a steady stream of people move on and off the elevators unchallenged. "How come no one is checking IDs?"

"We were told not to because it slows everyone down. Besides, the big brass really get pissed if you stop them."

Commandeering an elevator, Nolen took Devlin onto each floor for a tour, but when they came to the fourteenth, he bypassed it. "What's on the fourteenth floor?" Devlin asked.

"Research and Development."

"So let's take a look."

"I can't get on that floor. It's a high-security area and they don't use the regular access cards. All the doors are controlled by keypads."

"*You're* security and you don't have the passwords?"

"No."

"But what if there's an emergency and you have to get on the floor?" Devlin persisted.

Nolen, clearly embarrassed by Devlin's pointed questions, said, "We contact Dr. Biehl and he has someone meet us at the elevator. Of course, we've never had an emergency," he added quickly.

"Who's Biehl?"

"Dr. Kurt Biehl, the head of research and development."

Devlin grunted. "I think the good doctor and I are going to have to have a serious talk."

Most floors were very similar, with bland, pastel-colored walls, matching carpet, and mazes of claustrophobic cubicles that housed the dozens of departments and thousands of employees needed to run a major corporation.

But the atmosphere on the fortieth floor, where Jason Taggert, Gloria Salazar, and the other senior executives were ensconced, was markedly different. With its forests of potted plants, highlighted by strategically placed track lighting, modern paintings, and life-size sculptures, it struck Devlin as a cross between a very expensive whorehouse and the Vatican. The occupants on the executive floor seemed to float across the thick-pile carpet, speaking in reverential, ecclesiastical whispers. The good news was the eagle-eyed receptionist who challenged everyone coming off the elevators. She was the closest thing Devlin had seen to any real security.

Back on the elevator, Nolen took Devlin up one more floor. Most of the open cavernous space was unfinished concrete walls and floors and exposed wires and fixtures. But the southeast corner—much to Devlin's surprise—contained a sprawling penthouse apartment complete with formal dining room, kitchen, screening room, and other amenities.

Devlin peeked into the screening room. "How many rooms in this complex?"

"Including the maid's quarters, fifteen. The whole apartment is over twenty thousand square feet."

Devlin's eyebrows shot up. The house he'd grown up in on Long Island had been 2,000 square feet. "What does Taggert do with all this space?"

Nolen shrugged. "Hell if I know. He's got mansions and condos all over the place. He doesn't spend a lot of time in any one of them."

By the end of the building tour, Devlin had a roaring headache that was part hangover and part dismay.

When he got back to his office, Carla was brewing the third pot of coffee for the morning. A long beige cigarette dangled from her mouth. "There's an envelope on your desk from Gloria Salazar," she said, squinting through the smoke. "It's marked confidential, so I didn't open it."

Devlin thought he detected a note of sarcasm in her voice and wondered whether it had to do with Gloria or with Carla's not being sure she should open the envelope. Better learn the office politics, he thought to himself.

Inside the envelope was a handwritten memo from Gloria.

> *Welcome aboard, Mike.*
> *If you need anything call me.*
> *G*

Attached to the memo was Taggert's death-threat note: *The wages of sin are death/Jason Taggert prepare to die very soon.*

The note reminded Devlin of a seminar he'd attended on executive protection. One of the speakers, a gnomish psychiatrist who wore a rumpled tweed jacket, had given an impressive lecture about the meaning of threatening letters. Those that contained name calling and vague threats about future retribution were the mildest form. The most severe threat was one that talked of imminent death. Such letters, he cautioned, should be taken very seriously. Devlin picked up the letter, read the words *very soon,* and decided that the psychiatrist might be right.

Clearly, the security around here was a mess, but he'd take care of that shortly. The one thing he had to take care of immediately was Jason Taggert. It was cover-your-ass time. He grabbed the telephone and dialed a number. As the phone rang, he thought about Gloria's assurance that money was no object. He hoped she was serious.

"Tenth Squad, Detective Mangi."

"Nick, Mike Devlin."

"Hey, Mike, how's the outside world?"

"About as screwed up as the police department. Listen, I got a proposition for you."

"I'm listening."

"How'd you like to do some moonlighting? Make a few extra bucks."

"I gotta kill somebody?"

"No. Just stop my *boss* from getting killed."

There was a pause. "You serious?"

Devlin looked at the note again. "It's probably

nothing. It's just . . . I think I got a crank on my hands. Probably the worst thing we have to fear is someone pelts him with an egg. Still, no point in taking any chances."

On the other end of the line, Mangi chuckled. "Damn right. If he gets popped, you're out of a job. What do you want me to do?"

"Pick up Taggert here at the office and stay with him."

"All night?"

"Yeah."

"Mike, there's this thing called sleep. I indulge in it once in a while."

"That's why I want you to talk to the other guys in TAC. I can find work for all of them. You arrange it any way you want, but I want twenty-four-hour protection on this guy starting tonight. Can you do it?"

Nick thought about it. "We're talking nice money, right?"

"Always the accountant," Devlin said. "Don't worry about the dough—there may even be enough to buy a pair of glasses. It'll help your shooting."

Nick laughed. "Okay, I'll line up the troops. What about guys from *outside* TAC?"

"No. I want only top shooters."

"You sure you're not expecting trouble?"

Devlin glanced at the note. "Pretty sure," he said, sounding more confident than he felt. "Besides, with what we'll be paying, why shouldn't we get the best?"

"Okay, consider it done. Listen, I'm off tomorrow, so I can take the first shift tonight. When and where?"

"Six o'clock, my office."

Devlin hung up and sat back. "Gloria," he said

softly to the ceiling, "we're about to find out if money really *is* no object."

At 6:15 P.M., Nick Mangi and Devlin walked into Gloria Salazar's office. It wasn't quite as large as Taggert's, but it was more tastefully furnished with English antique furniture that complemented the stately Georgian decor.

Gloria was wearing a simple high-necked white silk blouse with ruffles on the front that on anyone else would have looked ordinary. Her hair hung loose around her shoulders and the auburn highlights gleamed like satin.

She hung up the phone and pushed her hair out of her eyes, a move that Devlin found pleasantly provocative. "How is it going so far?"

"Good. Gloria Salazar, say hello to Nick Mangi."

She shook Mangi's hand and gave Devlin a quizzical look.

"Nick works in the TAC unit," Devlin explained. "I've hired him and a few other cops part-time to provide around-the-clock protection for Mr. Taggert."

Gloria studied the trim cop. Dressed in a well-tailored charcoal-gray suit, white shirt, and maroon polka-dot tie, he looked more like an MBA graduate than a police officer. "Well," she said, turning her dazzling smile on Mangi, "they sure don't make cops like they used to."

The twenty-eight-year-old detective, unaccustomed to compliments from someone as attractive as Gloria, reddened. "It's all part of our training," he mumbled. "People involved in executive protection should blend in with the corporate culture."

Gloria looked at her watch and then at Devlin. "Sounds good to me. If there's nothing else, I have a meeting."

Devlin leaned forward. "This twenty-four-hour protection isn't going to come cheap," he whispered.

She looked at Mangi and shrugged, unconcerned. "If you're hiring the best, I guess not. Do what you have to do."

On their way to Taggert's office, Mangi said, "She's some piece of ass."

"Not bad."

"Not bad! She's dynamite." He elbowed Devlin. "You gonna hit on her or what?"

"Not my type."

"Bullshit. That woman is everybody's type."

Devlin had to admit that she was. He'd always been attracted to beautiful, elegant women, and the combination of his rugged good looks, easy manner, and ability to make being a cop seem like the world's most fascinating profession had made many available to him. But since his divorce he'd successfully uncomplicated his life by shying away from the tonier type. For the moment, simple, unpretentious Tammy was all he needed.

"Nick," he deadpanned, "I can't screw my boss. It wouldn't be right."

Mangi grunted. "Why not? You've been screwing bosses for years."

Laughing, they turned into Taggert's office just as the CEO was coming out of the conference room.

"Mr. Taggert," Devlin said, "I want you to meet your bodyguard, Nick Mangi."

The CEO stared at Mangi as though he were a lab specimen. "Bodyguard? What bodyguard?"

"I'm putting twenty-four-hour protection on you."

Taggert scowled. "I don't need twenty-four-hour protection. I told you—"

"I know most CEOs don't need that kind of heavy-duty protection," Devlin said in a confidential tone. "But that's because they aren't high-profile types like you. I'll bet nine out of ten people couldn't identify the top five CEOs in the country, but most people recognize you. You're practically a celebrity."

Taggert puffed up at the compliment. "Well, I don't know about celebrity, but my public appearances are beginning to generate notice."

"Right. That's why you need twenty-four-hour protection."

"Well, I don't know—"

"They're all from the TAC unit," Devlin whispered.

As Devlin suspected, Taggert's eyes lit up. "What are you packing?" he asked Mangi.

"Excuse me?"

"Gun," Taggert snapped. "What kind of gun are you carrying?"

"Oh, a Glock 19."

"How many in the clip?"

"Fifteen."

Taggert opened his suit jacket, revealing his holstered 9mm Beretta. "Mine's only a nine-shot, but I'm thinking of moving up to a higher capacity."

Mangi cast a baleful look at Devlin, who was suddenly busy brushing some lint off his lapel. Like most cops, Mangi was not in favor of civilians carrying firearms.

On their way to the elevator, Mangi hissed, "You didn't tell me I was going to be guarding Rambo."

Devlin grinned. "You can handle him. But if anyone starts shooting at you, I suggest you disarm Taggert first for your own protection."

"Thanks a lot," Mangi muttered as the elevator doors opened.

ELGIN TOSSED ASIDE THE HARD rubber ball he'd been squeezing and pressed the light button on his watch: 12:10 A.M. For almost two hours he'd been parked across the street from Jason Taggert's Sutton Place apartment building, watching the gold-braided doorman hailing cabs and opening limo doors.

The exclusive building overlooking the East River was home to some of the most wealthy and influential people in the city. Since he'd been watching, he'd recognized several familiar faces emerging from the steady stream of limos, including a famous violinist and a high-profile network anchorwoman.

He pried open a peanut and popped it into his mouth.

The frigid March air had long since sucked the warmth from the car's interior, but Elgin didn't turn on the engine: an idling engine attracted attention. The bone-chilling cold was uncomfortable, but he'd suffered worse. In Vietnam and Cambodia he'd lain in muddy ditches beside well-worn trails for hours,

patiently waiting for his target to appear while preda-
tory mosquitos sucked the blood from his exposed
flesh and scorpions skittered across his hands.

Most men would have found this a tedious vigil,
but Elgin's training and experience had made him a
patient man. This mission was too important to rush:
Haste meant a botched job.

He'd been staking out the building for almost a
week and last night had decided that this was the
place where Jason Taggert would die. Like most men
Elgin had stalked, Taggert was a creature of habit.
Two nights earlier, Elgin had broken into the building
through the service entrance and had discovered that
he could use the fire stairs to gain access to Taggert's
floor. Then it was a simple matter of picking the lock,
confronting Taggert, and— He patted the black bag
next to him that contained his surgical knives.

Suddenly his opaque eyes snapped up from the
bag and focused on Taggert's stretch limo coming
down Sutton Place.

To a casual observer it looked like all the other
gleaming black limos that pulled up in front of the
Sutton Place apartment building, but Elgin knew this
one was Taggert's. Three nights earlier, he'd smashed
the right parking light to make it easier to identify.
That, too, had been part of his training: Do what you
can to help identify the target.

From his darkened car Elgin saw the approaching limo slow down. After five nights of observing
the same scene, it was like watching a familiar play.
Each character performed his role exactly the same
way night after night. The limo always made a U-
turn, so Taggert, who sat on the right side, didn't
have to get out on the street side. Then, as he did

every night, the doorman came running out of the
lobby to open the door with his ever-present, ingratiating smile.

Elgin observed the robotlike regularity of the
play's participants with satisfaction. He knew what
would happen next. Taggert would get out and
punch the doorman's shoulder. They would both
laugh at some inane remark and Taggert would stroll
on into the lobby. Within an hour the lights in the
fourteenth-floor apartment would go out, signaling
that Taggert was in bed. Then . . .

Elgin stiffened as an unfamiliar figure emerged
from the seat next to the driver. The man, not part of
the usual cast, unbuttoned his trench coat and looked
up and down the street. He said something to the
doorman, who quickly opened the back door. As
Taggert appeared, the man took his arm and rushed
him into the lobby while scanning the street surroundings.

Elgin blinked once, slowly. *A bodyguard.* His first
instinct was to go ahead with his plan anyway. Killing
two men was just as easy as killing one. But it was
obvious from the way the bodyguard carried himself
that he was a professional, and there was no point in
complicating matters. He'd wait until the man left.
He popped another peanut into his mouth and
resumed squeezing the hard rubber ball.

By 3:00 A.M., long after the lights had gone out on
the fourteenth floor, Elgin realized that the bodyguard was staying the night. He started the car. As
he drove past the lobby, he saw the gold-braided
doorman seated by the front door, bathed in the blue
light of his portable TV. Elgin looked up at the building's upper floors. "There's always another way," he

said, squeezing the rubber ball until his forearm ached.

The next morning Devlin was back in his office reviewing the long list of security problems he'd spotted the day before. He'd barely waded in when he heard Carla's gruff voice in the outer reception area. Seconds later she was standing in the doorway. "Mike," she whispered, "are you expecting someone named Otis Royal?"

"Yeah, show him in."

Carla hesitated, then stepped aside as a six-foot-seven black man wearing a garish multicolored dashiki eased past her. "Michael," he said, flashing a mouthful of large white teeth. "It's good to see you, mon."

Royal's spirited bear hug enveloped Devlin, and as the smaller man stepped back, he gave his friend an appraising look. "Understated as usual, Otis."

The ex-con turned security expert had been Devlin's first telephone call, right after he agreed to accept the job. Devlin knew how to protect Taggert, but he didn't know a damn thing about protecting a building and that was where Royal came in.

Otis had begun his criminal career while still in his teens. Not a fussy man by nature, he'd entered Manhattan office buildings and stolen computers, fax machines, copiers, cellular telephones, and anything else that wasn't nailed down and had good street resale value. That he was six-foot-seven, possessed an impressive profusion of dreadlocks, and had a penchant for wildly colored dashikis should have been a hindrance to his criminal enterprise. Fortunately—or unfortunately, depending on your point of view—

Royal also possessed a winning smile and personality that could charm a wily secretary right out of her personal computer, which is exactly how he came into possession of most of his contraband.

It was inevitable that Otis's unusual description and his M.O. would eventually spread among the network of alarmed Manhattan security directors. Forced to change his M.O., Royal began breaking into the buildings at night. And as frustrated security personnel erected ever more sophisticated barriers to thwart him, he had to work harder and harder to succeed. In the process the high school dropout became a self-taught security expert, developing an encyclopedic knowledge of CCTV systems, microwave transmission, infrared motion detectors, and multiplex microprocessors.

When he was finally captured, an army of irate security cops and their employers wanted to send Royal to prison for life, but Devlin, one of the members of the NYPD task force cobbled together to capture him, suggested an alternative: Get him to go straight and tap into his expertise to train security directors on how to protect their buildings from the other Royals of the world. The disgruntled list of complainants reluctantly agreed and a grateful Royal, terrified at the idea of going back to jail, became Devlin's friend for life.

Devlin sat down and put his hands behind his head. "Like I was telling you on the phone, the security around here sucks and I'm counting on you to help me whip it into shape."

"That may not be as easy as you think, my friend." Otis still hadn't sat down. "One moment." He went out to Carla's office and returned carrying a painting.

A surprised Devlin eyed the brightly covered canvas. "For me?" Carla *had* been telling him he needed something for the walls. This particular painting wasn't really to his taste, though. "Thanks, Otis. It's real nice."

Otis admired the painting cradled in his arms. "It tis nice. A genuine Matisse."

Devlin studied the painting suspiciously. "A Matisse? Where'd you get it?"

The white teeth flashed. "From a wall in the executive dinin' room."

Devlin shot forward in his seat. "Jesus Christ! And nobody stopped you?"

"No one. I was prepared to tell them I was takin' it for a cleanin', but no one asked."

Gingerly, Devlin took the valuable painting from Otis and placed it on the floor. "Let's see how long it takes for someone to notice it's missing."

Otis fingered a dreadlock. "I am afraid you will wait a long time."

Devlin grunted. "Why do you say that?"

"Before I came here I took a tour of the buildin'." Royal opened a notebook and read from it. "In the lobby station there are two security guards tryin' to watch fifteen CCTV monitors."

"Is that too many?"

"It would be, but six monitors are not workin'."

"Why?"

"There's probably no maintenance contract on the equipment."

"What else?"

"There's too much piggy-backin'."

"Pig—?"

"When an employee uses his access card and others

follow him through the door. That's how I got on the ninth floor and stole the paintin'." He shut the notebook. "Such foolery, you know? I had free rein of the buildin'. Except for the fourteenth and fortieth floors, no one stopped me or even questioned me." He shook his head and his dreadlocks swayed from side to side. "Very bad, Michael," he said with his deep lilting voice. "Very bad."

"So what's the bottom line?"

"The bottom line is that your forty-story Taggert Industries corporate headquarters is a sieve, mon. It gives new meanin' to the term 'open-door policy.'"

Devlin grimaced. "I wish you'd stop saying 'your.'"

Royal grinned. "But it tis yours, Michael. You are the security director." The grin turned to a look of puzzlement. "Which leads me to a most interestin' question. How did you get this job?"

Devlin flashed his best Cheshire cat smile. "They said they wanted the best. Why? Don't you think I'm qualified?"

Royal snorted. "Brother, I *know* you are not qualified. For sure, you can put a bullet where you want it, but you know nuthin' about buildin' security."

"Well, hell, besides you, who does?"

"You would be surprised. There are a lot of people around with experience protectin' government buildin's and installations."

Devlin shrugged. "Maybe they hired me because of my charming personality."

Royal smiled broadly. "That must be it."

Devlin was making light of it, but he was troubled by Otis's question. *Why had they hired him?*

Carla buzzed him on the intercom. "Mike, Miss Falcone is here to see you."

Devlin jumped up. "Here comes the rest of the cavalry," he said to Royal.

Marie Falcone, an attractive, petite woman with short, curly black hair and large, mischievous brown eyes, came into Devlin's office lugging a stack of printouts. Devlin touched her lightly on the shoulder and kissed her forehead. "Hey, how are my godkids?"

"They're fine, Michael," she said in a pronounced Brooklyn accent. "But they would like to know where the fuck their godfather has been hiding."

Devlin scratched his chin. "I've been kinda busy," he mumbled.

Marie cocked her head, something she always did when someone, especially Mike Devlin, was giving her a line. "At *Toomey's*? Please. Spare me the bull-shit."

When Devlin turned to introduce Marie, he saw Otis Royal staring wide-eyed. It was a typical reaction from someone meeting Marie for the first time. Somehow the combination of those big brown eyes, a penchant for salty language, and an angelic face didn't square. And if that wasn't bad enough, listening to her discourse knowledgeably about computer security in her Hollywood-Brooklyn accent only added to the mental vertigo.

At thirty-five, Marie Falcone would still be an activist in the PTA and the scourge of the Canarsie school board had her life not been irrevocably altered one day four years earlier when Richie—her husband and Devlin's ex-partner—stopped at a convenience store to buy his weekly lottery ticket. While he was filling out the numbers, two kids high on angel dust came in to rob the clerk. Drawing his gun, Richie caught the dopeheads off–guard, but he didn't know

there were three of them. The third one, carrying a
sawed-off shotgun, popped up from behind an ice
cream case and blasted away with both barrels. The
kid was so wired he hit both his friends. But it was
Richie Falcone who caught the full impact of the
double–0 buck. He was dead before the paramedics
arrived.

Marie, who hadn't worked since her marriage, was
faced with the daunting prospect of raising eleven-
year-old twin boys. She knew she needed to make
herself marketable in the business world and took a
computer course at the local community college. It
was enough to get her a job with a law firm. To her
surprise, she discovered that she was very much at
ease in the arcane world of bauds, gigabytes, and pix-
els, so she went back to school and took every computer course in the catalogue.

The law firm took advantage of her growing
expertise and put her in charge of their extensive
computer system. Soon she was designing new systems and running training sessions. Then one of the
firm's clients, a small telecommunications company
that was getting ripped off by hackers, asked her to
help them make their system more secure.

The law firm, which had always been ill at ease
with her salty language and outspokenness, reluctantly recognized her expertise, but they were unwilling to pay for it. And so, much to the consternation of
her friends, including Mike Devlin, she left her reasonably well-paying job to start her own security consulting business.

In the beginning things were slow, but soon her
natural talent for uncovering and plugging security
holes in computer systems became known in the

industry and her client base expanded dramatically. In the four years since her husband's death Marie Falcone had become one of the most knowledgeable and sought-after computer security consultants in the city.

Devlin took the stack of papers from her. "What's this?"

"Oh, just some printouts of Taggert Industries' files containing salary records, passwords, and a piece of the company's five-year plan."

"Where'd you get 'em?"

"The garbage. After you called and said you needed some help, I started trashing the Taggert building."

"Trash—?"

"A hacker term—looking through the garbage for useful information."

Devlin made a face. "You were *garbage* picking for the last two weeks?"

"It's not as bad as it sounds. You only pick through the computer stuff. Of course, once in a while some asshole throws a chicken bone in with the printouts and things get messy, but usually it's real clean. You'd be amazed what you find."

"And you found . . . ?"

"A current list of passwords used by employees to gain access to the computer data banks."

Devlin chuckled. "Son of a bitch . . . "

"Yeah. The good news is that the sysops changes the passwords monthly. The bad news is that the schmuck throws the master list in the garbage without shredding it."

"What's a sysops?"

"System operator. The person who controls the computer system. The traffic cop."

"How'd you get the five-year plan?"

Marie shook her head disbelievingly. "It was embarrassingly easy."

"So let me in on it."

"Default codes."

"Huh?"

"Standard passwords that installers use while they're setting up the system. When they're done the sysops is supposed to get rid of them and create new ones. But sometimes that doesn't happen and you wind up with a system without a front door. Naturally, hackers know all the default passwords. We call them trap-door passwords."

Devlin rolled his eyes. He thought of Gloria again and mumbled, "Tighten security, my ass."

"Huh?" Marie looked perplexed.

Devlin rubbed his temples. "Nothing." He tapped the stack of printouts. "How did you get these salary records?"

"That was a little more difficult: Information about what people make is usually guarded like the friggin' family jewels. God forbid someone should find out! I had to run one of my customized password programs."

"How does that work?"

"I dial in and my program attacks the system by presenting a long list of common passwords—test, diag, password. Eventually one of 'em hits and I'm in. Another—"

"You mean some people use the word *password* as a password?" Royal interrupted.

"It's one of the *most* common," Marie replied. "Lots of imagination out there."

As she continued, Devlin began to feel less sure of

himself and his abilities. He was getting the clear message that the nature of white-collar crime was changing. Corporations no longer had to fear the big, burly guys with jacks, hammers, and torches. Sitting there in his office, Marie was painting the profile of the new criminal: any intelligent man or woman with a computer, a modem, and the willingness to break the law.

"You ever do any hacking, Marie?" Devlin was geniunely curious.

She chuckled. "Does a bee buzz? When I first got into computers, I became a phone freak. Lemme tell ya, it's a real rush dialing into systems and roaming through the electronic landscape. Then one day I heard the Secret Service raided the house of a friend of mine and confiscated all his equipment. It scared the shit out of me and I never hacked again. But the experience did come in handy. Now I make a good living stopping people who give in to the temptation."

"It takes one to know one," Royal pointed out knowingly.

"It couldn't hurt."

Devlin eyed the computer printouts with amusement. "Security around here really does suck."

"That would be putting it mildly."

He looked at his two friends. "Hey, guys, I'll be straight with you. I know how to protect Taggert— that is, if he's within arm's length. But I don't know diddly-squat about building security and computers. So what do we have to do?"

Royal frowned, contemplating the daunting task. "To tell you the truth, I would rather be stealin' from this buildin' than protectin' it. But that not bein' the case, I'll check out the present system to see what we can keep and what we'll have to scrap. Then you can decide what level of security you want."

"What are my options?"

"Anythin' from a simple computer-controlled card-access system to state-of-the-art biometric systems using eye-, voice-, and palm-print technology."

"All right. Do the survey. Then we'll decide what we need. Money is no object," Devlin said, cheerfully echoing Gloria Salazar's words.

"A good thing. You know, to do it right may cost a bundle."

Devlin turned to Marie. "What do you have to do?"

"Sit down with the sysops people. Personally, if it were up to me, I'd fire their lazy asses and—"

"Marie—"

"I know. That's neither here nor there. First, we get rid of all the old passwords and set up a program for password confidentiality. Then I gotta run virus checks on all the systems. Then I gotta design a security program that will protect the company's computers from outside attack. When that's done, I'll run a security-awareness training program for everybody."

"Sounds like that's gonna take a lot of time," Devlin said. "How's your schedule, Otis?"

"No problem, mon. I can give you my undivided attention for the next four weeks. Then I'm on a plane to Jamaica, where there's a lady waitin' for me," he said, smirking.

"How about you, Marie?"

"I have to juggle my schedule, but I can probably give you three weeks."

Devlin looked at the calendar. "That's not a lot of time. If we're going to get this thing off the ground, it'll mean a lot of OT."

"The timing is good for me," Marie said. "Spring break is coming up and I'm shipping the twins off to Grandma's house."

"Let me know when. I'll drive you to the airport."

"That's all right. I—"

"No. It'll give me a chance to see the kids."

Marie shrugged. "Okay, sounds good to me."

Devlin put his feet up on the desk and grinned. "Well, you're both gonna be real busy for the next few weeks."

Marie cocked her head. "You find this amusing?"

Devlin shrugged. "No need to stress out. You've found a few holes, we'll plug 'em. I didn't take this job to break my ass. That's what consultants are for."

Royal glanced uneasily at Marie and then back to Devlin. "You think it will be that easy, my friend?"

"Why not? With you handling the building hardware and Marie handling the computer software, it'll be a piece of cake."

"Michael," Marie Falcone said dryly, "a cake like this you've never bitten into."

THE NEXT MORNING DEVLIN barged through the revolving doors at exactly 8:00 A.M. He was in a foul mood and didn't care if anyone knew it. When he'd agreed to take this job, he'd had no intention of becoming a twelve-hour-a-day man, but four hours before a nightmare had caused him to bolt upright in bed, covered in sweat. He'd dreamed he was handcuffed to a potted plant in the Taggert Tower lobby and forced to watch an endless parade of men wearing ski masks empty the entire building of its furniture and equipment. After the dream he couldn't go back to sleep.

As he was walking toward the elevator bank, Tommy Nolen slid up beside him, looking surprised. "Hey, boss, you're in early."

Devlin shot him a look. "Yeah, I couldn't wait to get here."

"Good news," Tommy said, smiling. "I've got four cops who are interested in working here."

"You tell them to call Carla?"

"Yeah." Nolen scratched his head. "There's a little problem, though."

"What?"

"The other guards have heard they're going to be replaced and they're kinda upset."

"So we're even. I'm kinda upset that these clowns are my guards in the first place." He saw the distressed expression on Nolen's face and added, "Tell them that anyone who is doing a good job will stay. I'm only looking to get rid of the deadwood."

Nolen's face brightened. "They'll be glad to hear that."

Even in his mad-at-the-world mood, Devlin appreciated Nolen's attitude. The retired detective knew some of his guards were useless, but they were still his people. Devlin respected that kind of loyalty.

"Have you worked out access to the fourteenth floor?" Devlin asked.

"That's another problem."

Devlin stopped and spun around. "Why?"

"I went to Biehl like you told me."

"And—"

"He said no."

"Son of a bitch! *I'm* the security director for this whole building. You tell him ... Never mind," he said, getting on the elevator. "I'll tell him myself."

As soon as he got into his office he thumbed through the corporate telephone directory and dialed Biehl's number.

"Research and Development," a haughty female voice answered.

"I want to talk to Dr. Biehl."

She sniffed at his belligerent tone. "May I ask who's calling?"

"Mike Devlin. The security director."

"I'm afraid Dr. Biehl isn't available right now, Mr. Devlin. If you'd like to make an appointment—"

"No, I wouldn't. I want to talk to him *now*."

There was a pause. Then, "Just a minute. I'll see if he's free."

A moment later Biehl was on the line. "What can I do for you?" The voice was deep with a slight Eastern European accent.

"For openers, you can give me the access codes for the fourteenth floor."

"I'm afraid that's out of the question. I informed your guard this morning that—"

"What's out of the question," Devlin snapped, "is *not* giving me the access codes."

Biehl's tone was patient. "The fourteenth floor is the heart of our research and development. It contains highly secret information. I control the security on this floor and I will be responsible. I'm sorry, but you'll have to—"

"Hold it. Let me make this as simple as I can. The way I see it, there are two options: You can give me the passwords or I can go up there and take the door off the hinges."

"You wouldn't do that," Biehl said, sounding not at all certain of his convictions.

"You be at the elevator bank in three minutes and you can watch it happen."

Biehl cleared his throat. "Let me get back to you."

Five minutes later he called back. This time his tone was much more reasonable. "Why don't I meet you at the elevators and show you around."

"And you'll give me the codes?"

"Yes."

❉   ❉   ❉

The gangly Dr. Kurt Biehl possessed the disheveled look of a man who is so busy solving equations in his head that he has no time to tend to mundane chores like combing his hair and keeping his tie on straight. He was a lot younger than Devlin had imagined. He guessed the man to be in his early forties; surprisingly young, he thought, for someone to be the head of R&D at Taggert Industries.

Biehl peered down at Devlin through thick wire-rimmed glasses that made his brown eyes appear soft and childlike. "Mike," he said, offering his hand tentatively, "I think there may have been a misunderstanding."

Devlin, quick to anger and just as quick to cool down, was in a conciliatory mood. "No problem, Kurt. I think we're both interested in protecting the company's assets."

Biehl led Devlin to a reinforced steel door and punched a code on the number pad. The door sprung open and they stepped into a labyrinth of cubicled offices and wall dividers. Devlin had half expected to see a gathering of weird men in white lab coats hunched over smoking beakers. But except for an atmosphere that was more intense and somber, it could have been any of the other floors he'd visited earlier.

Devlin went on tiptoes and looked over a row of cubicles. "So where are all the mad scientists yelling 'It's alive, it's alive'?"

Lacking a sense of humor, Biehl smiled tentatively. "We do very little of that kind of pure research here. Our satellite labs located throughout the country

handle most of our experimental work. Here we concentrate on theoretical concepts and computer-based
mathematical solutions. We're also the central reposi-
tory for all of Taggert Industries' research. So, as you
can imagine, we have a great deal of valuable proprietary information to protect."

"I'll bet you do. Where do you store it?"

"On computer databases."

Devlin nodded. "Your computers secure?"

Biehl looked startled at the thought of them being
otherwise. "Of course. We have strict access and
password control."

Devlin grunted. Nice answer, but the good doctor
didn't know about a secret weapon named Marie
Falcone. She would determine just how secure the
R&D computers really were.

As they continued the tour, which led them
through a series of doors, all protected by keypad
locks, Biehl pointed out where the various research
teams worked. These teams, he explained, were
responsible for a wide variety of products ranging
from new drug development to looking for new
applications for fiber optics. There was even a section
that Biehl called "the center for pure research,"
where several men and one woman sat around all day
working on any idea that pleased them. They
appeared to be the happiest workers on the floor.

As they passed one room that looked like a library,
Devlin stopped. "What's in there?" he asked.

"That's where the research log books are stored."

"Log books?"

"Each scientist maintains a log book in which they
detail all their experiments, trials, tests, ideas. When
it's full, it's stored here."

"For how long?"

"Indefinitely. Those logs contain valuable information and we may need to refer to them at some time in the future. One throws away nothing in a research laboratory."

By the time the tour was over, Devlin had begun to like the shy head of research and development. When he'd first spoken to him on the phone, he thought he was dealing with an egomaniac with a power problem, but after having spent some time with him he realized that the soft-spoken man was genuinely concerned about protecting the secrecy of his work. He seemed a little suspicious and high-strung, but Devlin attributed that to the kind of work that he did. Devlin didn't know any scientists personally, but he supposed they were all odd in one way or another. And he was sure that his threat to kick the door down hadn't helped the man's mental stability.

Back at the elevator banks, Biehl reluctantly handed Devlin the list of passwords for the floor. "Frankly, I'm opposed to this," he said.

"Why?"

Biehl ran his long fingers through his already tousled hair. "I'm not impressed by the caliber of your security guards."

"Neither am I. But don't worry. Until I get some real talent on board, the only ones with these passwords will be me and Tommy Nolen."

Biehl nodded, but it was clear that he still wasn't overjoyed at the prospect of outsiders having access to his domain.

As Devlin stepped into the elevator, the doors started to close. "So, Doc," he said, holding the doors open, "what made you change your mind about giving up the passwords?"

Biehl's frown caused his two bushy eyebrows to meet over his nose. "I called Gloria Salazar to protest, but she said to do whatever you asked."

"Huh," Devlin said, letting the doors close. *And all this time I thought it was because I was such a smooth talker.*

As Biehl and Devlin were finishing up their tour of the R&D section, a bicycle messenger purposefully strode across the lobby downstairs and stopped in front of the directory opposite the elevator banks. Dressed in the typical bike messenger's uniform— one-piece spandex suit, sneakers, helmet, mirrored sunglasses, and canvas over-the-shoulder pouch—he looked like just one more of the multitude of messengers whose bicycles cut swaths on a daily basis through crowds of unwary pedestrians.

But Elgin's pouch contained nothing urgent—just a handful of blank envelopes and a few empty boxes. He wasn't in the lobby of Taggert Industries to deliver anything. He was here to receive. Information.

Last night the presence of the bodyguard had convinced Elgin that he had to develop an alternative plan. By training it was something he knew he should have done in the first place, but he'd been lulled by the ease with which Taggert had cooperated in making himself a target. He wouldn't make that mistake again.

He stood in front of the directory smiling at his good fortune. There it was: a list of all the departments and the names of department heads, including the office of the CEO: JASON TAGGERT, ROOM 4050. In less than three minutes Elgin had memorized a name assigned to several different floors.

Without a glance at the guards, he walked past them and got on the elevator, confident that no one would stop him. Earlier in the morning he'd been in the lobby and had observed that the guards stopped no one. He took the elevator to random floors and slowly walked the corridors, making mental notes of the location of exit doors, emergency lighting, presence of CCTV cameras, and electrical power closets. He didn't have the access card needed to get through the doors leading from the elevator lobby to the interior corridors, but that was no problem. He waited for an employee to use his card and followed him in.

On some floors a few people looked at him as though they wanted to challenge him, but he glared at them through his mirrored sunglasses and they turned away. Some even held the door open for him. This confrontational tactic worked on every floor except two. On fourteen no one would permit him to pass through the keypad-locked doors. On the fortieth an officious receptionist made him stand in front of the desk while she looked through the corporate directory for the room number of the name he'd given her. By the time she was able to tell him that he was on the wrong floor, he'd fixed in his mind the location of the CCTV camera, the fire exit doors, and, more important, Jason Taggert's office.

The EDP center was on eighteen and he was amazed that not even this floor, which housed the computer banks that were the lifeblood of Taggert Industries, was properly protected.

An hour later, he'd worked his way down to the

tenth floor. As he was passing a room marked SECU-
RITY DEPARTMENT, a gray-haired woman carrying an
empty coffeepot came out and eyed him suspiciously. He tried to stare her down, but the pugnacious woman wouldn't be intimidated. "Excuse me,"
she said, holding the empty pot in front of her like a
weapon. "Who are you looking for?"

"Walton Reade. I have—"

"Wrong floor. Reade is on eleven."

Elgin knew that. "Damn," he said, feigning annoyance. "The guy downstairs said the tenth." He turned
and started walking back toward the elevators. "I
don't get paid for walking all over this damn building," he muttered.

When Elgin got to the end of the corridor where
the elevators were located, he looked back. She was
still standing there, watching him. He got into the
elevator and punched the lobby button. It was time
to end the reconnaissance. The meddling old bitch
might call Reade to tell him a messenger was on the
way. He'd wanted to see more of the building, but
still the hour had been well spent. He'd return
another day. There was no rush. It was important this
be done right.

As he stepped off the elevator, pleased with what
he'd learned, his body stiffened. Jason Taggert was
walking toward him. Another bodyguard, not the
same as last night, shadowed him, his eyes constantly
sweeping the handful of people in the lobby.

With focused intensity, Elgin watched through his
mirrored sunglasses as the silver-haired CEO stopped to
joke with a cluster of employees waiting for an elevator.

Soon, Elgin said to himself, as Taggert brushed
past him to get on the elevator. *Soon.*

THE NORMALLY LIGHTHEARTED OTIS ROYAL was un-characteristically gloomy as he took Devlin for a tour of the building. He'd spent the past two days conduct-ing a top-to-bottom survey and he'd never seen a more poorly protected facility.

"You know," he said, continuing his nonstop criti-cism, "seeing a buildin' like this almost makes me wish I was on the other side of the law again. With what I could take out of here over a three-day week-end, I could retire to Jamaica and live like a king."

Devlin reached out and tugged Otis's bright yel-low dashiki. "But you wouldn't sleep the sleep of the just."

Royal chuckled. "I don't need much sleep."

"All right, all right," Devlin said. "Enough fanta-sizing. Tell me what it's going to take to button this place up."

Royal stopped in front of the lobby directory and nodded. "You be lookin' at Step Number One."

"Huh?"

"This directory is a road map for criminals, for goodness' sake." He ticked off the points on his long, slender fingers. "It tells me where every key executive office is, includin' the big man himself. It lists the departments, so I know just where to find the equipment I want to steal. It tells me that the security department is on the tenth floor, so I know to stay off that floor. It tells me who is on what floor. That way I can memorize names and if someone stops me I tell them I'm lookin' for someone on another floor and I'm lost."

"Sounds like you're speaking from experience."

Royal grinned broadly. "In the old days, I never met a buildin' directory I didn't like."

"Okay, it comes down today."

They stopped by the lobby elevator banks to watch a stream of people entering and exiting the elevators. "What's wrong with this picture?" Royal asked.

"The guards don't stop anyone. I noticed that the first day I was here."

"Correct. What else?"

Devlin shrugged. "I give up."

"Messengers and couriers shouldn't be allowed beyond the lobby, mon. Most aren't a worry, but others have thievin' on their minds."

"Okay, I'll take care of it. Maybe even write a memo," Devlin said. He smiled to himself, thinking of the promise he'd made when he was twenty: Never set foot in a corporation—always have a job doing something *real*. Something that affected people directly without a layer of paperwork in between. Funny how time changed your perspective.

"Another thing," Royal continued, "when they

opened this buildin' some damn fool ran wild with a stencil and labeled every door. So even a complete stranger can quickly find the computer rooms, the payroll department, the security department, the electrical closets, and the telephone switchin' rooms."

"Okay, we'll get rid of the signs."

Royal waved his access card at Devlin. "Also, there are forty-two hundred employees in this buildin', but over five thousand cards have been issued."

"Where are the other eight hundred?"

Royal shrugged. "Most have probably been lost or stolen. What's really incredible is that the company lets you keep your card when you leave or retire."

"It's cheaper than a watch?" Devlin offered.

Royal was not amused. "Michael," he said as if explaining patiently to a child, "they don't deactivate the card. *None* of these missing cards have been deactivated. Look"—he jabbed a long, slender finger at the Taggert Industries logo embossed on his card—"any rascal who finds one of these on the street knows exactly where it came from. Which means we have no idea who's comin' and who's goin'."

Devlin rubbed his temples, feeling the onset of a real head-banger. This security business was proving to be more difficult than he'd imagined.

As they walked behind the lobby security desk Devlin pointed at the vast array of monitors and blinking lights. "Looks pretty simple to me," he said, tongue firmly in cheek.

Royal grunted. "Simply awful is what it is. As I suspected, the blank screens mean the CCTV cameras or the monitors or both are out of order. This mornin' I checked all the alarms on the fire stairway doors. Forty percent of those are on the blink as well."

"Why?"

"Tommy Nolen tells me there's no maintenance contract for any of this equipment."

"When was this stuff installed?"

"A couple of years ago."

Devlin seemed puzzled. "Only two years old. It should still work."

Royal shook his head. "We're not talkin' about that TV set you use to watch the Playboy channel. This equipment is extremely delicate. It requires constant upkeep and calibration."

"So what's your recommendation?"

"The basic system is sound, but it's in serious need of an upgrade. Many of the CCTVs, monitors, and alarm sensors will have to be replaced."

"All right," Devlin said, realizing he was out of his depth. "How soon can you do it?"

"You give me the okay, I can start workin' on it right away."

"This sounds like it's gonna be big bucks."

Royal grinned. "You got it, mon. Big bucks."

"I'd better check with Salazar. I'll get back to you."

"Okay. Just make sure she understands that I can't replace everythin' at once. This is triage, mon. I'll take care of the most important things first."

By the time Devlin got back to his office he'd talked himself into believing that Otis would soon fix all the bugs in the system, at which point he could turn to more important things, like reading the sports pages.

His newfound euphoria quickly evaporated, though, when he read a copy of Taggert's schedule of public appearances for the next six months. The CEO was going to speak at twenty-seven luncheons and dinners, six of which were out of town. "Jesus H. Christ!" he shouted, slamming the paper on the desk.

Carla stuck her head in the door. "You called?"

"Did you see this?"

Carla sat down and lit a thin, lavender-colored cigarette. She'd never asked him if he minded the smoke. He did mind, but he figured there was no point in voicing his objection. She'd probably tell him to go fuck himself.

"Yeah," she said, blowing a long line of blue smoke toward the ceiling. "JT has been bitten by the political bug. About a year ago he gave an inflammatory speech to some of his right-wing buddies suggesting that the government should stop meddling in the affairs of America's downtrodden entrepreneurs. And, as they say, the crowd went wild. Old JT hasn't been the same since."

Devlin rested his chin in his hands. "Carla, so far you're the only person I've met here who isn't afraid to say what you think of Taggert."

She shrugged. "That's because I know him. He's like the Wizard of Oz hiding behind the curtain—just a little guy who makes a lot of noise."

"You've known him a long time?"

"I started out with him back in '75 when he was running a small scrap-metal company."

"No kidding. What'd you do?"

"Gal Friday. It was a real loose operation in those days."

Devlin sat back. "So how come you're not his number one secretary up on the fortieth floor?"

"It's a long story. The short version is that in the late seventies he hired a young kid just out of high school to do typing and stuff. She and I didn't get along, although I gotta admit she had brains. Soaked up information like a sponge. With his encouragement she went back to school and picked up a degree. Then she quit to get her MBA. By the time she came back, JT had started to make his move and his 'empire,' as they say, was expanding. He hired her as a VP of sales and she's been climbing the corporate ladder ever since."

"So who is this mystery woman?"

Carla squinted at him through a blue haze. "You've met her—the dragon lady of the fortieth floor."

Devlin stopped toying with a paper clip. "Gloria Salazar?"

"The same."

"No kidding," Devlin said. "So what was the problem between you two?"

"Gloria is superambitious and a control freak. You do things her way or not at all."

"So how come she didn't fire you?"

"She wouldn't dare. She has JT jumping through hoops, but one thing about him, he's loyal to his people. He'd never let her get rid of me."

"So she tossed you in the security department Dumpster."

"Yeah, this *is* sort of the company gulag. But things have picked up since you got here. It's kinda fun watching you get in people's faces." She gave him a strange look. "You know, it's even money you'll either shape this place up or get canned."

"Why's that?"

"You might have been a good cop, but you don't know a damn thing about corporate culture. You're a rock thrower in a city of glass."

Devlin smiled. "So what if I do break a few windows. I have the dragon lady in my corner."

Carla's laugh turned into a phlegmy smoker's cough. "Don't turn your back on her," she said, pounding her chest.

Devlin waited until Carla resumed normal breathing to ask his question. "Back then . . . now. Are Taggert and Gloria . . . you know, anything going on?"

Carla flicked a long ash into her empty coffee cup. "Who knows?" she said noncommittally.

Apparently there was more to the story than Carla was willing to talk about right now. Maybe someday he'd pry it out of her.

He changed the subject. "So JT is using these speaking appearances to test the political waters?"

"To see if he can walk on them is more likely," she said. "He's got a big ego, but he'd better watch his ass."

"Why?"

"JT is one hell of a businessman. He could bottle Ganges River water and give Perrier a run for its money. But there are visions of politics dancing in his head and he's not paying attention to business the way he should. He forgets this is a public company with an independent board of directors. If he's not careful Gloria will pull the rug out from under him."

"You think she can do that?"

"She can and she will if she gets the chance."

Devlin noticed the concern in her tone when she spoke about Taggert. "It sounds like you really like him."

"I do. Lord knows, he has his faults, but under that blustery exterior he's a decent man."

Devlin thought of the interview he'd had with Taggert. "Are we talking about the same guy?"

"What you and the rest of the company see is Jason Taggert, tough-as-nails CEO. What few people get to see is the Jason Taggert who put his first chauffeur's three kids through college. The Jason Taggert who still visits his first sales manager in a nursing home every month, which, incidentally, he pays for. Like I said, he's got his faults, but he's not the heartless bastard people think he is."

Devlin nodded, trying to reconcile this very different image of Taggert. He slipped the schedule in his pocket and stood up. "I'll be right back."

"Where are you going?"

"To see Saint Jason about cutting down on these appearances."

Carla snorted. "You might as well ask him to cut off his right hand. Those speeches feed his ego. He's not gonna give 'em up."

"We'll see."

Carla flicked a long ash into a potted plant on Devlin's desk. "If I were you, I wouldn't worry about those speeches now. I'd start worrying about the shareholders' meeting."

Devlin stopped halfway to the door. "What shareholders' meeting?"

Carla pushed her bangs out of her eyes. "No one told you about it?"

"No. When is it?"

"Next week."

"Next—He'll have to cancel it. I'll need more time to—"

Carla shook her head. "You don't cancel a shareholders' meeting. They're planned a year in advance and they're required by corporate charter to be held on a certain date."

Devlin slumped up against the wall. "Where is it going to be held?"

"The grand ballroom of the Excelsior Hotel."

"Who's invited?"

"Anyone who owns one share of Taggert Industries stock."

"That's gotta be a lot of people."

"More than you think. A lot of people buy stock that's held in the brokerage house's name. So there's really no way to tell if someone is a stockholder or not."

"So you're saying I can't keep anyone out?"

"You got it."

Devlin rolled his eyes. *Let's hope the person who wrote that note is just some old lady who needs a pen pal. Otherwise, things could get sticky real fast.*

Preoccupied by the bombshell Carla had just dropped on him, Devlin had to wait outside Taggert's office while a skittish band of pinstripe-suited men with flip charts and reams of spreadsheets tucked under their arms filed into the inner sanctum to make a presentation. Within minutes, even through thick oak doors, Devlin could hear Taggert's shouts and curses. Fifteen minutes later, the pinstripers reappeared, looking battle-weary and defeated as they shuffled toward the elevator banks.

Devlin walked into Taggert's office just as the CEO was slamming the phone down on the hapless man responsible for preparing the flip charts. "Look at that," Taggert said, jabbing his cigar at the offending chart. "The goddamn numbers don't add up. I got

an army of bean counters on my payroll and not one
of 'em can add worth a damn."

Devlin glanced at the multicolored bar graph
showing a bewildering array of figures and percentages, and shrugged. If he had the rest of the week he
couldn't find the mistake on that chart. He was surprised that Taggert had, but then he remembered
reading about the man's legendary ability to absorb at
a glance staggering quantities of numbers and statis-
tics. It was a feat that would have been remarkable in
a Wharton MBA, but it was nothing short of miracu-
lous for a high school dropout like Jason Taggert.

The CEO glanced at his watch. "I got another
meeting in five minutes. What's up, Devlin?"

"I wanted to talk to you about your speaking
schedule."

"What about it?"

"I think it would be a good idea to cut down on
the public appearances."

Taggert stuck out his well-tanned jaw. "Why?"

"Until I get a better handle on who sent you that
note, you should keep a low profile."

Taggert shook his head. "Out of the question. I've
made a commitment to speak to these people and I
keep my commitments."

"Mr. Taggert," Devlin said in a reasonable tone,
"it's not easy guarding someone in public places,
especially crowded hotel ballrooms and convention
centers."

Taggert scowled. "What are you talking about?
They guard the president in places like that all the
time."

Devlin groaned inwardly. As far as Carla was concerned, this guy might be a candidate for the Mother

Teresa Award, but the son of a bitch had an ego the size of Central Park. Struggling to maintain a reasonable tone, he said, "The president has hundreds of Secret Service agents and local police to protect him. All I have is me and a handful of bodyguards."

"And they're good, too. That guy Mangy is very good. He really knows his guns."

"Nick *Mangi* is good. So are the other guys, but they don't have big red S's on their chests. There's only so much we can—"

The voice of Taggert's secretary came over the intercom. "Mr. Taggert, your eleven o'clock is here."

Taggert punched a button. "Bring them in, Sylvia." He looked up. "Listen, Devlin, your job is to protect me. You just gotta work a little harder, that's all."

Before Devlin could say anything else, the secretary appeared, followed by three smiling Japanese men in identical blue suits. Already forgetting that Devlin was still in the room, Taggert rose with a smile to greet them.

MARIE FALCONE HAD BEEN IN the building since
seven that morning going from office to office checking the security of computer workstations. As she
entered Gloria Salazar's outer office, the secretary, a
young woman with long brown hair, was heading for
the door. "May I help you?" she asked Marie.

"Yes, I'm doing a computer survey in the building." She dangled an authorization memo signed by
Devlin.

"Oh, right," the secretary said. "I know about this.
Listen, I gotta deliver this fax." She pointed to her
desk. "There's the computer. Help yourself. I'll be
right back."

Marie slid behind the secretary's desk and, as
she'd been doing all morning, inspected the usual
places where forgetful employees jotted down their
passwords. She checked under the keyboard; she
read the half-dozen Post-it notes stuck to the side of
the monitor and the adjacent wall; she checked the
back of the company telephone directory where

there were two pages of penciled telephone numbers; and she checked the Rolodex under *C* for
computer and *P* for password. Nothing. So far so
good.

The monitor screen was blank. She pressed enter,
and PASSWORD: appeared on the screen. She tried
some common passwords: TEST, GUEST, and HELP,
with no results. The secretary's name was Gale
Bruno. Marie typed GALE, then BRUNO. Again, nothing. Marie smiled, pleased that she'd found a secure
terminal. She was about to get up when she noticed
a photograph on the desk of the smiling secretary
holding a chubby baby. She read the caption: *James's
first birthday*. Marie typed JAMES, then JIM. Nothing.
Then she typed JIMBO and groaned as the screen
filled up with a list of files.

She read through the long list and selected a
promising one called TALGON MERGER. Just as she was
about to bring it up, a sharp voice behind her said,
"What are you doing?"

Marie hit the exit command, clearing the screen,
and turned around to face Gloria Salazar, who was
standing in the doorway with her hands on her hips.

"Marie Falcone," she answered, wondering why
the hell she was feeling so guilty. "I'm doing a computer security survey for Mr. Devlin."

"Where's my secretary?"

"She went down the hall to deliver a fax."

"You shouldn't be at her computer without—"

"She gave me her permission." Marie could feel
her anger rising.

Gloria pushed a wisp of hair away from her eyes.
"What exactly were you trying to do?"

"I'm checking the workstations to make sure

they're secure. Sometimes employees leave passwords around or—"

"That's ridiculous. Gale is very conscientious.
Besides, I trained her myself. She knows how to protect the confidentiality of this office."

"I'm sure she does," Marie said noncommittally.
She wanted to tell this arrogant bitch that she'd broken into her secretary's files in less than three minutes, but she knew that Salazar's response would
probably be to fire the woman.

Gloria came over and looked down at the blank
screen. With a sideward glance Marie stared envi-
ously at Salazar's expensive and well-tailored suit and
alligator pumps. Her perfectly manicured nails—a
high-gloss coral—matched her earrings. *Marone!*
Marie had to admit it: the bimbo really knew how to
dress. But then again anyone could look good in
those expensive clothes.

"I'll have to talk to Mike," Gloria said. "I don't
think it's a good idea for you to be fooling with these
computers. You might accidentally erase something."

It took all of Marie's effort to smile. "How could
I," she asked innocently, "if the computer is secure?"

Gloria's eyebrow went up, but before she could
respond to Marie's sarcasm, the secretary reappeared. Gloria turned toward her with a flash of
anger in her eyes. "Gale, come in. I have some dictation for you." She turned to Marie. "Miss—?"

"Falcone," Marie answered through clenched teeth.

"Are you through here?"

"Yeah." Her instinct was to tell this plastic excuse
for a woman what she thought of her, but she didn't
want to get Michael in trouble.

Without another word, Gloria spun on her expensive heels and went back into her office, trailed by her apprehensive secretary.

"Michael," Marie said softly a few minutes later as she entered Devlin's office, "I do not like that fucking woman."

The quiet tone made Devlin uneasy because he knew from experience that the quieter the tone the more pissed she was. He handed her a cup of coffee. "Don't take it personal. Gloria is a human buzz saw. She—"

Marie trained her big brown eyes on him. "I don't give a rat's ass if she's an atom bomb. I'm not going to take that crap from anyone."

Devlin retreated behind the safety of his desk and studied Marie over his coffee cup. He knew that one of her most difficult-to-cope-with—and yet most attractive—features was her volatility. No one knew that better than Richie Falcone, her husband. It still made Devlin smile, remembering the tough street cop cringing and stuttering when Marie was on his case.

When he'd decided to bring Otis Royal aboard, Devlin anticipated some flack from the uptight corporate suits, but he didn't expect a problem with Marie—especially one between her and Gloria Salazar. *Jesus.*

"I'll talk to her," he said. "It'll be okay." He quickly changed the subject. "So what fun facts did your survey turn up?"

Marie rolled her eyes. "It's worse than I thought. I checked fifteen workstations and found the passwords for seven of them. Using intuition and luck, I

hacked into four more. Extrapolating those numbers,
73 percent of the computers in this building are not
secure."

Devlin wondered if this poor level of security was
atypical, or if the only difference between Taggert
Tower and any other Manhattan office building was
that they'd gone over it with a fine-tooth comb.
"Okay, give me a list of the computers you hacked
and I'll send a memo to Glo—Salazar. Once we identify who—"

Marie put her cup down. "Michael, get real. I'm
not going to tell you whose computers I broke into."

"Why not?"

"Think about it. A report like that will embarrass a
lot of high-level executives, and guess who's going to
bear the brunt of that embarrassment? The secretaries. Assuming they don't get fired, they'll take a lot
of shit from those pompous asses. Besides, I'm going
to need their cooperation if I'm to make this company computer-security conscious. As far as the individual workstations are concerned, you can issue a
report in general terms, but no names." She grinned
maliciously. "On the other hand when it comes to the
EDP guys, fuck 'em. They think they know everything."

Devlin heard the gloating in her voice and said,
"What did you do?"

"I had a preliminary meeting with them yesterday.
The sons of bitches actually laughed in my face when
I suggested that they might have a security problem.
So this morning I let them watch me while I hacked
their systems. They went bonkers!"

Devlin cradled his head in his hands thinking of
the flack he was going to get from that. "Marie—"

"Hey, those guys deserve to have their noses rubbed in it. Not for nuthin'," she said, in a low confidential tone, "but it wasn't quite as simple as I made it seem. I did the serious hacking at home. By the time I sat down with them, I already knew all the passwords. I let 'em look over my shoulder and I said, 'Hmm, let me try a few default passwords. . . . Uh, how about a couple of educated guesses'. . . . You should have seen the looks on their faces when I got in."

In spite of himself Devlin had to laugh, imagining the sight of Marie busting into their multimillion-dollar computers like a runaway train. "Do you think maybe you were too tough on them?"

"Absolutely not. These guys get paid a lot of money to run a system properly. Hey, if a guy is dumb enough to leave default passwords in the system, he deserves to get his nose rubbed in it."

"You're a fanatic."

Her grin vanished and she was suddenly very serious. "Maybe I am, but this computer technology is a powerful force. It's the future. We have to respect it and we have to understand it."

Devlin suddenly saw her in a different light. She wasn't just a tough-talking mother supporting two sons, a woman struggling for recognition in a man's world. She was a professional, one of the few who truly understood cyberspace and its implications for companies like Taggert Industries. It was a strange feeling, being with a woman who could outthink you in a lot of areas that mattered. He'd never had to worry about that with Tammy.

Carla stuck her head in the door. "You wanted an appointment to see Salazar? Seems she wants to see you, too."

"When?"

"Right now."

Gloria Salazar paced up and down on the plush maroon carpet while Devlin tried to look contrite. But it wasn't easy. She had terrific legs and Devlin was finding it hard to keep his mind on business.

"It's only ten-thirty," she said. "And already I've received four phone calls from EDP managers complaining about your Miss Falcone."

"*My* Miss Falcone? Gloria, it was *your* idea to do a survey on the computer system."

"I know that, but I didn't think you'd hire someone to conduct guerrilla warfare on my systems managers."

"They're ticked because they got caught with their pants down. The bottom line is that Marie exposed a real security problem in the company's computer systems."

Gloria stopped pacing and sat on the edge of her desk. Her skirt hiked up, not enough to be immodest, but enough to get Devlin's attention. He wondered if she was doing it on purpose, didn't realize she was doing it, or didn't give a damn either way. "I understand Marie Falcone is a personal friend," she said.

"Yeah, she is."

Gloria stared intently at Devlin. "She's an attractive woman. Anything between you two?"

Devlin bristled at Gloria's implication, but he wouldn't give her the satisfaction of showing it. "I hired her because she's one of the best computer security consultants in the business," he said evenly. "If you don't believe me, check it out yourself."

"I have."

Devlin didn't know which surprised him more—
that she'd checked out Marie or that she admitted
doing it. "And?"

Gloria shrugged. "They say she's good."

Just then the secretary came in carrying a silver
tray with bone china cups and saucers. Devlin,
who'd been in Gloria's office at least once a day
since he'd been hired, had heard that she had her
coffee served on fine china, but he didn't believe it.
Even Jason Taggert drank his coffee from an old
chipped mug.

"Leave it on the credenza, Gale. I'll take care of it."
She turned to Devlin. "How do you like your coffee?"

"Black."

She handed him a cup and saucer and offered a
tray of miniature danishes. He waved them off.

Gloria piled three onto her plate and sat down
behind her desk. The secretary's arrival seemed to
break the tension.

"These are so good," she said.

"Better watch it," Devlin cautioned. "They look
fattening."

"Don't I know it." She studied the tiny cheese
Danish in her hand. "I figure each one of these
babies is about an extra half hour on the Stairmaster."

Judging from the firmness of her body, she spent
a lot of time climbing stairs. But Devlin wondered
when she found the time. She was in her office
before seven every morning and he'd heard that she
seldom left before nine at night.

Gloria dabbed at her mouth with a linen napkin
and smiled. "Mike, you and your 'deadly duo' have
caused a lot of anxiety throughout the building."

"The computer people? They'll just have to—"

"Not just them. I'm talking about removing the lobby directory. It's made a few executives very unhappy."

"Why?"

"For some of these men the directory is a form of recognition. Name-up-in-lights kind of thing."

Devlin studied her carefully, trying to decide if she was kidding, but her face said she was serious. "Kinda petty, don't you think?"

She poked at some crumbs on her plate with her index finger. "You don't understand the corporate world. What may appear petty to you can be a crisis for someone else. A couple of years ago, we rearranged the office space on this floor and an executive lost his corner office. He tried to commit suicide. But it's not just the executives. The secretaries are annoyed with your order banning the messengers from the floors."

"Why?"

"It means they have to go down to the lobby."

"So?"

"It affects their image of themselves; they see it as assault on their position in the pecking order."

Devlin shook his head in bewilderment. "And I thought the criminal mind was devious and unfathomable."

She put her cup and saucer down on the edge of her desk. "Mike, you need to learn about the corporate culture. It's an important survival tool." She studied him with her emerald eyes. "I can help you with that."

Devlin, not exactly sure of what was implied in that offer, didn't know how to respond. The telephone saved him. Gloria picked it up. "Okay, Gale. I'm on my way."

She stood up. "Duty calls. A meeting with JT."

Devlin put his cup on the credenza. "Gloria, about these changes I've been making—"

She put her hand on his arm and squeezed. It was the kind of intimate gesture she did often. He didn't object, but he wondered what she would say if he did that to her. "Keep it up," she said. "They're long overdue."

"There'll be more and I'm sure I'm going to ruffle some feathers."

She opened the door and gently rubbed his back as she pushed him ahead of her. "If anyone has a problem, tell them to call me."

FOR THE NEXT FRANTIC WEEK, Devlin left Otis and Marie to their work while he scrambled to prepare for the upcoming shareholders' meeting.

First he met with the people responsible for organizing the annual event. The meeting went badly from the beginning. Every time Devlin mentioned security, Neil Thornburg, the self-important VP of shareholder relations, winced as though Devlin had uttered a profanity. It didn't take Devlin long to realize that the respective roles of shareholder relations and corporate security were at odds. Thornburg saw the shareholders' meeting as a wonderful public relations opportunity for Jason Taggert to bask in the glow of a roomful of happy, dividend-receiving stockholders, while Devlin saw this same meeting as an open opportunity for every psychopath in New York City to show up and take a whack at his boss. One thing was certain: If the writer of the threatening note was serious, at least one individual wanted Taggert dead.

After an hour of heated discussion that quickly escalated into haggling, then thinly veiled threats, and finally to not-so-thinly veiled threats, Thornburg reluctantly agreed to the use of portable metal detectors and X-ray scanners. But the sticking point was how to make the security devices as unobtrusive as possible.

Earlier in the meeting Thornburg had waxed eloquent about the theme of this year's meeting: spring— as in rebirth and renewal of Taggert Industries as it advanced toward the new millennium. Half in jest, Devlin suggested that the metal detectors could be festooned with flowers and leaves so that they would resemble garden arbors. To his surprise, Thornburg loved the idea and made a note to talk to a floral arranger.

Next, Devlin visited the hotel security director and almost gave the medical-disability-retired detective his second heart attack with his long list of demands and requirements.

Finally, he called Nick Mangi and told him he wanted to hire every TAC cop available.

The night before the shareholders' meeting, the entire board of directors, and enough employees to take up two whole floors, converged on the hotel. While the directors partied with Taggert, platoons of employees went about the behind-the-scenes business of making the annual shareholder meeting appear as effortless as a small-town church social. Swarms of men and women spread out to check audio levels, visual aids, seating arrangements, flowers, and meeting room assignments, while others held last-minute parleys with the catering staff to ensure that everything from ice-water pitchers on the dais to enough coffee and buns for a hundred-plus shareholders was in readiness.

The hotel staff was busy as well. While teams of maintenance men moved partitions, others vacuumed carpets and set up folding chairs and tables. Amid the organized chaos of preparing the ballroom for the next day's meeting, no one paid any attention to one worker, dressed in the khaki uniform of the hotel's maintenance section, who was kneeling by the speaker's lectern. Elgin slid a box onto the shelf under the podium. It fit perfectly, as he knew it would. Two days earlier he'd measured the space.

He'd decided on a nail bomb because it was simplicity itself. All that was required was a small charge of explosives, a detonator, and a handful of nails. The detonator ignited the explosives and sent the spinning, razor-sharp nails propelling through the air at high velocity, shredding clothing, lacerating skin, and penetrating bone.

The nail bomb was also a very versatile weapon of destruction. In Nam he'd constructed hundreds of them, each specially tailored to the need at hand. Harass the enemy? Place the device at knee height, reduce the amount of explosives and the number of nails. The idea was to destroy the target's legs so that his buddies would have to carry him to an aid station in the rear. Kill the enemy? Set the device at chest height. Increase the explosives and number of nails. Make an example of someone? Add even more explosives and more nails. The body of a man shredded by thousands of nails was barely recognizable. But the sight of the mutilated corpse always left a lasting impression on a village of VC sympathizers. Elgin's personal touch included dipping each nail point in human feces. Even if the man survived the initial impact, he was certain to die a slow, lingering death from infection.

He reached around behind the box and connected a wire sticking out of a hole to another wire that he'd run from an electrical box. The thin wire was barely noticeable nestled among the clusters of microphone and audiovisual equipment wires.

As he spread a napkin over the box and placed a tray with a water pitcher and glasses on top, he pictured in his mind's eye what would happen tomorrow. At detonation, the thousand nails he'd meticulously attached to the lump of C-4 would rip into Taggert's midsection, instantly disemboweling him. Elgin had carefully calculated the charge so that Taggert wouldn't die immediately. He smiled at the thought of a roomful of Taggert's admirers witnessing his slow, excruciating death. *What goes around comes around, asshole.*

Everything was in readiness for tomorrow morning. His work completed for now, he made his way to the back of the ballroom where two men in dark suits, obviously cops, were watching the installation of portable metal detectors.

"Tight security, huh?" Elgin said to them.

One of the men turned and gave him a cursory glance. "Yeah."

"Expecting trouble?"

The other man, possessing a perpetually suspicious squint, studied Elgin. "No, pal. Are you?"

Elgin grinned. "I sure hope not. Hey, you guys have a good night."

°   °   °

Ten minutes after Elgin left the ballroom, Devlin and
Harry Tedesco, whom Devlin had hired to supervise
the security detail of twenty-five men, came in to
watch four maintenance men install a three-foot-
square quarter-inch steel plate directly in front of the
seat where Taggert was to sit.

"What do you think, Harry?" Devlin asked as one
workman covered the plate with the decorative table
bunting.

"Looks good to me. Think we'll need it?"

Devlin wished he knew the answer to that question. How seriously should he take an unsigned letter
that hadn't been followed up by an overt act? Was it a
warning from a guy who was out for blood or somebody's sick idea of a joke? He was inclined to think
the latter, but he wasn't about to bet Jason Taggert's
life on it. "I hope not," he said finally.

"Does Taggert know about these precautions?"

Devlin grunted. "Hell, no. He's dangerous enough
as it is."

"That reminds me. I told Nick you wanted him to
try and get the gun away from him. He said he'd try
but that it would be easier to convince a pimp to join
the priesthood."

Devlin grinned. "Nick is resourceful. He'll think
of something." He tapped the hard steel underneath
the bunting and felt better about the prospects of
keeping his boss alive—at least through this meeting.

Tedesco pressed his finger against his earpiece
and paused. Then he said "Ten-four" into the microphone attached to his wrist. "Taggert's here."

"Good. Who's got him?"

"Mangi and Tyler. They're going to stay in his suite with him all night. I checked it out earlier. There's no balcony and the nearest windows are fifty feet away. I told Nick to keep the drapes drawn."

"Who'll be outside in the corridor?"

"A four-man detail. They'll rotate two on and two off."

"All TAC guys?"

"Yep." Tedesco tapped the earpiece. "I'm impressed. Same communications equipment as the Secret Service. Can we have this stuff when the meeting is over?"

"'Fraid not. I only rented it."

Tedesco shrugged. "No harm in trying."

Devlin knew Tedesco was only half kidding. Every unit in the NYPD, including one as essential as the TAC unit, was underfunded and, consequently, short of modern equipment. He knew Harry would love to have the use of such state-of-the-art communications equipment. In the two weeks he'd been with Taggert Industries, Devlin had come to really appreciate the saying "Money is no object." He scanned the neatly aligned rows of folding chairs. Tomorrow they'd all be filled and he wondered if the letter writer would be in one of them.

"Harry, are you all set with this room?"

"Yep. I have people stationed at all the entrances and exits. From now on any hotel employee coming into the ballroom will have to come through the east corridor doors. My people will scan them with portable metal detectors and check for ID."

"Good. No ID, they don't get in," Devlin said firmly. "I went through hell getting those photo ID badges."

"How'd you convince the hotel to issue the badges on such short notice?"

"Shekels. I had to pony up the cost of processing the badges."

When he'd made his unusual request to the hotel security director, the man had thought that Devlin was overreacting. But he didn't understand the special burden that came with protecting a public figure. It didn't matter how well you planned for his safety. In the executive protection business, if your subject was killed or injured, then by definition you didn't do enough.

Tedesco studied his friend's face. "You're looking a lot better than you did the last time I saw you. You like this new gig?"

Devlin nodded. "Can't complain about the pay. And protecting people is something I'm good at. Computers and security hardware—well, that's another story. I have Marie and Otis, but still, I don't like being in a position where I don't know what the hell's going on."

Tedesco raised his eyebrows. "Am I hearing correctly? Does the who-gives-a-shit Mike Devlin I know actually give a shit?"

Devlin chuckled. "Let's not get carried away. There's nothing in this world that's worth taking seriously. It's just that I want to understand this technical stuff better. That's all."

Tedesco nodded. In the beginning he'd had his doubts when Devlin told him he was leaving the police department to take this security job. He was afraid that it was a knee-jerk reaction his friend would soon regret. But he was satisfied with what he saw. Devlin gave no sign that he missed the police department and he seemed to be enjoying himself. "You've got a good job here," Harry said to Devlin. "Don't blow it."

"How could I blow this job?"

"By not taking it seriously."

A grinning Devlin patted Tedesco's cheek. "Don't worry, Mom. I'll be fine."

"I hope so," Tedesco said.

It was after eleven by the time Devlin finished inspecting the hotel from the basement to the roof with the wheezing, overweight hotel security director trailing after him.

Then he went to his room and unpacked his overnight bag. He was just about to call room service for a nightcap when there was a knock at the door to the adjoining room. *Oh, God,* he thought. *With my luck I'm next door to that pompous ass Thornburg.* Reluctantly, he opened the door and to his surprise found Gloria Salazar standing there. The black silk pajamas were certainly modest—sort of a boutique version of a martial-arts uniform. Still, between the pajamas and the long auburn hair hanging down to her shoulders, she looked nothing like the high-powered, no-nonsense executive he'd grown accustomed to seeing at the office.

"Did you have dinner yet?" she asked.

"No ... well, sort of," he stumbled. "I had a burger a few hours ago."

She turned around and went directly to a mirrored cubicle containing a wet bar. "Come in. I thought it would be a good idea for your room to be next to mine. Want a drink?"

"I was just thinking about that."

"What'll you have?"

"Scotch?"

"Chivas Regal okay?"

"Fine. A little ice."

He slid into a wing-back chair. As he watched her prepare his drink, a peculiar sensation come over him and he realized immediately what it was: It was a heady experience having a powerful, beautiful woman cater to him. He'd felt the same sensation when she'd served him coffee in her office.

Since that first day in Taggert's office, he'd had ambivalent feelings about her. He was naturally attracted to her, but he knew from his own painful experience where that could lead and he was determined, for once, to follow the advice of his inner voice. It was telling him to stay away from her.

He thought he'd been kidding when he'd told Mangi that he couldn't get involved with his boss, but maybe that was it. In any event, he'd made up his mind. Their relationship would be strictly business.

She handed him his drink, sat down on the edge of the bed, and kicked off her satin slippers. She was drinking scotch, too, but it was mostly water. "To the end of this madness," she said, holding her glass in the air.

Devlin, who'd been admiring the firm outline of her thighs through the silk, looked up. "You don't like shareholders' meetings?"

"God, no. They're such a waste of time. Every year we do this ridiculous dog-and-pony act to entertain a bunch of pathetic people who come for the free goodies package and a chance to give advice to the head of a big company."

"Is that any way to talk about the shareholders?"

Her eyes flashed in anger. "Shareholders," she said with contempt. "They own a few shares and they think they know how to run the business. Well, they're wrong. Running a company like Taggert Industries is a full-time job requiring a lot of blood, sweat, and tears."

"Okay," Devlin said, shocked by the vehemence in her tone. "I was only kidding."

Gloria pushed the hair out of her eyes and sat back with a long sigh. "Do you know we have forty-nine employees staying in this hotel tonight, not counting the board of directors?" she asked in a more moderate tone. "Do you have any idea of the cost of all this in terms of money and lost man-hours? And when we take the show out of town it costs five times that and takes three times as long."

Devlin could only grin at the incongruity of the moment. Leaning back on the bed with her hair cascading around the pillow, she was breathtakingly sexy, but her hard-edged, businesslike speech didn't match the image.

"What's so funny?" she asked.

"Nothing. It's just that you're so . . . intense about everything."

"I guess I am." Idly, she pulled at a loose strand of hair and for a moment looked like a sad little girl. "I find it hard to relax. I never go on vacation without a notebook computer, a cellular phone, and a portable fax machine." She looked up, caught him staring at her, and the little girl vanished.

"A hamburger isn't dinner," she said, jumping up from the bed. "I'll order something from room service and you can tell me what you're doing to protect our founder."

By the time Devlin concluded telling her about the extra guards, the metal detectors, and his meeting with Thornburg, which she thought was hilarious, room service had arrived. She dismissed the waiter, telling him that she would serve the food herself.

With childlike playfulness she uncovered a silver dish with a flourish. "This is a really good Brie from the south of France and this sausage is from Lyon. And this," she said, brandishing a wine bottle, "is a not-so-bad '83 Bordeaux." She pulled him out of his seat and handed him the wine. "You open that. I'll cut the sausage and cheese."

He perched on the edge of the wing-back chair and she sat cross-legged on the bed, her bare feet just visible under the black silk pants. While she talked nonstop about the joys of wine and good food, he ate silently, trying to figure out what the hell was going on. Suddenly, she stopped. "Oh, I never even asked you if you like this stuff."

Devlin popped a piece of Brie into his mouth. "I come from a long line of hewers-of-wood and drawers-of-water," he said. "But, yeah, it's not bad."

She bit her lower lip. "I come from peasant stock, too."

Devlin caught a fleeting glimpse of the vulnerable little girl again, but it quickly vanished.

He changed the subject. "Where did you learn so much about wine?"

"I spent eighteen months in France trying to apply CPR to a turkey of a bottle manufacturing plant. It was a lost cause, but I did learn a lot about food and wine."

She rubbed the rim of her glass with the tip of her long, elegant finger, a movement Devlin found erotic.

"I do come from peasant stock, Mike. I started working for JT when I was eighteen, just out of high school. Carla"—she looked up—"your secretary broke me in."

"Carla?" Devlin said, feigning surprise. "No kidding."

"She was so good to me when I first started. Both her and JT encouraged me to go back to school. After I got my finance degree, I went on for my MBA. Then I came back to work for JT."

"So you three have been together a long time. How come Carla is working in the security department?"

Gloria looked thoughtful. "Something happened back then. I thought we were friends, but then she started to undermine me. Actually, I think she was jealous of my success. I put up with it for a long time, but then, through her carelessness, she caused us to lose an important contract. JT was furious. He wanted to fire her, but I intervened and suggested we transfer her to another department. Unfortunately, I think she blames me and has held it against me ever since."

As she spoke, Devlin watched her face carefully for signs that she was lying, but all he saw in those captivating eyes was the hurt of someone who believed that she'd been misunderstood.

Devlin was curious. When Carla had told him her story, she seemed genuine, too. One of them was not telling the truth. He wondered which one.

Gloria was still talking. "I came up the hard way," she said almost defensively. "I wasn't to the manor born."

"Not many of us are."

He half expected to see the little girl emerge again, but Gloria pushed the platter toward him. "More cheese? Sausage?"

"No, I'm stuffed."

She jumped up, pushed the cart aside, and pointed to a two-seated couch. "Sit over here," she said, gleefully rubbing her hands together. "I want to show you something."

Devlin did as he was told. She dimmed the lights until the room was almost dark. Then she went to the window and pulled open the drapes. "Look. Isn't that beautiful?"

The floor-to-ceiling window looked out over a spectacular forest of blazing skyscrapers, and towering over everything was the Empire State Building with its needle top bathed in red, white, and blue lights.

She rested her forehead against the glass. "Before . . . I told you that I'm not good at relaxing, but this is how I get my enjoyment—in small snatches that don't make me feel guilty. I've stood on a hotel balcony in Singapore and watched sampans glide across the indigo waters like so many fireflies. I've sat by my window in Paris and watched dawn dim the lights of the Eiffel Tower."

"Why always at a distance?" Devlin asked. "Why as an observer?"

She tapped the window pane with a long, glossy red fingernail. "Because sights like these are so much more beautiful from a distance. When you get too close, you see the dirt, the misery, the crowding. . . ." She turned to him. "Can you understand what I mean?"

"Yeah. I've never been to Singapore or Paris, but

I've spent over twenty years wandering the streets of this city. It certainly looks a hell of a lot better from up here."

She sat down beside him on the couch. "I'll bet you've seen a lot."

"Enough."

"Too much?"

He looked at her sharply. "Why do you say that?"

"I sense a certain . . . pent-up hostility, an aggressiveness in you. I heard it just now when I asked you if you'd seen too much."

"You sense wrong. I'm fine."

"Okay." She handed him his refilled glass. "To the city," she said, clinking glasses.

"To the city," he mumbled.

Since he'd first opened the door and saw her standing there, a jumble of questions had been churning through his mind. Was this a setup? Some kind of wacky test? Was she crazy? A nympho? The one possibility that didn't occur to him was that she was really interested in him. Granted, he didn't know her well, but from what he'd seen, she was the consummate hard-charging female executive. Women like that had no time for men like him. And men like him were not compatible with women like her. Tammy was more his speed. She was fun, she liked sex, she wasn't a deep thinker, and best of all she didn't ask a lot of questions.

Gloria's touching his thigh brought him out of his musings with a jolt. "Mike, when I look out at this city I can pretend for a moment that it's all mine."

"It *is* all yours," he said, reminding himself, once again, that he wasn't going to get involved with her.

"You're young, you're smart, and you're successful. For you, the sky's the limit."

She turned to face him. "And is the sky the limit for you?"

Devlin stared into his glass. In the subdued light the wine was a murky brown. "No, I don't have any aspirations."

"Why not?"

"Because it's all bullshit," he snapped, surprised at the vehemence in his tone.

She pulled away to get a better look at him. "Why is it bullshit?"

He pointed to the window. "Look out there. Thousands of people chasing their dreams. And for what? Tomorrow they could be the victims of a drive-by shooting; next year they could be dead from cancer."

"There are no guarantees in life."

"Right. So why bother knocking yourself out?"

She looked at him in genuine puzzlement. "You mean you have no goals?"

He returned her gaze. "None. I take it one day at a time."

"My God, what happened to make you feel this way?"

He shrugged. "Probably an occupational hazard. I've seen too much lying; people chasing impossible goals . . . " He stopped and gazed out the window. "Let's just say I've seen an awful lot of very disappointed people," he said softly.

"So that means you don't try?"

"It means you don't set yourself up for a fall."

"But—"

"Gloria, can we change the subject?" The conversation was beginning to dredge up memories that he'd invested a lot of time burying.

"Okay." In the strained silence that followed, the only sound to be heard was the gentle humming of the refrigerator under the wet bar. Then she held her glass up to the window and leaned against him, her silky, fragrant hair brushing against his cheek. "Look at the way the lights reflect in the wine," she said in awe. "I have a whole world in my hands!"

In spite of the emotional turmoil her questions had aroused in him, he had to smile. Under that tough exterior, Jason Taggert's right-hand woman was a carefree spirit, amused by the simplest things.

He looked into her eyes and saw the light of a thousand buildings shining there. His anger subsided. Suddenly, as if by some unspoken communication, she slipped her hand behind his neck and pulled him toward her. She brushed her lips against his, and his resolve to remain detached melted. As he ran his hands up inside her top, the pajamas became undone and his fingers found her erect nipples.

A wineglass fell to the floor with a wet tinkling of glass. He started to pull away, but she held him. "Never mind," she murmured into his ear. "Someone will clean it up."

She tugged at the front of his shirt and he felt a pop as a button gave way. Then her long nails were scraping his chest. He slid her pajama top off her shoulders, exposing her firm, taut breasts. With an urgent gasp she arched her back and pulled his head down to her, and Devlin, feeling himself being sucked into a swirling vortex of fragrant hair and soft, yielding flesh, let himself go.

Neither of them was willing to stop, so they made

love there, half on and half off the couch, heedless of
the broken wineglass lurking perilously close. After
they'd spent themselves, they moved to the large
bed, undressed each other, and made love again. The
second time was just as intense but without the
urgency born of an unspoken fear that they might
come to their senses and stop.

Completely comfortable in her nakedness, Gloria
came padding back from the bar with two brandy
snifters and slipped back into bed beside him.
"Nothing like a good brandy after making love," she
said, nuzzling his cheek.

Devlin put his arm around her. He felt good, but he
was also furious with himself. He'd promised himself
that he wouldn't get involved with this woman. It was
important for him to be in control of things and he was
definitely not in control of this situation. Still, he wasn't
about to climb out of bed and go back to his room.

"So what's next?" he said, staring into his snifter.

She swirled her brandy. "I'm not sure. Let's take it
one step at a time."

"Any regrets?" he asked, hoping to get a clue as to
what she was thinking.

She squeezed him. "Absolutely not. I trust my
instincts. You?"

"I don't know."

She pulled away to look at him. "What's that supposed to mean?"

"It means that this complicates things. I've never
gone to bed with my boss before."

She giggled. "Maybe you should have. You might
have gone far in the police department."

An image of Gloria with Taggert flashed in his mind, and he immediately felt guilty. "Humor aside, it does complicate things."

She poured a dribble of brandy on his chest and licked it with her tongue. "Let me worry about that," she murmured.

"What the hell do you see in me?" he blurted out.

She sat back and rested her glass on her flat stomach. "What do I see in you. Well, of course there's the usual stuff. You're good-looking." She squeezed his bicep. "You keep yourself in shape. You're very different from the kind of men I'm used to encountering. You're a little wild, untamed, dangerous. At the same time I see a man who harbors a secret that someday he'll trust me enough to tell me about. All and all, someone I find very intriguing." She nibbled on his earlobe. "Is that enough to satisfy your suspicious police mind?"

"I guess so," he said, pulling her on top of him. He didn't know if it was enough, but he didn't want to think about it right now. For the time being he just wanted to enjoy her and the moment. There was always time to think.

10

"COME ON, SLEEPYHEAD," SHE SAID. "Time for the circus to begin."

Devlin rubbed his temples. The combination of scotch, wine, brandy, and lack of sleep had given him a dull headache. "What time is it?" he asked, opening one eye.

Gloria was standing in front of a mirror putting on her earrings. "Six-thirty."

Devlin propped himself up on one elbow. "You look like you've been up for hours."

"I have. I don't need a lot of sleep." She smiled at him in the mirror. "Especially when I've had such a wonderful evening."

She was dressed in a conservative gray suit with dark stockings and plain black pumps. But she still managed to look enticing. Remembering the wild, uninhibited things they'd done the night before, he said, "Gloria, I don't suppose—"

She saw the look on his face and shook her head.

"Not now, sweetie. We have a very busy day ahead of us."

"Yeah," he said, reluctantly pulling himself out of bed. "Let's hope not too busy."

It was seven-thirty by the time he got downstairs. Harry Tedesco and most of the security detail were waiting for him in the ballroom. Dressed in non-descript business suits, the moonlighting cops looked very much like the young company assistants scurrying about making last-minute changes. But the cops possessed two important pieces of equipment that set them apart from the corporate types. The first was a small earpiece and a tiny microphone attached to their wrists that allowed them to communicate with their fellow police officers. The second was a fifteen-shot semiautomatic pistol.

Tedesco took one look at the puffy-faced Devlin and said, "Jesus, you look like you had a tough night."

"I don't sleep well in hotel beds," he mumbled. "Where's Taggert?"

"Still in his room. Nick told me he's scheduled to attend a committee meeting on the fourth floor in a few minutes."

"Do we have it covered?"

"Yep. Three of our guys are posted outside the room."

Devlin signaled the men to gather around. He knew them all personally. They were experienced cops and they didn't need a lot of instruction. "This should be a piece of cake, guys, but let's think of the worst-case scenario. Jason Taggert is a high-profile executive. That means someone—a psycho, a disgruntled employee, a shareholder—may want to take a piece out of him. We're here to see that that doesn't happen." At Gloria's request Devlin had reluctantly agreed not to tell them, not even Harry Tedesco, about the threatening letter.

"Remember, guys," he continued, "the imminent threat code word is *gun*." Devlin had chosen the same word that the Secret Service and most protective agencies use. It didn't matter if the threat came from a gun, a knife, or a bomb. The word *gun* was short, not easily misunderstood, and said all that needed to be said.

"If there's a direct physical move against Taggert while he's on the stage, Mangi and Tyler will secure him behind the metal plate. Anywhere else, we get him out of the hotel immediately. Harry, is the trapdoor exit ready?"

"Yep. There's a direct route through the kitchen. The elevator is standing by, and the limo is in the garage waiting to go. We can clear him out of the building in under three minutes."

"Okay," Devlin said to the assembled men. "Harry has given you your assignments. The meeting starts at ten o'clock. Let's have a nice, quiet day."

Twenty minutes later an agitated man wearing a white carnation in his lapel cornered Devlin outside the ballroom. "Are you responsible for security?"

"Yeah. Who're you?"

"Dale Fisher, the banquet manager. Your security precautions are disrupting the work of the hotel's staff. You can't have our employees going through metal detectors every time they come in and out of the ballroom."

"Why not?"

"Because it's too time-consuming and it's un-necessary."

"It might be time-consuming, but I'll be the one to judge if it's necessary."

Fisher sniffed. "I've been a banquet manager for more than twelve years and in that time I've never seen such outlandish precautions."

Devlin leaned forward. "I'll bet in all that time you've never had to deal with a terrorist threat, either," he said in a confidential tone.

The man's right eye twitched. "Do you mean . . . are you saying—"

Devlin raised his eyebrows knowingly. "I can't say," he whispered. "But you can't be too careful."

"Well, yes . . . um . . . is there something I should know?" he said in a tone that said he didn't want to know.

Devlin patted the man's arm and winked. "Everything's under control," he said reassuringly.

"Yes, of course," the man muttered, walking away with a preoccupied look on his face.

While Devlin was humoring the banquet manager, Elgin had come into the hotel lobby. As was the case before every mission, he'd been up before dawn and had already run five miles, followed by a hundred pushups and two hundred situps. He felt energized as he strode across the crowded lobby. The hard physical exercise had toned his muscles and sharpened his mind. Now he was ready, totally focused on the target: Jason Taggert.

He glanced at the Schedule of Events board, which advertised that the Taggert Industries Shareholders'

Meeting was to be held in the Grand Ballroom at 10:00 A.M., and stepped onto the elevator.

Wearing a trench coat, which covered his khaki maintenance uniform, and carrying a Macy's shopping bag, he looked very much like all the other out-of-town tourists on the elevator. But there were no New York City souvenir purchases inside his shopping bag, just a change of clothes.

The first thing he saw when he came off the elevator were the metal detectors. Since last night they'd been covered with flowers and branches. As he stopped to watch a handful of people pass through the detectors, a group of hotel waiters and maintenance people were walking toward him. He frowned. *Something was wrong.* What was different about them? Then he saw it. *They were all wearing photo ID badges.* He swore softly. The ID badges were going to make it more difficult for him, but it was too late to do anything about it now. He'd have to improvise.

Several men wearing radio earpieces were standing near the ballroom entrance scanning the crowd. Grudgingly, he had to admit the security precautions were impressive, but he wasn't overly concerned. In fact, penetrating the security barriers would make killing Taggert all the more enjoyable. When the time came, his maintenance uniform would allow him to blend in with the other hotel workers, rendering him—for all intents and purposes—invisible, even to a small army of sharp-eyed security people. Despite the radios, the metal detectors, and all the other ridiculous security precautions, he was going to kill Jason Taggert right before their eyes.

He had plenty of time and for the next half hour he casually strolled around the corridors outside the

ballroom, carefully noting the locations of security
guards and exit doors. As he did, he reviewed, once
again, the plan in his mind's eye. He would enter the
ballroom just before the meeting started, take up his
position at the electrical fuse box, and wait for the
moment when Jason Taggert got up to speak. Late
the night before, as he lay awake in his Bowery hotel
room, he'd decided that he would let Taggert tell his
opening joke, then, while everyone was having a
hearty laugh, flip the circuit breaker. The hot wire
would trigger the detonator, and the spinning nails,
like thousands of tiny buzz saws, would do the rest.
Let them laugh at that.

He could have used a remote triggering device,
but he wanted to be there to see it happen, to physi-
cally flip the switch. Even in Nam he had favored
seeing his targets die close-up, preferring a knife to a
gun: the "hands-on approach," as he described it to
his stunned counterparts in the South Vietnamese
army.

Devlin and Tedesco had received the message on their
radios that Taggert was on his way down, and they
were waiting for him when he came off the elevators
accompanied by an entourage of senior executives.
Watching Gloria in animated conversation with
Taggert and the others, Devlin was astonished at the
radical change in her demeanor. She'd once more
become the consummate businesswoman. He looked
away, almost believing that last night hadn't happened.

Suddenly a swarm of well-wishers surrounded
Taggert and Devlin became concerned. Undoubtedly,
most of them just wanted to shake the hand of the

man who was making them so much money, but the
letter writer could be among them.

"Mr. Taggert," Devlin said, wading into the crowd,
"we'd better get inside. It's almost time for the meeting to begin."

Taggert, who didn't appreciate anyone taking him
away from his adoring fans, scowled. "The meeting
doesn't start until I'm there," he snapped.

Gloria raised her eyebrows as if to say "Don't rush
him."

Devlin backed away and pulled Mangi aside.
"Nick," he whispered, "give him a couple of minutes
in the sun, then get his ass inside."

A few minutes later, as Mangi and Tyler expertly
herded their charge toward the ballroom doors,
Mangi whispered to Devlin, "I couldn't get the gun
away from him, but I did the next best thing. I took
the round out of the chamber."

Devlin grinned. Without a round in the chamber,
the gun couldn't fire.

Elgin, who'd been standing near the elevator
bank when Taggert arrived, mentally graded the two
bodyguards who were scrutinizing everyone who
approached Taggert. They were no "square badges,"
he concluded. They were professionals, probably
cops. His attention shifted to another man, obviously
the one in charge of security. The security chief
spoke to Taggert and then whispered something to
one of the guards.

As the entourage swirled past him, Elgin ignored
Taggert. Instead, his flat black eyes fixed on Mike
Devlin, the man he assumed was responsible for
making the killing of Taggert so difficult.

He waited until Taggert disappeared into the

ballroom, then he ducked into a restroom, stuffed his trench coat into the shopping bag with the other clothes, and went down the hall to where he knew there was an unlocked utility closet. He hid the bag on a shelf behind some cleaning materials.

Dressed in his maintenance uniform, he walked around to the west side of the ballroom, away from the crowds streaming through the main doors. As he started to open a side door, a tall, well-built black man walked toward him. "Hold it, pal," he said. "You can't go in that door."

Elgin saw the earpiece and the wire running down into his collar and shrugged. "My boss told me to meet him inside right away."

"Okay, but you gotta use the employee door."

"What employee door?" Elgin said, feigning irritation.

The security guard stared at Elgin more closely. "Didn't anyone tell you what door to use?"

Elgin glanced around. He and the guard were alone in the corridor. For a brief moment he considered taking him out. The guard was taller and heavier, but Elgin had the advantage of surprise. One quick chop to the windpipe and he was a dead man. Easy enough, but there was no time to dispose of the body. He saw the guard looking him over suspiciously and said, "No one tells me shit around here. Where do I gotta go?"

"The east corridor. Back the way you came and make two lefts."

As Elgin started to walk away, the guard called out, "Hey, wait a minute."

Elgin stopped and his body tensed. Had the guard noticed his khaki uniform? It wasn't exactly the same color as the hotel's, but it was close enough. Or was it the missing ID badge? As the man walked toward him, Elgin measured him for a quick, sudden chop to the throat.

"Where's your ID?" the man asked.

Elgin was prepared for the question. He patted his chest in surprise. "Damn. I must have left it in my locker."

The man nodded grimly. "You'd better get it. You won't get into the ballroom without it."

"Okay." Elgin walked away.

At the end of the corridor, he looked back and saw the security guard talking into his mike. Aware that the meeting was about to begin, he hurried down the corridor toward the other side of the ballroom. As he turned into the east corridor, three waiters in white jackets were wheeling carts filled with ice water pitchers and glasses toward a set of double doors. He stepped up his pace, planning to enter the ballroom with them. Then two security guards in civilian clothes with hand-held metal detectors stepped out into the corridor. Elgin did an about-face. He stopped at the end of the corridor and watched one security guard run the magnetic wand over the three waiters while the other guard examined their ID badges.

Elgin turned around and went back the way he'd come. *There has to be a way past these dickheads.* He picked up his pace. Suddenly, from inside the ballroom he heard a smattering of applause and then an amplified voice welcoming the crowd to the annual shareholders' meeting of Taggert Industries.

Elgin's black eyes blinked once, slowly. The meeting had begun.

❖   ❖   ❖

Standing just inside the doors, Devlin heard someone calling him through his earpiece, but the booming voice at the lectern was drowning out the message. He stepped outside and cupped his hand over his ear. "Ten-five that last transmission."

"Mike, this is Lester. I just had an unusual incident with a maintenance man. You got a second?"

"Yeah, where are you?"

"The west corridor."

"I'll be right there."

On his way, he called Tedesco on the radio and told him to meet him there with the maintenance supervisor.

When Devlin got to the west corridor, the two men were already there talking to Lester. Tedesco turned to Devlin. "Lester stopped a maintenance man from using this door. The guy didn't seem to know about the east corridor door."

Devlin turned to the maintenance supervisor, a fat, swarthy man in need of a shave.

"Didn't you tell your people?" Devlin asked.

"They was told."

Devlin turned to Lester. "Why did he want to get inside?"

"He said his boss wanted him."

"Did you ask any of your men to meet you inside?" Devlin asked the supervisor.

The foreman scratched his stubble. "Everyone in this friggin' hotel thinks he's a boss when it comes to the maintenance department. Anyone coulda told him that."

"What'd you tell him, Lester?"

"To go around to the east corridor."

"Who's on the door?"

Tedesco consulted his assignment list. "Dave Moller."

Devlin keyed his mike. "Dave, did a maintenance man come through there a while ago?"

"Negative. Just a few waiters with ice water."

Tedesco shrugged. "Maybe he changed his mind?"

Devlin turned to the young cop. "What'd he look like?"

"About five-ten, athletic build. Weird fucking eyes. Flat, like a rattlesnake. A spooky-looking son of a bitch."

"What color hair?"

"Sandy brown. But it was a rug. A good one, but it didn't fool me."

"If it was good, how can you be so sure?" Tedesco asked.

"My uncle makes toupees. When I was a kid I used to work in his shop every summer. I can spot a toupee from a hundred yards. I don't care how expensive it is."

Tedesco grunted. "So we don't even know what color hair he has. Anything else?"

Lester scratched his chin. "There was something about that guy that didn't seem right." The young cop was looking down at the carpet and his eyes rested on the maintenance supervisor's hard-tipped boots. "Shoes!" he said, snapping his fingers. "He was wearing street shoes."

The supervisor shook his head. "He's not one of mine. Last year the union had a big OSHA beef with the hotel about protective shoes. You get caught wearing street shoes now, they fire your ass."

Tedesco looked at Devlin as the same thought occurred to both of them. "We have a hostile in the area," Tedesco said grimly.

Devlin keyed his mike. "Code Red!" he said evenly. "We have a Code Red."

Upon hearing those words, each member of the twenty-five-man detail felt a shot of adrenaline surge through his body. *Code Red: Immediate danger present.* He didn't know what form it would take, so everything became a potential threat. The pleasant public relations smiles vanished, replaced by long, hard stares as each man scrutinized the sea of strange faces, looking for a telltale gesture, some sign of imminent hostility.

Mangi and Tyler, who'd been standing off to the side of the dais, unbuttoned their jackets and hurried out to stand behind Taggert. Because of the elevated dais the audience couldn't see them, but they stood no more than twenty-five feet from the CEO, prepared to unceremoniously stuff their charge under the table at the first cry of "Gun."

While Devlin was talking to Lester and the others, Elgin had gone back to the utility closet to retrieve his clothes. He changed in the restroom and stuffed the uniform and the toupee into the paper-towel receptacle. Then he ran his hands through his close-cropped hair, slipped on a pair of dark glasses, and studied himself in the mirror. Satisfied that he looked nothing like the maintenance man, he came out of the restroom determined to find another way to get to that electrical box.

This time he went into the ballroom through the front doors.

The two security guards carefully scrutinized him as he passed through the metal detectors, but Elgin simply smiled back. He took a seat in the rear, where he could study the layout of the room. The raised dais ran almost the full width of the room, but positioned at each end were two security guards. There was no way he could get past them. Then he saw a waiter, wheeling a serving cart, disappear behind the dais. *There has to be a kitchen back there.*

He got up and went back outside. Near the elevator he found what he was looking for: a posted fire-escape floor plan. It showed all the entrances and exits on the floor. The diagram didn't indicate a kitchen, but it showed a large space behind the ballroom with several doors. There had to be a cooking and serving facility back there. With an absolute concentration that blotted out the sounds and noise around him, he began to memorize the maze of corridors and doors that would lead to the kitchen area.

Confused and angry, Gloria Salazar accompanied Tedesco to the west-side corridor where Devlin was waiting.

"Mike, I have to give a speech in a few minutes. What's this about?"

Devlin didn't like her petulant tone, but with Harry Tedesco standing there, he had to go along with the superior-subordinate role. "Something's come up."

She listened intently as he explained what had happened and what he thought it meant. When he was finished, she said, "So what are you doing about it?"

"I have men searching every room on this floor

and I've clamped down on security. No more hotel workers are permitted inside the ballroom unless Lester personally gets a good look at them."

She nodded. "Good."

He hesitated. "There's one more thing I want to do."

"What's that?"

He turned away from her inquisitive emerald eyes. "I want to scuttle the videotape portion of the meeting."

"Impossible. That's the heart of this meeting. The show-and-tell that everyone comes here to see. Shareholders want to hear about all the great things we've done and the great things we're going to do. My God, we spent a fortune putting this tape together. We can't scrap it."

Devlin fought back his anger. Only last night she'd said herself that this was nothing but a dog-and-pony show. Now she was acting as though showing the tape was the most important thing in the world. She was being unreasonable. If he could talk to her alone, he knew he could convince her. But Tedesco was standing there, watching and listening. "Gloria," he said calmly, "the tape runs ten minutes. The lights are out the entire time. Taggert will be at the podium. I don't know if this guy got inside, but the darkness is an open invitation to someone who wants to do harm."

Gloria was unyielding. "Mike, we will show the tape."

"But I can't guarantee—"

"For God's sake," she snapped. "You have an army of cops here. Are you telling me they can't protect one man?"

"All right, I'll protect him," Devlin snapped. "But

on my terms. I'm going to put every available cop I have in front of the dais. It may interfere with your idea that this meeting is some kind of trip to Disneyland, but I do it that way or I walk out of here and *you* can protect him."

Tedesco saw the familiar signs of self-destruction erupting in his friend and said, "Mike, I think we can—"

Gloria silenced him with a wave of her hand. "Look, do what you have to do to protect JT, but the tape will be shown and this meeting will continue."

"Fine," Devlin said. "But it's going to be a big-time display of force."

"No problem. I can finesse that. Now I have to get back. I have a speech to give."

Tedesco watched her walk away. "Wow," he said. "That woman pisses ice water."

"We'll see," Devlin said, silently fuming at her obstinacy.

Patiently, but mindful that time was slipping away, Elgin explored the east corridors with no success. He'd found three exit doors, but one was locked and the other two led down corridors away from the kitchen.

Now he was on the west side of the building. Access to the kitchen, he decided, had to be there. He walked down a long corridor, turned a corner, and spotted a service entrance at the end of the hallway. He pushed the door open and peered down another long corridor.

As Gloria was giving her speech on the progress that the health-care division had made this fiscal year,

Devlin came behind the dais to give a description of the maintenance man to Mangi and Tyler.

When he finished, Mangi said, "Mike, the zone is contaminated. Shouldn't we get him out of here?"

Devlin nodded glumly. That was the basic doctrine of executive protection: If you know, or seriously suspect, there's a real threat to your subject, get him the hell out of the area. But Devlin wasn't calling the shots. Gloria was, and he was beginning to regret letting himself get involved with her. Clearly, he wasn't in control, and he didn't like the feeling.

Devlin was looking down at the tangle of wires running across the dais floor and his eye focused on a wire that was different from the others. He bent down, jiggled it, and his eyes followed the wire's course toward the podium. "Nick, get the hotel electrician on the horn. I want him here on the double."

Getting down on his hands and knees, he followed the wire, startling a couple of half-dozing senior VPs who were seated on the dais. He winked at them and continued following the path of the wire. As he got to the podium, Gloria glanced down at him. She raised an eyebrow, as if to say "What the hell are you doing there?" but she never missed a beat as she explained the significance of the slides being flashed on the three projection screens located around the room.

As he traced the wire up through the inside of the podium, he could smell her perfume and memories of last night came rushing into his mind. He fought the impulse to run his hand up her leg. There was nothing inside the podium except a tray with a water pitcher and glasses on a shelf covered with a white napkin. He peeked under the napkin and froze. Beads of sweat formed on his forehead as he stared

at a box no more than eight inches from his face. The
wire terminated there. He looked back. Mangi,
standing with another man, was waving at him. He
turned and slowly retraced his steps.

Except for two men mopping the floor, the huge ballroom kitchen was deserted. The men, loudly arguing
about the Mets' shot at a pennant, paid no attention
to Elgin as he walked to the back of the kitchen
toward the ballroom. There were four doors that
opened into a long corridor separating the kitchen
from the ballroom. He heard an amplified woman's
voice and knew that Taggert hadn't spoken yet. He
peered cautiously down the corridor and saw a security guard sitting on a folding chair at the far end.
From his vantage point he had a commanding view of
the entire length of the corridor. There was no way
Elgin could duck across the twelve-foot-wide corridor without being seen.

    As he was trying to decide his next move, a door
opened behind the guard. A woman pushing an
elderly man in a wheelchair tried to get through the
opening, but it was too small. As the guard turned
around to open the second door, Elgin saw his
chance and darted across the corridor and through
the door. He was once again in the ballroom—this
time, though, he was close to the fuse box.

"This is the house electrician," Mangi said to Devlin.

    Devlin pointed at the wire. "Do you know what
it's for?"

    The electrician, a black man with an unruly walrus

mustache, squatted down and fingered the wire. "Beats me. It ain't for the AV stuff, I know that."

"It's connected to a box under the podium," Devlin said.

The man frowned. "Ain't no control box there."

The three men's eyes followed the course of the wire in the other direction, but it disappeared under raised skids abutting a curtain. "Come on," Devlin said. "Let's find out where it leads."

Now that Elgin was in the ballroom, it took a moment to orient himself because he'd come in from a different direction than the night before. When he was certain which way he had to go, he cautiously picked his way through a deserted storage area where extra chairs and folding tables were stacked. The electrical box was just on the other side of a curtain fifty feet away. He smiled. The woman was still speaking. He had plenty of time.

When he got to the curtain, he peeked around and quickly jerked his head back. Three men were standing in front of the electrical box. Elgin watched in silent rage as one of the men, dressed in a maintenance uniform, detached his wires from the box. Powerless to do anything about it, he silently backed away and went out the way he'd come in.

Devlin looked down at the wire in the electrician's hand. "So what's its purpose?" he asked.

The electrician examined the wire with a puzzled expression. "I don't know. It was hooked up to an unused circuit breaker."

"Was it live?" Mangi asked.

The electrician shook his head. "The circuit breaker was off."

"And if you threw it?" Devlin prompted.

"Then it's live."

Mangi looked at Devlin. "A bomb?"

Devlin nodded. "Could be."

"*Sweet Jesus*," the electrician muttered, dropping the wire and taking a step backward.

"It's all right," Devlin said. "If it's a bomb, it's been deactivated."

"*Sweet Jesus*," the man repeated with more emphasis.

Devlin put his arm around the electrician. He didn't need a panicky man yelling "Bomb." "Listen, it's okay. I think someone has been playing a practical joke. Hey, don't you have someplace else you gotta be?"

The electrician gulped. "Yeah, somewhere outta here."

"Okay. Thanks for your help."

After he left, Mangi said, "You think it's a bomb?"

Devlin nodded.

"You think it's deactivated?"

Devlin looked into the troubled eyes of the young cop. "I haven't the slightest idea."

As Gloria was finishing up her presentation, she saw two rows of security guards begin to file into the ballroom and work their way down the aisles as Devlin had ordered. She kept a smile on her face, but she was silently cursing him. They were so obvious that a quiet murmur began in the audience.

Taggert, who was to provide the narration for the videotape, leaned forward in his seat and hissed, "Gloria, what the hell's going on?"

"Don't worry," she said, bending down, "this is all part of the show."

By the time the noise had died down, there was a line of grim, well-dressed men standing in front of the podium.

"And now," she said brightly, "we have a real treat for you. We've prepared a short but informative videotape that will summarize what Taggert Industries has accomplished in the last year and what it is that we intend to accomplish for you in the coming year."

She paused to glance at the men lining the front of the podium. "I'm sure you've noticed the sudden increase in security." She stopped while the nervous titter died down. "Let me explain. Given the economic climate today, some CEOs are hiring guards to protect them from the shareholders. But that's not true at Taggert Industries. If you've been following the stock market, and I'm sure that you have, you will know that we have outperformed every competitor by a wide margin. These serious-looking men you see before you today are not here to protect Jason Taggert from you." She flashed a confident, winning smile. "They're here to protect him from his competitors."

The nervous titters erupted in wild applause.

Jason Taggert stood at the podium smiling and waving at recognized faces in the audience. "Gloria," he said out of the side of his mouth, "I don't know what's going on, but you're a goddamn genius."

She patted his arm. "Jason, this is your day. Have a wonderful time."

Just before the lights dimmed, she saw Devlin waving to her and she went to him. "What was that all about?" she said curtly.

Devlin told her about the wire and the box. Then he said, "We have to stop the meeting. I think the bomb has been disabled, but I'm not sure. The wire could be a decoy. There might be a timer ticking away right now."

She folded her arms. "Mike, let's look at this logically. First, you don't even know for sure that it's a bomb, do you?"

"No, but—"

"Second, the electrician disconnected the wire."

"Yeah, but that doesn't mean—"

"And third, if there is a bomb, don't you think that it would have gone off by now?"

As they were talking, Tedesco had joined the group and was listening to the discussion.

Gloria continued. "So you want to stop a very important meeting because you think that there *may* be a bomb. Have you any idea what that piece of information will do to our stock price? Last year we lost ten points in one hour on a rumor that JT had pneumonia!"

Devlin looked at her in disbelief. "You're willing to risk the lives of everyone in this room to avoid losing a couple of points on your stock?"

"Don't be simplistic," she snapped.

"I'm not being simplistic. I just want to know what's valuable around here. Lives or stock prices?"

"That's not the issue. There is no bomb, and if there is, it's been rendered harmless."

Devlin glared at her. "You want to bet everyone's lives on that?"

She returned his belligerent look. "If you want to leave, go ahead."

Devlin snorted. "I'm not leaving. I wouldn't miss this for the world."

Tedesco could hardly believe he was listening to this conversation from two supposedly sane people. "Wait a minute," he said. "I don't know what the hell's going on between you two. If you want to risk blowing yourselves up, that's your business, but you can't risk other lives."

Gloria turned to him. "If you'd feel safer being out of this room, go."

"Don't tell me what to do, lady," Tedesco snapped.

"All I'm saying is, if any of you want to leave, please do so."

Mangi, fuming at the implication that he was afraid, said, "I'm not going anywhere."

"Me neither," Tyler added.

Devlin started for the stage.

"Where are you going?" Gloria demanded.

"To make an announcement. I've had enough of this bullshit. The meeting is over, Gloria. Nick, call 911. Tell them we have a suspected bomb. Harry, round up your people and clear the room. Make sure they take it easy. I don't want a panic."

"Mike," she said evenly, "you make that announcement and you're fired."

Devlin, who'd started for the dais, stopped to look at the beautiful woman he'd spent the night with. It had been a mistake getting involved with her. He knew that now. But he had to admit it had been the best one-night stand he'd ever had. He was just about to tell her to take her job and shove it when there was a burst of applause. Taggert had finished his speech, concluding the meeting. The lights came back up. The standoff ended.

He turned to Mangi and Tyler. "Use the trap door. Get him out of here. Now."

"There are people he should see," Gloria said, tight-lipped.

Devlin regarded her with barely suppressed anger. "Ms. Salazar," he said quietly, "he leaves right now or I do. It's your call."

Gloria turned on her heels and walked away.

Mangi and Tyler came up behind Taggert and took his arm. "This way, sir."

Taggert pulled his arm free. "What the hell are you doing? I have people to talk to."

Mangi stepped in front of him. "Mr. Taggert," he said in a soft but firm voice, "we have reason to believe that there is someone in the hotel who wishes you harm. We have to go. Now."

Taggert looked down and paled. Both Mangi and Tyler were holding their automatics by their sides. "Which way . . ." he muttered.

Mangi took his arm and led the stunned CEO through the doors and into the kitchen. The two cleaning men, still arguing about the Mets, barely looked up as Mangi and Tyler, flanking the ashen-faced Taggert, rushed their charge toward the elevator and safety.

As people spilled out into the vestibule outside the ballroom, three elderly women stood by the door like aging groupies in heady anticipation of Taggert's appearance. Devlin was the last one out the door and one of the women approached him.

"Where's Mr. Taggert?" she asked, peering around his shoulder.

"I'm sorry. Mr. Taggert had to attend an important meeting."

The disappointed woman believed him, but Elgin, who was standing near the elevator bank, knew better. They'd taken Taggert out the back way. It was something he'd anticipated, but there was nothing he could do about it. He was, after all, only one man and he couldn't be in two places at once.

He popped a peanut into his mouth and pressed the down button. As he waited for the elevator to arrive, he studied Devlin with a mixture of grudging admiration and growing fury.

This was the second time this man had interfered with his plans. Something might have to be done about him. The elevator door opened and Elgin stepped inside. In the meantime, he thought as the doors closed, Taggert could wait. The CEO's name wasn't the only one on his list.

Charlie Stanville, a lanky Bomb Squad detective, carefully wiped the lens of the video camera mounted on top of Bruce, the bomb retrieval robot. "Wanna get the best picture I can," he said over his shoulder to Devlin.

The ballroom had been cleared and a makeshift ramp had been constructed so that tank-treaded Bruce could get up on the dais. The only people outside the ballroom were the two Bomb Squad detectives and Devlin. At the far end of the corridor, a curious cluster of hotel employees, safely out of range, watched from behind a barricade of folding chairs and tables.

"Think it's still active?" Devlin asked.

Stanville shrugged. "Ya never know. The wire could be a decoy. There might be a mercury switch designed to set it off if it's moved. Could be a timer inside. Could be a mercury switch that'll set it off when the lid is raised." He took his wet, soggy cigar out of his mouth and flicked an inch-long ash onto the rug. "On the other hand, there could also be somebody's pastrami sandwich in there. I've seen 'em all."

He manipulated the controls as Bruce used short, jerky movements to disappear through the doors. The three men bent over the control console to watch the video monitor. Bruce had no trouble negotiating the ramp's steep incline, but there were several chairs in his way and, as he rumbled toward the podium, he swept them aside, knocking them off the dais. Stanville maneuvered Bruce to a position directly in front of the podium. Then he zoomed the camera in on the shelf. In the gloom, it was difficult to see the water pitcher and glasses. "Let's throw some light on the subject," he said, flipping on a flood lamp that bathed the shelf in bright light.

The detective and his partner squinted at the screen. "See anything, Ronnie?"

Ronnie Wilson studied the screen for telltale signs of trip wires. "Nope. Get that shit out of the way."

Bruce's arm, appearing on the bottom of the screen, went straight out and swept the glasses and pitcher away with a loud crash of breaking glass.

"A little clumsy for a bomb handler, isn't he?" Devlin said, trying to lighten the tension.

Stanville chuckled dryly. "Brucie would never make it as a waiter, but he's good at what he does. He doesn't sweat, he doesn't flinch—"

"And he doesn't take summer vacations," Ronnie Wilson added, peering intently at the screen.

Carefully, Stanville brought Bruce's two arms to either sides of the box. "Here's where we find out if the device has an antipickup switch." He manipulated the controls and Bruce lifted the box a few inches off the shelf. "So far so good," he whispered.

Bruce backed up and put the box on the floor. "Okay, let's see what's inside." With surprising delicacy, the robot claw lifted the lid and the detective zoomed the camera in. "Jesus Christ," he muttered.

The three men hunched over the video monitor. Illuminated by Bruce's spotlight was a lethal-looking ball of clay studded with sharp-pointed nails.

"Look familiar, Ronnie?" Stanville asked his partner.

"I never saw one here," Wilson said. "But I saw plenty of them in Nam."

Stanville sat back and looked up at Devlin with the kind of weary, haunted expression that came from working with too much tension. "Most people who plant bombs want to make a statement," he said. "They blow up a building because they want to get attention for their cause. Sometimes innocent people get killed, which may or may not be part of the plan."

He tapped the video monitor. "What you got here is an antipersonnel device, designed for one reason only: to hurt somebody bad. Whoever did this is one pissed-off, crazy son of a bitch."

Devlin stared at the sharp-pointed nails, remembering that his face had been less than eight inches from the box. "How much damage could that thing cause?"

Stanville studied the screen, mentally calculating

the explosive power of the ball of C-4. "Anyone standing in front of that podium when it went off was dead meat." He jammed the cigar in his mouth. "You'd have to pick up the sorry son of a bitch with a squeegee."

WHILE MANGI AND TYLER WERE hustling him out of the hotel Jason Taggert had been too stunned to say anything. It wasn't until an hour later, when he was safely back in his office, that he began to loudly question what he considered to be Devlin's overreaction.

Gloria, understanding JT's mercurial moods, had spent the last hour assuring him that Devlin had acted properly. But she didn't believe it. She, too, thought he'd overreacted and, worse, had missed a chance to capture the phony maintenance man.

When Devlin called to say he was on his way back to the office, she concealed her displeasure and tried to repair whatever damage their disagreement might have caused between them. But he'd cut her off bruskly, saying that he wanted to have a meeting with her and Taggert right away.

Jason Taggert drummed his thick fingers on his glass-topped desk. "Well, where is he?"

"He's on the way, JT. Take it easy."

Taggert yanked on his monogrammed cufflinks.

"Don't tell me to take it easy. Hiring this guy was your idea, not mine. I still don't think we need a god-damn private cop around here, especially one who's screwing up the building and everyone in it."

Gloria smiled patiently. "It's not his fault this corporation is totally lacking in security. Don't shoot the messenger."

He slammed his hand down on the glass desktop. "The man's a goddamn bull in a china shop and you know it."

"I'll admit he lacks finesse. But I'm working on it. It'll be fine."

An unappeased Taggert continued. "The guy makes me uncomfortable. He's always got that god-damn smirk on his face like he's laughing at some private joke. I—"

The intercom interrupted his tirade. "Mr. Taggert, Mr. Devlin is here."

"Send him in," Taggert growled.

As soon as Devlin came through the door Gloria could see that he was still angry.

"So what have you found out?" Taggert asked.

Devlin stood over Taggert's desk. "There was a nail bomb in the podium."

The CEO paled. "A nail—? What the hell is that?"

"Several hundred nails embedded in C-4 explosive. If it had gone off, it would have gutted you like a buzz saw."

Involuntarily, Taggert hunched over. "Good God. Who'd want to do that to me?"

"The letter writer?" Gloria offered.

"Probably," Devlin said. "So now we know we're not dealing with a crank. This guy means business." He took a sheet of paper out of his pocket and tossed it on Taggert's desk. "Here's your speaking schedule. I've crossed out the speeches that I think are too dangerous." A numbed Taggert glanced down at the list. Most of the speeches were crossed off.

Devlin continued. "From now on I want you to hold as many meetings as possible right here in the building. If you have to go outside, I don't want it advertised. I've already instructed your driver to take different routes to and from the office. From now on there'll no more routine patterns."

Taggert recovered his voice. "What are you doing to find this man?" he asked.

Devlin looked down at the CEO, trying to decide which version of Taggert he liked the least: the blustery, in-your-face bantam or the frightened executive. He concluded he liked neither. "The bomb was intact. They're going to dust for prints. The detective handling the case will run an MO check to see if this guy has surfaced before. I've also asked Personnel to compile a list of everyone who's left the company in the past year. There might be something there."

Chastened, Taggert slumped back in his high-backed chair and turned to Gloria. "What do you think?"

Gloria fingered a gold pendant hanging from her neck. Outwardly, she was calm, but she was seething at Devlin's coarse handling of JT. Early this morning in her hotel room she'd told him the secret to handling Jason Taggert. He was like a big kid, she explained. The best way to deal with him was to humor him. Devlin had bridled at the suggestion, but she'd made him promise. So much for promises.

"I think in the short term, at least until Mike can

get a handle on this person, you should limit your public exposure."

Taggert's eyes narrowed. "What does that mean?"

"Like Mike said, cut down on some of your public appearances."

Taggert's pugnaciousness returned and his jaw jutted out defiantly. "You know damn well—"

Gloria raised her hands in supplication. "JT, not every appearance. Some of these speeches are open to the public. Let's knock out those for a start. Then Mike can check out the setup for the others. You'll go to the ones where he's confident he can secure the setting and control audience access."

Taggert, who didn't like the idea of Devlin controlling his schedule, glared at the ex-cop. "We'll take it one step at a time. Now get out of here, the both of you," he said, reaching for a briefcase full of papers. "I have work to do."

Gloria headed for the door. "Mike," she said over her shoulder, "I'd like to see you in my office."

Gloria paced up and down while Devlin sullenly stared out the window. "You have to get away from that cop mentality, Mike. You simply don't browbeat someone like JT."

"He's not a goddamn child. Somebody's trying to kill him and he ought to know it."

She whirled around. "I know that. But there are better ways of telling him. When he gets frightened he gets angry. When he gets angry he does stupid things." She sat down on the edge of the desk and her dress hiked up, but Devlin was too irritated to be affected by it. "We're working on a very important merger," she said in a conciliatory tone. "I need him to have a clear head."

Devlin shook his head. "You talk like he's a retarded child, for chrissake. How'd he make all that money before you came along?"

"Things were different then. Those were free-wheeling times and he was extremely lucky. You don't succeed in today's business world by shooting from the hip. Every move, every strategy has to be carefully orchestrated."

"And you can do that better than him?"

Her eyes flashed. "You're damn right. I can do it better than him or anyone in this company."

Devlin was stunned by the intensity in her tone. It was as though she viewed Taggert Industries as her own private fiefdom.

Gloria walked around behind the desk, sat down, and glanced through a stack of telephone messages. "So how close *are* you to finding this guy?"

Devlin grunted. "You gotta be kidding."

Her eyes turned cold. "I don't kid about things like this. Are you saying you can't find him?"

"What I'm saying is that right now I don't have a damn thing to go on. The key is motive. If I can figure out why this guy wants to kill Taggert, maybe I can figure out who it is. It could be a disgruntled employee, someone he screwed in a business deal, or some psycho who hates rich guys. Who the hell knows?" Devlin exhaled sharply to release his pent-up anger. "Maybe we'll get something from the prints. Maybe the MO check will turn up something."

She tossed the telephone messages on the desk and sat back. "I think you blew your chance to catch this guy."

Devlin's head snapped up. "How do you figure that?"

"You knew he was in the area. Displaying that show of force was very impressive, but I'm sure it scared him away."

Devlin couldn't believe what he was hearing. "That was the whole point. What do you think I should I have done?"

"Set a trap. Let him try to get to JT and then grab him."

Devlin grunted. "Why don't you stick to business, because you don't know anything about police work."

"I know it would be a risk, but the cost benefits of—"

"Gloria, read my lips. There's no way I'd risk Taggert's or anybody else's life to capture the guy."

He stood up. "I gotta go. I have a meeting with Otis and Marie."

She came around the desk and stood in front of him. "Are you coming over tonight?" she asked.

"No," he said, astonished at the rapidity with which she changed moods.

She straightened his tie. "Why? Are you mad because I yelled at you?"

He pulled away. "Gloria, last night was a mistake. Let's not make that same mistake again."

"Mike, this has been a rough day. I'm always testy at shareholders' meetings and the bomb incident only made it worse. I'm sorry."

"It won't work, Gloria. I can't be arguing with you all day and going to bed with you at night. It's crazy."

She stroked his cheek. "Ah, but the making up part can be very good, no?"

Devlin thought he'd figured out the female

species, but this Gloria was something else. Even as a part of him knew she was leading him around by the short hairs, another part whispered, "Sure, anything you say." He chided himself for being so easily manipulated.

She slipped her arms around his neck and nibbled on his earlobe. "I want you, Mike."

He felt her warm body press against him and the subtle musk scent of her perfume almost made him dizzy. "All right," he said as if in a trance. "What time?"

"I have a business dinner, but I should be home by ten-thirty."

She pulled away and opened her office door. Her secretary wasn't there and the outer office was deserted. She ran her fingers across his cheek. "See you tonight."

Just then Marie came through the door and stopped abruptly. Gloria pulled her hand away from Devlin's face.

"Michael"—Marie looked at the floor—"they . . . they said you were here. I just wanted to tell you that Otis and I will meet you in your office."

"Okay. I'll be right there."

She nodded curtly and left.

"My, my," Gloria said. "I think Miss Falcone is jealous."

"Marie? No way." He shrugged it off, but he was dimly aware of a slight feeling of guilt.

Gloria studied Devlin's face. "Sure you two aren't more than friends?"

"She was my best friend's wife, for chrissake. I'm her children's godfather. It'd be like . . . "

"Incest?"

"Jesus, Gloria."

She smiled at his obvious discomfort. "Mike, you're so quaint. But I do like it." She pushed him gently. "Go to work, Devlin. Little Miss Muffet and the Jolly Green Giant await."

Otis and Marie sat quietly as Devlin described what had occurred at the shareholders' meeting. When he finished, Otis said, "Was the bomb the work of an amateur or an expert?"

"The Bomb Squad guys say that whoever rigged it knew what he was doing. They also said that nail bombs were included in the bag of tricks the Phoenix Project used in Vietnam."

"What's that?" Marie asked.

"Well, the way it was explained to me, the idea was for our guys to expose high-ranking VC officials running for office in South Vietnam so people would know who they were voting for. But somewhere along the way somebody decided that using the ballot box was too slow and they started whacking the officials."

"You mean we murdered them?" Marie asked.

"Terminated with extreme prejudice is the way they phrase it."

"I think I've heard about this Phoenix thing before," Otis said. "Wasn't the CIA involved?"

"The CIA, yes, and Special Forces *and* South Vietnamese intelligence people."

Royal frowned. "So you think the guy who wrote the letter and planted the bomb could be one of them?"

Devlin sighed. "It's a theory."

Marie seemed pensive. "So where does this leave us?"

"This leaves us running way behind schedule locking up this building," Devlin said.

"If you'll recall, you said there was no urgency," Marie reminded him.

Devlin heard the petulant tone in her voice and knew where it came from. "I thought we were dealing with a crank, not a murderer." He smiled ruefully. "Guess I'm out of the running for this year's Clairvoyant Award." His expression turned serious. "Bottom line: We have to tighten up this building immediately."

Otis fingered his dreadlocks. "That's one tall order, mon."

Devlin tried to sound upbeat. "What are you talking about? I know there're a lot of problems, but you said you could handle them."

"True enough. But I thought I was protectin' the buildin' from ordinary burglars and cranks. Not professional killers."

"Let's not jump to conclusions. We don't know that for sure."

Royal absentmindedly fingered a deadlock. "But let's assume we are. It'll be almost impossible to protect the buildin' from him."

"Why?"

"Behind all those mysterious doors that say 'Authorized Personnel—Keep Out' is the machinery that keeps the buildin' alive and breathin'. At the center of this buildin' is the core—a huge cavity runnin' right up the middle and containing thirty elevator shafts, hundreds of air shafts, and thousands of pipes. Take the water supply, for example. Where do you think it comes from?"

Devlin shrugged. "Underground pipes."

"That's only the beginnin'. It's piped into the basement, but then it has to be pumped up to the six water tanks dispersed throughout the buildin'."

"Six? When I took a tour of the building with Tommy I saw only *two* tanks on the roof. Where are the other four?"

"The buildin' is divided into three zones and each of those zones is supplied by separate water tanks. There are two on the thirteenth floor, two more on the twenty-seventh, and two on the roof."

"You mean there are four wooden tanks *inside* the building?" Devlin asked, surprised.

"You got it, mon."

As a city kid Devlin had grown used to the sight of those wooden water tanks on every rooftop and he'd always assumed that they supplied all the water for the building. "Okay, so if they're inside, what's the problem?"

"They're not secured. Someone could open a hatch, throw poison into the tank, and it would kill anyone drinkin' that water."

Devlin started writing. "I'll have locks on them before the day is out."

"Good. What do you know about electricity?"

Devlin shrugged. "It comes in through feeder lines from Con Ed."

"Right. It enters the buildin' through a vault in the cellar. But this is high-voltage electricity and must go through step-down transformers. Otherwise you'd fry your computers, fax machines, and coffeepots. The transformer room is vulnerable. If it were flooded, it would short-circuit the transformers and interrupt the supply of electricity to the buildin', and that would mean, among other things, no power to the security system. That's what water would do. You can imagine what a bomb would do."

"Isn't there a backup generator?" Marie asked.

"A diesel generator. But it's in the same room."

"We'll secure that room, too," Devlin said.

Marie said, "While we're on the subject, I want a dedicated backup generator for the security computer."

"You've got it."

"On the roof, away from all that other stuff in the basement."

Devlin jotted a note. "Done."

Royal continued. "Michael, what do you know about—"

Devlin tossed his pen down and threw his hands up in supplication. "Okay, Otis. I get the picture. It's not going to be easy making this building airtight."

"No, it isn't. And you know why? The people who created this buildin' designed it for commerce, not for defense. There are so many ways he can attack us. We must be diligent about protectin' vital elements like the water supply, the electrical supply, the air. Countin' the garage and three delivery bays, there are sixteen ways into the buildin' and—"

"It'll be difficult, but not impossible."

Royal drummed his fingers on the desk. "Not impossible," he said finally. "But it will take money and time."

"Money is no object," Devlin said. "Time is the problem." He turned to Marie. "What's the threat from your side?"

"If he hacks into the system, he can really fuck things up. Every second of every day data are being entered, deleted, retrieved, modified. The computers keep track of payrolls, expenses, business plans, inventory, record storage, financial data, you name it. Lose just a part of that information and you're screwed. People have no idea how much they're dependent on computers. Not for nuthin', but you can't even make a phone call out of this building without the aid of a computer."

"How close are you to correcting the problems you found?"

"I've been tightening the screws, but there are still too many windows of vulnerability to suit me."

"You gotta close them, Marie."

"There are only so many hours in the day."

"I know, but you both recognize the urgency here."

Royal nodded. "Don't get vexed. We'll do our best."

Devlin looked at his watch. It was almost 7:00 P.M. He'd called a meeting with all the TAC cops at Toomey's and it was time to get over there. He slapped the desktop with both hands. "Go on home and get some rest, you two. Tomorrow's going to be a busy day."

Tammy planted a big wet kiss on Devlin's lips. "Hey, stranger," she said accusingly, "where you been?"

Devlin disengaged himself. "The new job. Busy as hell."

Tammy pouted her voluptuous lips and it almost made Devlin forget why he'd come there. "So you have no time for your old friends?"

Devlin smiled. "I always have time for you."

"Yeah, sure you do. The usual?"

"No. Make it a beer." He was here on serious business and it was best to keep a clear head. Later, after he had said what he had to say to the guys, he'd think about something stronger. Maybe something a lot stronger. "Are the guys here yet?"

She slid the bottle across the bar. "Yeah. In the back."

"Put their drinks on my tab."

"Hmmm, big spender."

Ignoring the sarcasm, Devlin scooped up his bottle and walked into the back room, where there was a heated discussion going on about which was better, the 9mm Glock or the 10mm Colt.

Tedesco looked up. "Hey, Mike, which gun do you think is the best?"

"The one that takes down the target," Devlin said, pulling up a chair.

When the laughter died down, he said, "I asked you guys to meet me here because I've got something to lay on you." When the room grew quiet he said, "A few weeks ago, Jason Taggert received an anonymous death threat in the mail. As a result of that letter, Taggert Industries hired me to beef up protection for him and the building."

"Did Chief Lynne get you the job?" someone called out.

"No," someone else said. "Mike wrote the letter himself."

Ignoring the good-natured gibes, Devlin continued. "To tell you the truth, when I took the job I figured I was dealing with a crank or at worst a disgruntled employee. Well, as you know, we found a nail bomb under the podium this afternoon."

"Was it live?" someone asked.

"Yeah. They blew it up at Rodman's Neck a couple of hours ago."

There was a somber silence as every man in the room thought about what the bomb would have done to Jason Taggert.

"When I saw that nail bomb on the robot's TV monitor," Devlin continued, "I realized that it was a whole new ball game. I hired you guys mainly for psychological reasons—to make Taggert feel more secure. The company could afford the expense and you guys could use the extra money. But now, with a psycho on the loose, I can't ask you guys to risk your lives anymore. Christ knows, the department doesn't pay you enough for what you do, and I pay even less. So . . . thanks for your help, but I can't use you anymore."

Mangi spoke up. "Are you saying we're fired?"

Devlin's smile was wan. "I wouldn't put it that way. What's the politically correct term . . . dehired? Consider yourselves dehired."

"Is the department going to provide security?" Tedesco asked.

Devlin shook his head. "I asked, but you know how it is . . . too expensive, not enough manpower, not a serious enough threat."

"So how are you going to protect him?" Mangi asked.

"I don't know," he answered truthfully.

Tyler said, "Mike, there's no way you can do this by yourself."

"Fuck 'em," someone said in jest. "Taggert's a surly bastard. He deserves to get popped."

"Sure he does," Tyler said with a straight face. "But Mike's not a bad guy. *He* needs protection."

Devlin knew what they were doing. Like most cops, they were dealing with a very serious and dangerous situation by making a joke out of it. "Guys, I appreciate your concern for me, but I can't let you do it."

Mangi slammed his beer bottle on the table. "Mike, you can't do this to me. I'm this close to scoring with Gloria Salazar."

That obvious lie raised a chorus of derisive hoots and a handful of tossed soggy napkins.

"Let's get serious," Tedesco said. "Mike, I think you hear what the guys are saying. They want to stay on."

"I can't—"

An angry Tyler growled, "Who the fuck is this guy? Superman? There's no way he's going to take Taggert out if we're baby-sitting him."

Mangi raised his hand. "Who wants to continue this assignment?"

All nine men raised their hands. Devlin knew they'd want to continue protecting Taggert, but he wanted to hear them say it. In the somber faces before him he saw the pride and confidence of an elite, highly trained group of men who were absolutely convinced that no one could get to a man they were protecting. And he saw something else—that special aura that surrounds men who willingly confront danger. But none of this was a revelation to Devlin because he knew that men who volunteered for a unit like TAC needed that adrenaline rush.

"All right," he said, relieved that he could count on the best nine cops in the police department. "We're back in business. From now on I'm doubling the detail. Two men on him at all times. Nick, you coordinate it." He stood up. "Oh, one more thing. Drink up. Jason Taggert is buying."

It was almost nine-thirty and everyone had gone home except Tedesco and Devlin. Tedesco, feeling no pain, propped his elbows up on the bar and said with a slurred voice, "I'm really happy to see you like this."

Devlin shook his head. "Gee, thanks, Harry, I got a lunatic trying to blow up my boss and you're happy."

"That's not what I mean." Tedesco slapped his old friend on the back. "You're really into this, aren't you, you old son of a bitch?"

"What are you talking about?"

Tedesco sipped his scotch. "Mikey, since your divorce, you haven't given a fuck about anything."

"You're full of shit."

"No, I'm not. You haven't given a royal fuck about anything and that's not you. You're a guy who always loved to grab life by the short hairs and give it a tug. It's something I've always admired about you."

Devlin popped an olive into his mouth. "Harry, you're drunk."

"Yes, I am. But I'm still happy. This is what you need, buddy. Something to dig your teeth into." He lurched to his feet. "I'll be right back. I gotta take a leak."

While Tedesco was gone Devlin studied his image in the mirror behind the bar. Harry was drunk, but he was right. The awesome responsibility of protecting Taggert, coupled with his concern for the men in the TAC team, had galvanized him. He hadn't felt this alive in a long time. It was crazy. He was responsible for protecting the life of the CEO of a major multinational corporation against a killer likely to have pro credentials and he was enjoying it. He downed the rest of his martini and called for the check.

Tammy handed him his credit-card receipt. "You going?"

"Yeah. I gotta see someone."

"Oh. I thought . . . you'd wait for me. Then we could—"

"I can't, Tammy." He'd promised Gloria that he would stop by her place. "Some other time."

"Yeah, okay."

What a shithead I am.

He waited for Tedesco to come back from the bathroom, then took him outside and poured him into a cab. Then he grabbed one for himself.

AFTER THE SHAREHOLDERS' MEETING, which he considered a monumental waste of his valuable time, Dr. Kurt Biehl went back to his office to finish up some work. Every Taggert Industries shareholders' meeting tended to be a three-ring circus, but this one had been even more bizarre than usual. First there'd been that commotion up on the dais, then there was the business of all those bodyguards and metal detectors. Others might have been curious, but not him. He was a scientist, not a businessman, and he made it a practice to stay out of corporate affairs as much as possible.

It was after midnight by the time he got home. When he unlocked the door to his apartment, he was surprised that Fritz wasn't there to offer his customary greeting.

"Hey, Fritz," he called out as he walked into the kitchen, "where are you, you lazy good-for-nothing cat?"

He rummaged around the half-empty refrigerator.

Finding nothing interesting to eat, he settled for a glass of almost-sour milk and two stale chocolate chip cookies.

As he was pouring the rest of the carton of milk down the drain, he shivered, suddenly realizing that the apartment was cold. He made a mental note to talk to the building super about it. This whole winter the heating had been very uneven, ranging from sweltering to frigid. He was paying way too much rent to put up with that.

Taking the glass with him, he went in search of the missing Fritz. He walked into the living room and stopped abruptly when he saw the reason for the chill. One of the windows was wide open. The drapes were pulled back and the blinds were up all the way, almost as though someone was preparing to pass something large through the window. But that was impossible. He was twenty-two stories up and there was no fire escape. "That damn super . . . " he muttered aloud.

As he started toward the window, two dark shapes on the rug, half hidden by the coffee table, caught his eye. He turned on a table lamp to get a better look. For a horrifying instant his mind refused to accept what he was seeing. Then the unspeakable image burst into his consciousness and the glass of milk slipped from his hand. The cat's head, with a frozen snarl on his face, stared up at him with lifeless eyes. A few feet away, the rest of the body lay in a congealed pool of blood. Biehl gagged.

As he staggered backward, a shadowy figure materialized from the darkened bedroom behind him. Two quick, silent steps and Elgin had Biehl in a choke hold. Biehl struggled, clawing at the arm around his neck, but he was no match for the stronger Elgin. Gradually, Elgin felt the rigid body go slack as the pressure on the carotid artery cut off the blood supply to Biehl's brain. He released his hold and, after the unconscious man had slumped to the floor, dragged him to the open window.

Lifting the body up, he slid Biehl's head and shoulders over the sill until he was evenly balanced half in and half out. Then he slipped a loop of a ten-foot-long nylon rope around one of Biehl's ankles and tied the other end to a metal bar jammed against the windowsill. Using another rope, he tied Biehl's ankles together.

Within seconds the oxygen returned to Biehl's brain, and his mind began to clear. But as it did he became aware of his body teetering on the edge of the windowsill. His eyes snapped open and he saw the street twenty-two stories below. Instinctively he tried to pull himself back inside the safety of the apartment, but someone was pinning his arms behind him, robbing him of the leverage he needed.

As he struggled to pull himself back from the precipice, he felt a hand grab his legs and yank them upward. The motion tilted his body forward and, bellowing like a petrified animal, he began to slide out the window.

Suddenly, he was a child again, reliving that dreaded, recurring childhood nightmare that had so often wrenched him from sleep, screaming and shaken. It was always the same: He was falling from a great height, his stomach churning from the sickening sensation of weightlessness. He always woke up before he smashed into the ground. But this time it was no dream.

He slid headlong out the window, catching his breath as he felt his body go weightless. Futilely, his arms flailed in the air as he sought a handhold on something solid. For one brief instant his mind, paralyzed by fear, cleared, and in that terrifying moment of lucidity, he knew he was going to die.

Then his body jerked to an abrupt stop and he slammed into the side of the building, gashing his forehead on the coarse bricks. Through a numbing fog of terror he realized that a rope was tied to his ankles. Partially blinded by the blood streaming into his eyes, he doubled his body over and frantically clawed at the rope.

It was at that moment that he saw a face looking down at him. With his flat black eyes and the shadows playing off his leering grin, the man looked like a medieval gargoyle. Holding onto the rope with one hand and fighting back the urge to vomit, Biehl extended his other hand. "Help me ... please ... help me."

"Sure. Put one hand over the other and pull yourself up. How's that for help?"

Biehl's biceps were beginning to cramp. "Please ... " His voice broke.

Suddenly, a knife appeared in Elgin's hand. Biehl cringed instinctively.

Elgin flipped the knife and offered it handle first to Biehl. "Your ankles are tied together," he said. "You'd be in better shape if they were free."

Biehl, too frightened to answer, merely nodded.

Elgin extended the knife handle. "Take it."

Tentatively, Biehl took it and after a great deal of exertion finally managed to cut the rope binding his ankles. With his feet free he was able to kick off the

wall and control his movements more easily. Thinking
he might have future use for the knife, he stuck it in
his belt.

The effort expended on cutting his ankles free
had tired him and his breathing came in short, quick
gasps. Pinwheels floated in front of his eyes. *Dear
God, don't let me pass out.* He looked up. "Why . . .
why are you doing this to me?" he gasped.

Elgin cracked a peanut shell with his teeth,
sucked the peanut into his mouth, and spat the husk
onto Biehl's head.

"You shouldn't be asking a lot of questions right
now. It seems to me you should be concentrating on
getting back into this room." He plucked the taut
nylon rope and shook his head. "Pretty thin. How
long do you think it can support your body weight?"

The man's condescending tone, as though he
were talking to a child, infuriated Biehl. But he
ignored his tormentor and turned his attention to
saving himself. He placed one hand over the other
and with great effort slowly began to pull himself up.
Every time he moved his body slammed up against
the building and his knuckles were soon scraped raw.
But he didn't feel the pain. With his whole being he
concentrated on climbing back up to the window. To
safety. To life.

From the shock of his predicament, Biehl had
entered into an almost dreamlike state and he was
having difficulty distinguishing between reality and
fantasy. Was this really happening? Was that man
above him real or a demon? Would he soon awaken
safely in his bed? *Please God, let me wake up.* As he
pulled himself up, one hand over the other, he drew
strength from the knowledge that every hard-fought,

painful inch was bringing him closer and closer to safety.

When he was less than three feet below the window, Elgin, with the absorbed expression of a boy watching a wingless fly, said, "There's an old saying that a coward dies a thousand deaths. Are you a coward, Dr. Biehl?"

"You . . . fucking . . . *devil*," Biehl hissed through his teeth. "Go away, I don't need you. I . . . can do this myself."

Elgin picked at his teeth with his pinky nail. "How did it feel to almost die? They say your whole life passes before you. Is that true?"

"You . . . are . . . a madman," Biehl gasped.

Elgin's black eyes narrowed. There was a sudden flash of steel and he was holding a long, gleaming knife in his hand. He scratched the side of his cheek with the blade edge. "I wanted you to die a thousand deaths," he said in a flat monotone, "but I couldn't figure out how to do that." A shimmer of pure hatred flashed in his forbidding eyes, stunning Biehl. "Still, I guess two deaths are better than one." He rested the blade against the rope. "The second time around, do you think your whole life passes before you *again*?" Elgin's wintry smile caused the hair on the back of Biehl's neck to rise. "If it does, maybe you could sort of give me a wave just before you hit the ground."

Elgin began sawing at the rope with the knife.

Biehl was less than three feet below the window's ledge. *So close to safety*. He felt a surge of murderous hatred that he didn't think was in him. Summoning all his strength, he snatched the knife from his belt and lunged upward, wanting with all his being to drive the blade through the man's heart. But the rope had become slippery from his bloody hands and he slid back down.

Elgin looked down on Biehl with a detached expression. "Is that any way to repay a kindness?"

Clutching his frail lifeline in exhaustion, Biehl watched the blade slice through the rope in horrified fascination. As each severed strand sprung away from the rope, bringing him closer and closer to death, his scientific mind wondered at what point the rope's integrity would be totally degraded. Whatever that point was, it would mean his death.

Biehl blinked away tears. "Why are you doing this?" he cried out.

Elgin stopped cutting. The sardonic smile vanished and his black eyes shimmered with hatred. "My name is Elgin."

Biehl sagged and felt the strength drain from his body. His tormentor had answered the question. Now he knew why he was going to die. There was no point in protesting. No use explaining.

Suddenly there was a sickening jolt, like the sensation of a falling elevator. Biehl's internal organs, free of the pull of gravity, surged up into his chest cavity, purging the air from his lungs, and he again felt the breathless sensation of weightlessness. "Nooo . . . "

Slowly, his arms and legs flailing in the air, Biehl cartwheeled in a downward spiral. As the ground rapidly approached, he caught one brief, horrifying glimpse of the sidewalk and the people below. An image of an elderly woman and her dog—the last sight he would ever see—etched itself in his mind: She was standing in the street and her dog was defecating on the sidewalk.

Elgin watched Biehl's body glance off a parked car and slam onto the sidewalk. Standing ten feet away, a stunned woman and her dog were spattered with the contents of Biehl's exploding skull. Elgin ducked his head back inside.

Before he left the apartment, he scattered three S&M magazines on the coffee table. He righted a chair that had been knocked over in the scuffle and methodically checked the apartment to make sure that everything was as it should be. To avoid leaving fingerprints, he'd worn rubber gloves. Satisfied that everything was as it should be, he let himself out and took the elevator to the basement. As he left the building through the service entrance the police cars were just beginning to arrive.

Gloria rolled over and threw her arm across Devlin's chest. "You gonna stay the night?"

"What time is it?"

Without her contacts she had to squint at the clock radio on the night table. "One-thirty."

"Might as well. I gotta get up soon."

Gloria slapped his chest playfully. "What a smooth talker you are. A woman would like to believe that a man might want to stay in her bed for reasons other than convenience."

Devlin fluffed up his pillow. "Smooth talking isn't one of my strong suits."

"I'll say. Especially tonight. You still angry about this afternoon?"

He was still angry about her unreasonableness over clearing the ballroom when they'd discovered the bomb. But what really bothered him was her mercurial mood swings. One minute she was soft and sweet, but then, in the blink of an eye, she was the cold, tough, professional businesswoman. He was finding it difficult to reconcile these two different personas, especially in the woman who was his boss and lover.

His thoughts were interrupted by the ringing of the telephone. She picked it up. "Yes?" she said curtly.

As she listened, her face drained of color. Then she mumbled a thank you and hung up.

Devlin saw a look of fear and total bewilderment on her face. "Who was that?"

She pulled the covers up around her protectively. "Charlie Floyd . . . the police just called him. Kurt Biehl is dead."

"Biehl?" Devlin recalled the tall, shy man who was the head of R&D. "How?"

"The window . . . they said he jumped. . . ."

"Was he having personal problems?"

"No. Kurt would never do something like that."

"People do strange things. I remember—"

"I'm telling you he wouldn't do that," she said fiercely.

"Okay, okay."

He wanted to leave, but clearly this news had genuinely thrown her and he didn't want to leave her in this state. "How about some coffee? I'll make it."

As he looked down at her, she was suddenly transformed from the frightened girl who'd just heard terrible news to the old, confident Gloria. "No, never mind." She threw the covers aside and got out of bed. "I have to get ready to go to the office."

"Gloria, it's not even two o'clock."

She wasn't listening. She was thinking of what she had to do next. "There's a lot to do," she said, more to herself than to him. "There'll be questions from the press. I'll have to sit down with our PR people and put the proper spin on this. JT will have to be called. We'll have to find an interim director so there will be no interruption in our research projects."

He tried to put his arms around her, but she pushed him away. "Go over to his apartment. Talk to the police; conduct your own investigation. Do whatever you have to do. I have to know what really happened."

Suddenly it occurred to Devlin what she was getting at. "You think the guy who planted the bomb is responsible for this?"

She bit her lip. "Yes."

"Why? Did Biehl get a threatening letter?"

"No."

"Then what makes you think—"

"Mike, I don't know." She ran her fingers through her hair in exasperation. "All I know is Kurt didn't commit suicide. It had to be murder. Will you please talk to the police and find out what happened?"

"All right," he said, studying her carefully. He'd never seen her so rattled before. This news had really upset her. "Are you going to be okay?"

"I'll be fine."

By the time he finished dressing she was already on the telephone with Taggert. He gave her a wave and slipped out the door.

13

Devlin went directly to Biehl's apartment on Fifteenth Street, but the detectives had already finished with their preliminary investigation and were gone. The door to the apartment was sealed with a Scotch-taped message warning that the apartment was under the jurisdiction of the public administrator. The note, signed by a Detective Victor Justes, also requested that anyone with information about this incident contact him at the Sixth Precinct squad office.

Before he went to the station house Devlin made some calls to see if any of his friends knew Justes. Normally he would have gone directly to the precinct, identified himself, and his badge would have been enough to open all doors. But he wasn't a cop anymore. Unless he could come up with a mutual friend, he'd be treated just like any other civilian. By nature, cops, especially detectives, were suspicious of anyone asking questions, and it helped to have someone smooth the way. On the third call he found a Bronx squad commander who knew Justes personally. He promised to call the detective and tell him that Devlin was on his way in to see him.

Detective Victor Justes, a beefy man in his mid-forties with slicked-back silver-gray hair and a penchant for loud ties, pushed a stack of reports aside. "So," he said, motioning Devlin into an old battered chair, "Timmy Latta tells me you're retired."

"Oh . . . yeah." Hearing himself described as retired had caught Devlin off guard. He was still getting used to his new status.

"So what can I do for you, Mike?"

"I'm the security director for Taggert Industries. Kurt Biehl worked for the company. Can you tell me what happened?"

Justes popped his collar button to relieve the strain on his thick neck. "He took a header out the window."

"Sounds simple enough. Suicide?"

"Probably."

"You're not sure?"

"It gets complicated. There was a rope attached to his leg."

"Cut or shredded?"

"Cut."

"Sounds like a homicide."

"Not necessarily. We found the knife on the street."

"So what do you think happened?"

"We come across a lot of kinky sex bullshit in this precinct. Guys using ropes and chains on themselves to get off. Whaddaya call it—"

"Autoerotic sex."

"Yeah, that's it. Just last week I had a case where

this guy hung himself while he was jacking off. Must've got too excited. Kicked the stool over and strangled himself. Go figure." Justes put one scruffy loafered foot up on the desk. "What is it with these guys? How come they can't go to the john with a copy of *Penthouse* like everybody else?"

Devlin had met the head of R&D only once. He had seemed straight, but . . . "You find anything in his apartment to indicate that Biehl was into kinky sex?"

Justes scratched his chin. "Yeah, a few S&M magazines. One of 'em featured an article involving ropes and trusses. Games to play alone or with a few close friends. Weird shit. I don't know what the hell he was doing dangling out the window. I've given up trying to figure out these assholes. Maybe he wasn't getting the thrill he was expecting, got pissed, cut the rope." He shrugged. "Who knows? Who cares?"

"Is there any chance it's murder?" Devlin asked.

"Naw. Nothing taken from the apartment, no sign of a struggle . . . oh, except for the cat."

"What about the cat?"

"The head was cut off. Probably more kinky bullshit. Unless we find someone else's fingerprints on that knife, it's going to be ruled a suicide."

Listening to the detective talk, Devlin was convinced that Gloria's hunch was wrong. There was no murder here. All the evidence pointed to suicide.

He stood up. "Thanks for your time, Victor."

By the time Devlin got to the building, it was almost 5:00 A.M. All the offices on the fortieth floor were still dark, except for Gloria Salazar's. She was just winding up a meeting with a puffy-faced Charlie Floyd and three equally tired and grim members of corporate public relations.

"Terrible thing," Floyd muttered to Devlin as he left the office. "Terrible thing."

Gloria closed the door and motioned Devlin into a seat. "Coffee?"

"Yeah, I could use a cup."

He knew that she, too, had had no sleep, but she looked remarkably fresh. He had to admire her boundless energy. Personally, he felt like shit.

She handed him a cup. "So what did you find out?"

As Devlin recounted his conversation with the detective she paled, especially when he described the manner in which Biehl had died. When he finished his narration, she said, "I don't believe it. Kurt was murdered."

"Gloria, they found S&M magazines in his apartment. An article on ropes, for chrissake. It adds up. Maybe Biehl picked up the wrong guy at a bar. Maybe—"

"Kurt wasn't gay," she said emphatically.

"Did you know him personally?"

"No, but I worked with him on several projects."

"Then you don't know."

"I do know. He was murdered."

Devlin, who had a low tolerance for amateur detectives, felt his anger rising. "Exactly what do you base that opinion on?"

"Just a feeling."

"Anything more substantial than woman's intuition?"

"No." If she heard the sarcasm in his voice she didn't let on.

"Let me see if I've got this straight. You think the guy who planted the bomb in the ballroom murdered Biehl."

"Yes."

"Then tell me this. What's the connection between Taggert and Biehl? What could they have done to become the target of this wacko?"

"I don't know."

"Think, Gloria. Were they involved in a joint business venture? Were they on the same board of directors?"

"I don't *know*. As the head of R&D Kurt had a lot of access to JT, but they had no personal relationship that I'm aware of."

"The secret to solving a murder is motive," Devlin explained patiently. "Find out why someone wants someone dead and you narrow the field of suspects."

"I know. You've already told me that. Mike, I want you to find this man."

Devlin, bristling at the lecturing tone in her voice, snapped, "Goddamn it, Gloria, I want to get this guy too, but it's not that easy. The son of a bitch doesn't leave a trail."

She slammed her cup down on the desk with such force that Devlin thought the saucer would break. "All I hear from you are excuses. There's a murderer loose. He's killed Kurt Biehl and he's trying to kill JT. You've *got* to find him."

"Gloria," Devlin said evenly, "there's no evidence that Biehl was murdered."

He put his cup down. He was getting fed up with her amateur sleuthing. "It's time to let the police know about Taggert's threatening note."

"No," she said firmly. "I don't want the police involved."

"Are you still worried about bad publicity?" he asked incredulously. "Try thinking about what's going to happen to your stock if Taggert gets whacked."

As she got up and came around the desk, her whole demeanor changed. The strident businesswoman was gone, replaced by the soft, sexy woman Devlin had come to know in their quiet hours together. She sat on the edge of his chair. "Mike," she said, stroking his cheek, "it's your job to see that that doesn't happen."

Refusing to be mollified, Devlin ducked away from her hand. "I'm glad you remembered what my job is."

"I know I've been testy and I'm sorry. Kurt Biehl's death has thrown me for a loop. This whole business is just . . . unbelievable. Murder, threatening letters. That may be part of your world, but it's totally alien to mine and frankly it scares me to death."

Devlin saw the fear in her eyes and immediately regretted his behavior. Gloria was right. She was a competent businesswoman, comfortable in her world of mergers, acquisitions, and power lunches, but none of that had anything to do with murder. He put his hand on hers. "I'm sorry, Gloria. I know this is rough on you."

She blinked away tears. "I didn't know him personally, but it's just dreadful that he had to die in such a horrible way."

Devlin stood up and put his arms around her. "There's something I want you to do. Convince Taggert to curtail his social activities and talk him into canceling all his campaign speeches. At least for the foreseeable future."

She looked up at him. "That's not going to be easy."

He kissed her forehead. "You can do it. I have to control his environment. I can put extra guards on him when he leaves the building for meetings, but there's always a risk. I'd prefer that he conduct his business right here in the building. Pretty soon we'll have the place wrapped up tight as a drum. Then he'll be safe here. Who knows," he said, trying to cheer her up, "the cops may grab this guy before the day is out and this will be all over."

She buried her face in his chest. "Oh, God, I hope so."

When Devlin got back to his office, Marie and Otis were waiting for him. Over a fresh pot of coffee brewed by Carla, he told them what he'd learned about Kurt Biehl's death.

"So," he concluded, "I can't see any connection between the swan dive Biehl took and our bomber, but I want to keep Taggert contained inside the building as much as possible."

"That's not going to be easy," Marie said. "He has a business to run and he can't do it all from here."

Devlin snorted. "You sound like Gloria."

Marie's right eyebrow arched. "Don't compare me to her."

"Sorry. Otis, how are you progressing?"

"Fair to middlin'. I spent most of yesterday afternoon schmoozin' with my suppliers, pleadin' and beggin' for monitors and cameras. I have a rather large lunch bill for you, Michael. Goodness, those men can drink!"

"Did I get my money's worth?"

"The equipment will be here by the end of the week."

"Good. How about the alarm hardware for the fire stairway doors?"

"I'm still havin' trouble procurin' that."

Devlin frowned. "I don't like the vulnerability. We have a set of unsecured stairs going from the basement to the top floor."

"That's the truth."

Devlin jotted down a note. "Until the hardware is installed, I'll have Tommy Nolen and his men patrol the stairs on a regular basis."

"With a little bit of luck I should get the equipment within the next two weeks."

"Too late, Otis. I need it now."

Royal shrugged. "I've been pestering them every day."

"Then pester them twice a day. Take *them* to lunch. Get them drunk if you have to."

Royal patted his stomach and looked queasy. "Mon, I don't know if my liver can take much more of this, but I'll try."

Devlin left with Otis to inspect the building's basement while Marie stayed behind in the office to work on plans to install a backup generator for the computer system.

Carla came into the office with a chocolate-brown cigarette dangling from her mouth and carrying her ever-present coffee mug. In the two weeks Marie had been here, she and Carla had become good friends. Although there was more than a twenty-year difference in age, they had much in common. Both women had a secure sense of who they were; both held themselves to high standards; and neither one hesitated to say exactly what was on her mind.

Carla sat down at Devlin's desk. "Coffee?"

"No thanks, Carla. I just had some."

"Too bad about Dr. Biehl."

"Yeah, did you know him?"

"About ten years."

"Was he married?"

"Three years ago. It lasted a year. Before he got married I told him it wouldn't work—that he was a workaholic. I told him he was married to his work—that loners like himself shouldn't get hitched. But he didn't listen. They never do."

Marie shook her head, sighed. "Tell me about it. Men are such assholes. You think it's in the genes?"

"For some. The others have to work at it." Carla blew a line of smoke toward the ceiling. "Speaking of loners, what's with Mike and you?"

Marie looked up. "What do you mean?"

"You're both available. Like each other. So where's the sparks?" She shimmied her shoulders. "Where's the electricity?"

"You in the matchmaking business or what?"

"It just seems like a natural. You not interested?"

A pensive Marie sat back and folded her arms. "I'm interested. He's not," she said softly.

"How come?"

"Six years ago he was married to an absolutely gorgeous woman. Christine had it all—looks, great body, wonderful voice."

"Sounds like she should have been in show business."

"That's what she thought. She used to sing at small clubs on Long Island. One night an agent was in the audience. He fed her a line of bullshit about her having the talent to make it big. Mike was against it, but she had stars in her eyes and he always did have a hard time refusing her anything. He took an extra job to pay for the singing lessons, makeup sessions, wardrobe, and God knows what else. A year later she ran off with the agent, leaving him with an empty apartment and a fistful of bills."

"A real bitch."

"You got it. It really knocked him on his ass. He changed after the divorce. Up until then he was on the fast track. He'd just made lieutenant and he was studying for the captain's exam. Unlike my husband, Richie, who just wanted to be a detective the rest of his life, Mike had ambitions of going all the way to the top. He'd have aced the test, too."

Marie traced angry circles on her notebook with a pencil. "After the divorce he started getting into arguments with his bosses. He finally got thrown out of the Detective Bureau over a stupid argument about an arrest." Marie shrugged her shoulders. "After that he just seemed to give up trying. It was like he didn't give a damn about anything. Richie was his best friend, but he couldn't do anything with him. Christine hurt him a lot more than Mike is willing to admit. So now he's afraid of making a commitment to anything."

"Is there a woman in his life?"

"Just a girl from the bar where he hangs out. You know the type—all boobs, no brains, no questions, no commitments."

Carla flicked her ashes into her empty coffee mug. "So you're saying he's woman-proof."

"You got it."

"Don't count out Gloria."

Marie studied Carla's wrinkled poker face. "What would a woman like Gloria want with an ex-cop like him?"

Carla shrugged. "Who knows what evil lurks in that woman's black heart."

The scene outside Gloria's office suddenly flashed into Marie's mind. At first she'd told herself that Gloria was probably brushing something from Mike's cheek, but the more she thought about their guilty reaction when she walked in on them, the more she realized she'd caught them in an intimate moment. "Carla, would Gloria use that body of hers to get what she wants?"

Carla squinted at Marie through a cloud of blue smoke. "The woman's a piranha. She'll do whatever she has to do."

"I don't doubt that. But what could Mike do for her?"

Carla lit another cigarette. "Damned if I know."

Devlin punched the down button on the elevator and looked at his watch. It was after 7:00 P.M. He'd been up for over twenty-four hours and he was so tired he couldn't see straight. The elevator doors opened to reveal a bedraggled Charlie Floyd, looking the way Devlin felt. "Tough day, Charlie," Devlin said, getting on.

"You said it. I don't know how you cops deal with this stuff on a regular basis."

"Ex-cop," Mike corrected. "You get used to it. Everything under control on your end?"

"I hope so. Taggert wants to keep the company out of the newspapers. Looks like we've managed to do that. Thank God, there've been no inquiries from the press." They rode the rest of the way in silence; then, just before they got to the lobby, Floyd said, "You know, I've been in the personnel business for over twenty-five years and this is the worst year I can remember."

"How so?"

"First Nisar Ahmad, then Ralph Brock, and now Kurt Biehl. All within a matter of months."

The doors opened and Floyd started to step out, but Devlin grabbed his elbow and pulled him back. "What are you talking about?"

"Three employees dying in such a short period of time. It's so unusual."

"How'd the other two die?"

"Freak accidents, really. In January Ahmad was electrocuted when a radio fell into his bathtub. Then, just a few weeks later, Ralph Brock died. His accident was even more bizarre. He had a summer home in Pennsylvania and he was out in the woods cutting firewood. Some freak thing happened—he must have tripped or fallen—and he cut off both his feet at the ankles with the chainsaw. There was no one to help him." Floyd shuddered. "He bled to death in the woods all alone. What a terrible way to die."

Devlin punched the personnel director's floor and the doors closed. "What are you doing?" Floyd asked.

"We're going back to your office. I want to see the files on those two men."

IT WAS ALMOST MIDNIGHT BY the time Devlin finished reviewing the personnel folders of the two men and making his telephone calls. He wanted to go home and get some sleep, but the information he'd found was too important to wait until morning. He called Gloria and told her to put a pot of coffee on the stove.

Devlin sat down at the dinette table while Gloria poured the coffee.

"I spoke to JT about his speech schedule," she said. "It was a struggle, but I finally got him to agree to cancel them until this man is found."

"Good. That'll make my job a lot easier. How about staying in the building?"

Gloria shook her head. "I couldn't get him to budge on that issue. He ranted about Taggert Tower becoming his tomb and he refuses to consider it. I must say, I agree. It's totally unreasonable to expect a CEO to conduct all his business at his desk. You'll just have to find a way to protect him."

Devlin nodded in resignation. "Okay. I'll put two men in the limo with him and add a two-man backup car. The chauffeur has already been instructed to take different routes daily. I'll talk to his secretaries. I don't want his movements advertised."

"That's not going to be easy. JT loves publicity. He has a woman on staff whose only responsibility is to keep the media informed of his schedule."

"Well, she's gonna be out of work. This bomber is too damn resourceful. If we telegraph Taggert's every move, sooner or later, he'll be waiting for us. I want a blackout on his movements. In fact, I want last-minute changes in meeting locations and times."

"It'll drive his staff nuts."

"Better that than a dead boss."

Gloria blinked, remembering the bomb in the podium. "So," she said, "what do you have to tell me that's so important it couldn't wait until tomorrow morning?"

Devlin rubbed his bloodshot eyes, and they felt like there was ground glass in them. "Did you know that two other Taggert employees besides Biehl have died within the last three months?"

"I really don't have the time to keep track of everyone who works for us, but I seem to recall hearing something about that. Why?"

"I think they may have been murdered."

Gloria put the cups down hard on the table, spilling some coffee. "Why do you say that?"

"The circumstances." Devlin wiped the spill with a napkin. "I did some checking. On January 21, Nisar Ahmad was electrocuted when a radio fell into his bathtub. A few hours ago I talked to the detective who handled the case. He called it an accident, but I finally got him to admit that the circumstances surrounding Ahmad's death were questionable."

"Why?"

"The radio was on a shelf about three feet away from the bathtub. It couldn't have just fallen in."

"So how do the police say it happened?"

"As the detective reconstructed it, he thinks that Ahmad probably leaned over to get a towel, lost his footing in the slippery tub, and accidentally pulled the radio in on top of him."

"You don't think that's what happened?"

"Sounds farfetched."

"So why didn't the police investigate it as a murder?"

"There was no evidence of a struggle, nothing was missing from the apartment, no one in the building heard anything, and the ME's autopsy didn't indicate anything suspicious. The detective was only too happy to label it an accidental death."

"But why? You said—"

"Paperwork. An accidental death is a closed case. A homicide stays open until a perp is arrested. From personal experience I can tell you an open homicide case, with few leads to work on, is a real pain in the ass."

Gloria stared at her untouched cup. "Maybe it was an accident."

"If it were an isolated incident, I would agree. But then on February 3, another employee, Ralph Brock, cut off both his feet with a chainsaw."

"Oh, my God. How terrible."

"The Pennsylvania state trooper who handled the case wasn't available, but I spoke to someone else in his office who was familiar with the incident. They think Brock was probably trying to climb a tree and lost control of the saw."

"Wasn't there anyone to help him?"

"No. It happened on a remote part of Brock's property. The cop said there was a trail of blood for over a hundred yards—evidence that he tried to crawl out of the woods. But he bled to death before he could make it back to the house."

An ashen-faced Gloria got up and poured herself a glass of water. Standing at the sink with her back to him, she said in a small voice, "Why do you think it was murder?"

"Accidents happen, but I find it hard to believe that a guy could cut off *both* his feet at the same time."

"What do the police think?"

"Again, without any supporting evidence to the contrary, they're always going to rule it an accident. But I don't buy it. As far as I'm concerned, there are just too many coincidences: Brock and Ahmad worked for the same company; they both died within a relatively short period of time; both deaths are questionable; and"—he paused—"they both worked for Kurt Biehl."

Gloria spun around. "They did?"

"They were chemists in Biehl's R&D department."

"So now you believe Kurt Biehl was murdered?"

Devlin drummed his fingers on the table. He hated to admit that she was right. After all, he was supposed to be the cop. "Yeah," he said. "In light of the other two questionable deaths, I think Biehl was murdered. Three people from the same division are dead. Remember I talked about motive? I think the answer to who did this lies somewhere in R&D."

Gloria shook her head. "How does that explain JT's threatening letter?"

Devlin scratched the stubble on his chin. "That's a problem." He stood up and yawned. All this conjecture and supposition were giving him a headache. "Gloria, I gotta get some sleep. I'm going out to Long Island tomorrow to see Brock's sister. Maybe she can tell me something." He didn't tell her that he was taking Marie and her kids to the airport first.

"Good. What about talking to Ahmad's relatives?"

"They're all in Pakistan. And there's no one else. Apparently he was a loner."

At the door, Devlin, too tired to do anything else, gave Gloria a perfunctory peck on the cheek. "Cheer up," he said, looking into her troubled green eyes. "You've been nagging me to find this guy. Maybe I'm finally on the right track."

She rested her cheek against his chest. "Mike, I'm worried about your safety. If what you say is true, this man tried to kill JT and has already murdered three others. Imagine," she said, shuddering, "cutting off a man's feet. How grisly."

"Yeah, grisly."

What he hadn't told her was that he was certain that after the killer had severed the chemist's feet, he'd stayed with him, following the maimed man as he dragged himself through the woods toward help. It had to have been that way. He would have wanted it to look like an accident. But the man who planted that bomb and killed three people without leaving a trace was too smart to have taken the chance that Brock might survive. But why, he wondered, would the killer choose such a cruel method of death?

Feeling protective of Gloria, Devlin put his arms around her and pulled her close. Her slender body trembled. Right now, Taggert's proficient "right-hand woman" was just a frightened little girl trying to come to terms with the malevolent and brutal world of murder.

As Frank and Richie Falcone, wearing the typical teenage uniform—baggy pants and unlaced high-tops—came out of the house lugging two enormous suitcases, Mike Devlin watched them from behind the wheel of his Honda. The sight of his two godsons evoked a feeling of real pride—and a tinge of envy. Despite the fact that they were in the full throes of that awkward and gangly stage teenage boys went through at fifteen, they showed the promise of becoming fine young men. Richie had the rugged good looks of his father and Frank had the sensitive alertness of his mother. If Devlin had stayed married he would have wanted boys just like them. Like most cops who'd seen their share of teen violence and drug abuse, he could be supercritical of teenagers, but Frank and Richie had never given him any reason for concern. They were reasonably well-adjusted kids who were doing well in school and were active in sports.

Marie came out and yelled at them for dragging the suitcases on the ground. The boys, already towering over their diminutive mother, laughed, but they picked up the suitcases. As he watched the three of them come down the driveway toward him, he realized that the primary reason the two boys were on the right track was because of her. As a single parent she'd managed to give them the requisite amount of TLC while earning enough to provide them with life's necessities. A neat trick in today's world.

They tossed the suitcases in the trunk and piled into the back. "Hey, Uncle Mike," Richie said, "where you been?"

"Busy with the new job, guys."

Frank slapped the back of the seat. "Cool! You're the head of security for some big company, right?"

"Yeah, and your mom's helping me straighten it out."

That got a big laugh out of them. Like most kids, they weren't overly impressed with what their mother did for a living.

During the first half of the trip to the airport the boys gave Devlin a nonstop, detailed rundown on who they were going to see when they got to California. The ambitious list included a dozen athletes, rock stars, and all the babes from *Baywatch*. Somewhere halfway through the list, they got into an argument about New York Ranger Brian Leetch's scoring record and they became so engrossed in the dispute that they forgot all about Devlin and their mother.

Devlin glanced at them in the rearview mirror. "They're really keyed up for this trip, huh?"

Marie rolled her eyes. "I *knew* I should have brought some Valium along."

Devlin smiled. Marie had a sense of the absurd that had always appealed to him.

They got to the airport with plenty of time to spare and went to a lounge near the gate. While the boys played video games, Devlin and Marie drank coffee. Soon it was time to go, and in an awkward confusion of hugs, kisses, hair smoothings, and handshakes, the boys disappeared into the tunnel leading to the plane. Devlin and Marie stayed to watch the plane taxi away from the gate.

As they stared back through the terminal, she said, "Thanks for playing chauffeur."

"I was glad to. It gave me a chance to catch up with them." Devlin felt a stab of guilt. After Richie's death, he'd promised himself that he would spend more time with his godsons. Marie did a great job, but he was convinced that growing boys needed a man's presence once in a while. He told himself he was doing it for Richie and the boys' sakes, but the truth was he liked being with them.

"You were right the other day, Marie. I haven't been around as much as I should. As soon as this mad bomber thing is cleared up, I'm gonna take them camping."

Marie's eyes lit up. "Can I come?"

"Nope. Men only."

Trying to hide her disappointment with humor, she said, "Are you trying to turn my sons into male chauvinist pigs?"

"I prefer to think of it as male bonding."

"Male chauvinist pig bonding," she corrected with a smile as she stepped onto the escalator.

When they pulled into her driveway Devlin turned off the ignition. "You gonna miss them?" he asked.

"Not yet. Give me another hour."

Devlin's face suddenly turned somber. "I kinda wish you were on that plane with them."

"Why?"

"Ahmad, Brock, Biehl. There are too many people dying around here and I don't like the idea of you being in the middle of it."

"What's that got to do with me? I work with computers, for chrissake. What could be safer than that?"

"I've been thinking . . . maybe I can find someone else to do the computer security—"

"What are you talking about? First, I'm the best there is, and second, I'm staying. Case closed."

"But I'm concerned about—"

"Case closed." She yanked the door open. "Wanna come in for coffee?"

"No. I have an appointment to see Brock's sister."

"Oh, yeah. I forgot. Hope you find out something."

"Yeah, me too. Marie, you're stubborn as hell."

"Tenacious. I like to think of myself as tenacious. I'll see you in the office later."

March 21 was officially the first day of spring, but winter was reluctant to release its frigid grip and the temperature was still in the low thirties. Later, as the weather warmed, the trees lining both sides of the street on Doris Miller's block would form a lush, verdant canopy. But for now the trees' bare, stark branches remained dormant.

Devlin pulled up in front of a neat ranch house that at one time had been identical to all the other tract houses on the block. But over the years each homeowner had added personal touches and now each house possessed its own distinct personality.

Devlin rang the bell and a woman propping a young child on her hip opened the door. "Yes?"

"Mike Devlin. I called you last night."

Doris Miller pushed the door open. "Oh, yes, come in."

She swept a GI Joe off the couch and tossed it on a pile of toys on the floor. "Sit down. You'll have to excuse the mess. Robert is a one-man wrecking crew."

Devlin took in the room at a glance. After years of entering houses and apartments he'd become adept at judging what kind of people a home's occupants were by its ambiance. There was something comfortable about this house and he decided that it was the easy casualness. There was a stack of newspapers and magazines on the coffee table and apparently the little boy had been playing with blocks, which were now strewn across the living room carpet. Devlin nodded at the blocks. "Is he going to be an engineer?"

"For today, anyway."

"I guess they're a real handful at that age."

Doris Miller ran her fingers through her hair. "Oh, God, yes. I'm dreading the 'terrible twos.' I'll probably wind up in a nut-house." She placed the baby in a playpen and handed him a stuffed animal. Then she came back and sat down on the couch next to Devlin. "So," she said, brushing an errant hair away from her eyes, "what can I do for you?"

"Well, first, Mrs. Miller, I want to say that I'm very sorry about Ralph's death."

"Thank you. It certainly was a shock losing my older brother, but I'm beginning to get used to it."

"As I said on the phone last night, I'm the benefits manager at Taggert Industries and I've started a new program in which we plan to keep in touch with the families of our deceased employees. We like to think of you as part of our extended family."

Last night he'd decided that he wouldn't introduce himself as the director of security because he didn't want to arouse her suspicions. It was bad enough that her brother had died a terrible death;

she didn't need to be concerned that he might have been murdered. At least not yet.

"Well, that's nice," she said, looking at him a bit oddly. She'd never heard of such a program before. "The people at Taggert *have* been very kind to us. Mr. Taggert even came to the wake. He seems to be a good man."

Devlin suppressed a grin. "Yes, he certainly is. Did Ralph have that home in the Poconos very long?"

"A little over three years. He loved the country. We grew up on a farm in Pennsylvania. Ralph left when he went to college and never came back. He's always worked in big cities, but his heart was in the country. After his wife died, he bought the house in the Poconos and spent every spare minute he could there. He was always busy, clearing land, repairing the old barn, adding an extension. He loved that place. It was going to be his retirement home."

After some more small talk, Devlin steered the conversation to Brock's death. "That was such a freak accident," he said. "But I know a chainsaw can be very dangerous. I have a doctor friend who lives upstate. He tells me that every weekend the emergency room is full of do-it-yourselfers who hurt themselves with power tools."

She shook her head emphatically. "Not Ralph. Like I said, he grew up on a farm using all kinds of power tools. Ralph was very careful with tools. He respected them."

"So what do you think happened?"

There was a faraway look in her misty eyes. "Just before he died, he wasn't himself. He was so . . . preoccupied. Maybe that had something to do with it."

"What do you mean?"

"He came to stay with us for the holidays. He was always a lot of fun, but this time his mind seemed to be someplace else. He was irritable and short-tempered. That wasn't like him."

"Do you have any idea why?"

"At first I thought it had something to do with Betty's death and the holidays. You know how that can be. But we talked and he finally admitted he was very unhappy at work."

"Did he say why?"

"No. He wouldn't talk about it. But one night he had a little too much to drink and he started rambling on about some project he was working on and the problems he was having with some doctor."

"What was his name?"

"I can't remember . . . a French name."

"Did this doctor work for the company?"

"I don't think so."

"Did Ralph say what the problem was about?"

"No. He didn't make a lot of sense. But he did say he was so upset that he was thinking of leaving the company. That surprised me. Ralph loved his work."

Devlin felt a rush of excitement, but remembering his cover story, he displayed just the right amount of concern. "That's too bad," he said. "A disruptive work environment isn't good for the employee and it certainly isn't good for the company. If you can remember this doctor's name, I'd appreciate your letting me know. I'd like to look into the matter."

She nodded. "I will. If I remember the name, I'll give you a call."

Devlin was about to stand up when he remembered a question he should ask. "Oh, another thing. I know you were Ralph's beneficiary. Any problem with getting your benefits?"

"None at all," Doris said.

"Good, good, happy to hear that," Devlin said, in a hurry now to get out of there. He'd heard enough. When he'd come here, he wasn't sure, but now that he'd spoken to Brock's sister, he was convinced that her brother had been murdered and that it had something to do with his work.

His eyes shining with excitement, Devlin paced up and down Gloria's spacious office. "Brock and Ahmad were chemists. What could they have been working on?"

Gloria tapped her long fingernails on the desk. "Kurt Biehl would be the man to talk to, but he's dead."

Devlin stopped pacing. "Who's taking his place?"

"For the time being, Dr. Philip Armond. He's been a senior consultant to our pharmaceutical division for the past nine years."

Devlin stood up. "Then that's the man I have to talk to."

"I think you'd waste your time talking to Armond. He's not going to know the inner workings of R&D."

"Maybe not, but the answer lies somewhere in that office."

She looked at him for a long moment. Maybe it was the light, but Devlin thought she looked very tired. "All right," she said, finally. "See what you can find out."

Dr. Philip Armond was a morbidly obese man with four cascading chins and a few wispy hairs jutting out of the top of his head. His turned-down mouth and hooded eyes imparted the impression of an arrogant man who was on the verge of falling asleep at any moment.

As he spun around in his chair, it groaned in protest. "Mr. Devlin," he said in a voice with just the hint of a lisp, "I'm afraid I don't know what Brock and Ahmad were working on before they died."

"Dr. Armond," Devlin said patiently, "this is a scientific laboratory, not a mom-and-pop candy store. Are you telling me that you don't know what two of your chemists were working on?"

Armond smiled and his eyes became mere slits. "It may sound preposterous, dear boy, but you must understand the nature of a research environment. Of course we're always meticulous in our research methodology, but some labs are quite loose in the way that they go about their research. Kurt was known for running a very casual and informal lab. That's neither good nor bad. It's merely a personal preference. Some scientists like to work in such an environment; others detest it."

"So you're telling me that you don't know what they were doing before they died?"

"I'm afraid so."

Devlin stood up. Gloria was right. Armond didn't know what time it was. "Well, if you find out anything, give me a call right away."

"I certainly will."

"Thanks for your time."

Armond nodded and all his chins quivered in unison. "Think nothing of it."

15

BALANCING THREE PLATES ON HER ARM, the waitress stood over their table. "Okay, who gets the burger and fries?"

Devlin took the platter from her.

"Pastrami?"

Marie took her plate.

The waitress slid a plate in front of Royal. "And you're the ham and swiss."

Marie pointed at Royal's plate. "I didn't think Rastafarians ate ham."

"They don't eat meat at all, child. They're strict vegetarians."

"So what's that on your plate? Brussels sprouts?"

Royal's booming laugh rumbled around the room. "I'm not a true Rastafarian," he whispered. "I'm an impostor."

Marie looked at Devlin. "I don't get it."

Royal grinned broadly. "This exotic look is very appealin' to the young girls, don't you know?" He pulled himself up to his full height, smoothed out his green, gold, and red dashiki, and shook out his dreadlocks. "Do I not look like a young African prince?"

Marie popped a french fry into her mouth. "You look like a big black guy in loud clothes."

"Guess you have to be a big black woman in loud clothes to appreciate it," Devlin said to Royal.

Marie fingered his dashiki. "But I really like this, Otis."

"I'll get you one," Royal said, cheering up.

"Great. I can wear it as a nightshirt."

While they ate, Devlin recounted what he'd learned from speaking to Doris Miller and Dr. Armond.

Marie dabbed a french fry into the ketchup. "It's not an open-and-shut case, but you make a good argument for murder."

"There's one big problem," Devlin said. "I can't picture the same psycho killing three guys from TI's R&D department *and* sending the threatening letter to Taggert. Why go to all the trouble of making the three murders look like accidents and then *advertise* your intention to murder the boss? The M.O. just isn't consistent."

"Does the guy have to follow a script?"

Devlin wiped his hands with a napkin. "Yeah. In multiple murders there's almost always some kind of pattern. We're not dealing with spur-of-the-moment murders here. This guy thought them through very carefully and he didn't make any mistakes."

Royal frowned. "I'll tell you one thing for sure. These murders, includin' the attempt on Taggert's life, were very . . . what's the word for it? Creative."

"Yeah," Devlin agreed. "This guy has a real sadistic streak."

"He can't be murdering these people just because he doesn't like scientists," Marie said. "He has to have a beef against the company."

After a few seconds during which the three contemplated the implications of that statement, Devlin rattled the ice cubes in his Coke. "Brock is the key to all this. It had to be something he was working on. I'd like to talk to that doctor Brock's sister mentioned."

Marie waved a french fry at Devlin. "But Dr. Armond said he didn't know what Brock was working on."

Devlin snorted. "Armond was pulling my chain. He had to know."

"You're so suspicious. He's new. He probably doesn't have a handle on how the R&D section works."

"Bull. This is a big corporation. There's no way Brock could have been working on a project without it being documented somewhere. You know that."

"So why would he stonewall you?"

"I don't know, but I'm beginning to think that Taggert Industries isn't the big happy family that it's cracked up to be." Discouraged, Devlin signaled for the check. "That's enough speculation for one day. Let's get back to work."

When Devlin came into the office Carla handed him a telephone message. "Mrs. Miller called. She was in a bookstore today and happened to see an author's name that made her remember the name of that doctor you were interested in."

Devlin looked down at the piece of paper and read the name. "Carla, have you ever heard of anyone named Malroux working for the company?"

An ash from Carla's cigarette dropped onto her computer keyboard and disappeared between the keys in a puff of black dust. "Nope, can't say that I have."

"Call personnel. Ask them to run a computer search to see if anyone named Malroux ever worked for the company."

"How far do you want to go back?"

"As far back as the records go."

Fifteen minutes later Carla buzzed Devlin on the intercom. "Personnel called. No one named Malroux has ever worked for us."

"Okay," Devlin said, trying not to sound disappointed. He thought for a moment. "Get me the telephone books for the five boroughs."

In the Manhattan directory he found three Malrouxs but only one, a Dr. Jean Malroux, was a doctor. There were two listings. He dialed the first number and listened to a recorded message stating that the line had been disconnected. When he called the second number, a woman answered. "Good afternoon, Clinique de Soissons."

"I'd like to speak to Dr. Malroux, please."

There was a long pause, then, "I'm afraid Dr. Malroux is no longer with us."

"Can you tell me where he is?"

The woman's voice dropped to almost a whisper. "Dr. Malroux is dead."

Without thinking, Devlin automatically fired off the questions of a police investigator: "When? Where?"

The flustered woman said, "In January. A terrible accident somewhere downtown."

"Can I speak to the new director?"

"Dr. Malroux was the sole proprietor. The clinic is

closed while the lawyers probate Dr. Malroux's estate.
I'm just here to answer the telephone. It's a terrible
mess. I don't know what's to become of us."

Devlin hung up and immediately looked up
Clinique de Soissons in the yellow pages. He found
a quarter-page advertisement prominently displaying a photograph of a good-looking man with
slicked-back hair. Under the photograph was a long
list of initials, testifying to Dr. Malroux's extensive
credentials. The ad copy stated that Clinique de
Soissons was a facility specializing in alternative
treatment for blood diseases.

A call to a friend in the Chief of Detectives Office
was all that was needed to find out that Dr. Malroux
had died on January 17 around the corner from the
Downtown Athletic Club. Fortunately, Devlin even
knew the detective who'd caught the case. Years ago
they'd played on the same Bronx detectives' softball
team. He didn't know Charlie Andrews very well, but
it was a good enough basis to dial him and ask him
out for a couple of drinks.

Devlin was at the bar when Andrews came in. The
tall black detective, moving with the grace of an athlete, weaved his way through the early evening cock-
tail crowd. Except for his salt-and-pepper hair, he still
looked the same. "Hey, Mike," he said, extending his
hand. "How've you been?"

"Good, Charlie, and you?"

"Can't complain. So how does it feel to be a
civilian?"

"I'm not sure. It hasn't been that long."

For the next few minutes they talked shop—who

went where, who was going where, and why so-and-so wasn't going anywhere. After they'd exhausted their list of mutual friends, Devlin got to the point. "Charlie, I'm conducting an internal investigation in the company and Malroux's name came up. I'm not sure how he fits into my probe, but I'd like to know a little more about how he died."

"What do you want to know?"

"Was his death a homicide?"

Andrews rattled the cubes in his glass. "At first I thought so, but it turned out to be a real freak accident. The dopey son of a bitch was fooling around with the engine of his car and caught his sleeve in the fan. What a way to go. The radiator branded crosshatches on what was left of his face. Looked like he got smacked with a waffle iron."

"Why did you think it was a homicide?"

"The fan cowling had been removed. Aha, I think, the plot thickens. Who goes to the trouble of removing a fan cowling so he can slam-dunk his victim's face into the fan?"

"The mob."

"Right. I figure it's gonna be a ground ball and I'll make first grade for sure. I checked Malroux out six ways to Sunday, but I couldn't find any mob or drug connections. He had big expenses, but he also made big bucks. Reluctantly, I had to conclude that it wasn't murder. There *was* one unusual thing. A couple of days before he died someone burglarized his office and trashed it."

"Could there be any connection?"

"Malroux didn't report anything missing. Probably some junkie looking for drugs."

Devlin masked his disappointment. He'd been

hoping that Andrews would say something to support his contention that Malroux and the others had been murdered. "That private clinic on the East Side sounds like a quack operation," he said.

"Yeah, it catered to the rich and the desperate. Malroux preferred rich patients, but he took anyone as long as they had some money. A real vacuum cleaner. Funny thing, they tell me he was a real good doctor, an authority on hematology. Wrote articles and stuff." Andrews downed the remainder of his drink. "Guess he sold out for the quick buck."

Devlin signaled for another round. "So what else is new?"

The two men stayed a while longer to discuss politics, baseball, and women. Around 8:30 P.M., Andrews left, and Devlin, still thinking about Malroux, ordered another martini. In spite of what Andrews had said, he didn't believe Malroux's death was an accident, especially in light of the other three questionable "accidents." By the time he finished his drink, he knew what he had to do. He went to the telephone and called the building.

Fred Holly, one of the newly hired retired cops, answered. "Taggert Tower."

"Freddy, Mike Devlin. Is Otis Royal still there?"

"Lemme check." After a few seconds, Holly came back on the line. "Yup, he's right here. Mr. Overtime, we call him. I'll put him on."

"Good evenin', Michael," Royal said in his lilting Jamaican accent. "What can I do for you?"

"Don't go anywhere. I'm on my way back and I have to talk to you about something."

"No problem, mon. This new card reader is givin' me conniptions. I may be here till next Sunday."

＊　　＊　　＊

It was just after 1:00 A.M. when Devlin and Royal drove past Clinique de Soissons, located off the corner of Park Avenue and 75th Street. Devlin peered up at the darkened four-story building. "Looks good."

"Yes, it does," Royal said, surveying the building with professional intensity. "Darkness is our friend."

Devlin pulled into a parking space around the block. When he'd gotten back to the building, he'd told Royal of his plan to break into Malroux's clinic and asked for a quick course in lock-picking. Royal had laughed at the absurdity of such a request and insisted on going along.

"Otis, you don't have to do this. You can still back out."

Royal's white teeth glistened in the darkness. "You know I wouldn't miss this for anythin'. Besides, it's a splendid opportunity to keep up my skills."

Devlin had serious reservations. He was about to commit a crime, and worse, he was making his friend an accomplice. If they were caught, his being an ex-cop wouldn't do them any good. What really surprised him was that he wanted to do this in the first place. He'd spent the last five years not getting involved. Now, here he was about to commit a felony. And for what? He yanked the door open. "Okay, Otis, let's do it."

Royal had no trouble picking the lock. The clinic was designed to be open twenty-four hours a day, so there was no alarm system to worry about. In a few minutes, they found Malroux's private office. Devlin was relieved to see a long row of file cabinets. He'd been afraid that the clinic might have had all their files on a computer. That would have meant using

Marie and that was out of the question. He'd never expose her to the possibility of arrest. He didn't even want her to know that they'd come here and he'd made Otis swear that he wouldn't tell Marie about this.

Royal quickly went down the row picking the cabinet locks almost as quickly as they could be opened with a key. Devlin opened a drawer and fingered through the files. "Bingo," he said. The cabinet contained patient files. "Otis, you start here. I'll look through his desk."

"What am I looking for?"

"I'm not sure. Anything marked Taggert, Biehl, Brock, or Ahmad."

While Royal sifted through the file cabinets, Devlin examined Malroux's desk, being careful not to disturb anything. The center drawer contained the usual heap of assorted business cards, pencils, and unimportant correspondence. Devlin went through it quickly to make sure there was nothing of significance. Then, methodically, he went from drawer to drawer, examining each piece of paper. When he got to the last drawer, he looked up and said, "Any luck?"

"So far just a bunch of names," Royal answered. "But not the ones we're lookin' for."

Suddenly feeling discouraged, Devlin sat back in Malroux's expensive leather chair. What the hell was he doing here? Had he let his imagination run wild? Four different detectives had investigated four deaths and they'd all concluded that the deaths were accidental. Was he trying to make connections where there were none? Had Gloria's insistence that Biehl was murdered affected his judgment?

Royal slammed the drawer, snapping Devlin out of his gloomy thoughts. "That's the last cabinet, Michael. Nothin' here."

"Okay, I have one more drawer to look through, then we're outta here."

In the back of the drawer was last year's leather-bound diary in which were written brief notes on patients and visitors. "Jesus," he said, squinting at the bold, scrawly handwriting. "This will take all night to read."

Royal peered over Devlin's shoulder. "Start with the date of Malroux's death and work your way back."

Devlin flipped to January 16, the day before Malroux died, and began to read the entries going back into the year. It was slow going trying to decipher Malroux's sloppy handwriting, especially by the light of a flickering flashlight.

He read the entry for November 26 and fell back in the chair. "Son of a bitch," he whispered.

Royal, who'd been dozing in a comfortable wing-back chair, snapped awake. "You find somethin'?"

Devlin read the simple, cryptic entry: "Call Brock re Elgin."

For a big man, Royal moved with surprising quickness. Before Devlin could tell him to look for the file, Royal was already thumbing through the E's. He yanked out the file, opened it, and began to read through it quickly. "Robert Elgin . . . age twelve . . . date of death January tenth." He looked up and frowned. "There's not much here. Most of the pages have been torn out of this file. Look, you can see bits of paper under the staple."

"Anything about Brock in there?"

"No, just a copy of the admission form."

Devlin tucked the file inside his jacket and carefully placed the diary back in the drawer. "Okay," he said, looking around to make certain they were leaving the office as they'd found it. "Let's get out of here."

16

It was almost 3:00 a.m. by the time Devlin got back
to his apartment. While he mixed himself a double
martini, he called Gloria, but she wasn't home. He
left a message on her machine and sat down to read
the Elgin file again. With the bulk of the file missing,
there wasn't a lot to learn. According to the admission form, the boy's mother, Kay Elgin, had admitted
her son and signed all the release forms. There was
no reference to a Mr. Elgin. She was the one to talk
to. Maybe she could make a connection between
Malroux's clinic and Taggert Industries.

The first thing he did when he awoke the next morn-
ing was call Gloria. Again, there was no answer.
Puzzled, he called her office and got the secretary.
"Hi, Gale. Is Gloria there?"

"No, Mr. Devlin. She's in Buenos Aires."

"Since when? I spoke to her yesterday. She didn't
mention anything about a trip."

"A decision was made late yesterday afternoon.

Apparently there's a big problem with a new plant
under construction and Mr. Taggert, Ms. Salazar, and
some of our engineers went down there to put out
the fire."

"When will she be back?"

"She wasn't sure. She said it could be a few days,
maybe longer."

Before he left for Kay Elgin's apartment in Astoria,
Queens, he called Carla. She told him that it had been
a last-minute scramble, but Nick Mangi had found
two cops to go to South America with Taggert. Devlin
hung up, pleased that Taggert had gone on this unexpected trip. With an unidentified psycho trying to kill
him, South America was the best place for him.

He left word for Otis and Marie to be available for a
meeting at 3:00 P.M. He needed to bounce some ideas
off someone and with Gloria out of town they were the
only ones he could rely on. Since the events of the last
few days, he didn't trust anyone else in the company.

Devlin got off the elevator on the eighth floor, found
apartment 814, and knocked on the paint-chipped
door. A gaunt woman, whom Devlin judged to be in
her early forties, opened the door.

"Yes?"

"My name is Mike Devlin. I'd like to talk to you
about—"

"I'm sorry," she said, starting to close the door.
"I'm not interested in whatever it is you're selling."

"I'm not selling anything," he said quickly. "I'd
like to talk to you about Dr. Malroux's clinic."

She froze and looked up at him with frightened,
haunted eyes. "It's about George, isn't it?"

Her unexpected question caught him off balance. Her son's name was Robert, so he assumed that George must be her husband or boyfriend. "It might be," he said. "May I come in?"

"How . . . how did you know where I live?" she asked in alarm.

"I used to be a policeman, Mrs. Elgin. There are ways."

She had moved from the address listed in the Elgin file, but it had taken only one telephone call to a retired cop, now a private investigator, to track her through telephone company records.

Devlin saw a flash of genuine fear in her eyes. "Does George know where I live?"

"Do you want him to know?"

She shook her head emphatically. "No."

"Why are you afraid of your husband?"

"Ex-husband," she said defensively. "I'm not responsible for anything that man does. I want you to know that."

"I understand."

She ran her fingers through her mousy-brown straight hair. "He's crazy and I want nothing to do with him."

Crazy? Maybe he's the one I should be talking to, Devlin thought. Clearly, the woman was terrified of her ex-husband. "Mrs. Elgin," he said, deliberately keeping his voice soft and reassuring, "I need to know where he is."

Her eyes welled up. "Has he done something bad? Tell me."

"I don't know. That's what I want to talk to him about."

Biting her lip, she stepped back. "All right, come in."

The dimly lit apartment was just the opposite of Doris Miller's cheerful living room. It was sparsely furnished and the bare walls were devoid of pictures or photographs. There were no personal touches anywhere to indicate that this was someone's home. It could have been a motel room.

He sat down on the sofa and felt an errant spring poking him in the back. She sat on a chair opposite him and folded her arms across her thin chest in a protective manner. She wasn't wearing any makeup and the dark smudges under her eyes gave her the wide-eyed look of a frightened fawn.

"Mrs. Elgin, I just want to say how sorry I am about your son, Robert."

She pursed her lips and nodded imperceptibly, as though she didn't trust herself to utter a word.

When he'd first knocked at the door he'd had no idea what he was going to say. As he'd done so often in the past, he fell back on his instincts to say the right thing. Now she'd given him an opening and he intended to take advantage of it.

"Why did you ask me if I was here about George?" Devlin asked. "What would I want with your ex-husband?"

"You work for that clinic, don't you?"

"I'm conducting an investigation for them," he lied.

"Well, George said he might do something and I guess he has."

"Mrs. Elgin, do you know where he is now?"

She looked up from a spot on the threadbare carpet as though she had forgotten he was in the room. "He moves around a lot. When I called him to tell him about Robby's death, he was living in an apartment in Hoboken. But he's not there anymore. I tried to call him a few weeks ago and the landlord said he'd moved out. He left no forwarding address."

Devlin was disappointed, but not discouraged. As long as Elgin didn't know anyone was looking for him, he shouldn't be too hard to find. "Why don't you tell me about George."

She pulled a yellowed handkerchief out of her housecoat pocket and dabbed at her eyes. "I don't know where to begin."

"Where did you meet him?"

Slowly, painfully, Kay Elgin related a story that was not unlike those told by thousands of other lonely young women who move from rural communities to large cities.

She and George Elgin met at work—a large payroll company located on the outskirts of Washington, D.C. He was a computer programmer and she was a secretary. The relationship started casually: a few shared lunches, then an occasional movie, and finally real dates. She was twenty-eight when they married. He was thirty-two.

Like so many other young women who had married badly, she couldn't articulate exactly what she'd seen in him in the first place. Instead, she alluded to vague generalities: "He was kind . . . attentive . . . fun to be with." It wasn't until after they were married that she began to see his flaws. He had a violent temper, which cost him his job at the payroll company two weeks after they'd come back from their honeymoon. He claimed it was his boss's fault, but then he was fired from his next job for getting into a fistfight with his supervisor. By the time he'd lost six more jobs for the same reason, she realized that it was he who was the problem. The first time she suggested that, he hit her. Later, he apologized, even bought her candy and flowers, but it happened again. And again.

In the beginning she attributed his violent behavior to his dysfunctional family. George had been the only son of strict Southern fundamentalists who were incapable of displaying affection. When George was nineteen, he and some friends were caught joyriding in a stolen car. Each boy called his father to come post bail. George's father hung up on him and he wound up in jail. While there, he was involved in a series of brutal clashes with inmates that caused his personality to undergo a dark transformation. The daredevil youth who entered the institution emerged a bitter, vengeful enforcer.

In the years that followed, George adopted a life of criminal behavior. Fortunately, before he could be implicated in a felony, a judge gave him two choices: a year in the county jail or the U.S. Army. He thrived in the army.

Two years after his marriage to Kay, Rob was born. The new baby gave meaning and joy to Kay's life, but George didn't know how to relate to the child. He never held him or played with him. Instead, he showed his love by becoming fiercely protective toward him.

Soon the novelty of a new baby wore off and Elgin went back to his habit of bar-hopping, not with his friends—he didn't have any—but alone. Often these nocturnal escapades resulted in drunken brawls. If he wasn't too drunk or too hurt, he took his frustrations out on his wife. She began to pray that he wouldn't come home.

Sitting there in the living room, talking to Devlin, Kay Elgin realized that she was painting a dismal picture of her ex-husband. "He wasn't *all* bad," she hastened to add. He did have a brilliant mind. He'd grown up in a dirt-poor farming community in the hills of West Virginia, but he'd parlayed his meager high school education, the technical training the army gave him, and his intelligence into a career as a computer specialist. He loved to tell her how his intuitive understanding of anything technical was forever astonishing the better-educated and -trained engineers he worked with.

She fell silent and stared at the threadbare carpet with a faraway look in her eyes.

"Mrs. Elgin," Devlin said softly, "why did you divorce him?"

She took a deep breath and focused on the worn-out rug. "An incident happened that made me finally realize that there was a streak of cruelty in him that I couldn't change and I couldn't live with. One day when Robby was about five, he came home crying with a bloody nose. An older boy—probably six or seven—had beaten him up. It was no big thing, but George went crazy. He kept yelling that no one could get away with hurting his kid."

She twisted the handkerchief in her hands. "The next morning I saw a handful of neighbors gathered in front of the home of the little boy who'd hit Robby and I went to see what all the fuss was about." She blinked away tears and swallowed hard. "The boy's dog was hanging from a tree in his front yard. It . . . it had been mutilated."

She bit her lip. "That night I asked George if he'd done it, but he denied it. Said it was divine intervention. Said that's what people got who hurt other people. I *knew* he did it and decided that night that I had to get away from him. Next day, I packed up Robby and we went to live with my sister."

"Did you get divorced then?"

"At first he refused to listen to anything about a divorce, but finally he said he'd agree if he could get Robby. Well, there was no chance of that. I would never give my son up to him. He didn't love Robby. His son was nothing more than a possession to him," she said bitterly. "It worked out all right, though. The judge found out about his history of violence and denied him custody."

"Did he keep in touch after the divorce?"

"Yeah. I moved around a lot, but he always seemed to know where I was. When Robby was diagnosed with leukemia he told me to get the best treatment for his son, but he never came to see Robby. Not one time.

"I took that boy to so many doctors, but they didn't seem to be helping him. Then, last November, I heard about this clinic where they specialize in treating blood disorders. I spoke to Dr. Malroux and he was very encouraging. He told me they were testing a new drug that might help Robby. I checked my son into the clinic the following week."

Not wanting to prolong her agony, Devlin cut in. "The treatment didn't work and Robby died."

She twisted the handkerchief around her fingers and nodded almost imperceptibly. "It was such a shock. I mean, Robby was sick, but we didn't expect him to die so soon."

"What was George's reaction?"

She looked up and Devlin saw genuine dread in

her eyes. "I've never seen him like that. He didn't go to the funeral, but he came to my apartment the next day. Outwardly he was very calm, but I could tell he was raging inside. He wanted to know what happened. I told him about Dr. Malroux and the experimental drug. George said, 'I'm gonna find out why my son died, and if that doctor did something wrong, he'll pay for it.' He walked out of the house and I haven't seen him since."

"Mrs. Elgin, do you know the name of the drug they gave Robby?"

"No."

"Have you ever heard of Taggert Industries?"

"I know it's some big company."

"Did Dr. Malroux ever mention the name?"

"I don't think so."

"Do the names Kurt Biehl, Ralph Brock, and Nisar Ahmad mean anything to you?"

She shook her head.

Devlin was disappointed. He was hoping she'd be able to connect the clinic with Taggert Industries. "Do you have a photo of George?" he asked.

"Somewhere, I suppose, but it'd be an old one."

"That's okay."

While she went to the bedroom to look for a photo, Devlin wrote his direct office number on a piece of paper.

She came back into the room. "I put his last address on the back." She handed him a dog-eared picture of George Elgin wearing camouflage fatigues. Obviously it had been taken in Vietnam. A close-cropped, muscular man with strange black eyes and a leering grin stared out of the photo. Devlin had seen that desperate, sardonic grin on the faces of emotionally disturbed people and he'd once asked a psychiatrist about it. The doctor said that some psychotics smiled like that to keep from screaming out their agony.

Devlin felt a cold chill. The odds were a hundred to one that he was looking at the man who'd written that threatening letter to Taggert. With a positive ID it wouldn't be too difficult to track him down.

Devlin tucked the photograph into his pocket. "If I may ask, what did your husband do in the army?"

"He got a lot of training in computers because he was so smart. But he found the work boring and volunteered for Special Forces. He served two tours in Vietnam."

A picture of the nail bomb flashed into Devlin's mind. "Did he ever say specifically what he did there?"

"Oh, yeah, he was very proud of his time there and talked about it all the time. He worked in some kind of secret assignment."

"The Phoenix Project?" Devlin asked, already knowing the answer.

"Yeah, that's it. He said it was the best time of his life."

WHEN DEVLIN GOT BACK TO the office, Marie and Otis were waiting for him. "I know who the killer is," he said triumphantly. He took his time pulling his chair out from behind his desk, enjoying the look of anticipation on their faces. "Kay Elgin practically announced—"

"Whoa," Marie interrupted. "Who's Kay Elgin?"

Devlin groaned inwardly. In his excitement he'd forgotten that Marie knew nothing about the break-in. "She's the mother of a boy who died recently in a clinic on the East Side," he said quickly. "She may be a link to—"

"Hold it. How did you find out about her?"

"From Malroux's files," Royal blurted.

Devlin glared at him.

Marie looked from one to the other. "What the hell is going on here? Who's Malroux?"

Royal started to speak, then looked at Devlin.

"I repeat," Marie said. "Who is Malroux?"

Devlin squirmed uncomfortably. "Marie, the details don't matter. The point is—"

"Michael," she said in that soft voice she used when she was about to explode. "Do not lie to me. Who the fuck is Malroux?"

There was no point in stonewalling her any further. Devlin knew she wouldn't stop until she had the whole story. Reluctantly, he told her about the break-in.

He hadn't even finished and she was rolling her eyes. "Are you *nuts*? That's a crime, for chrissake!"

"Well, so . . . so is hacking," Mike sputtered.

"It's not the same thing, Michael, and you know it. What was I supposed to say when the cops called to tell me they'd locked up you and Otis? Huh? Tell me that?"

"Okay, Marie, it's done. Let it go."

While she steamed, Devlin recounted his interview with Kay Elgin. When he finished, he tossed Elgin's photo on the desk. "That's him."

Marie scooped it up and studied it. "Looks like the poster boy for Psycho of the Month," she said. She dropped the photo onto Devlin's desk as if it were a dead rat.

Devlin handed the photo to Royal. "Yeah," Devlin said, "he'll never get elected president, but he's no dummy. According to his ex-wife, he's superintelligent and a whiz with computers."

"Hey, he speaks your lingo, Marie," Royal said with a grin. "Maybe you be judgin' him too quickly."

Marie glared. "Keep it up, Royal."

Devlin leaned back in his chair and folded his hands behind his head. "The thing is, I still can't figure out what the connection is between Elgin, Brock, and Taggert Industries."

Royal fingered his dreadlocks. "What *I* don't

understand is, if Elgin didn't give a fig about his son, why would he be so vexed over his death?"

"Because he's like those feuding families down south," Marie said. "Whaddaya call them . . . "

"The Hatfields and the McCoys," Devlin offered.

"Yeah, those guys. After a few generations of taking pop shots at each other, do you think the survivors had any idea why the hell they were doing it? Do you think they personally gave a rat's ass that a hundred years ago Billy Bob McCoy shot Jimmy Joe Hatfield in the keister? No. It was nothing personal. They were feuding over some fuzzy idea of family loyalty. From what the wife says, this guy Elgin is like a robot. He didn't give a fiddler's fuck for the kid. To him the kid was a possession, a piece of property. Someone destroys your property, you destroy them."

Devlin might have had a hard time accepting that rationale had he not witnessed, firsthand, a similar pattern when he'd worked in New York's Albanian neighborhood. Some Albanian immigrant families continued their ancient blood feuds, spanning hundreds of years, in the streets of the Bronx. It was very much like the Hatfields and the McCoys. When the killers were caught, they readily confessed, but most had only the vaguest notion of why they'd done it.

"So," Royal said, "what do Biehl, Ahmad, and Brock have to do with Elgin and the clinic?"

"That's what I'm waiting to talk to Gloria about," Devlin said, sitting forward in his chair. "She knows what's going on around here and she's the only one in this company I can trust."

"Why only her?" Marie asked incredulously.

"Because it's pretty clear she was the person who

got me hired. If she was part of the funny stuff that's going on around here, she'd still have Bozo the clown handling security."

"Maybe she isn't attractive to clowns," Marie said softly.

"What's that supposed to mean?" Devlin asked.

"Now, children, let us not quarrel," Royal soothed.

Marie put her hands up. "All right, all right. Let me see if I got this straight. You think Elgin is the killer, right?"

"Yeah."

"Have you told the cops?"

Devlin frowned. "For all the good it did. I called the Pennsylvania State Police investigator. He said the Brock case was closed and they had no intention of opening it again unless I could come up with more substantial evidence. I got the distinct impression that he was telling me to mind my own damn business. It was the same with the detective who handled the Ahmad case. Biehl's detective was a little more receptive, but he said he'd just caught a touchy case involving a Broadway star and he had to give it all his attention."

"What about the detective handling Malroux's death, Charlie Andrews?"

"He laughed at me and told me to accept retirement gracefully." Devlin felt a slight tinge of guilt. "Unfortunately, I couldn't tell him or the others what I knew about the other deaths or Taggert's threatening letter."

"Why not?" Marie asked.

"Gloria wants to keep Taggert's letter confidential. I guess I see her point," he added weakly.

The truth was that he was very uncomfortable

withholding information from the police. Taken separately, the four deaths, which Elgin had been careful to make look like accidents, had little meaning. Only he, Mike Devlin, knew the big picture. All four deaths had a common thread: Taggert Industries. And Devlin was convinced that all four deaths had a common killer: George Elgin.

The more he thought about Gloria's demand for secrecy, the more puzzled he became. She was the one who wanted him to catch Elgin, so why was she so insistent that he keep the police out of it? Her unreasonableness would be really irritating if he felt he wasn't already close to wrapping up the case himself.

"So how you going to find this guy?" Otis asked.

"With a little help from my friends," Devlin said. "Right after I left Kay Elgin's apartment, I called a buddy, John Canon—the FBI's liaison with the CIA—and asked him if he could put me in touch with someone from the agency who worked with Elgin in Vietnam."

"You think he can?"

"It's a long shot, but Canon knows a lot of people. I also called Kevin Clark, an ex-cop who runs his own investigating service, and gave him Elgin's last known address. He'll have no problem surfacing him."

Marie tilted her head and gave him a quizzical look. "So far this guy has gotten away with killing four people. What makes you so sure you're going to be the one to reel him in?"

Devlin sat back and put his feet up on the desk. "Because his luck's running out. And because for the first time since I took this job, I see the light at the end of the tunnel. When I saw Taggert's threatening

letter, I figured it was a crank. But then as these acci-
dent/murders popped up, I realized I was dealing
with a world-class psycho. Gloria has been on my
case to find the guy, but it was like looking for a needle in a haystack. Now I know who he is. As soon as
Clark tells me where Elgin is holing up, I go to
Charlie Andrews, tell him what I've got, and he
makes the arrest. Case closed. In the meantime I
don't have to worry about Jason Taggert, who is a safe
six thousand miles away."

Marie stood up. "Come on, Otis, we still have
work to do." At the door she turned to Devlin and
chuckled in that way that he hated because she only
did it when she knew she was right. "Michael," she
said, "you're fucking dreaming."

During the next hour Devlin chipped away at the
mountain of paperwork that had formed, and he was
still at it when the telephone rang. It was John Canon.

"Mike, the guy you want to talk to is Dwight
Allison. He was the CIA station chief at the same
time Elgin was in Vietnam."

Devlin pushed a pile of invoices aside and
grabbed a sheet of paper and a pen. "Where does he
live?"

"You won't believe it. Right here in the city. I've
cleared the way for you. He knows you're okay and
he's expecting you in forty minutes. I figured you'd
want to see him right away."

"You figured right. I owe you one, buddy." Devlin
scribbled down the address and headed for the door.

Dwight Allison, a ruddy-faced man in his early seventies, lived in a pre–Civil War brownstone in Brooklyn

Heights. The retired CIA station chief led Devlin into a spacious living room furnished with an eclectic mix of pieces he'd picked up during a lifetime of globe-trotting. He mixed a martini for Devlin and a club soda for himself, gave the log burning in the fireplace a gentle poke, and sat down opposite Devlin in a worn but comfortable wing-back chair.

"Cheers," he said with a pronounced southern drawl. "I'd sure love to join you in the hard stuff, son, but the doctors tell me my plumbing's shot."

Devlin grinned. "With that accent you can't be from New York."

"Amarillo, Texas."

"You're a long way from home."

"That's for damn sure." He looked around the room with a good-natured grimace. "My wife was born and raised in Brooklyn and this has always been home base for us. She died a couple of years ago, but I can't seem to get myself to move out of this godforsaken city."

"It grows on you."

"Maybe," he said. "Sometimes I worry that I'm becoming a damn Yankee." He studied Devlin with gray eyes that were alert and animated. "So what do you want to know about George Elgin?"

"As I told you on the phone, I'm the security director for Taggert Industries. My boss, Jason Taggert, received an anonymous threatening letter and George Elgin's name has come up. If he's the guy I'm looking for, I want to know as much about him as I can."

The easygoing smile faded from Allison's face and his gray, bushy eyebrows descended over his eyes. "There's only one thing to know. George Elgin is crazier than a hoot owl. That was my view the first time I set eyes on him in Vietnam, and in the year that I worked with him, I found no reason to change my mind."

"What was his connection with you?"

Allison's expression became guarded. "I've been told that you can be trusted, but let me make this perfectly clear. Nothing of what we say in this room is for public consumption."

Devlin nodded. "Understood."

"I presume you've heard about the Phoenix Program?"

"Yes."

Allison grunted. "All bad, no doubt. It was a combined CIA–Special Forces operation. The truth is, it started out as a worthwhile political program to identify North Vietnamese sympathizers holding, or running for, public office. But pretty soon some people got real impatient at the slow pace of the program and its limited results."

"Was Elgin one of them?"

"He was."

"What kind of guy was he?"

"A real loner, unpredictable, extremely hot-tempered. Even the other SF types gave him a wide berth. And that's saying something, because there were some real lunatics in that outfit.

"There was this one village chief, Boc Ho, who was giving us nothing but heartache. He provided safe haven to the VC, supplied them with food, and warned them of impending military operations. One night a bunch of us were drinking in the local watering hole, discussing how to shut down Boc Ho's operation. As usual, Elgin was sitting at the bar alone—off from the main group, listening in. All of a sudden he walks over to the table. 'I know how to stop that fucker,' he says. And with that he whips out his boot knife and drives it into the table. It was a real conversation-stopper, as you can imagine.

"The fact is, we were carpet-bombing the shit out of the country and killing God knows how many civilians, but at that time the thought of personally targeting and murdering an individual, even an evil son of a bitch like Boc Ho, was inconceivable. The party broke up and we all went to bed."

As Allison continued talking, he picked up a poker and prodded the log, sending a shower of sparks up the chimney. "I didn't think much of it, but then, a couple of days later, an intelligence report crossed my desk informing me that Boc Ho was dead, his throat slashed by party or parties unknown. Well, *I* knew damn well who the party was and I went ballistic. I stomped into the SF colonel's office and demanded a full investigation. The colonel called Elgin into the office and confronted him."

"Did he admit it?"

Allison shook his head. "He was the coolest son of a bitch I ever did see. He looked me and his colonel right in the eye and denied it. Not only did he get away with murder, worse, he gave other people ideas."

"There were other assassinations?"

"There were—although we didn't refer to them as such at the time. The truth is, you couldn't argue with the results. A dead enemy isn't a threat to anyone. Pretty soon, more and more targeted officials were popping up dead and we started making some real progress pacifying the provinces. We never once discussed it openly, but we all knew what was going on. That's when the boys started calling Elgin 'the Phantom.'"

"Why?"

"For his ability to fade into the jungle and suddenly reappear out of nowhere. Every time he did that, we'd hear that another village official was found dead. I can tell you, it really spooked the North Vietnamese."

Allison stopped talking and with a faraway look in his eyes studied the yellow and orange flames licking at the log.

Devlin decided to tread softly. "So . . . how come no one put a stop to it?"

Allison looked up, his eyes weary, resigned. "Son, you had to be in Vietnam at that time. It was a different universe—it had a reality all its own. To describe what it was like, getting through a day—well, you just can't."

The former CIA man struggled with the words. "In the morning you ate breakfast at a hotel . . . and then, a few hours later, you were in the field killing a few VC. And that night . . . well, that night you were back at the hotel having drinks at the bar like it was just another day at the office. A psychiatrist would probably come up with a fancy name for it. Me, I thought of it as survival. You did what had to be done."

"Mr. Allison, let me ask you something. Supposing Elgin is after my boss—how do I stop him?"

The retired CIA agent snorted. "You can't."

"Oh, come on, the guy's not supernatural. He—"

"Let me tell you about the episode that finally got Elgin thrown out of the country. He and I went to a village to interview the village chief and his two sons. While we're in the hootch talking, there's this godawful explosion. We run outside and Elgin's jeep is all blown to hell. I wanna tell you, it was ass-pucker time. I figure any minute the VC are going to pop out of the woodwork and blow up *our* sorry asses. I get on the horn and call for a gunship to come get us the hell out of there. What's Elgin doing? Choking the shit out of the village chief, demanding to know who blew up his jeep. When the chopper came in I had to practically drag Elgin away. All the way back all he keeps saying is, 'They destroyed my property.' I told him, 'It's only a jeep, for chrissake. Get another one from the motor pool.' He looks me right in the eye— and I wanna tell you, son, the look on that man's face gave me chills—and says in a low, flat voice, 'That's my property and nobody destroys my property.'

"The next morning we go back to the village. Only this time we're accompanied by three squads of South Vietnamese Rangers. It's just dawn and as we approach through the mist we see a cluster of villagers standing around, silently staring at something. Suddenly the mist blows away and we see what they're looking at." Allison stopped talking, stared at the fire for a long moment, and then continued. "The village chief and his two sons were impaled on sharpened stakes. I said to Elgin, 'You did this, you crazy son of a bitch.' He looked at me with those flat black eyes of his and said, 'Not me. It must have been divine retribution.'"

"Was he arrested?" Devlin asked.

"No. By this time the Phoenix Project had become one hot political potato. I wanted him court-martialed or at least given a Section 8, but I was overruled. The agency couldn't afford a scandal. The folks back home were fed up with the war and the administra-

tion was getting a lot of heat from the press. The last
thing they needed was an exposé about some Green
Beret who thought he was Vlad the Impaler."

"So what happened to him?"

"We rotated him back early and gave him a medical discharge."

By this time Devlin's stomach was churning. From
Kay Elgin's description of her husband, he figured he
was dealing with a Looney Tune, but he would never
have guessed the man was this far around the bend.
"He murdered three men because of a *jeep?*" he asked.

Allison leaned forward in his chair, and the sense
of wonder was still evident in his eyes. "That ain't the
half of it, son. That village was twenty-five miles into
VC territory. After dark, the entire area was a notori-
ous hot zone crawling with VC. No American troops,
and certainly no South Vietnamese, went anywhere
near that area at night. Think of it. Elgin, alone, in
the dark, making his way twenty-five miles through
enemy territory just so he can kill three men. And all
because of a damn jeep."

Allison drained his glass and looked at Devlin with
sympathy in his eyes. "If George Elgin is after your boss,
I wouldn't want to be his life insurance agent. And you,
well, I'd say you're in for a heap of trouble." He pointed
at Devlin's glass. "Want another one of those?"

Devlin looked down at his empty glass and suddenly realized his throat was dry. "Yeah," he said.
"Make it a double."

The next morning Marie and Otis arrived at the
reception area outside Devlin's office, only to be
warned by Carla that "the boss is in a bad mood."

Confident he could cheer Devlin up, Royal nudged Marie forward and called out, "Good news, Michael. We've been making excellent progress on installin'—"

"Sit down," Devlin said abruptly. "I've found out a few things."

"Michael, you don't look so good," Marie said, noting the bags under his eyes. She lowered herself slowly to the chair. "What's wrong?"

"Last night I heard a few war stories," Devlin said. "George Elgin war stories. You'd better sit down." He recounted his meeting with Allison, leaving out only a few details.

When he'd finished, Marie and Otis were like statues—paralyzed by the implications and still unable to fully absorb it all.

"Well, say something," Devlin prodded. "I'm going to need—"

Carla's buzzer interrupted him. He snatched up the receiver. "Yeah, fine. Okay, put him on the speaker." Devlin looked at Marie and Otis, mouthed the words "Kevin Clark."

"Kevin, what you got for me?"

"Good news and bad news, Mike. The good news is I got all my documentation. Usually this stuff takes days, but you said you needed it right away, so I pulled out all the stops—"

"I appreciate that, Kev," Devlin said, rolling his eyes. The PI was always selling himself. "Cut to the chase."

"Well, the bad news is that the subject has dropped out of the system."

Devlin sat up. "What do you mean?"

"I mean that after January 16, there's absolutely

no paper trail. No electric bills, no telephone bills, no car payments, no nothing. I checked out Elgin's last address. He moved out on that same date. Left no forwarding address. From January 16, he ceases to exist—at least on paper."

January 16 was the day after the clinic burglary and the day before Malroux died. "How about credit cards?" Devlin asked.

"Master and Visa. On the sixteenth he maxed out his cards. Couple of purchases, the rest cash advances. Looks like the credit-card companies are gonna eat this one."

"What were the purchases?"

There was a shuffling of papers over the speaker-phone as Clark looked for his documentation. "Here it is. Kimball Medical Supplies in Bayonne, New Jersey."

"Do you know what he bought?"

"I made some inquiries," Clark whispered in a confidential tone, which Devlin knew meant that he'd greased somebody's palm. "Assorted rolls of surgical tape and some surgical instruments: scalpels, knives, shears. That sort of thing."

Devlin looked down at the photograph of George Elgin on his desk and felt the knot in his stomach growing tighter.

"He also spent over two grand at TKD Supplies in South Carolina."

"What kind of company is that?"

"Military surplus. I couldn't find out what he bought. Those guys at TKD are a tight-lipped bunch of bastards." Devlin knew that meant that Clark couldn't grease anybody's palm. "The company specializes in all kinds of sophisticated and exotic stuff, laser sights, night-vision goggles, rapelling equipment, that sort of thing."

"Weapons?"

Clark's voice again dropped to a whisper, as though whispering on the telephone would make any difference if someone were listening. "If you know the right people to talk to, I hear you can get all kinds of stuff: flashbang grenades, silencers, armor-piercing rounds, C-4 explosives. You name it. Probably a friggin' Stinger missile if you got the dough."

Devlin shook his head as Marie and Otis exchanged looks with each other.

Clark continued. "I don't know why you're looking for this guy, Mike, but he ain't gonna be easy to find. I've chased deadbeat dads who'd thought they could beat the system, but they were amateurs. They don't realize it, but these days, it's damn near impossible to drop off Big Brother's electronic screen. Unless you're a real pro. This guy shows all the signs of being just that."

"No shit, Sherlock," Marie mumbled under her breath.

Devlin told the PI to keep looking for Elgin, promising him a hefty bonus, then slammed down the receiver. When he looked up, Marie and Otis were staring at him with a mixture of fear and compassion. Their expressions were easy enough to read. He'd been thinking the same thing. It was a whole new ball game. Elgin had not only made himself invisible, he'd embarked on a plan that promised more mayhem than they'd ever dreamed of. So much for "wrapping up" the case.

"I think I was a tad too optimistic," Devlin said morosely.

"Yes, you were," Marie said.

"So what's Plan B?" Royal asked, straining to sound upbeat.

"Step one of Plan B is for Marie to wrap up what she's doing tomorrow," Devlin said. "I won't be needing her anymore."

Marie met his level gaze. "Why?"

"The computer stuff can wait. Right now the important thing is to zip up this building. Otis and I—"

"Michael, don't chase me away."

"Marie, this is not open for discussion. Later, when Elgin is caught, you'll come back and—"

"You're not chasing Otis away."

Royal tugged at his dreadlocks. "I wouldn't mind if he did," he said half in jest.

"Marie, Elgin is coming after Taggert and he'll take out anyone in his way. I don't want you around."

"Listen to me," she said in a low voice. "If Elgin is as good with computers as his wife says he is, he's a real threat. He could crash the entire system. It might not be as satisfying as killing Taggert, but it would cause a hell of a lot of damage. You *need* me."

Devlin recognized the truth of what she was saying. Still, some deeper part of him wanted her safe. He was too cynical to be chivalrous and under too much pressure not to appreciate what she could do for him. *Then why did he desperately want her out of harm's way?*

He kept shaking his head, unable to frame an argument for her departure. "Marie, for once just do what I—"

"No, goddamn it, unless you can sit there and tell me I can't be of use around here."

An exasperated Devlin sat back in resignation. "All

right, we'll see," he said, keeping his options open. Feeling a sense of desperate urgency, he said, "This changes everything. I thought I could protect Taggert with a couple of bodyguards, but that's not going to be enough. For all I know, Elgin does have a Stinger missile and he's planning to blow up Taggert's limo."

Marie thought furiously, trying to come up with a computer systems angle that would alleviate the situation, but she drew nothing but blanks. "Michael, short of imprisoning Taggert, how else can we guarantee his safety?"

Devlin went to his file cabinet and took out a thick folder. "Imprisoning him might not be too far off the mark. I've got to quarantine him somehow until Elgin is caught, and I'm thinking of isolating him in one of his houses or apartments."

He spread the contents of the file on his desk. "These are photos and blueprints of the various places Taggert calls home."

Marie picked up a photograph of a sprawling multicolumned mansion nestled among a stand of magnolia and oak trees. "*Marone*. The only thing missing is Scarlett and Rhett dancing on the front veranda. How many residences does he have?"

"Four." He pointed to the photo in her hands. "That's his horse farm in Kentucky—a couple of thousand acres." He tossed more photographs on the table. "That's the Sutton Place apartment; here's a condo on Maui; and finally, a small villa in southern France."

Royal studied the photos and blueprints with interest. "I'm impressed, Michael. You've been very diligent in your security functions."

Devlin grunted. "I didn't put this stuff together.

Apparently the lucky guy who had this job before me had a yen to see Maui and France. Wish I'd thought of it first. I've never been to—"

"Well, well, glad to see you're burning the midnight oil."

The three spun around and gaped at Gloria standing in the doorway.

"I thought you were in Buenos Aires?" Devlin blurted.

"I was, but the problem was solved by the time we got there. I told JT there was no need to rush down there, but he—"

"Taggert!" Devlin started for the door. "Where is he?"

"He's still there. He found a nude beach and decided he had to stay a couple of more days. Your bodyguards didn't seem to mind." She gave him a curious look. "What's the matter with you?"

Devlin exhaled in relief, thankful that Taggert was still out of the country. He pulled out a chair. "Sit down, Gloria. A lot of things have happened since you left."

WHILE DEVLIN WAS TELLING Gloria what he'd discovered—leaving out the details about how he'd learned about George Elgin—Marie studied her with barely concealed envy. The woman had just made a six-thousand-mile journey and she looked as though she'd stepped off the cover of *Vogue*. Her makeup was perfect, not a hair out of place. Her expensive Margo Tintano suit wasn't even wrinkled. *What'd she do, stand all the way home, for chrissake?*

Reluctantly, Marie made a quick comparison with her own clothing. She was wearing a pair of off-the-rack slacks from JC Penney, the right knee of which, she had just noticed, was sporting a loose thread. She unconsciously covered the offending blemish with her hands, causing her to focus on her nails. They were cut short—easier to type with, she'd often told herself. But there was no denying it, they paled in comparison to Gloria's long, high-gloss talons.

Marie didn't know what brand of shoes Gloria was

wearing, but they looked like the shoes Marie had
wistfully seen displayed in the windows of those
expensive Italian shoe stores along 57th Street. She
refused to look at her own feet. She already knew
what she was wearing: a pair of slightly scuffed flats
from Macy's. Self-consciously, she tucked her feet
under the chair.

Marie had comforted herself with the thought
that anyone could look good in expensive clothes,
but, she had to admit, she was kidding herself. The
truth was that Gloria Salazar was one of those irritating women who could look good wearing a sleeping
bag.

When Devlin told Gloria he'd identified Elgin,
her eyes lit up, but then when he said that Elgin had
dropped out of sight her elation turned to a smolder-
ing anger.

When he finished telling his story, she said, "So
where does that leave us?"

"We were just talking about it when you came in.
I've got to get Taggert off the street and into a safe
and controlled environment."

"Where's that?"

"One of his residences."

Gloria looked doubtful. "You mean stay there
until Elgin is caught?"

"Yes."

She shook her head. "He'll never go for it."

"I don't care if he goes for it or not. That's the only
way I can protect him. I don't want to get melodramatic, but this is literally a matter of life and death
and it's no time to be bullheaded. He could wind up
the most stubborn corpse in the cemetery."

Gloria drummed the desk with her long fingernails. Then she said, "All right, I suppose that could work. At least for the short duration. All he really needs is a fax machine, a computer, a telephone, and a squad of secretaries. We might even be able to set up a teleconferencing center. And if there's anybody he needs to see in person, we'll send them over. Which residence do you have in mind?"

As Devlin leaned over her to point to the photo of the villa, he caught a whiff of her perfume. *Goddamn it, she makes it hard to concentrate.* He cleared his throat. "There's the villa—"

Gloria shook her head. "It can't be out of the country."

"Why not?"

"Too impractical. If we do have to set up a meeting, we don't want to have to be flying people to Europe."

"I guess we can rule out Maui, then?"

Gloria nodded.

Royal, who'd been studying the blueprints, looked up. "The farm is no good, you know. It's too big. It wouldn't be possible to secure it properly in such a short period of time."

Devlin reached for a photo of the Sutton Place apartment. "Then this is—"

Royal shook his head and his dreadlocks swayed back and forth. "That's no good either, Michael. Look . . . " He stabbed at the blueprints. "There is a fire stairway runnin' up through the center of the buildin'. We couldn't secure that. Besides, I'm certain the other tenants would object to additional locks and armed guards patrollin' their halls."

Devlin pushed the Sutton Place photo away in disgust. "So where the hell do we put him?"

"Right here."

The three turned to Marie.

"Why not?" she said. "We control the entire building, there's a penthouse on the top floor where he can stay, and this is where he works."

Gloria's smile was grudging. "I think she has something."

A doubtful Devlin said to Royal, "Can we secure an entire building?"

Royal idly fingered a dreadlock and contemplated the ceiling. "It certainly would be a challenge."

"That's not what I asked you, Otis. Can we secure the building?"

"Secure is a relative word. If by that you mean guarantee that Elgin can't get into the buildin', the answer is no. *But* with Taggert confined to the top floor and through a process of layerin'—"

"What's that mean?" Gloria asked.

"Increasin' the sophistication and complexity of the security hardware the closer you get to the thing or person you want to protect. Say the lowest level of security is a one and the highest a ten. I could set up a level one in the lobby, a level three up to the twentieth floor, a level eight to the thirty-ninth floor, and a level ten for the fortieth and penthouse floors."

Gloria was intrigued. Security was a field that was totally alien to her. Like everyone else who worked in a modern office building, she'd been controlled or observed by various types of security systems, but she'd never paid any attention to the ubiquitous unblinking eyes of CCTV cameras or understood what happened when she swiped a card through a black box and the door magically sprung open. To her, security was the amiable retired cop who stood by the elevators and said good morning.

"What would be the difference between level one and level ten?" she asked.

"Level one could be CCTV cameras—"

"Which are?" Gloria asked impatiently.

"Sorry. Closed-circuit television. I would mount CCTV cameras at every entrance and exit out of the building, including the garage and service bays."

"Whoa," Gloria said, mentally counting up the number of doors in the tower. "There's gotta be over a dozen doors. Who could watch that many monitors?"

"A multiplexer can accept sixteen cameras and channel all of them into one monitor. The guard has the option of watchin' one, four, nine, or all sixteen pictures at once or sequencin' through all sixteen."

"You can't expect one man to watch all that."

"No. I'd install video motion detectors at all sites where there is little activity. A fire emergency door, for instance. I set my VMD so that any movement in the camera view will generate a response. With digital pipeline processing and an EE-PROM memory for backup—"

Gloria put her hands up in mock surrender. "Wait, you're losing me. Speak English."

Royal grinned sheepishly. "Sorry. When the VMD is triggered by movement, the camera instantly captures the monitor at the guard station and displays the door. So he can see what is happenin'."

Gloria, always analytical, said, "What if someone doesn't go through the door? They just walk in front of it. Won't that create a false alarm?"

"To prevent that, I can configure the VMD in what is known as a museum mode. I can define the VMD so that it will ignore the movement of people and respond only if the door is opened."

Gloria turned to Devlin. "This stuff is fascinating, isn't it?"

Devlin shrugged. "I've heard it all before." He winced as Marie kicked him under the table.

Basking in his role as teacher, Royal continued. "To complete level one security in the lobby, I issue employees access cards that can be programmed to permit access to certain doors only."

"Okay," Gloria said, "level one sounds pretty sophisticated. So what can level ten be like?"

Royal rubbed his hands together. "This is the part I like the best—usin' exotic security devices. Level ten would mean employin' biometrics."

Gloria's eyebrows went up. "Which are—?"

"A reader that uses some unique body feature— palm print, eye retina, or voice—for identification. From a security standpoint, the good thing about bio- metrics is that it uses body parts. Unlike a card, you can't lose them and no one else can borrow them."

"How does it work?"

"Very simple. A person puts his hand on a pad and the computer records and remembers its peculiar geography."

"Doesn't that take a long time?"

"Less than two seconds to verify identity. I would use this very secure system, in conjunction with CCTV cameras and access cards, to protect the forti- eth floor. A computer, controlled by one person, can interface all these third-party platforms and make modifications as necessary. Then—"

Gloria shook her head and stood up. "That's enough *Star Wars* for me." She turned to Devlin. "Sounds good to me. Let's do it."

"There is one problem," Royal said.

"What's that?"

"It will take time to purchase these systems and put them in place."

Gloria's easy smile faded. "Mr. Royal, we don't have time. Get the equipment any way you have to. Have them rip it out of new construction if necessary. We'll pay any and all additional costs."

Royal nodded. "I'll do my best."

Gloria patted his hand. "You won't do your best, you'll just do it." As she turned to leave she said, "Mike, could I see you in my office for a moment?"

"Sure," he said. "I'll be right there."

Devlin gathered up the photos and blueprints. "I know what Otis is going to be doing for the next few days. What's your game plan gonna be, Marie?"

"Make sure the company's computers are secure from outside assault."

Devlin stuffed the file back into the drawer and slammed it. "There's an awful lot we have to do in a short period of time. We're talking about around-the-clock work. Anybody have problems with that?"

Marie shook her head. "It's okay with me. It's boring as hell being home with no kids to yell at."

"No problem, mon. Playing with all these gadgets tickles me."

Devlin looked at Marie. "I know there are a lot of systems in the building," he said. "Just do the best you can."

"No," she said, repeating Gloria's line. "I'll just *do* it."

They all laughed.

As Devlin came into Gloria's office she was just kicking off her shoes. She slid up to him and put her arms around his neck. "Aren't you going to say hello?" she whispered in his ear.

Pulling her tight against him, Devlin smelled her delicate fragrance and felt a rush. But he still wasn't quite comfortable with this lover-boss arrangement. There were times when he was almost afraid to initiate anything personal between them, half expecting that she'd pull away in astonishment and demand to know what the hell he was doing.

She slipped out of his arms and slid a mirrored panel aside, revealing a bar. "I can use a drink. How about you?"

He fell into a chair. "Sounds good."

While she was making him a double scotch on the rocks and a light scotch for herself, he said, "I think Armond is stonewalling me."

She handed him his drink and sat down on the couch next to him. "Why would he do that?"

"I don't know. But when I spoke to him about Ahmad and Brock, I think he was being evasive."

Gloria stuck a long fingernail into her glass and spun her ice cubes. "You cops are so paranoid. I told you, Armond is new. He's still feeling his way around. The R&D section is involved in a lot of heavy projects and he doesn't have a handle on it yet. He has a learning curve to deal with, that's all."

Devlin tugged on her chin. "And that's the man you want me to see for information? Very clever."

She smacked his hand away. She tried to make it appear playful, but Devlin knew he'd hit a raw nerve. Gloria didn't like being made fun of.

Still, why was she making excuses for Armond? From the little that Devlin had seen of him, he wasn't impressed. The man seemed vague, out of touch—

incompetent was the word that came to mind. Nothing like his predecessor, Kurt Biehl. Why was a perfectionist like Gloria defending him? It was out of character.

She clinked his glass. "Here's to you catching Mr. Elgin."

Devlin stopped smiling. "Gloria, let's not start that again."

Her eyes widened. "Start what?"

"This thing about me getting Elgin. My job is to protect Taggert. It's the cops' job to get Elgin."

"But you said yourself the police aren't interested. You have to be the one to get him."

"They'd be interested if they knew what I know about these four murders. I think it's time we let the police in on the whole story. That way—"

"No. I told you, we can't afford the negative publicity."

"Publicity?" Devlin sat forward quickly and his drink splashed over his hand. "Gloria, I may sound like a broken record, but there's a lunatic trying to kill your boss. Do you think maybe you have a priority problem here or what?"

"I'm well aware of the seriousness of the problem," Gloria said stiffly. "It isn't just the merger and how the stock price may affect it, we're in the middle of negotiating an important bond issue which we desperately need to finance new construction. If word gets out that someone is trying to kill our best asset, it'll scare off investors. I've discussed this with JT and he concurs. There'll be no police involvement. Is that clear?"

"Yeah, that's clear. Now let me make something clear to you. I don't have the resources or the manpower to go after Elgin. The man is a phantom. The best I can do is to throw up a protective wall around Taggert. *That's* my job."

"Are you afraid to go after him?"

The challenge was like a slap in the face. *Was he afraid?* Of course he was. He'd be a fool not to be afraid of someone like Elgin. The question she really meant was: Was he a coward? He knew the answer to that question, but he was disappointed that she would even have to ask.

He put his drink down and stood up. "When Elgin comes after Taggert," he said wearily, "I'll be waiting."

"Where are you going?" she said.

"I have a lot to do," he muttered, heading toward the door.

She ran around the desk and stepped in front of him. "Mike, I'm sorry. I didn't mean that."

He pushed her hand away. "You say a lot of things you don't mean."

She threw her arms around him and pressed her soft body against his. "Mike, I *am* sorry. It's just that . . . I'm so terrified of all this that I'm not thinking straight."

Devlin, getting weary of these crazy mood swings, removed her arms from around his neck. "Everything is going to be all right," he said. "We'll keep Taggert out of harm's way while my PI locates Elgin. Then we'll see what happens."

19

AFTER HE LEFT GLORIA'S OFFICE, Devlin took the elevator to the penthouse to make a detailed inspection of what were going to be Jason Taggert's living quarters for the foreseeable future. All too aware of Taggert's irascible nature, he hoped that wouldn't be for long.

A lot of the layout he remembered from his first day's inspection with Tommy Nolen, but he hadn't paid much attention to the details, and it was now that he fully appreciated how many perks there were. In addition to an office and a conference room, which were as large as the ones on the fortieth floor, there was a thirty-foot-square master bedroom with floor-to-ceiling windows overlooking the southern tip of Manhattan. Along the entire wall opposite a raised king-size bed was a built-in closet containing a giant-size TV, VCR, and state-of-the-art stereo system.

The kitchen, which Taggert had probably never seen and would never use, was equipped with a professional stove and appliances worthy of the finest

four-star restaurant. A formal dining room, complete
with a huge Waterford crystal chandelier hanging over
an ebony table, was large enough to accommodate a
dinner party of twenty.

Farther down the hall was a screening room; a
mini-theater with a twenty-five-person seating
capacity; a glass-mirrored gym furnished with a
Stairmaster, a treadmill, and the latest Nautilus
equipment; and a dark-paneled library lined with
leather-bound volumes of the classics—something
else Devlin doubted Taggert used very often. The
rest of the rooms, stretching down the hall and
around U-shaped corridors, were used for storage.

As Devlin toured the rabbit warren of rooms and
corridors, he was satisfied that from a SWAT team
tactical standpoint the penthouse would be a nightmare to negotiate. Trying to find your way through
this maze wouldn't be easy without a good floor plan
and the time to memorize its many twists and turns.
Devlin was pleased with his good fortune. At least he
had the advantage of defending an objective that
would be hard to infiltrate. Not that he expected that
to happen. After what Otis had said about "layering,"
it was highly unlikely that even someone as resourceful as Elgin could get this far.

By the time Devlin got home, it was after 1:00 A.M.
He was exhausted—it seemed like days since he'd
had a full night's sleep—but he was too keyed up to
go to bed. As he rethought the feasibility of defending Taggert Tower, he vacillated between confidence and apprehension. One minute he was
convinced that between him, Otis, and the best

security technology money could buy they could make the building invincible. Then he'd think of George Elgin, ex–Special Forces assassin, crawling through the jungle to administer payback for the burning of his jeep, and he wasn't so sure.

He fixed himself a martini and sat down to do some channel surfing. After clicking through a few channels, he settled on Clint Eastwood's *High Plains Drifter.* In the middle of a scene where Eastwood was mowing down a gang of bad guys, Devlin suddenly had a thought. He ripped off a piece of the *Daily News* and scrawled across the margin: *Get submachine gun . . . flashbang grenades . . .*

Devlin was in his office the next afternoon waiting for Taggert to arrive from the airport. The telephone rang: It was Tommy Nolen.

"Boss, you wanted me to let you know when Mr. Taggert got in. He's on his way up to his penthouse office."

The penthouse office was as large as the one on the fortieth floor, but instead of the minimalist look of glass-and-steel furniture, this office was copiously furnished with massive antique pieces.

Looking tanned and relaxed, Taggert glanced up from the *Wall Street Journal.* "What's going on now? When I got off the plane there were two more bodyguards."

Devlin shut the door behind him. "There have been some new developments."

As Devlin told Taggert what he'd uncovered, the CEO listened with his usual impatience, firing questions as they occurred to him. But then, as the import of what Devlin was saying hit home, he fell silent. By the end of the narrative, he was tight-lipped and somber.

"So what are you doing to catch this guy?" he asked.

"A private investigator is tracking his whereabouts."

"What about the cops?"

"They're not interested."

"Why the hell not?"

"They don't believe these so-called accidents are murders." Devlin sighed. "To put it more accurately, they don't want the headache of reopening a can of worms when they have so little to go on."

Taggert hurled the newspaper into the wastebasket in disgust. "So that leaves just you and a handful of moonlighting cops to protect me against Rambo and The Terminator all rolled into one?"

"It looks that way."

Taggert got up and went to look out the window. "Exactly how do you plan to do that?"

"I want you to stay here until Elgin is caught."

"Stay here? You mean the city?"

"I mean the building."

Taggert chuckled mirthlessly. "Funny, Devlin. Very funny."

"It wasn't meant to be a joke."

Taggert turned away from the window. "You're nuts."

"It's the only way I can ensure your safety until Elgin is out of the picture."

Taggert looked at Devlin for a long moment to make sure he wasn't kidding, then he exploded. "Goddamn it! I'm not gonna become a prisoner in my own building because you can't do your job."

Devlin stepped up to Taggert and poked his finger into the CEO's chest. "Let me tell you what my job is," he said in an even voice. "You hired me to protect you and make this a secure facility. That's what I'm doing. I didn't hire on as a private cop to track down psychos who want to kill you.

"The truth of the matter is this guy isn't just your run-of-the-mill fuck-up. He has expertise. He's *very* capable. We *know* how capable he is—he's killed four people already. And he has a special hard-on for you." Devlin jabbed his finger at the city stretched out below them. "You can't walk those streets and think you can avoid him, because you're a target. He's a patient son of a bitch. He'll stalk you until he finds the right moment, and when he does, you're dead meat. And this"—he thrust his hand inside Taggert's coat, yanked the pistol from his holster, and slammed it on the desk—"isn't going to save you. Your only hope of staying alive is to plant your butt in this building and pray like hell that I can protect you from him. *That's* my job description. You don't like it, fire me."

A red-faced Taggert poked back at Devlin. "You don't like me much, do you?"

"Not particularly."

"Why? Because you think I have an easy job? Because you think I'm just another fat-cat business-man earning more money than he's worth? Well, I got news for you. I'm worth every goddamn penny they pay me. And you know why? No, of course you don't." Taggert's eyes bored in. "You've been feeding off the public trough your whole life. Every two weeks, no matter what, they hand you a paycheck. You've never had to make a payroll. You've never had to show a profit."

"Listen—" Devlin countered.

"No, *you* listen," Taggert said. "I have thousands of people whose livelihood depends on the decisions I make daily. If I guess wrong, some people lose a couple of points on the stock, but others lose their *jobs*, which means they can't pay the mortgage, can't send their kids to decent schools, maybe can't even get the medical care they need. Let me tell you, that's an awesome responsibility. It *wouldn't* be if I didn't give a goddamn about the people in this organization, but I do.

"You think a company like Taggert Industries just makes money? You're wrong. We serve a useful purpose. It may sound like PR bullshit, but we change people's lives."

Devlin had taken a step back, less sure of himself now, and Taggert moderated his tone.

"Here, let me show you something."

He went to his desk and pointed at a beaker that was filled with a clear liquid. "I leave this on my desk to remind me of the good things this company does. Our R&D people made a significant breakthrough with this industrial acid. They chemically altered the polymer chains, making the acid ecologically friendly while still retaining its full strength.

"Watch." Taggert carefully removed the lid from the beaker, then theatrically picked up a half-inch bolt and carefully dropped it in. By the time it hit bottom, it had almost fully dissolved. "That," he said, "is big business in action."

Devlin would have been more impressed with the demonstration if he hadn't already heard about the famous "screw-in-the-acid" routine. Every first-time visitor to Taggert's penthouse office got the same show and the same spiel.

"So what's this got to do with me?" Devlin asked.

"You've been playing cowboys and Indians too long, Devlin. To you, there are good guys in white hats and bad guys in black hats. Well, that's simplistic horseshit. The world is a whole lot more complicated place than that. So get off your moralistic high horse and stop judging me."

Inwardly, Devlin conceded that maybe Taggert had a point. Did he dislike the abrasive CEO because he saw him as a spoiled, rich executive? Or because he took what he did so seriously—something Devlin had strenuously avoided until very recently?

Taggert carefully placed the lid back on the beaker. "Look, Devlin, I'm not dazzled by your personality either, but I'm gonna have to rely on you to protect me. I know you've got balls and that you're good with a gun, so I'm placing myself in your hands. But *I'm* the one who makes the big decisions."

Devlin grunted, trying to mask the fact that the Taggert he was seeing now for the first time didn't actually seem half-bad. Full of piss-and-vinegar, but fair.

"Okay," said Devlin finally. He put his hand out. "Maybe I misjudged you."

A startled Taggert tentatively took his hand. "All right," he said gruffly. "It's good to clear the air once in a while."

"So you'll agree to stay in the building until Elgin is caught?"

Taggert exhaled slowly and turned to look down on the bustling traffic on Park Avenue. "I'm one of the most powerful businessmen in the world," he said. "I know presidents, Hollywood stars, champion athletes. I have more money that I can count. And"—

he laughed bitterly—"where does it get me? I'm a prisoner in my own building." He turned around, and Devlin saw a glimmer of fear in the CEO's pale blue eyes. "Devlin, don't let this building become my tomb."

"I won't," Devlin said, for the first time seriously committing himself to keeping Jason Taggert alive. "We'll get through this."

Jason Taggert. Elgin violently crushed the mound of peanut husks against the scored bartop with the bottom of his beer bottle. Since Taggert had eluded the nail bomb at the shareholders' meeting, images of the smug CEO had continued to invade Elgin's thoughts, denying him any peace. Just thinking about how the greedy, self-important tycoon had been saved at the last minute made him furious.

In subsequent surveillances Elgin had learned that Taggert was being protected by two guards twenty-four hours a day. But just this afternoon, as he waited outside the corporate headquarters on Park Avenue, he'd seen Taggert's limousine pull up to the entrance. This time there were *four* guards. Clearly, they were creating a fortress around the CEO. He would have to act soon.

While Elgin was considering possible tactical solutions, two boisterous construction workers came in and sat down a few bar stools away. The taller of the two, a jowly man with a barrel-shaped belly, slammed his beefy hand on the bar. "Hey, what do ya have to do to get some service around here?"

Another bartender might have declined to serve them, but this one, a thickly muscled Italian, catered to a Bowery clientele of mostly bums and near bums who, if nothing else, tolerated other drunks. It didn't pay to be choosy. The barkeep quickly took the customers' order and returned with two Budweisers.

The shorter of the two workers, a wiry, ferret-faced man, snatched up his bottle. "Hey, Tony," he said, nudging his friend, "get a load of that guy."

Tony turned to look at Elgin, who was staring straight ahead, lost in his own thoughts. He spotted the mound of peanuts in front of Elgin and said in a loud voice, "You know what, Charlie? This place smells like a fuckin' circus." When he didn't get a rise out of Elgin, he said in a louder voice, "Hey, pal, don't eat all them nuts. Save some for your elephants."

Assuming his usual role as troublemaker, Charlie said, "He ain't laughing, Tony. He don't think you're so funny."

Tony's grin quickly faded. In a louder voice he said, "Yo, circus clown. You got peanuts in your fuckin' ears or what?"

Still looking straight ahead, Elgin took a peanut out of the bag next to him, slowly stripped the husk, and popped it into his mouth.

"He's ignoring you," Charlie whispered in the big man's ear.

Tony slid unsteadily off his stool and walked down to where Elgin was seated. "Hey, clown. You ignoring me?"

Elgin turned toward Tony and fixed him with black, shining eyes. "I'm doing my best."

As Elgin reached for another peanut, the construction worker snatched the bag off the bar, threw it on the ground, and stomped on it with his large orange work boot.

As Elgin looked down at the crushed peanuts, the old, familiar rage began to well up in him and he was, once again, a nineteen-year-old kid in the cafeteria of the Henderson County Jail.

The big guy, the one they called T-Bone, had just taken his blueberry pie off his tray. This was Elgin's third day in the lockup, and ever since he'd arrived, T-Bone had been needling him.

Elgin glared across the table at the big, thick-necked man with the small pig-eyes. "Give me the pie back," he said.

T-Bone flashed a gap-toothed grin. "Why should I?"

"Because it's my property."

The big man chuckled. "You ain't got no property, asshole."

As Elgin watched T-Bone cram the entire piece of pie into his mouth, something snapped inside him. A sound like the rushing whoosh of an exploding boiler filled his ears. Then there was a blinding flash and, as if watching fragments of film projected in slow motion through a crimson haze, he saw himself clawing his way over the table, scattering trays and dishes. He saw T-Bone smashing a fist into his face, but there was no pain. Then he saw himself pummeling his tormentor and felt an overpowering surge of pleasure as the fat, ugly face contorted in pain.

Then everything went red.

As the blows from the guards' nightsticks rained down on his head and shoulders, the red fog dissipated as quickly as it had come. Unseen iron-grip hands restrained his arms and legs. A stick, roughly thrust against his throat, pressed the air out of him and pinwheels floated before his eyes.

He was still on his back when his hearing returned,

more acute than ever. Despite the deafening clatter of a hundred tin trays beating on metal tables and the wild roar of a hundred voices reverberating off the tiled walls, he heard snatches of awed comments. . . . *Jesus Christ, he bit the guy's nose off! . . . I think T-Bone's dead. . . . That fucking guy is crazy. . . .*

As the guards dragged him away by his feet, Elgin looked up and saw a sea of faces staring down at him. And every one of those faces showed fear and respect. In spite of his own pain, he smiled. At nineteen years of age, George Elgin had found life's key to success: *You gain respect by inflicting pain and instilling fear.* As the guards dragged him across the cafeteria's cement floor, banging his head as they went, he experienced a second revelation: Administering pain gave him intense pleasure.

"All right, that's enough."

The bartender's words brought Elgin back to the present. The man had vaulted over the bar and was standing between a seated Elgin and Tony. He was as big as the construction worker, but younger and in better shape. Clutching a sawed-off baseball bat by his side, he said, "That's enough. The party's over."

Elgin gathered up his change and stood up. "I was just leaving."

Charlie had been hoping for a fight and was disappointed. "You're a real pussy, peanut man," he called from his bar stool.

Tony, feeling victorious because he'd made the other guy back down, roared in delight. *"Peanut man! I like that."*

As Elgin walked toward the door, Tony yelled after him, "If I ever see you again, peanut man, I'll stick those peanuts up your ass."

An hour later, the two drunken construction workers left the bar. As they staggered down a dark side street toward Tony's van, they didn't notice a shadowy figure emerge from a darkened doorway and begin to follow them.

Moving at a faster pace, Elgin quickly caught up to them. When he was right behind them, he said softly, "Hey, fatso."

As Tony turned, Elgin swung the two-by-four and caught the big man flush on the nose. The blow shattered his cartilage and drove him backward, knocking him into a row of garbage cans.

Charlie froze as Elgin came toward him with the two-by-four held out in front of him like a sword. "Mister . . . wait. We . . . we didn't mean no harm—"

Without a word, Elgin swung the two-by-four and caught the side of the small man's right leg. There was a loud crack as the knee dislocated. As Charlie fell to the ground screaming and writhing in pain, Elgin swung again, dislocating the other knee.

He grabbed Charlie's hair and yanked him to a kneeling position. "Now you can't run," he whispered, "and your fat friend can't see."

Blinded by the blood streaming down his face, Tony stumbled to his feet and tried to run, but he tripped over an overturned garbage can and sprawled to the pavement. As he tried to rise again, there was the whoosh of the two-by-four and a sickening snap. As Tony rolled on the pavement, clutching his broken knee, Elgin swung again, breaking the other one.

Now that the big man was immobilized, Elgin threw the two-by-four aside, grabbed the man's right arm, and, bracing the back of the elbow against his knee, snapped the joint. Tony bellowed in pain and

RETRIBUTION   249

swung his good arm toward Elgin, but Elgin ducked
and delivered a withering kick to the man's testicles.
As Tony sagged to the ground, vomiting, Elgin
grabbed the other arm and, using the same technique, snapped that joint.

With Tony unable to use his arms or legs, Elgin
silently and methodically went about the task of
breaking every joint in the man's body. When he was
done, he turned to a whimpering Charlie, who was
curled up on the sidewalk in a fetal position.

Elgin looked down at the terrified man, his black
eyes glistening. "It's your turn, Charlie."

Breathing hard from the exertion, Elgin stepped back
to view his handiwork. Both men were sprawled on
the pavement, semiconscious and whimpering in
pain. He knelt down by Charlie and lifted the man's
mangled arm, which dangled at a grotesque angle.
"Save that thought about the circus," he said, staring
into Charlie's glazed eyes. "Maybe you and your big-
mouth friend can get jobs as rubber men in a freak
show."

OVER THE NEXT TWO DAYS, Taggert Tower buzzed with around-the-clock activity as squads of technicians swarmed over the building, installing CCTV cameras, magnetic locks, and card readers. Devlin didn't know how Royal had done it, but in less than twenty-fours hours he'd managed to procure a brand-new state-of-the-art access card system.

Proudly, he led Devlin to the guard station to demonstrate his new toy. He tapped the screen with a stubby pencil. "Look. Every time someone goes through a door, I know who it is and what door he used. That information is filed on the hard disk. Later, I can query the computer for a history of that employee and it will print out a listin' of every door that employee went through, includin' time and date."

"What if a card is lost or stolen?"

"I can lock out a card with a couple of keystrokes. I can also program each employee card so that he'll have access to only certain doors at certain times. The control features are almost limitless."

He answered a guard's question having to do with passwords, and then continued. "By the end of the day the changeover to the new system will be complete. All the old cards will be obsolete and we start over from scratch." He whispered, "If, perchance, Elgin has one of the old cards, startin' today, it will do him no good." He took Devlin's arm. "Let's go to forty. I want to show you somethin'."

Royal led Devlin to the corridor leading up to Taggert's office and stopped. "Michael, how many cameras do you see?"

"Two. One at each end of the corridor."

"Any more?"

Devlin looked around carefully. "Nope."

Royal grinned. He was thoroughly enjoying himself. "You must be blind, mon. There are three more."

"Okay, I give up. Where are they?"

"There's one in the exit sign, there's another in the emergency light box, and there's one in the clock."

Devlin peered closely at the emergency light box, but he couldn't see anything, not even a peephole for the lens.

"It is very difficult to spot," Royal said. "Just a tiny pinhole. The best thing is that all these devices are functional."

"Why so many cameras?"

"Layerin', backup, and precaution. Suppose Elgin wants to get down this corridor without being seen. He could disable the cameras by tiltin' them away or sprayin' paint in the lenses. But there would be no way for him to know that there are three more cameras here. We're installin' several hidden cameras on the penthouse floor as well."

Devlin liked that idea. When you're defending

against a man like Elgin, there is no such thing as too
much redundancy.

"Tomorrow the supplier promises that he will
deliver my hand geometry reader. Unfortunately, he
can only deliver one for the time bein'. I will use it to
protect the tenth-floor command and control station.
Right now that is the most important room in the
whole buildin'. When I get the others, they'll be
installed on the executive floor, the R&D floor, and
the penthouse."

"What's going to be in the C&C room?"

"Let's go downstairs and talk to Marie. She's the
software expert."

When they entered the C&C room, Marie, seem-
ingly oblivious to the chaos surrounding her, was
hunched over the computer terminal while a small
army of workmen went about the business of installing
the rows of metal racks needed to house the computer,
monitors, VCRs, multiplexers, and switchers.

Devlin carefully stepped over a bewildering rat's
nest of multicolored wires that crisscrossed the floor.
"I hope you know what you're doing."

Marie looked up from the screen and blew her
hair out of her eyes. "If I don't, we're all in real fucking trouble."

"Do you have time to explain this to us?"

"Yeah, sure. This C&C room is going to be the
nerve center of the system. As soon as Otis gets all
the hardware installed, I'll begin working on a program that will tie all the building's systems together:
elevators, fire, electrical, telephone, security. From
this room we'll have the capability of shutting off
electricity on any floor, shunting individual elevator
banks, locking and unlocking every door in the

building—effectively shutting out all access cards. The key to this system will be flexibility and simplicity. I'll build in user-friendly pull-down menus, color graphic displays, and hot keys for frequently used functions and emergencies."

"Sounds like something out of NASA."

Marie shrugged. "Not really. There are systems like this in most new office buildings. Oh, I guess you should know that Otis and I have temporarily installed another C&C room on the penthouse floor."

"How come?"

"When this room becomes operational tomorrow, it's going to be crowded in here. Otis has to teach the guards how to use the new system. I can work in peace and quiet upstairs. How do you like it so far?"

Devlin turned to Royal. "I see one problem."

"What's that?" the Jamaican asked.

"If this room is the brains of the building, it's also our most vulnerable location. What would happen if Elgin got in here?"

"That's why I'm installin' the first palm reader right here. That, plus the reinforced-steel-hardened door, will keep him out."

"And," Marie added, "even if Elgin were to get in, he couldn't do any serious damage."

"Why not? You said the computer will control everything in the building."

"Yeah, but there'll only be two people with sysops status: Otis and me. Right now we're the only ones who can get into the system and reconfigure it. Later, when the guards are fully trained, you can assign a few of them sysops status."

Devlin was still uneasy. "I don't know. Elgin is supposed to be a real hotshot with computers. What if he finds a way to circumvent the system?"

Marie looked at him defiantly. "Take my word for it, with the safeguards I'm building into the system, *no one* will be able to hack into it."

Devlin looked her right in the eye. "You guarantee it."

She winked. "Fuckin'-A."

"Okay."

Satisfied that Otis and Marie had everything under control, Devlin was about to leave when Marie pulled him aside. "So tell me, how did Taggert take being confined to the building?"

"His reaction was rather loud."

"You guys don't like each other, do you?"

"We had an interesting talk. We'll never be best buddies, but there's more integrity there than I thought."

She gave him an assessing look. "You seem sort of down. Something eating at you?"

Devlin shook his head in frustration. "I don't know. Four men dead—evasive answers from the new head of R&D. There's something very wrong in this company and I can't seem to get a straight answer from anybody."

A workman called out to Marie, "Hey, yo, where do you want this rack set up?"

"Just a sec." She flashed a sympathetic smile. "Gotta go. You're right—something about this company does smell. Hope you find some answers."

Sitting at the computer terminal in the C&C room on the penthouse floor, Marie looked at her watch. It was almost 8:30 P.M. and she still had a couple of hours of work ahead of her. But she didn't mind. With the kids gone the house was too damn quiet anyway.

She supposed it was wrong to cure loneliness with work. But a person did what she had to to get by. The thing about computers was they demanded too much concentration for the mind to drift very far. And since Richie died, it had helped to stay in the here-and-now. She knew that if she spent too much time thinking about might-have-beens, she'd drive herself nuts.

She was so intent on her work that she didn't notice a figure slip into the dimly lit room. As she tapped the keys the figure came closer. Then a hand reached out and touched her shoulder. She screamed.

Taggert jumped backward. "I'm sorry," he stammered. "I didn't mean to frighten you."

Marie backed away from her overturned chair. "Don't you *ever* do that again," she shrieked. "Whaddaya wanna do, give me a fuckin' heart attack, for chrissake?"

"I'm sorry. I spoke to you, but you didn't respond."

"I was working. Who listens when they're working?"

"You mean . . . you didn't hear me?"

"Do you think I would have hit the ceiling if I'd heard you?"

Taggert shook his head. "I admire your concentration."

She gave a sheepish grin. "It has its downside."

Taggert pulled a folding chair toward him and sat down. "You're working late."

She bent down and picked up the notes that

she'd thrown up in the air. "The work's gotta be done."

"I guess this is all my fault."

"Don't apologize. I like working with computers. They're the perfect companions. They respond quickly, they don't lie, and they don't talk back. Oh, once in a while they spit out 'bad command' or 'access denied.' But I forgive them."

Taggert found himself intrigued. This woman reminded him of the way he was when he was just getting started. Time meant nothing when he was working. Except for Gloria, he'd never met another person who seemed to revel as he did in the sheer joy of work. "You're the computer consultant Devlin hired?"

"Yeah."

"How'd you like to work for me?"

"Thanks, but no thanks. I'm making more money working for you as a consultant than I could working as an employee."

Taggert laughed, but it was an uncertain laugh. He hated the thought of anyone, even an attractive woman, making a profit off him. "Have you eaten?" he asked, changing the subject.

"Um, not since lunch, I think."

Taggert was like an awkward schoolboy. "Well, I, uh . . . I hate to eat alone. What do you say—would you like to have a bite with me?"

Her impulse was to say no, but then she thought about Michael and his frustrating attempt to find out what was *really* going on in the company. Maybe she could pry something loose from the Big Man himself. "Okay," she said. "I guess I could eat something."

"Great. Under the circumstances, I'm afraid I'll have to order in."

"No problem. I live on Chinese food."

"I was thinking of something . . . a little more substantial."

"Like . . . ?"

"Le Bambou has excellent duck. How does that sound?"

Marie was stunned. Le Bambou was one of the most exclusive restaurants in the city. "Oh. Yeah, sure."

"Is something the matter?"

"No. It's just that I didn't know Le Bambou did takeouts."

"They don't. But the chef is a personal friend."

While they waited in Taggert's dining room for the food to arrive, the CEO opened a bottle of wine. She'd forgotten the name and the year, but he'd made such a big deal out of it that Marie knew it had to be good. And expensive.

"How do you like the wine?" he said, swirling it around in his glass and holding it up to the light.

"Great." Actually, she would have preferred a beer, but she didn't want to hurt his feelings.

Ten minutes later, a waiter from Le Bambou arrived with a cart full of gleaming silver-dome-covered dishes. After a careful patdown by the two grim-faced moonlighting cops, the anxious waiter served the first course while Marie told Taggert her life story since Richie's death.

During the entree, Taggert told her—in poignant detail—about his two failed marriages. It was clear that he was still fond of both women despite their inability to deal with his passion for

work. While conceding that his obsessiveness had
squeezed out any chance for a normal family life,
he was enough of a realist to concede that "normal-
ity" was something that would never factor into his
personal equation.

By the time they got to the dessert Marie decided
to turn the conversation to present matters. The wine
seemed to have put him at ease.

"I think it's terrible that this man wants to kill
you," she said, taking a small sip of cognac.

"You know"—he gave a grim smile—"there are
some people in this town who would actually be quite
pleased were they to know of my situation."

"Give people more credit than that," Marie said.
"There's a difference between rivalry and hate."

"Yes, I guess so." The features of his face suddenly
darkened. "What's really frustrating is, I haven't the
vaguest idea what this man's quarrel with me is. I've
negotiated some tough deals in my time, even
ducked a punch once in a takeover battle, but I never
worried about anything like this."

They talked for a few minutes more, then Taggert
pushed his chair away from the table. "Let's go into
the library and give the waiter a chance to clean up."
He picked up the cognac bottle from the table. "A
half glass more?" He gestured.

"No, thanks. I've had enough."

He stumbled slightly as they approached the den,
spilling a small quantity of cognac onto his jacket.
"Damn. I guess I've had enough, too," he said.

She was reaching out to help him get his jacket off
when Devlin suddenly appeared in the doorway.
"Marie," he said, startled. "I . . . I've been looking for
you."

She spun around and felt herself redden. "Michael!" It had been a perfectly innocent dinner, so why did she feel as though she'd been caught in a compromising situation?

Devlin turned on his heels. "It can wait until tomorrow."

"No," she said, nodding at Taggert. "I was just leaving. Jason," she called over her shoulder, "thanks for dinner. The wine was great."

She caught up to Devlin at the elevator. "Michael, what's the matter?"

"Nothing."

"What did you want?"

"It can wait until tomorrow. Why don't you go back for dessert?"

The elevator door opened and he stepped inside. She followed. "Don't be sarcastic," she said through clenched teeth.

They rode the elevator down to the lobby in silence. When the doors opened, he stepped outside and started walking toward the exit. She grabbed his arm and spun him around. "It isn't what you think. I was trying to get some answers for you."

"I don't need you to get answers for me, Marie. I hired you to work with the computers—not to be a lonely-hearts club for Jason Taggert."

The roundhouse smack echoed throughout the empty marble-floored lobby. Devlin touched his reddened cheek. "Thanks."

Through tears of frustration she watched him walk through the exit door and slam it. The sound reverberated in the lobby like a shot. A lone security officer, watching from the guard station sixty feet away, quickly turned away when he saw Marie looking at him.

Weary and heartsick, she got back on the elevator and went back upstairs. To her computer.

THE NEXT MORNING DEVLIN took the elevator straight to his office. Usually the first thing he did when he got in was find Marie and Otis and check on their progress. But he wasn't up to seeing Marie just yet. . . .

When he'd gotten home the night before, he'd opened a bottle of scotch, sat down in his darkened living room, and endlessly replayed the night's events. He started out pissed at Taggert, thought about it some more, and grew incensed at Marie. Soon, however, he was directing his anger at himself.

He knew he had a tendency to slot people into categories—what Taggert had called the "black hat/white hat" thing. In his personal filing system Taggert was simultaneously the "irresistible force" and the "immovable object"—the thing he was always bucking up against. Over the years he'd had a tendency to slot all his bosses into this category. He didn't really view them as people, as human beings with needs—for him, they were just the "rule makers" who made life difficult. So the fact that Taggert might actually be someone looking for a little companionship, that he might actually have honorable intentions—that hadn't occurred to him.

And what about Marie? What category did she fit into? He shook his head, thinking about when he was a kid and Moe Kramer from down the block first told him what sexual intercourse was. He had refused to believe that his mother could have had any involvement with *that*.

It was like that with Marie. He didn't see Marie as a virgin, exactly. It was more complicated. He supposed it was that he'd always seen her as someone who was permanently out of circulation, a woman who'd offered up her sexual life to the memory of her dead husband. Viewing her as someone who might want a *physical* relationship—well, his feelings for Richie, for the camaraderie they'd shared, had always gotten in the way.

Sitting in that darkened room, he poured another glass of the warm amber liquid. Hell, why *not* Taggert and Marie? What was the big deal? Certainly his opinion of the man had risen considerably in the past couple of days.

The trouble was, all this logical thinking wasn't keeping him from feeling like shit. He knew he'd fucked up in at least two major ways. First, he'd spoken without knowing what he was talking about. And second, he'd mouthed off about something that was none of his business. He'd had no right to come down on Marie like that. No right at all. He winced, thinking about how uncomfortable it would be when they saw each other the next day. . . .

And he was still wincing when Carla entered his

office, carrying his cup of coffee. The first day they'd met she'd told him in no uncertain terms that she didn't serve coffee. But somewhere between then and now she'd forgotten her own rule.

"A package from UPS," she said, nodding toward a box on his desk. She flopped into a chair and lit a vermilion-colored cigarette. "Well," she said, blowing a jet stream of smoke toward the ceiling, "aren't you going to open it?"

Devlin pulled himself out of his funk and tore open the carton. Looking pleased, he took out a device about the size of a mailbox and placed it on the desk. "This is my first line of defense against Elgin."

"What is it?"

"A smoke machine."

Clara waved a cloud of smoke away from her face and coughed. "Just ... what ... this city needs," she gasped. "More smoke. Where are you going to use it?"

"In the vestibule by the penthouse elevator. These things are very effective in relatively confined spaces."

"How does it work?"

"It's activated by breaking an infrared beam. In a few seconds the area is filled with dense smoke. At the same time an alarm condition is sent to the guard station in the lobby."

"Is it some kind of tear gas?"

"Nope. Harmless smoke. The point is to disorient Elgin until help arrives."

"How long does it last?"

"A few minutes. But long enough to slow him down."

Carla flicked an ash into a potted plant on Devlin's desk. "You're talking about Elgin as though you're sure he's coming. It gives me the creeps."

Devlin grunted. "I hope Kevin Clark catches up to him first, but in the meantime, I have to assume the worst-case scenario."

The telephone rang on her desk. As she went out to answer it, she said over her shoulder, "If Elgin is as bad as you think he is, it seems to me a little smoke ain't gonna stop him."

Devlin looked down at the black box, confident it would serve its purpose. When Elgin came he knew exactly how he would come—the same way Devlin had trained as a SWAT team member: with stealth and speed. The element of surprise would be a critical factor in Elgin's plan and anything that delayed or harassed him was to Devlin's advantage.

Once again dressed in his bicycle messenger outfit, Elgin stopped in the middle of the Taggert Tower plaza and gazed up at the soaring structure. He was standing almost in the same spot where Devlin had stood three weeks earlier when he'd contemplated his new job at Taggert Industries.

Now that he'd taken care of Biehl, it was time for Elgin to refocus his attention on his main target: Jason Taggert. Three days before, Elgin had taken a position across the street from the garage entrance and watched Taggert's limo arrive. In addition to the usual two bodyguards, he spotted a tail car with two more men. He'd maintained his vigil ever since and Taggert still hadn't come out. Had he decided to hole up in his own building? It was possible. In fact, it made sense. He worked here and he had a place to stay. From his research Elgin knew there was a penthouse on the building's top floor.

Clearly, this extra protection and siege mentality were obstacles, but not insurmountable ones. At least he knew where to find Taggert. He'd learned a valuable lesson from his experiences in Vietnam: Sometimes the best place to terminate your target is right in his own backyard—a place where the target feels safe and secure. That place could be a hootch, a guarded encampment, or a safe house in a bustling city. Or an office building.

Today he was here to see if security in Taggert Tower was as tight as the security he'd seen at the shareholders' meeting.

As he was heading for the elevators a guard called out to him, "Hey, buddy, where you going?"

Not expecting to be stopped, Elgin was momentarily caught off guard, but he quickly recovered. Remembering a name he'd memorized from his earlier visit, he said, "Got a letter for James Pearson."

"Let me have it," the guard said. "I'll see that he gets it."

"Can't do that." Elgin studied the guard through his mirrored sunglasses. He was an older man and he didn't look very sure of himself. Elgin was confident he could browbeat his way onto the elevator if he made a big enough scene. "I gotta deliver it myself," he said loudly. "He's gotta sign for it."

"His secretary will come down and sign for it," the guard said patiently.

"Bullshit," Elgin said, feigning indignation. "I don't get paid to stand around here waiting for people. I bring the stuff to them, they sign, and I'm outta here. What's the big fucking problem?"

Tommy Nolen heard the raised voice and came over. "What's up, Ray?"

"This guy wants to personally deliver a letter to Mr. Pearson."

Elgin studied the big man. Unlike the older guard, Nolen looked like a cop and he didn't appear to be the kind who was intimidated easily. Elgin looked at the name tag and flashed an ingratiating grin. "Hey, Mr. Nolen, I've been delivering stuff to this building for months," he said reasonably. "There's never been a problem before."

"New rules, pal. Only employees are allowed upstairs."

Just then an elderly black man with a shoeshine box slung over his shoulder walked by waving an access card in the air. "Hey, Raymond," he called out to the guard, "I'm on my way up to do Mr. Taggert."

The guard picked up the telephone. "Okay, Walter, we'll let his secretary know you're coming."

"Who's that?" Elgin asked, watching the man disappear into the elevator. "He don't look like an employee."

Nolen's easygoing smile vanished and he fixed Elgin with a hard look. "Hey, pal, I'm not going to spend the rest of the day playing twenty questions with you. You got two choices: Leave the letter here or take it with you."

"Fuck it," Elgin said, turning away from the guard desk. "I don't get paid to wait around. Let him come and get it."

As he walked away, Elgin's body language— hunched shoulders, determined gait—said he was angry, but inside he was smiling. He'd just found his entree into the building.

As Elgin was exiting through the revolving doors,

Devlin stepped off the elevator. He saw Tommy Nolen and Ray Towne laughing. "What's so funny?"

"We just had a messenger here with a real bug up his ass," Nolen said. "He insisted on going upstairs to personally deliver a letter and left in a huff when I said he couldn't do it."

"Been having much trouble with them over this new policy?"

"Naw. Most of 'em like it. They give us the stuff and they're outta here. Actually, it saves them time. I don't know what was wrong with him."

Towne chuckled. "I'd be pissed, too, if I was still delivering packages at his age. My opinion, nobody over thirty should be spending his workday on a bike."

Devlin had started to walk away, but he stopped and came back. "How old was he?"

Towne shrugged. "Hard to tell with the sunglasses and helmet, but he had to be in his late thirties, early forties."

"And he was insistent about going upstairs?"

"Yeah. He was really pissed when we told him he couldn't."

"Which way did he go out?"

"The Park Avenue entrance."

"How was he dressed?"

"White helmet, black spandex suit. Why—"

Devlin bolted for the revolving doors. Once outside, he sprinted to the top of the steps at the edge of the plaza and scanned the busy avenue. It was clogged with noontime traffic, and a cacophonous symphony of horns blared at a spillback that had stopped northbound traffic on Park Avenue.

He caught a glimpse of a white helmet bobbing

up and down as a black-suited messenger weaved his
bike through traffic. Devlin leaped down the stairs
and elbowed his way along a sidewalk swarming with
people on their way to lunch. He found it slow going
and ran out into the street. The white helmet was still
a long block away, but fortunately he'd been slowed
by the spillback.

As Devlin closed the distance, a brown-suited
traffic agent stepped into the intersection and began
to clear the logjam. Beyond the intersection, Park
Avenue was wide open. If the traffic started flowing,
Devlin knew he'd have no chance of catching a man
on a bike.

Afraid to take his eyes off the bobbing white helmet, he darted blindly among the cars. The front
fender of a taxicab brushed against him, knocking
him to the pavement. The driver slammed on his
brakes, waved his fist out the window, and roundly
cursed Devlin in Arabic. Devlin scrambled back to
his feet and, ignoring the sharp pain in his leg, hob-
bled up the avenue.

By now the traffic agent had cleared the last of
the spillbacked cars and stepped back to wave the
traffic on.

The impatient drivers, seeing a clear avenue in front
of them, began to inch forward. With a final burst of
speed that seared his lungs, Devlin reached the messenger just as he was getting up a head of steam.

Gasping for breath, he yanked the cyclist backward and the riderless bike wobbled forward, car-
oming into the side of a taxicab. The startled
messenger, no more than twenty years old, stared at
Devlin, wide-eyed. "Hey, man, what the fuck's the
matter with you?"

Devlin let him go and backed away. "Sorry," he mumbled. "Wrong guy."

An elderly woman, part of a sidewalk crowd that had gathered to watch the encounter, shouted, "You got the right guy, mister. Those fools are always running into someone. Poke him in the nose for me."

The messenger jumped back on his bike. "You people are crazy," he muttered, and sped off down the avenue.

By the time Devlin limped back to the building his breathing had returned to normal, but the pain in his leg had become more pronounced.

It was after 7:00 P.M. when Walter Simpson finished shining shoes on the executive floor. It had been a surprisingly lucrative day and the thought of all that money in his pocket brought a broad smile to his face.

Tommy Nolen was standing at the security desk when Simpson stepped off the elevator. "Hey, Walter," he said, "you look like you swallowed the canary."

Simpson put his shoeshine box down. It wasn't heavy, but his arthritis was acting up again. He opened and closed his hands slowly to relieve the stiffness. "I had a *good* day, Tommy," he whispered. "Musta done a dozen shines, not counting Mr. Taggert. I ain't never seen so many bigwigs up there all at the same time. What's goin' on?"

"Board meeting."

"I figured it was something like that." He shook his head and chuckled. "Those gentlemen really tickle me. They all gotta have what the other have.

You do a shine for one, they all want a shine." He elbowed Nolen. "Not that I'm complainin', mind."

Nolen slapped Simpson on the back. "Never complain about making money, Walter. You heading home now?"

"Uh-uh. Goin' over to Duffy's and get me something to eat." He picked up his shoeshine box and winked at Nolen. "Then I'm gonna have a couple of beers and watch the Knicks wup the Bulls. But I'll be back tomorrow. Mr. Taggert bought six pairs of shoes in South America and he wants me to shine 'em up real good."

22

DUFFY'S BAR & GRILL HAD BEEN on the same corner of Lexington Avenue since the mid-fifties and had changed little in that time. It wasn't in the same league with the dimly lit trendy bars that had sprung up around it in the last ten years. Still, the shabby saloon was always packed with an eclectic clientele of yuppies, businessmen, and blue-collar workers. Many years ago, Jack Duffy had discovered the magic formula for running a successful bar: provide a three-hour happy hour, reasonably priced sandwiches, and a big-screen TV tuned to the latest sporting event.

Simpson came in, waved to a few friends, and stopped in front of the steam table to study the daily specials. After considerable reflection he ordered the knockwurst with sauerkraut and boiled potato. He would have preferred the roast beef hot plate special, but it was a little too expensive. His disability check wasn't due for another five days and he would have to make do with the money he'd made today.

He elbowed his way into a tight spot at the bar

and settled in to watch the pregame show. He was so intent on watching the highlights of the Knicks' previous matchup against the Bulls that he never noticed a man wearing a black windbreaker come in. Elgin walked to the other end of the bar and ordered a beer.

Soon the game began and all eyes focused on the TV screen—all except Elgin's. While he methodically shelled peanuts and nursed a beer, he kept his unblinking eyes on the back of the shoeshine man's head.

By 10:00 P.M., it was clear that the Bulls were going to win the game. Shaking his head in disgust, Simpson picked up his shoeshine box and said goodnight to the bartender.

Elgin followed Simpson the three blocks to the subway station and boarded the same uptown train. At this hour there were few passengers. He sat down across from the shoeshine man and began shelling a handful of peanuts.

"The Knicks suck," he said.

Simpson, who was nodding off, opened his eyes. "Excuse me?"

"I saw the game." Elgin picked his teeth with a pinky nail. "The Knicks suck."

Simpson shook his head from side to side. "Ain't that the truth." He closed his eyes again. He'd wanted to tell the man that he was dead wrong, but he was a veteran subway rider and knew it wasn't a good idea to get into an argument with a stranger, especially one with flat black eyes that didn't blink.

As the train pulled into 116th Street, Simpson got up and stood in the door. In the reflection in the glass, he saw the man in the black windbreaker get up, brush the peanut husks of his jacket, and come stand behind him. Simpson wondered what a white guy was doing getting off the subway in the middle of Harlem. He could spot a plainclothes cop a mile away. This dude was no cop.

The man spread his arms out and grasped both poles. Simpson felt a chill. With his close-cropped head, shiny black jacket, and black, spooky eyes, the man loomed over the smaller Simpson like a bird of prey.

The doors opened and Simpson stepped out onto the platform. As he started walking toward the exit at the far end of the station, he was suddenly aware that he and the man in the windbreaker were the only two people on the platform. He picked up his pace, but the damn arthritis in his knee was shooting a dull pain through his leg and he had to slow down.

"Think they got a chance for the playoffs?"

Simpson jumped. He hadn't realized the man was that close behind him. He didn't turn around. "I sure hope so," he said. He peered down the dimly lit platform, praying that he'd see a cop. But the platform was deserted.

Now, Walter, don't look like no damn victim. Walk tall, like you're not 'fraid of nuthin'. He shifted the shoeshine box to his other hand. The exit was only thirty more yards and he forced himself to slow down. He heard the low rumble of a train in the distance and felt a rush of air on the back of his neck from the pressure wave.

As they were passing a shallow alcove, an arm went around his neck and yanked him off his feet. He felt the man's hot breath on the back of his neck and smelled the sharp aroma of peanuts. Even though he

was half expecting it, he was still surprised. As his
shoeshine box clattered to the ground, brushes, rags,
and shoe polish scattered across the platform floor.
Stay calm, he reminded himself as he was dragged
into the alcove. *This isn't the first time you been
mugged, Walter. Don't fight it. Give the man what he
wants and you'll be on your way.* Then he thought
about all that money in his pocket and regretted that
he hadn't spent the extra couple of dollars on the
roast beef dinner. "Mister, I ain't got much money,"
he gasped, struggling to catch his breath. "But you
take what you want."

"I'm going to let go now," Elgin whispered in
Simpson's ear. "Don't do anything stupid."

"Don't worry, mister. I don't want no trouble."

Elgin slammed Simpson against the wall and
snapped his fingers. "Wallet."

Simpson handed it over with shaking hands. Elgin
pulled it apart, casting onto the ground old photos
and a lifetime's collection of yellowed pieces of paper
with long forgotten names and telephone numbers.
Elgin flung the wallet aside. "Empty your pockets."

Sighing, Simpson emptied his pockets. Stuck
among a handful of bills was the green ID card that
he used to get around the Taggert building. Elgin put
the ID card in his pocket. Simpson looked longingly
at the bills. "Mister, do you think you could spare me
a couple of dollars? Just so I could get home."

Elgin studied the frightened man with soulless
black eyes. "Sure. Why not?" He peeled off a ten-
dollar bill.

"Thank you, sir," a surprised Simpson mumbled.

Elgin counted the money. "You make all this shining shoes?" he asked in a conversational tone.

"Yessir."

"Not bad. Tax free, too. Right?"

Simpson chuckled nervously. "Yessir." Simpson had never encountered a mugger like this. He seemed to be in no hurry. It was almost like he was waiting for something.

Elgin offered another ten-dollar bill. "Here, take this one too." He seemed to be enjoying this game. Simpson tentatively took the money and stuffed it back into his pocket. "Thank you."

"Think nothing of it."

When he'd been pulled into the alcove, Simpson had heard a train approaching and was hoping it was a local. That would mean more people on the platform. But it was an express. It was almost in the station and it wasn't slowing down.

Elgin held out the rest of the bills. "Here you go, old-timer," he said. "Take it all."

Hesitantly, Simpson reached out, half expecting some trick, but Elgin shoved the bills into his hand. "God bless you," Simpson said.

Elgin stepped aside. "Pick up your shit and get out of here."

As Simpson bent over to retrieve his tools scattered across the platform, the train came roaring into the station in a whirlwind of sound and turbulence. The high-pitched grating of metal wheel on metal track was reaching an ear-shattering crescendo when a thought that had been nagging him exploded into his consciousness. *Almost like he was waiting for something.* He looked to his left and saw the train rapidly approaching. *Oh, dear Lord!* He shoved the shoeshine box aside and stood up to run, but the man stepped in front of him. Simpson looked into those cold, dead eyes and his legs buckled. In that moment he knew he was going to die.

Sobbing, he pleaded for his life, but the sound of the oncoming train drowned out his words. Elgin grasped the old man's arms in a vicelike grip and looked down the track. When the train was less than fifty feet away, he shoved him.

Simpson stumbled over his shoeshine box and fell sprawling onto his hands and knees at the edge of the platform. He looked down at the gleaming tracks lighted by the train's headlights and his heart pounded in his ears.

Grunting in terror, he tried to crab away from the edge, but Elgin blocked his path. He looked up and those scary opaque eyes, betraying no emotion, fixed him in a paralyzing gaze.

Without warning, Elgin kicked Simpson in the face. The unexpected blow rocked the old man back on his heals. His arms flailing wildly, he tried to stop his momentum, but he was too close to the edge. For what seemed like an eternity he teetered on the edge of the platform. Then, almost in slow motion, his body arched backward. The last sight he saw was those two black eyes, still serenely watching him.

The screech of the braking wheels drowned out Walter Simpson's screams as the train rumbled over his body.

Devlin rolled over in bed and grimaced.

"What's the matter?"

"My leg," he said. "It hurts like hell."

Gloria kissed the angry bruise. "Poor baby."

She ran her tongue up his leg, his stomach, his

chest, and stopped at his throat. "Hey, I hear your computer expert had dinner with JT the other night."

Why bring that up? Devlin thought. He hadn't run into Marie all day and had managed to push the whole incident into the back of his mind.

"None of *my* business," he said.

"Not mine either. Still, it *is* interesting."

"Ah, I'm sure Marie just thought it would be fun to get to know a celebrity. You know, 'I had dinner with the great Jason Taggert'—that sort of thing."

Gloria flashed an impish smile. "You don't think there could be more to it? He's rich, attractive for a man his age, and, I hear, pretty good in the sack."

Devlin scowled. "Does he post his results?"

"I do believe you're defensive."

He tried his best to look nonchalant. "I don't care. It's just that . . . Marie isn't like that."

"Isn't like what?"

"Look, let's just drop it, okay?"

She pulled away from him. "What's the matter with you tonight? You're so touchy."

"I told you, my leg hurts. I . . . no, it's not that." Devlin laced his fingers behind his head and stared up at the ceiling. "I thought I had him today, Gloria."

She threw her arm across his chest. "Do you think it was Elgin?"

"Yeah."

She curled her fingers in his chest hairs. Suddenly she yanked a handful. "Damn it, I wish those guards would have stopped him. They have a photo of him. Why didn't they—"

"Ow, that hurt." Devlin rubbed his chest. "It's not their fault. He was wearing mirrored sunglasses and a bike helmet. He could have been Bill Clinton and they wouldn't have known. Besides, maybe it wasn't him."

She propped herself up on one elbow. "Do you believe that?"

"No," he said quietly.

She lay back down. "How are you coming along with replacing those guards?"

"I've hired four retired cops and I have a few more coming in for interviews."

"How many of the old crew is still there?"

"Five. I've already sent the rest back to their old jobs. Charlie Floyd is pulling his hair out."

"It's the mission of personnel directors to cry about everything," she said. "Who was the guard who spoke to the messenger today?"

"Ray Towne."

"Get rid of him."

Devlin, startled by the cold tone of her voice, sat up. "You mean send him back to the mailroom?"

"No, I mean fire him."

"What for? He's one of the guards I intend to keep."

"He blew it. You said yourself it was Elgin."

"Yeah, and I also said that Towne couldn't have known that."

"Mike, why do you keep making excuses for your people? They had a chance to grab Elgin at the shareholders' meeting and they blew it, and now this."

"Gloria, you don't know what you're talking about."

Her emerald eyes hardened. "I want him fired."

Devlin sat up. "No."

She stared at him for a long moment. Finally she

said, "Then I want him out of the security department. Send him back to the mailroom."

Devlin got up and grabbed his robe.

"Where are you going?"

"Home."

"Oh, Mike, don't be so thin-skinned."

"Thin-skinned? Five minutes ago I'm making love to you, now I'm taking orders from you about something you don't even understand. You've been watching too many cop movies, Gloria."

She pulled the sheet up around her neck. "All right, I'm sorry. I know I keep making the same excuses, but this whole thing has me off balance. We have a company to run and Elgin is draining too much of our resources. I just want this guy caught. I want him stopped."

"So do I, Gloria," Devlin said, suddenly realizing that he'd never wanted anything more in his life. "So do I."

23

THE NEXT MORNING ELGIN, dressed in a conservative business suit and trench coat, drove into the Taggert Tower garage. Once there, he confidently strolled up to the door that led from the basement garage to the building's interior. Ignoring the TV camera staring down at him, he waved Simpson's access card at the reader and tensed, prepared to bolt if the card was rejected. A rejection would mean that they knew the shoeshine man was dead. The soft clicking of the door mechanism unlocking told him he'd successfully penetrated their first line of defense.

It was only a matter of time before they learned that the shoeshine man was dead and then the card would be useless. He wasn't sure what doors the card would open, so he'd planned a busy itinerary. There were several parts of the building he wanted to study and there was no time to waste. He stepped into the elevator and pressed the button for the subbasement.

Twenty minutes later, he was back on the elevator, feeling pleased with his results. "This is going to be easier than I thought," he said aloud. Whistling softly, he punched a button and, while the elevator quickly ascended to the tenth floor, popped a peanut into his mouth.

He'd had to stop his reconnaissance the last time he was here because of that old bitch with the coffeepot. Keeping an eye out for her as he walked the corridor, he noted that they'd added surveillance cameras since his last visit. *What other security devices had they installed that* weren't *so obvious,* he wondered.

Two security guards, laughing over a joke, hurried past him and stopped in front of an unmarked door. Elgin saw the hand geometry reader and knew that it had to be protecting something very important. He slowed to give the guards a chance to use the reader. Then, as they went through the door, he glanced over their shoulders and saw a tall black man wearing a dashiki talking to a woman. They were standing in front of a computer console. Behind them was a bank of CCTV monitors and a computer console. He'd found the nerve center of the building's security system.

He completed his tour of the floor, went back to the elevator, and pressed the up button.

While Elgin was exploring the upper floors, Devlin was on his way to the C&C room on the tenth floor. He and Marie hadn't spoken for two days and he'd decided it was time to apologize.

He put his palm on the hand geometry reader and the C&C room door popped open. Marie was inputting data and Otis was instructing two guards on how the system worked. She looked up from the

computer and quickly turned away when she saw
him. Devlin walked up behind her and peered over
her shoulder. "How's it going?"

"Fine."

"Getting a lot done?"

"Yeah."

Devlin sighed. She was still mad. This wasn't
going to be easy. "Marie, can I talk to you outside?"

"I'm busy."

"Marie—"

"All right. A couple of minutes."

She stood in the hallway with her arms folded,
silently glaring at him. He preferred the old Marie,
the one who yelled and screamed. At least then he
knew what she was thinking.

"Marie, about the other night . . ." He paused, hoping she would help him out, but she didn't. "I'm sorry,"
he blurted out. "I overreacted . . . actually it was none
of my business . . . I mean, if you and Taggert—"

"Michael, you are such a fucking jerk."

Devlin looked up at the ceiling. "Thanks."

"Did you think I went there to get laid?"

"Marie—"

"Oh, does that shock you? Hey, you gotta know
I've gotten laid at least once. I didn't get the twins by
sitting on a dirty toilet seat."

"Marie, why are you saying this?"

"Because I want you to stop treating me like a
goddamn child. I'm a woman and I can take care of
myself."

"Okay, I'm sorry. Okay? I'm sorry."

She exhaled slowly, releasing her anger. "Okay."

But it wasn't okay. She wanted to say that she
wished he would see her as a flesh-and-blood woman.

But what was the point? Either you affected a man in a certain way or you didn't.

Devlin decided her grudging acceptance of his apology was as good as he was going to get, and quickly changed the subject. "So, any news from the boys?"

"I talked to them the other night," she said. As she spoke, her features brightened. "Of course, as you'd expect, I had to phone *them*. God forbid they should be viewed as wimps, checking in with their mother. They flapped their lips about getting a great education, seeing the sights and all. I don't want to even think about what they're really doing out there."

Devlin, trying to keep her in a good mood, almost made the mistake of commenting on the "special qualities" of male hormones, but he checked himself just in time.

When they went back inside, Royal looked up. "I'm just showin' these gentlemen how the system works."

"Everything okay?"

Royal frowned. "No, it's not." He tapped the screen, which was displaying the names of people who were using their cards.

"Look. A *shoeshine* man has an access card. I thought we had agreed to limit cards to employees only." He shook his head. "This really vexes me."

Devlin studied the screen. "Who the hell issued—"

One of the guards looked up from the computer manual he was reading. "Is Walter in the building? Mr. Taggert has been looking for him."

"Okay," Royal said to the other guard who was sitting at the monitor. "Here's a chance to use the system. Let me see you get hold of Mr. Simpson."

The guard squinted at the screen. "All right. Simpson just went through the west doors on the thirty-ninth floor." He picked up a phone and dialed the receptionist on that floor. "Hey, Mary, Simpson just came through the door. Would you—" He paused and his brow furrowed in a puzzled expression.

"What is it?" Royal asked.

"She says she hasn't seen Walter all day."

Royal glanced back at the screen. "Impossible. He just passed her seconds ago."

Devlin and Marie moved closer as the guard spoke to the receptionist again. "Mary, according to the screen here, he had to pass you." He put his hand over the telephone. "She says the only one to pass in the last minute was a guy in a business suit."

"Does she know what Simpson looks like?" Devlin asked.

"Oh, sure. He's been here so long, he's like one of the family. We all know Walter."

Devlin looked back at the screen and suddenly it made sense. "Elgin!" He snatched a portable radio off the console. "Code Red. Repeat. This is a Code Red." He ran for the door. "Backup team, meet me at the receptionist desk on the thirty-ninth floor forthwith."

Nick Mangi and Bill Tyler, lounging in Taggert's outer office reading magazines, heard the signal and responded immediately. Tossing the magazines aside, they rushed into Taggert's office. The CEO was dictating a memo. Without waiting for him to finish, Mangi took him by the arm. "Come on, Mr. Taggert. We have to go now."

Taggert pulled away. "What the hell are you talking about? I'm in the middle—"

Mangi leaned down and whispered, "It's a Code Red, sir. We have to go."

Taggert paled. Just yesterday, Devlin had told him that a Code Red would mean that Elgin was in the building. At the time he'd thought it was a bit melodramatic. With all the security in the building, how could Elgin get anywhere near him? He stood up.

Mangi led him toward the safe room, an interior room that Devlin had selected because it had no windows. With the reinforced steel door that Devlin had added, it was probably the most secure room in the building. "We'll let you know when it's all clear," Mangi said, locking the door.

About the time Mangi was securing their charge in the safe room, Devlin bolted out of the elevator onto the thirty-ninth floor. Two moonlighting cops with guns at their sides were waiting for him, partially obscuring a wide-eyed receptionist who stood a few steps to their rear.

Ted Munson, a short, muscular cop with a gossamer blond mustache, said calmly, "Dark-blue business suit, five-eleven. He went this way."

Devlin realized that the nondescript description probably fit half the men in the building, but he keyed the mike. "Tommy, start calling all the offices in the west corridor. We're looking for a man, five-eleven, dark blue business suit."

While Nolen was polling the offices, they searched the utility closets and spare rooms. Munson stopped in front of the men's restroom and pointed. Devlin nodded. They turned off their radios and silently slipped inside. Munson crouched and looked down the row of stalls. He pointed to the third stall and mouthed the word: "Occupied."

Devlin crouched down and saw a pair of feet with the trousers bunched up around the ankles. It could be an employee, Devlin thought, but it could also be Elgin. He was certainly ballsy enough to use this subterfuge.

Devlin went to the sink and turned on the water to mask their movements. Watching the two men through the mirror, he used hand signals to position Munson and the other cop to either side of the stall. When they were in position, he held up one finger, then two fingers. At the third finger, he spun around and kicked in the door while the two cops popped up over the top of the stall.

A young man from the accounting department, startled by the sudden and unexpected invasion of his stall, looked up, saw three guns pointed at him, and promptly slid off the commode in a faint, clutching his *Wall Street Journal* in a death grip.

Devlin hurled the printout across the room. "Goddamn it, how did that shoeshine man get a card?"

Tommy Nolen studied the weave of the carpet and tried to look contrite. "I gave it to him."

Devlin looked up sharply. "You? Why?"

"Mr. Taggert told me to."

Devlin glared at Gloria. "Since when does—"

"Walter has been coming into this building for years," she said with a calmness that made Devlin even more furious. "He's not a security threat."

"Maybe *he* isn't, but his card in someone else's hands is." Devlin turned to Royal. "I want him out of the system."

"Done."

"Enough about him. What I want to know is, how did Elgin get away?" Gloria asked pointedly.

Devlin ran his fingers through his hair. "We were watching all the elevator banks. As best we can figure it, he got out of the building through the fire stairs."

Gloria looked at Royal with an arched eyebrow. "I thought they were alarmed?"

It was the Jamaican's turn to look embarrassed. "Not yet. We're in the process of installin' the hardware."

"Oh, for God's sake!"

Devlin came to Royal's rescue. "Gloria, we're doing the best we can. Otis has worked miracles getting this equipment as quickly as he has. But it's going to take time to install it and get the bugs out."

"Well, I hope Mr. Elgin will give us the time to get everything in order," she said.

Devlin smarted at the snide remark, but she was right. As long as they were in the process of installing the equipment, they were vulnerable. In a week the building would be sewed up tight, but right now there were some major gaps in their security umbrella, the fire stairs being one painful example.

There was no doubt in Devlin's mind that Elgin had been in the building. But how much had he seen? And did he know enough about security systems to assess their vulnerability? If he was knowledgeable, he had to know that this was his window of opportunity. In another few days it would be too late.

Gloria stood up. From the expression on her face it was clear that she wasn't pleased with this latest fiasco. "I'll tell JT that we're doing our very best."

He said nothing, but her refusal to understand the

logistics of securing a forty-story building exasperated him. So she was pissed because Elgin had gotten away again. Well, hell, so was he.

As Gloria was walking out of Devlin's office, she almost collided with Marie, who was just coming in. Neither woman spoke.

Nolen stood up. "I guess I should be getting back."

Devlin put his arm around the gloomy ex-cop. "Tommy, it wasn't your fault. When the big boss tells you to do something, you gotta do it."

"Yeah, but I should have told you about it."

"Don't worry. From now on no one except me, Otis, or Marie will have the authority to issue cards."

Nolen nodded. "Okay by me."

Marie waited until Nolen left, then she said, "I have more bad news."

Devlin fell back into his chair and pressed his hands against the sides of his head, but it didn't stop the jackhammers. He'd taken this goddamn job because it was supposed to be a ground ball, a no-brainer. But he'd never had so many headaches in his life. "I'm afraid to ask."

Marie handed copies of a printout to Devlin and Royal. "Tommy said he saw Simpson last night, so I ran a chronological tracking history of the card from midnight until the time it was used on the thirty-ninth floor. And it ain't good."

"Why?"

"Elgin has been all over the building. He started out in the subbasement. Spent twenty minutes there."

Devlin turned to Royal. "What's down there?"

Royal shook his head glumly. "Things we don't want him to see. The electrical vaults, step-down transformers, water supply lines, backup generators.

Sabotagin' any one of those systems could knock this buildin' out of commission."

Royal glanced down at his blueprint for the sub-basement. "Oh my goodness. More trouble you know?"

Devlin stiffened. "What?"

"The buildin' engineer's office is there."

"So?"

"That is where they keep complete sets of blueprints for the buildin's electrical, water, and HVA systems, as well as floor plans for each individual floor."

"Jesus Christ! Including the penthouse?"

"Includin' the penthouse."

Devlin's spirit sagged. His whole game plan was coming apart. No matter what he did, Elgin always seemed to be one step ahead of him. "Where else did he go, Marie?"

Marie consulted her printout. "There's some good news. He was on ten, eleven, and thirty-nine. At least he never got a chance to go on forty."

"Or the penthouse," Otis added hopefully.

"He didn't need to," a dejected Devlin said. "He has the goddamn floor plans."

Cupping his chin in his hands, Devlin looked down at the two-page printout, every line representing another door that Elgin had passed through. *The son of a bitch knows more about this building than I do.* He'd seen everything: the cameras, the access card system, the vital innards of the building. He could attack any of them. But which one? Devlin had a queasy feeling that he wouldn't know the answer to that question until *after* it had happened.

❖   ❖   ❖

With a sense of gloom Devlin went up to the penthouse alone. As he walked from room to room, he remembered how pleased he'd been with the convoluted labyrinth of rooms and hallways—a natural obstacle against an aggressor. But that was before Elgin had the floor plans.

As a SWAT team member, Devlin knew the value of floor plans. Anytime they had to go into a house or an apartment after a barricaded target, the first thing they asked for was floor plans. In unfamiliar surroundings, knowing the whereabouts of your target was critical to a successful mission. And if things went bad, knowing the quickest way out could mean the difference between life and death. Devlin wished he could erase the whole penthouse and start over. Suddenly, standing in the corridor, an idea came to him and he sprinted back to the elevator.

"Carla," he said, hurrying into his office, "find out the name of the contractor who did the penthouse and get him on the phone for me."

Fifteen minutes later, Carla yelled in, "I have Bert Kohler from Empire Construction on the line."

"Bert, Mike Devlin, the corporate security director for Taggert Industries. I understand your company built the penthouse."

"Yeah, that's right," he said with a thick Brooklyn accent. "I supervised the job personally and I wanna say I'm real proud of what we—"

Devlin interrupted the commercial. "I have a simple question for you. Is it possible to alter the configuration of those rooms?"

"Yeah, sure . . . but it would depend on . . . What do you wanna do?"

He would have preferred to start over from

scratch: Level the penthouse. But that was out of the question. So he'd decided on the next best thing. "I want to change the locations of doors and I want to reroute corridors."

"That could be done. None of the interior walls are bearing walls."

"Good. How long would it take?"

"That depends on the extent of the changes. We might have to reroute electrical lines, water, and so forth."

"I'll keep it simple. How long?"

"By the time I get permits, get the drawings completed, line up my people, you're looking at four to five weeks."

"Too long."

"When did you need this by?"

"Tomorrow. The day after at the latest."

On the other end of the line Devlin heard Kohler choking on his cigar. "You gotta be kidding," he said in a raspy voice. "We're not talking about building a doghouse here. This is—"

"Bert, here's the bottom line. Right now you do all the construction for Taggert Industries. Right?"

"Yeah," Kohler answered cautiously.

"Well, let me make this as simple as I can. You don't do this on my timetable, you've done your last job for Taggert Industries."

There was a long pause as Kohler calculated how much business that would cost him. Finally, he cleared his throat and said in a more servile tone, "You don't know what you're asking. I gotta line up electricians, carpenters, tin knockers, plumbers, painters, carpet people. . . ."

"Yes or no?"

There was a long sigh, like the sound of air being let out of a very large balloon. "Okay," he said in a barely audible voice.

"Good. Be over here in ten minutes and we'll go over the changes."

"*Ten*—I got an appointment—"

"Bert, you're working for me now. Clear your calendar for the next two days. You're going to be a very busy man."

BERT KOHLER WAS BORN with thick lips and dark smudges under his eyes. His five-o'-clock shadow, which made him look in constant need of a shave, didn't come until he was sixteen.

He rested his hands on an enormous belly that appeared to be all fat, but which Devlin knew contained a good deal of muscle as well. In the past forty-eight hours he'd seen the fifty-five-year-old contractor lend his considerable brawn to a number of tasks that would have winded men half his age.

"Sorry we got a late start the other day," Kohler said, watching two of his men painting the molding for the new door leading to Taggert's office. "But I hadda pull some of my men off other jobs."

"It did concern me," Devlin said, effecting a look of mild, if benevolent, annoyance. But the truth was, he was delighted. The morning after Devlin had spoken with him, Kohler had arrived at 10:00 A.M. with a small army of men, and they'd immediately set about the task of ripping out openings for new doors and building frames for walls that would seal off corridors.

"When do you think you'll be finished?"

Kohler rubbed his chin. "I'm hoping by tonight."

"Hoping?"

"I'm gonna do my best, Mr. Devlin. But—"

Devlin shook his head. "Bert, you *will* be done by tonight."

Kohler assumed a hound-dog expression. "Yeah, I'll be finished."

"Have all the electric shutters been installed?"

"Yeah, I tested them myself. They work fine. They're timed to close at dusk and open an hour after sunup." He scratched his chin stubble. "Could I ask you something?"

"Shoot."

"Why would you want to block off that terrific view by putting shutters on all the windows?"

Devlin couldn't tell him it was a precaution against Elgin's using a telescopic rifle, so he said, "Mr. Taggert has very sensitive eyes. Sometimes he can't take a lot of light."

"Ah, I see." But from the expression on his face it was clear that he didn't. He looked at the blueprints and his beetle brow creased in a furrow. "Could I ask you another question?"

"Go for it," Devlin said, amused by the contractor's bewildered expression.

"I don't get it. All we did was change door locations and wall off a few hallways. The way it is now, you can't get very far without going through at least two different rooms. It's like a friggin' maze. How come?"

"Mr. Taggert bores easily," Devlin said with a

straight face. "He likes variety. Some people redecorate, he reconstructs."

Kohler nodded gravely. "You know," he said in an awed tone, "rich people are different from us."

"I guess so." Devlin looked at his watch. "Gotta go."

As he was walking away, he said, "Add more people if you have to, but I want this finished by tonight."

But Kohler wasn't listening. He was busy chewing out a carpet technician who was working too slowly.

Devlin found Royal at the lobby guard station.

"Otis, how we doing?"

The big man flashed Devlin a big toothy grin. "Just fine. The rest of the hardware came in yesterday afternoon and we're just finishin' up installin' the locks for the stairwells. Come, let me show you what I've done."

On their way up, Otis explained the newly installed elevator card reader. "Startin' today, people going to the fortieth floor will have to use their access cards. Only those authorized by the computer will be permitted beyond the thirty-ninth floor."

He pointed at the ceiling. "There's a surveillance camera up there. If anyone tries to fool with the system, it'll create an alarm condition and the guard will be able to see immediately what's goin' on. If it's an intruder, we can stop the elevator between floors until the police get here." He grinned slyly. "This system also takes into account the 'J' factor."

"What's that?"

"Jackass, mon. If one of the bigwigs screws up because he doesn't know how to punch the right buttons, the guard can override the system and send him on his way. No problem."

They got off on the thirty-eighth floor and Royal took Devlin into the fire stairwell. "We have a special problem with fire stair doors," he said. "Fire Department regulations say we can't lock these doors, so all we can do is alarm them. If Elgin enters the stairwell on any floor, we would know immediately where he went in because of the alarm, but we would have no way of knowing if he went up or down. What I've done is installed infrared motion detectors in conjunction with surveillance cameras on thirty-eight, thirty-nine, forty, and the penthouse floor landings."

Devlin looked around, but he didn't see a camera. Then he pointed at the fire extinguisher. "There?"

Royal grinned. "You're gettin' more perceptive."

"So everything is in place?"

"There are some minor glitches in the system that Marie and I have to work on, but—"

"Do they compromise the system?"

"No. Essentially, everything is in place."

Devlin smiled. "You've done a hell of a job, Otis."

"Marie did most of the work, you know."

"I had a feeling that was the case," Devlin said. They both laughed.

As they walked back to the elevator, Devlin reflected that now that all the security precautions had been taken, it was up to him to provide Taggert with the final measure of protection. And he felt confident about it. He was certain that Elgin would make an attempt to kill Taggert, but he was just as certain he wouldn't succeed. And now that the security system was in place, Marie would soon be off the premises. Safe from this psycho.

Royal pressed the up button. "I have to meet Marie in the penthouse C&C room."

"What's the problem?"

"The alarm condition reports are not loggin' on the system as they should. Probably—"

Devlin snapped his fingers. "Logs! Of course." He punched the down button. "I forgot about the god-damn logs."

Royal scrunched his forehead. "What are you talkin' about, mon?"

The doors opened and Devlin stepped in. "All the scientists in R&D keep logbooks," he explained. "Brock's and Ahmad's will tell me what they were working on when they died."

The corpulent Armond waddled around his desk and offered a flabby hand. "Come in, dear boy," he said, sliding out a chair. "Come in. Would you like some coffee?"

"No."

He pointed at a desk strewn with paper and reports. "I'm so busy. I just got back from speaking at a pharmaceutical convention in Los Angeles." He rolled his tiny eyes. "They can be *so* tedious. I don't mind the speeches, it's those terminally boring cock-tail parties that I'm required to attend as the guest of honor. But I suppose it's my duty to—"

"Dr. Armond," Devlin interrupted, "the last time I spoke to you, you told me you didn't know what Ahmad and Brock were working on."

Armond studied Devlin with eyes that were mere slits in the folds of his fleshy face. "Correct."

"Did you subsequently check their logbooks?"

"Yes, of course."

"Well, what did they say?" Devlin asked impatiently.

"Routine matters, really. Reviewing colleagues' research data, excerpts from the latest scientific literature—that sort of thing. Though I did think you'd want to know"—Armond's voice dropped to a whisper as if he were now imparting top-secret information—"that their area of specialization was our cold remedy product line."

Devlin frowned. "These men weren't killed because of nasal decongestant. It had to be something else. Let me have the logs. Maybe I can—"

Armond pursed his thick lips in distress. "I'm afraid I can't."

"Why?"

"The logs . . . well, they appear to be missing."

Devlin snapped forward in his seat. "Missing? From where? When?" His first thought was that Elgin had gotten into the R&D section, but then he remembered Marie's printout. Elgin had been nowhere near the fourteenth floor. Besides, it wouldn't have mattered; the shoeshine man's card was not authorized for the R&D section.

"Just yesterday I went searching for them in the archives room," Armond said, shrugging, "but . . . they were missing."

Devlin slammed his hand on Armond's desk. "Goddamn it, stop saying 'missing' like they were mislaid or something. They were stolen, right?"

Armond tucked his chins in, causing his cheeks and jowls to flare out like a bullfrog's. "Well, I don't know that I would characterize it that way."

"Why wasn't I told about this?"

"Frankly, I didn't see any urgency. The librarian is

conducting a search for them even as we speak. I'm sure they'll turn up."

"If they do, I want to be notified right away." But Devlin knew he was wasting his breath. Those logs were long gone.

"By all means," Armond called after him as Devlin stormed out of the office, cursing himself for not remembering the logs the first time he was here.

When he got back to his office, Carla was loading paper into her printer's paper tray. "Carla," he said, "leave that and come inside. I want to talk to you."

She followed him into his office clutching a full pack of cigarettes as though it were a life support system. "What's up, boss?" she asked, having picked up Tommy Nolen's way of addressing him.

"What do you know about Dr. Armond?"

Carla fired up a long, thin purple cigarette, a color he hadn't seen before. "He's been a consultant with our pharmaceutical division for about ten years."

"What do you think of him?"

She tucked her head under a billowing cloud of smoke to peek at Devlin. "He's fat?"

"Don't be cute."

"Why are you asking me about him?"

"Because you've been with the company for a long time and that makes you a valuable resource; because there's something going on in this company that I don't like, but I don't know what it is; and . . . because I trust you."

That last admission didn't come easy. He'd liked Carla since the first day she'd told him she wouldn't balance his checkbook, but he wasn't sure if he could trust her fully. Since he'd started to work for the company, he'd sensed strong undercurrents of informal politics that he was certain were based on shifting loyalties. He knew it was the same in all large organizations—it was certainly like that in the police department. But at least there he knew who the players were.

So far, Carla's read on the company and its employees had been right on target and he wanted to get the view of someone who worked on the tenth floor. Later, he would get Gloria's view from the fortieth floor. Together, he might be able to get a better picture of what was going on in Taggert Industries.

Carla blew three perfect circles toward the ceiling. "I was wondering when you would get around to trusting me," she said.

Devlin grinned. "Sorry, I'm naturally suspicious."

She waved her cigarette like a wand. "Forgiven." She took a long drag of the purple cigarette and waited until she'd fully exhaled a lungful of smoke. Then she said, "Philip Armond is full of hot air. He did some important work early in his career, but he's been riding on that since. He makes most of his money consulting for the company. He likes to complain about wasting his time on the speaking circuit, but the truth is he gets invited to speak at those meetings only because there's a lot of wily businessmen who see him as an entree into Taggert Industries."

"If he's such a lightweight, why is he under consideration as Biehl's replacement?"

"Gloria is pushing him for the job."

Devlin shook his head in the negative. "Gloria is more gung-ho about this company than Taggert. Why would she put an incompetent in the R&D slot?"

"It makes no sense, I'll admit. I'm no Gloria Salazar fan, but I'll concede that she's shrewd. All I can say is, she must have her reasons for wanting Armond on her team."

"What team?"

"You want things done around here, you need a power base. Which means recruiting the right allies—and Gloria is a master at it. She even has a few board members in her pocket."

Devlin was puzzled. "But Gloria is Taggert's right hand, for chrissake. Why does she need a power base?"

"To overthrow him."

Devlin was dumbstruck. "What are you talking about?"

Carla smiled knowingly. "Last year Gloria was appointed president of the health-care division, our biggest division and our biggest moneymaker. Next to CEO, it's the most powerful job in the company." She looked at him curiously. "You've been kind of . . . close to Gloria. I thought you knew all that."

Devlin shook his head slowly. The truth was that he'd been so busy chasing Elgin and scrambling to secure the building, he'd had no time to observe office politics. When he and Gloria were alone their talks had always been about them, or the threat from Elgin.

Carla continued. "She's almost at the top of the pyramid, so what's her next move?"

"CEO," Devlin said automatically.

Carla grinned, baring nicotine-stained teeth. "Bingo."

25

GEORGE ELGIN STOOD IN FRONT of a paint-chipped wall on which he'd tacked up floor plans for Taggert Tower's fortieth floor and penthouse.

"Off the elevator on forty," he said aloud with his eyes closed. "Turn left . . . down corridor seven doors . . . turn left again . . . across open area . . . second door on right to reception area . . . " While he recited the most direct path to Taggert's office, he took a magazine clip out of his pocket, and with his eyes still closed, jammed it into his AK-47 submachine gun. Then he worked the bolt to drive a round into the chamber and released the safety—"straight across through double doors . . . and"—he opened his eyes and spat a peanut husk at the floor plan—"I'm in Jason Taggert's office."

His flat black eyes followed the highlighted yellow marker trail that led from the elevator bank to Taggert's office. He'd done it so often that he could picture in his mind the floor plan as though it were in front of him. The penthouse had been more difficult, but he'd memorized its labyrinth of halls and rooms as well.

He pushed the tattered curtain aside and looked out the soot-stained window of his one-room rental in the Bowery. Below, small clusters of drunks, having been rudely awakened by the rumble of the morning's rush-hour traffic, anxiously gathered together to pool their resources so they could buy the first wine of the day.

Elgin gazed down on those weak, pathetic men with contempt. He'd been up since 5:00 A.M., had already done his five miles, one hundred pushups, and two hundred situps while they were still rolling on the ground in a drunken stupor.

Elgin let the curtain fall back into place and went to the sagging bed, where he had laid out his gleaming surgical implements. One by one, he placed the saw, shears, scalpels, and cutting knives back into a black knapsack with his other equipment.

He sat down at a table and hunched over a towel covered with dozens of springs and parts. He punched the stopwatch button on his watch, closed his eyes, and with lightning speed unerringly reassembled his 9mm Sig Saur automatic pistol for the third time that morning. When he was done, he hit the stop button and smiled, pleased with his improved time.

Then he looked around and studied the small, dingy room containing only a bed, a table, and a rickety chair. This was his second day here. Since he'd started this mission, he hadn't stayed in any one place for more than three days. He was growing tired of the routine, but it was going to end tonight.

He shut his eyes tight and began to recite in a

monotone: "Off the elevator on forty . . . turn left . . . down corridor seven doors . . . "

Devlin groped for the switch at the front door and flipped on the lights. As he stepped inside the stuffy apartment and closed the door behind him, he was assailed by the faintly sour smell of dried blood.

He walked quickly into the living room, threw open the window, and took a deep breath. The cold air seared his lungs, but it cleared his nostrils of the smell of death. He pulled his head in and turned around to inspect the room.

After the police had finished their investigation, they'd allowed the superintendent to clean up Biehl's apartment, but he'd done a poor job. There were still two blackish-maroon stains on the carpet where the cat and its severed head had been found. He hadn't even tried to clean the sofa, which was still dotted with dried flecks of blood.

Devlin ran his fingers over the two indents on either side of the window frame where the bar had held the weight of Biehl's body. He peered out the window and tried to imagine what it must be like to fall twenty-two floors to your death.

He turned away. That wasn't why he was here. He'd come to look for some clue that might connect all the deaths, a clue that the police wouldn't have found because they wouldn't have been looking for it.

Except for the customary police search for valuables and personal effects, the apartment hadn't been touched since the night of Biehl's death. Biehl had no next of kin, so the apartment and its contents were sealed until the ponderous bureaucracy of the Public

Administrator's Office decided what to do with it. It had taken all Devlin's persuasiveness to convince Charlie Andrews to give him the key to the apartment. The detective finally agreed only after Devlin promised not to disturb anything.

He started in the bedroom. Systematically, he went through each drawer looking under socks, shirts, and underwear in search of—what? Did he expect to find secret documents? Some smoking gun that would neatly tie up the mystery of why four men were dead and another one was in danger? He knew better. He'd been a cop too long to expect that kind of luck. The truth was, he was here because he'd exhausted all his other options and he didn't know what else to do.

He moved on to a small desk in Biehl's bedroom. In the drawers there was the usual clutter of old electric bills, insurance papers, articles cut from newspapers and magazines, old statements from his mutual fund and his checking account. Devlin read them carefully, hoping to find something unusual, but all he discovered was that Biehl's mutual fund was doing poorly and he maintained a minimum balance in his checking account.

He was there almost an hour by the time he got into the kitchen. The only drawer worth checking was the clutter drawer, common to all kitchens.

Getting bored, and coming to the realization that he was wasting his time, he quickly flipped through a stack of coupons, receipts, and photographs. Suddenly, he froze and stared unbelievingly at a photograph of a thin and pale Kurt Biehl, looking ill at ease in baggy swimming trunks. He was squinting into the sun with his arm around a smiling Gloria Salazar, who was wearing a red thong bikini that showed her perfect bronzed body to great advantage. Sprawled on the back of the photo in Gloria's bold handwriting was the inscription: *K, Thanks for a wonderful weekend. The Caymans will never be the same. G.* The photo was imprinted with the date December 14.

She'd lied to him. Slowly, he slid into a chair and stared vacantly at the photo as his thoughts drifted to his ex-wife, Christine. *Devlin, what a schmuck you are.* Why did his judgment so dramatically fail him when it came to women? Why was he so eager to believe their excuses, so willing to make allowances for the inconsistencies in their behavior?

Now, all the little contradictions he'd refused to acknowledge in Gloria began to fall into place: her mercurial mood swings from passionate lover to uncompromising businesswoman willing to fire any-one who displeased her; her puzzling protective stance toward the incompetent Armond; her genuine fear of Elgin, yet her maddening insistence on keeping the police out of it.

Sitting at Kurt Biehl's kitchen table, he could no longer remember what made him think that he and Gloria could ever have a successful relationship. Had he ever really thought that? No. The truth was, he enjoyed being pursued by her. *What a joke.*

After a minute or so, his anger was overtaken by curiosity. Gloria had gone to great pains to manipulate him. But why? He put the photograph into his pocket and stood up. It was time to use what he'd just learned to get some answers.

When he got back to his office it was almost 7:00 P.M. Carla had just put on her coat when he came in.

"Carla, you got a minute?"

She saw the expression on his face and followed him into his office. "You look like your dog just died. What happened?"

He looked at her for a long moment. Finally he said, "Did you know that Gloria Salazar and Kurt Biehl were having an affair?"

Carla lowered herself to the chair, her coat still on. "I didn't know about Biehl, but I'm not surprised."

"Why?"

"You remember the first time we talked about Gloria, JT, and me?"

"Yeah."

"Well, maybe now's the time to give you the full story."

Devlin wasn't sure he wanted to hear it, but he nodded for her to continue.

"When Gloria first came to work for us, she was terrific," Carla said, wriggling out of her coat. "Not just smart—scary smart. Tell her something once and she had it down cold. And she was ambitious. She made no secret of it, she wanted to go to the top. Some people thought there was something sexual going on between her and JT, but there wasn't. He admired her because she was a workaholic like him. He could *relate* to her. He saw something of his younger self in her, I guess. Anyway, he became her mentor."

Carla took a deep breath. "I said she didn't use sex to get ahead with JT, but she had no aversion to using her body to get ahead with others." She saw the uncomfortable look on Devlin's face but went on. "She was good at it, too; very discreet. In fact, I was the only one who saw what was going on. When she realized I was on to her, she decided to get rid of me. She deliberately sabotaged a very important contract so she could blame me. When the deal fell through, she demanded that JT fire me. But JT and I went back too far. To protect me he sent me here to the security department where I'd be as far away from her as possible." Carla smiled. "Until you came on board, I don't think she knew where the security department was."

As Devlin sat there, listening to Carla describe a Gloria he hadn't known existed, a question that had been bothering him for a long time was finally answered. She'd hit on him because she wanted something from him. But what?

Carla continued. "Gloria is the most amoral person I've ever met. She uses people until she gets what she wants, then she discards them. You met Kurt Biehl. Do you think someone like Gloria could fall in love with a guy like him?"

Remembering the photograph of the tall, ungainly man in the baggy swim trunks, Devlin said, "No, I guess not."

The truth was, he'd asked the same question about himself and, until today, had been willing to believe that the answer was yes.

It was almost 8:00 P.M. by the time Devlin picked up the telephone and called Gloria at home.

"Yes?"

"Gloria, I have to talk to you about—"

"Can't do it now, sweetie. I'm running out the door. A black-tie benefit at the Waldorf."

"It's important. When will you be home?"

"I'm coming back to the office after the dinner—probably around one-thirty. JT and I are expecting a two A.M. call from Jakarta. Some out-of-control Japanese drilling operation accidentally cut through our underwater cable and—" She paused. "'Important,' you said?"

"Very."

"Well . . . if you don't mind staying up that late, you *could* meet me there."

Two in the morning? Didn't she ever sleep? He and Otis and Marie had been planning to stay quite late, but . . .

"All right. I'll be here."

26

LONG AFTER HE HUNG UP, Devlin sat at his desk try-ing to sort out the tangle of questions that this new image of Gloria had created. Clearly, she wanted something from him. But what was it? She was throwing her support to an incompetent Dr. Armond. Why? Obviously, she'd had an affair with Biehl so she could use him. But for what? And then there was the big question: What did all this have to do with Jason Taggert, Elgin, and the four men he'd murdered?

Devlin got up to adjust the blinds. It was almost 10:00 P.M., but some lights were still on in the build-ing across the street. Each lighted office window cre-ated its own distinct tableau: in one window a cleaning woman was shaking her hips to the rhythm coming from her earphones as she dusted a book-case; in another a young man in suspenders was intently hunched over his computer. Working on an important project or his own resume? And in a third window a bald-headed man with apparently no place else to go sat with his feet up on the desk watching a portable TV.

Devlin turned away from the window. As he did, he realized what had been nagging him about his conversations with the head of R&D. The first time he'd questioned Armond, he'd told the scientist to call as soon as he learned what Brock and the others had been working on. In their follow-up talk, Armond had confided that business about the cold remedy. The question was: Why hadn't he contacted Devlin as soon as he'd uncovered the information? There couldn't have been any doubt that Devlin wanted to know Brock and the others' research focus, no matter how innocuous. Nor could there have been any doubt about Devlin's sense of urgency. Why had it been necessary for Devlin to seek him out again? More than ever, he had a feeling that Dr. Amond was playing with him.

Devlin picked up the telephone. There was a good chance that Armond might still be in the building. Since Taggert had taken up residency in the penthouse, most of the top executives were reluctant to go home early. As soon as he heard Armond's voice, Devlin hung up. He didn't want the doctor to know he was about to get a surprise visit.

When Devlin walked into Armond's office he thought he detected a fleeting look of alarm on the doctor's face. But it quickly gave way to a sleepy smile.

"Well, hello there," Armond said cheerily. "Apparently I'm not the only one working late tonight. I find I can get a lot more done without the endless interruptions during the day. Is that your experience, too?"

Devlin, looming over him, ignored the out-stretched hand. "Give me the logbooks."

Armond withdrew his hand as though it had been burned. "I told you they're—"

"Missing. I know. And you're the one who's got them."

Armond intertwined his sausagelike fingers and rested them on his stomach. "I have nothing further to say to you," he said.

For effect, Devlin, feigning outrage, reached across the desk and yanked on Armond's necktie. The petrified look in Armond's eyes confirmed Devlin's suspicions: The man had never been treated this way before.

"Listen, fat ass. You lied to me once. Now I want the truth."

The tightened tie was cutting into Armond's flabby neck and his face was turning purple. "I . . . didn't . . . lie . . . "

Devlin let go of his tie and sat on the edge of Armond's desk. He'd planted the seed of imminent violence, always a real attention-getter. Now it was time for the bluff.

"Armond," he said in a reasonable voice, "you're in real deep shit. What do you think the police will do when I tell them that you took valuable company research documents? And what will the medical societies do when they find out you've taken part in a research coverup?" Devlin shook his head sadly. "Too bad. I hear you're in line for the director's slot here. You can kiss that job good-bye. Same goes for those lucrative consulting contracts, the speeches, the par-ties . . . " Devlin let Armond complete the rest of the gloomy scenario in his own head.

Armond, looking like he was about to cry, screwed up his face in anguish. "I didn't do anything wrong," he whined.

Devlin picked up the telephone. "We'll let the police decide that."

"No . . . wait. Isn't there something we can do without involving the police?"

Devlin put the telephone down. "That depends. You tell me the truth, I'll see what I can do."

Armond glanced at the telephone anxiously. "I would like to talk to Gloria Salazar first."

Devlin's stomach knotted. He'd been expecting to hear that Gloria was in the middle of whatever Armond had done, but it was still a jolt. "No," he said. "You're on your own."

Armond cleared his throat. "Frankly, I don't know much. Right before you came to see me that first time, I got a call from Gloria. She said you'd probably be stopping by to ask questions about two chemists who had worked here. She said there were reasons she couldn't go into, but I was not to give you any information about them. I was to fall back on my unfamiliarity with the organization."

"What happened to the logbooks?"

Armond broke eye contact. "She asked for them and I . . . I gave them to her."

"What was in them?"

"I didn't look. Frankly, I didn't want to know."

Devlin sat back, feeling suddenly spent. After what Carla had told him about Gloria, none of what Armond said surprised him. What amazed him was how gullible he'd been. She'd been manipulating people and events all around him and he never knew it.

"Why did you take those logs?" he asked Armond.
"Why would you risk your reputation?"

Armond laughed bitterly. "What reputation? I've
been a hack for the last fifteen years. By the time I
became a consultant with Taggert Industries I was
ready to sell my services to the highest bidder and
Gloria knew it. Oh, yes, she doesn't mince words,
that one. Told me my career was washed up, but that
she could help me. She gave me a job as the company's primary drug consultant."

"And in exchange, you did what?"

"Conducted studies and research on the company's products."

"And those research findings were always favorable to the company."

Armond's eyes flashed in indignation at the sarcastic tone in Devlin's voice. "I never fudged my figures,
nor did I intentionally lie about my results." He
turned away. "It isn't necessary. When one is controlling the scope of the research, it's not too difficult to
arrive at a predetermined conclusion. It's quite common in the corporate research field, really. Think of
the tobacco and automotive industries, pharmaceuticals, food—well, you read the newspapers. You know."

Devlin did know, but he didn't understand. As a
cop he'd dealt with a different class of criminals. It
was easier to understand the motivation of thieves,
muggers, and murderers—disenfranchised people
who lived on the fringe of society, people who didn't
have a stake in the future. What he found harder to
understand was the motivations of the Salazars and
Armonds of the world—bright, highly skilled people
with everything going for them—risking it all for a
few dollars more or fake prestige.

"What did she promise for your cooperation this time?"

Armond smoothed out his tie. "The directorship of the R&D section. You've got to understand . . . it's the chance of a lifetime," he said, not yet fully realizing that chance had flown out of his grasp. "Becoming the director of R&D for a prestigious company like Taggert Industries at this stage in my career is—" His face brightened. "Well, it would reverse everything . . . put me back where I was. At the top."

Devlin stood up, feeling more pity for Armond than anger. Like himself, he was just another one of Gloria's victims.

"Okay, I'm through with you," Devlin said. "Get out of here."

With a speed belying his size, Armond jumped up and hastily threw on his coat. As he was heading for the door, Devlin grabbed his sleeve. "Don't even think of contacting Gloria," he warned. "Or, I promise you, as bad a situation as you're in now, it'll get much worse."

"No, no, of course I won't." He clutched his briefcase in his arms like a schoolboy who has just been told he's suspended. "What . . . what will happen now?"

"I don't know. Go home." He made a mental note to have Armond's access card deactivated.

After Armond left, Devlin walked through the deserted R&D section. Without people to give it life, the empty rooms exuded a tomblike atmosphere. As if to verify that life really did exist in these sterile offices, the occupants had left their marks behind: sweaters casually tossed over the backs of chairs, comfortable shoes tucked under desks, and on almost every work-station Styrofoam cups and soda pop cans arrayed like sentinels guarding abandoned computer terminals.

As Devlin viewed the dozens of darkened computer screens, it occurred to him that the answers he was looking for had to be concealed somewhere in the R&D computers. And he knew only one person who could retrieve that information.

Devlin went downstairs and found Marie and Otis by the lobby guard desk hunched over a technical manual. Tommy Nolen sat in a chair observing as Ray Towne worked with the system, attempting different commands.

Otis looked up. "Michael, you still here?"

"Yeah." He stared at the security console. "What are you doing?"

"We've just spent the last hour trying to eliminate a couple of glitches," Marie said. Her eyes still scanned the technical manual. "Some of the door sensors aren't reporting properly. We were just about to go up to the tenth-floor C&C room to check out whether the problem's in the hardware or software."

Devlin nodded. "Otis, can you get started without Marie? I need her."

"Sure, no problem, mon," he said, shrugging. "Marie, I'll see you later—either on ten or in the penthouse."

"Okay," Marie said, looking slightly baffled as Devlin led her by the arm toward the elevator.

"Come on," he said, "I'll explain on the way."

By the time the elevator got to the fourteenth floor, he'd told her the whole story about Gloria.

She'd listened with calm detachment, but inside she was delighted. Well, maybe *delighted* wasn't the right word. Her joy was tempered by the sense of pain and betrayal she saw in his eyes.

As the elevator doors opened she said, "So what do you want *me* to do?"

"I think the answer to what's going on around here is in the R&D computers and I want you to find it. Can you do that?"

She waved her access card in front of the card reader. "It might be possible. It's worth a shot, I guess," she said, pushing the door open.

She sat down at Biehl's desk and logged on. That was the easy part. As a systemwide sysops, she had automatic entry into the R&D computer, but once inside it was another matter entirely.

She quickly found that scientists had their own peculiar way of setting up directories and subdirectories, and the use of arcane jargon and scientific notation made the going even more tedious.

While Devlin peered over her shoulder, Marie muttered cryptically about trees and root directories, and attacked the keyboard. As her fingers flew over the keys, a bewildering array of lists and numbers appeared on the screen and disappeared just as quickly. *Goddamn,* he thought. Even if he had decades to bone up on computers, he couldn't imagine himself ever having this level of expertise.

After almost fifteen minutes of running down electronic dead ends, she finally began to understand the logic of the system.

"Okay," she said, peering at a screen full of names and numbers, "here are the major directories. *Marone!* There's gotta be a million of 'em."

Devlin's heart sank. "What does that mean?"

"It means that this is going to take a little longer than I thought. What do you want me to look for?"

"Biehl's correspondence. Does he have his own file?"

"He must, but I don't see a directory with his name on it. It's gotta be listed under something else. Look at some of these directory names—Doc, Dopey, Sneezy, Plato. Weird sense of humor, these scientists. Let me try a name search."

After several minutes of quietly tapping on the keys, she said to the screen, "There you are, you little bastard." To Devlin she said, "His directory is called Fritz. Go figure." She drummed on the desk with her fingernails and peered at the screen. "There's a lot of files here. Where do you want to start?"

"Robby Elgin was admitted to Malroux's clinic on November 9. Let's start with that date and move forward."

One by one, Marie brought up the files beginning with that date. Most of them contained mundane correspondence to medical universities, laboratories, and internal memos.

An hour later, they came to the date when Biehl was murdered. Marie hit the exit command and sat back. "There was nothing there. What next?"

Devlin slammed his hand on the desk. "The key to this thing has gotta be in here somewhere."

Marie stared morosely at the screen, which was still displaying Biehl's directory. Suddenly, she bolted upright. "Michael, give me a calendar and Biehl's appointment diary."

Devlin tossed her a calendar and, while she jotted down a list of dates, he rummaged through Biehl's desk looking for his diary. He found it and slid it across the desk to her. "What do you see?"

She typed a command and tapped the screen. "Look, I've gone back to September. If we exclude weekend dates, there's a file for every working day in September and October. Then we come to November and there's a file for every day except the twenty-sixth. Three more workdays in December and four more workdays in January are missing."

Devlin stared at the screen as though the answer should be self-evident. "So?"

"So, according to his appointment diary, he was in the office on all those days." Marie waved the diary in the air. "He was the director of R&D, Michael. Think about it. Wouldn't a man in that position have files to save every day?"

Devlin finally saw what she was getting at. "He erased them?"

"I think so."

"Can you get them back?"

Marie bit her lower lip. "I doubt it."

"Why not? They got Ollie North's files back after he thought he'd erased them, didn't they?"

"Let me explain how a computer works. When you delete a file you're really deleting only the file name from the index. The file itself is still on the hard drive until it gets overwritten." She tapped the terminal. "All these workstations are networked into a main-frame, so any files Biehl deleted back in November would have been written over a long time ago."

Devlin's growing optimism quickly waned. "That son of a bitch. We're back to square one."

Marie snapped her fingers. "Wait! The LAN admin! The files might be there."

"Who the hell is the LAN—?"

"The local area network administrator. It's his job to back up the entire system's work every twenty-four hours."

"Then he has Biehl's deleted files?"

Marie frowned. "That depends. If Biehl deleted the file before the backup took place, then it's gone for good. But let's say that he went back and deleted the files, even a day later, then he'd be too late. The files would already have been backed up and in storage."

"Wouldn't Biehl know that?"

"Not necessarily. Unless you're seriously into computers, very few people understand the mechanics. They operate computers with blind faith. They press delete, a line disappears from the screen, they think it's gone."

"Where do they store these backups?"

"Right upstairs in EDP."

Devlin jumped up. "Let's go."

"Wait." Marie said. "I need to print out a copy of Biehl's directory for the three-month period."

Devlin impatiently drummed his fingers on the console top as Marie's hands flew over the keys. When the last sheet of paper spilled out of the printer, he checked his watch.

Twelve-thirty A.M. Another hour until Gloria was due back in the building.

As expected, the electronic data processing section was relatively quiet at this time of night. Only a handful of people were needed to run the high-speed machines, which hummed away at their task of recording, retrieving, and storing the electronic paperwork of a huge multinational corporation.

When Devlin and Marie came through the door, the night supervisor looked up. "Hi, Marie. Can I get you anything?"

"No thanks, Hank. I just want to check a couple of backup tapes."

The man nodded. "You know where they are. If you need any help, give a yell."

The reception she got now from the people in the computer section was a lot different than when she'd first arrived. After the initial shock of discovering that their computer systems were vulnerable to outside attack, they'd begun to listen to her and accept her advice and suggestions. The gallons of coffee and dozens of boxes of donuts she'd brought as peace offerings hadn't hurt, either.

After she found the tapes for the dates she was looking for, she loaded November 26 into the machine. Soon the now-familiar R&D menu popped up on the screen. She exhaled slowly. "Okay, now let's see if there's anything for Biehl." She typed a command, and his directory, listing six files, appeared on the screen.

Marie pumped her clenched fist. "Yes!"

Devlin sat down slowly on the edge of the desk. "Okay, let's see them."

The first file was an internal memo about Christmas vacations. The second had to do with new reporting procedures. The third and fourth were routine memos to the Food and Drug Administration. "Nothing he'd want to erase here," she said.

Devlin felt his hopes fading. "Let's see what's on the last two."

She typed a command and a memo from Brock to Biehl popped up on the screen.

26 NOVEMBER
FROM: R. BROCK
TO: K. BIEHL
RE: XP-115

I had a disturbing call today from Dr. Malroux re dosage rate for patient XP-115. As per our prior instructions he has increased the dosage of Hemotolin, but the patient's blood count continues to drop precipitously. I have conferred with Ahmad and our preliminary computer modeling tests indicate that the drug may be attacking the immune system. I know this is the only case in which this has happened, but until we discover if this is an anomaly or a flaw in the drug, I recommend we stop all field protocols immediately.

R. Brock

"Son of a bitch," Devlin whispered. "The smoking gun."

"XP. Experimental patient?" Marie asked.

"I guess so."

"Oh my God! That means there are at least one hundred and fifteen people on this drug and there's no official record of what's going on."

"I wouldn't say that," Devlin said. "I'm sure someone in R&D is still monitoring this program."

"Who?"

"I don't know, but I'm going to find out. Let's see the other files."

The last November file was of no consequence, as were three for the month of December. Then Marie retrieved a memo from Biehl to Gloria.

CONFIDENTIAL

6 DECEMBER

FROM: K. BIEHL

TO: G. SALAZAR

RE: DRUG: H

Enclosed memo from R. Brock indicates potential serious problem. I know your strong feelings on this, but I think you should reconsider. We face liability exposure, problems with the FDA, etc. Let's talk.

K. Biehl

enc.

Devlin stared at the screen for a long time as though he couldn't believe what he was seeing. Finally, Marie hit the exit key and the memo vanished from the screen.

I sure know how to pick 'em, Devlin thought. He ran his fingers through his hair, feeling both embarrassed and stupid. Then he turned sheepishly to Marie. "Guess you were right about her."

She shook her head. "I knew she was a bitch, but I never dreamed she'd be capable of this."

"No"—he gave her a direct look—"you're right about a lot of things." He took a deep breath, seeming to make up his mind about something. "Okay," he said, slapping the desk. "Let's see what's in the rest of the files."

At 12:45 A.M. Elgin slipped into the Taggert Tower garage. From his earlier reconnaissance, he'd determined that the garage entrance was his best way into the building. There were no guards present, nor was there much traffic through the door at this time of night. Of course, there was the surveillance camera and a card reader to contend with, but that was no problem. In fact, the presence of the camera was a necessary part of his plan.

Double glass doors led from the garage into a well-lighted twelve-foot-square vestibule. Opposite the glass doors was a steel door leading into the building. On the ceiling to the left of the door a surveillance camera monitored anyone using the card reader or door.

Elgin slipped through the glass doors. Hugging the left wall out of range of the camera, he took a telescoping wand out of his knapsack. Carefully he touched the camera with the extended wand and pushed it so that the lens pointed toward the ceiling.

Nolen looked up from his newspaper when he heard the insistent beeping of a motion detection alarm and saw that one of the monitors was displaying a view of a tiled ceiling. "Where the hell is that?"

Ray Towne looked at his monitor display. "The garage entrance. One of the damn parking-lot attendants screwing around. I'll take a look."

"No," Nolen said, patting his belly. "You stay. I can use the exercise."

Elgin folded his telescoping wand and put it back in his knapsack. Then he selected a gleaming, thin-bladed knife from his bag and crouched by the side of the door to wait.

Nolen was in a good mood and came off the elevator whistling. He was at the end of his shift and was scheduled to leave the next day for a three-day visit to his grandchildren. *Can't wait to see those little guys,* he thought. As he opened the door to the vestibule, he was so intent on looking up toward the ceiling camera that he never saw the figure crouching in the corner.

Elgin sprung up and drove the knife through Nolen's throat with such force that the protruding blade tip broke off as it struck the steel door. Instinctively, the ex-cop grabbed Elgin's arm with one hand and with the other tried to free his gun. But Elgin grabbed his wrist and kneed the big man in the groin.

Blood spurting from his mouth, Nolen sagged slowly to the floor while Elgin kept the knife lodged firmly in place. When he saw Nolen's eyes rotate upward, he gave a final twist and pulled it out. Nolen shuddered and was still.

Elgin dragged the body inside and closed the door after him. Then he stripped off his trench coat and threw it aside. Underneath, he was wearing his old combat fatigues, the uniform he'd always felt most comfortable in. It was only fitting that he wear it now on his final mission.

He removed a small, battery-powered noise generator from his knapsack and, using duct tape, secured Nolen's portable radio to it with the transmit key taped in the open position. He turned on the noise generator and a wave of white noise went out over the channel, effectively jamming all the security radios in the building. Then he lifted a panel from the hallway's false ceiling and placed the radio and generator inside.

He returned to the body and after a quick search found Nolen's access card. Next, he wiped the knife off, returned it to the knapsack, and laid out on the floor three stainless-steel surgical implements: a scalpel, shears, and a saw.

He recognized Nolen from his earlier encounter with him. "Hey, Nolen," he whispered to the lifeless body, "I wonder if you could give me a hand?"

When Dr. Philip Armond left his office after his confrontation with Devlin, he'd had every intention of going home as he'd been told. But on the way down in the elevator, he thought about Gloria's fierce tem-

per and decided he feared her wrath more than
Devlin's. Devlin would try to make good on his
threat, he was sure of that. But his instincts told him
that the president of Taggert's health-care division
still held better cards. It was wiser, he thought, to
stay on her good side and depend on her to get him
through this.

He'd stopped at the guard desk to inquire about
Gloria's whereabouts and was pleased to hear from
Tommy Nolen that she was expected back from the
Waldorf shortly.

He went back upstairs to Gloria's office suite.
While he waited alone in the outer reception area, he
reflected on the best way to break the news to her.
She'd be angry, of course, but he intended to offset
her ire by assuring her that he'd told Devlin nothing
about the existence of the new drug project.
Nervously, he drummed his fat fingers on the briefcase on his lap, hoping he was doing the right thing.
If there was still a possibility he might get the director's job, damage control was crucial.

After fifteen minutes, he decided that perhaps she
wasn't coming back after all. He hurried down the hall,
suddenly afraid he'd run into Devlin. Inside the elevator, he pushed the button for the basement garage
and tried to think good thoughts as the elevator
plunged toward the garage level.

The doors opened, and as Armond stepped off the
elevator, he saw a figure dressed in a military uniform
crouching over something on the floor. It took the
preoccupied biochemist a second to realize that it was
a body. Then the fatigue-clad figure spun around. His
hands were covered with blood, and his flat black eyes
locked on Armond with a look of pure rage.

Oh my God . . . no, please no. Gagging, Armond staggered back into the elevator.

Elgin sprung forward as Armond frantically slapped at the close button. "Close, damn it . . . god-damn you!" Armond wailed.

With tears of relief the scientist watched the doors begin to move. But they moved with agonizing slowness and he felt an overwhelming urge to urinate as the gap between the doors narrowed inch by inch. Just as they were about to meet, a bloodied hand wielding a shiny knife thrust through the opening and began slashing the air.

Grunting in terror, Armond blindly pawed at the control panel, trying desperately to make the elevator go up. Then, to his horror, the doors opened and the man stepped inside. Armond, hyperventilating, staggered to the back of the elevator and squeezed his back up against the rear wall. "No . . . no . . . "

Elgin, holding the knife partially hidden behind his back in the classic knife-fighting position, stepped forward. With one fluid motion he brought his hand up, driving the blade into Armond's unprotected mid-section.

The doctor exhaled sharply as the wind was taken from him. At first he thought he'd been punched. Then he looked down and saw the knife handle protruding from his stomach. His knees buckled and he slid to the floor.

Upstairs at the lobby guard station, Ray Towne was fiddling with the squelch button on his radio, trying to get rid of the static. He had his back to the surveillance camera monitors and never saw the black-and-white, grainy, live transmission of Elgin dragging Armond's body out of the elevator.

Elgin left the body next to Nolen's. Then he took the elevator to the tenth floor. When he got to the C&C room, he placed Nolen's severed hand on the palm reader and the door clicked open.

Except for a spotlight over the workstation, the rest of the room was dimly lit. Otis Royal was sitting at the terminal, intent on running a system diagnostic test. Without looking up he tapped a schematic spread out in front of him. "I think I found the problem, Marie. It's probably—"

Elgin tossed Nolen's bloody hand in the air. "Let's give the man a hand," he said, as the severed appendage hit the schematic.

"*Ahhhggg . . .*" Royal jumped from his seat and spun around. He hadn't even had time to process what had happened when an AK-47 round slammed into his left knee. The big Jamaican fell writhing to the floor.

"It's best that you're incapacitated," Elgin said flatly. He righted the chair. "Sit here." When Royal didn't respond, he pointed the weapon at his other knee. "Should I do it again?"

In great pain, Royal crawled across the floor and lifted himself into the chair; his chest pounded with the physical exertion.

Elgin took a roll of duct tape out of his knapsack and tossed it to Royal. "Secure your left arm to the chair's arm." When that was done, Elgin clamped his right arm down and wrapped the tape around it. Royal winced in pain. "That's too tight, mon."

Elgin smiled. "No. You'll see it isn't."

He secured Royal's long legs to the chair with more tape. Otis screamed in agony when Elgin roughly pulled his shattered knee into position. "Bite the bullet, man," Elgin said disgustedly. "I've seen gut-shot men who didn't carry on like that."

When Royal was securely tied to the chair, Elgin wheeled him to the side and sat down at the console. He was about to type a command when he looked up at the monitor and saw Jason Taggert sitting behind his desk. "Ah," he said aloud. "The target." Then Gloria walked into the picture and handed Taggert a glass. "Who's that?"

Royal looked up at the screen. Taggert and Gloria were clinking champagne glasses. "I don't know."

Without comment Elgin turned back to the computer. After several futile attempts to gain access at the sysops level, he spun around in his seat and faced Royal. "What's your name?"

"Otis."

"I'm impressed with your work, Otis. Usually I have no trouble hacking into a program, but you've built a lot of safeguards into it."

Royal said nothing. It had been Marie who had built the security into the system, but he wasn't about to tell him that. In fact, since Elgin had taken him prisoner, he'd been trying to think of a way to warn her. If he didn't, sooner or later, she was going to come walking through that door.

Elgin pinned Royal with his deadened eyes. "I have to make a few changes around here. Make this system more user-friendly. What's the password?"

"I'm just a technician, mon. I don't know all that—"

"Wrong answer," Elgin said. Without warning, he smashed Otis's nose with the heel of his hand.

Otis coughed, spit out blood. His eyes seemed to lose focus for a few seconds, then they cleared. "I'm tellin' you, mon," he said, gasping, "I do not know—"

Elgin brought the gun butt down on Royal's splintered knee. The Jamaican screamed as hot, searing pain convulsed his leg.

"I . . . don't know. . . ." Pinwheels floated across his field of vision and then, mercifully, he passed out.

When he awoke Elgin had wheeled his chair in front of the computer. Royal's eyes widened and his body involuntarily jerked to attention when he saw the array of gleaming surgical instruments laid out on the desk.

"You've got two choices," Elgin said in a flat voice. "You can tell me the password or you can let me persuade you. The same outcome, but the process is very different. Trust me."

The irony of the situation was not lost on Royal. He thought of all the money spent, all the state-of-the-art equipment, all the time and rush to get it installed, all of Marie's efforts to make the system hackproof. All that time, money, and effort spent to stop Elgin, and now it came down to him. *Hold on, mon . . . hold on. Don't give this man what he wants.*

"Well?"

Royal met his stare. "Look, I'd be crazy to lie to you. I'm tellin' you, I don't know how to get into the system."

Elgin's face darkened. He grabbed the shears and placed a pencil between the gleaming blades. Holding the pencil a few short inches from Otis's face, he snapped the pencil in half. The crunching sound made Royal blink involuntarily. Tears formed in his eyes. "Please, I don't know no password, mon."

Elgin lightly rested the shears on Royal's long, slender fingers.

"Last chance. The password."

Royal thought of Devlin and Marie somewhere in the building. If he gave Elgin access to the system, they'd be totally unprotected. So would Taggert. "I don't know no password."

Elgin gripped Royal's middle finger between the blades of the shears. "The password," he whispered.

"I don't—Ahhhh! . . ."

Elgin squeezed the shears and Royal entered a place he'd never been before. The pain seemed to lift him off the floor, push his brains through his skull. In that horrible moment, he was not really a person, but one giant nerve ending screaming for mercy.

Darkness came an instant later and the Jamaican's head lolled forward.

Elgin slapped Otis in the face a few times, waiting a full thirty seconds for him to stir. "Hey, Otis . . . you're not gonna bleed to death. Remember me tying your wrist tight? It's a tourniquet, man. No, don't thank me."

"I don't—" Otis started to slip into unconsciousness again.

A few more slaps brought Otis back around. He stared up into Elgin's evil, grinning face.

"Now, let's see, for some reason the last time I asked for that password you couldn't put your finger on it." Elgin waved Otis's severed digit in the air. Then he tossed the digit into the wastebasket. "Hey, maybe you're one of those guys who thinks with his dick."

Elgin jabbed the shears into Royal's crotch.

The intensity of the pain had reached a level where Royal could stand it. But he knew shock was playing a part in controlling his agony. Soon it would wear off and then . . . How long could he last? Should he keep trying?

Elgin unzipped Royal's fly and exposed his penis. "The password," he whispered.

Royal felt the cold steel of the shears next to his penis. *The password.* The path away from pain. Tears rolled down his cheeks. "Please, mon . . . "

"The password." Elgin's tone was soothing, beckoning Otis to a world where there was no pain.

Royal felt the the razor-sharp blade closing on his penis and screamed. "No more . . . " he sobbed. "No more . . . "

28

IN THE EDP SECTION, MARIE continued to retrieve Biehl's deleted files. As she and Devlin read them, she printed a copy. When they finished, they had a small stack of memos that painted a picture of intrigue and cynical duplicity.

Memos to and from Gloria, Biehl, Ahmad, and Brock described the development of a new wonder drug, Hemotolin, that promised to treat and arrest one type of leukemia. The laboratory tests had been encouraging. So had most of the field tests on 125 patients. Everything had been progressing according to plan. And then Robby Elgin entered the program.

For reasons unknown, he failed to respond to the drug. The dosage was increased, but his condition worsened. Eventually, the R&D team ran the data through a computer model and concluded that the drug was attacking the boy's immune system.

Malroux had conferred with Biehl, Brock, and Ahmad on numerous occasions and the memos underscored Malroux's growing concern that the drug was contraindicated. But Biehl and the two chemists reassured Malroux that there was often an initial dip in the white blood cell count, and that it was only temporary. They assured him that favorable results would be forthcoming. From the blizzard of memos back and forth discussing changes in dosage, symptom interpretation, and systemic reactions to these changes, it was clear to Devlin that these guys didn't know what the hell was going on.

Up until this point, the four Taggert Industries participants were of one mind. But when the possible cause of the problem was identified, there was a sudden break in the group's cohesiveness. Brock and Ahmad wanted to suspend the human testing, Gloria was adamant about continuing, and Biehl vacillated between the two positions.

Gloria prevailed and the experiments continued— even after the boy died. But on February 4, the day after Brock died on his Pennsylvania farm, Gloria sent a terse memo to Biehl instructing him to suspend all field tests on Hemotolin, to gather together and store all records of Hemotolin under a different name. Her final instruction to him was to delete all records, including computer files and E-mail, having to do with Hemotolin.

Devlin was jolted by what he'd read. Not only had Gloria lied to him, she'd directed the entire operation under his nose. But the Biehl file had answered some questions. By early December, it had become clear that Biehl wanted to stop the field testing. Apparently, Gloria's response had been to use her body to make him see things her way. The photo he'd found of the two of them was dated December 14.

He also knew why Gloria had backed Armond for

the R&D director's position: She knew he'd do anything to get the job, including covering up the existence of the Hemotolin experiment. He was also fairly certain that Dr. Armond was monitoring the Hemotolin project under a new name. But this time no lowly lab scientists, who might quibble about the methodology, would be privy to test information. Only Gloria and her hireling, Armond, would be trusted to protect the interests of the company.

Marie thought of her twins, of what she'd do if she'd been Kay Elgin. "How could they do that to a little boy?" she asked, her anger mounting.

"That's easy," Devlin said. "Taggert Industries must have blown big bucks on Hemotolin R&D, and the company wasn't about to let all that money go down the drain just because some little kid refused to respond to their new wonder drug."

"Do you think Taggert is part of this?"

"Damn right," Devlin said, angry that he'd been fooled by him as well. "Taggert's a hands-on guy. He had to know what was going on."

Marie looked numb.

"Now all the pieces of the puzzle are coming together," Devlin continued. "Charlie Andrews said someone broke into Malroux's office two days before he died. He assumed it was a junkie looking for drugs, but it had to be Elgin looking for Robby's medical records. He found the file and ripped out the pages he wanted. The memos must have come from Biehl, Brock, and Ahmad. Together, in Elgin's mind, these four men were responsible for Robby's death."

"What about Taggert?" Marie asked. "He's not mentioned in the file."

"No, he isn't, but he *does* own the company that made the drug that killed the boy. Elgin must have assumed Taggert knew about the drug's risks. And even if he didn't, it's Taggert who stands to profit from the drug more than anyone else. In Elgin's mind, that makes him target number one."

Marie thumbed through the memos. "You're right. The chronology fits." She took out a pencil, wrote down dates as she talked. "Robby Elgin died on January the tenth. He was buried on the thirteenth. According to Kay Elgin, George came to see her the day after the funeral; that would be the fourteenth. The clinic was burglarized the next day. Two days later, Malroux is dead." She looked up. "Elgin wasted no time. Four days later, he got Ahmad, and less than two weeks after that, he got Brock."

Devlin grunted. "You know what's really ironic? Gloria's in the clear. All the memos to and from her were internal. None went to Malroux. So there was no way for Elgin to know she orchestrated the whole thing."

Marie tapped the pencil against her cheek. "There are a couple of things I still don't get. Gloria is up to her neck in this. So why did she hire you to investigate the case? She had to know you'd eventually get to the bottom of it. And why did Elgin disguise his murders as accidents, and then advertise his intent to kill Taggert by sending a threatening letter?"

He looked at his watch. It was almost 1:45 A.M. "Gloria must be back by now. Maybe she and Taggert can answer those questions."

Marie followed him into the elevator.

"Where do you think you're going?" he asked.

"To the penthouse with you."

"No, you're not."

"Fucking-A," she said defiantly. Marie didn't know who she was more mad at—Taggert, for having convinced her he was a nice guy, or Gloria, for pulling Michael's chain. "I'm gonna tell those two what—"

Devlin put his hands on her shoulders. "Marie, let me handle it—alone."

"But . . . "

"I'll let you work them over—*after* I find out what I need to know."

She gave an exasperated sigh, slapped the reader with her card, and pressed the penthouse button.

"Marie, I told—"

"I'm going to look for Otis," she said, heading off his protest. "Don't get your ass in an uproar."

When Devlin and Marie got off the elevator at the penthouse, the two moonlighting TAC cops assigned to guard Taggert were checking their radios.

"What's up, Frank?" Devlin asked.

"Static on the radio."

"Bad battery?"

"No. Tony's having the same problem with his."

"Is Otis up here?" Marie asked.

"He was, but he went back to ten."

"Maybe he's causing this," she said to Devlin. "I'll call him from here." As she walked off toward the C&C room at the northwest wing of the floor, Devlin said to the cops, "Is Gloria Salazar here?"

"Yeah, she's with the big man in his office."

As Devlin started down the corridor, Tony called after him. "I should warn you, she's dressed to kill. Wearing an evening gown. And it looks painted on."

But Devlin didn't share in the lewd laughter. He was thinking about strategy.

Gloria was wearing a clinging red satin dress that highlighted the trim, taut body that Devlin had come to know so well. She was standing near Taggert's desk holding a glass of champagne and laughing at something he'd just said.

As Devlin came into the room, Taggert spun around in his chair and waved his glass in the air. "Come in, Devlin. We're celebrating. Looks like we turned a crisis into a windfall for the company. Gloria, pour him some champagne."

Gloria reached for a glass.

"Not for me," he said, halting her with his tone. "While you've been engaging in crisis management, I've been doing some problem solving of my own, and I've come up with some interesting findings."

Taggert, already a bit light-headed, missed the sarcasm in Devlin's tone. "I'm always happy to hear my employees are being productive. What do you have?"

"Good news and bad news."

Taggert grinned. "I'm in the mood for more good news. Give me that first."

"I know why Elgin is trying to kill you."

Slowly, Taggert put his glass down, and Gloria, with the concentration of a lip reader, studied Devlin's face for a clue as to what he was about to say. Unable to read his expression, she said, "And what's the bad news, Mike?"

Devlin smiled at her. "I know why Elgin is trying to kill him."

Taggert scowled. "Is this a riddle? What the hell are you talking about?"

Devlin rested his hands on Taggert's mirror-finished desk and leaned forward. "Confused? I'll give you a one-word clue. Hemotolin."

Royal had been slipping in and out of consciousness since he'd given Elgin the password. Elgin had been diligently working at the computer terminal, but suddenly he spun around in his chair. "You're one hell of a computer guy. I've been around your system, and I want to tell you, it's really elegant. Anti–trap doors; anti–Trojan horses. Very exotic. You really know your shit."

Thankful that this madman didn't know about Marie, Royal nodded numbly. Since Elgin had started working on the computer, Royal had been trying to stay awake, but he kept passing out. It was crucial that he know what Elgin was doing so he could warn Marie. "What are you trying to do, mon?" he asked.

Elgin looked at Royal with a quizzical expression. Then he said, "You'll appreciate this." He popped a peanut into his mouth and held a handful out to Royal. "Want one?"

Royal shook his head and noticed that the floor under the console was stained with a mixture of peanut husks and dried blood.

"First, I've installed my own program. It's not as sophisticated as yours, but it'll do. It's designed to override your program, lock out everyone else, and make me the only sysops on the board."

He typed a command. "There, I just invalidated all the access cards in the building, except mine, which is now programmed for universal access. While you were out, I programmed a series of system shutdowns. At exactly zero-two-hundred hours, three things will happen simultaneously. First, all the elevator banks will shut down, except one, which will be at my disposal. Second, the telephones on the penthouse floor will shut down, effectively breaking communication between the penthouse and the outside world. Third, all surveillance camera transmissions from the penthouse will terminate.

"I give myself ten minutes to set charges on the thirty-eighth, thirty-ninth, and fortieth floors." He shook his head. "It isn't easy hiding trip wires in a bare stairwell. There are no trees, no bushes, no dirt. But with the lights out it's a lot easier.

"At exactly zero-two-fifteen hours, the lights go out in the stairwell. The first guy to hit that wire is dead meat and it's going to scare the shit out of whoever is with him. On thirty-nine and forty, I alternate the wires—some at chest height, some at neck height. By that time they'll know what to look for and they'll probably be able to avoid them. Still, it'll slow 'em down.

"So, I'm done with the trip wires. I get in my private elevator, and at exactly zero-two-ten hours, I head for the penthouse. Just as I get there, the electricity to the penthouse shuts down."

There was something about the unemotional, methodical way Elgin was describing his plan that gave Royal a chill. He sounded more like a computer than a human. "How are you goin' to get around in the dark?" he asked.

Elgin pulled a device out of his knapsack and held it up. "Night-vision goggles."

Royal made an effort to remember the details of what he'd just been told. Yet, even in his numbed state, he knew it was futile. Elgin might be crazy, but he wouldn't divulge his plan—except to a dead man.

As Royal sat there, contemplating his fate, an image came to him from his boyhood in Jamaica. He and a friend had foolishly defied their parents' instructions and put out to sea in a ten-foot sailboat. When a squall rose up five miles out and the boat capsized, the boys had clung desperately to the overturned hull. Despite deep chest lacerations, sustained when he'd slammed hard against the boat's tiller, Otis kept his grip on the overturned craft for hours, counting on a passing boat to spot them. It was nearly dusk when he was jarred to full consciousness by his friend's hysterical screams and frantic pointing. Terrified, he'd looked out over the darkening water and saw the large dorsal fin of a shark slicing toward them. The shark had taken his friend that night, sparing him. Now he asked himself, How many chances did one man get?

Elgin looked at his watch and stood up. "Time to get on with the mission."

Royal watched with grim acceptance as Elgin checked the mechanism on his submachine gun. Then, with a sudden violent jerk, Elgin turned the weapon on Royal and fired a single round into his chest. The big man shuddered for a moment and then was still.

Elgin glanced up at the screen. One of the cops, a smile on his face, was showing the other a cartoon in the newspaper. "You're next, smiley," Elgin said aloud.

As he was starting for the door, the monitor sequenced to the penthouse camera, and he came back for a closer look. The man whom Elgin recognized as the security director was in the office. "A bonus," Elgin said to the screen. He smiled. *Let's see if you can protect him now, asshole.*

Ray Towne was in a quandary. It had been almost a half hour since Nolen went to check on the camera in the basement and he hadn't come back yet. He'd tried to reach Nolen on the radio, but with all the static, he couldn't get through. Suddenly, blinking lights caught his attention. He turned around and stared slack-jawed at the elevator status board as one by one the elevator banks began to shut down.

He picked up the telephone and tried to call the penthouse, but the line was dead. Then he looked up at the monitors and muttered an oath. All the monitors for the penthouse surveillance cameras were black. Contact between him and the penthouse was completely severed. He picked up the telephone and punched 911.

29

"WHAT THE HELL IS HEMOTOLIN?" Taggert asked.

"The drug that's going to make you millions. The drug that, just coincidentally, kills the same people it's suppose to help."

"Now, listen here—"

"No, you listen. This 'windfall' you just pulled off in Indonesia. Will it be safe for the people who work for you? For the environment? Oh, I forgot, you don't worry about minor details like that. The bottom line is all that counts."

Taggert's already crimson face turned a bright, beet-red. "Goddamn it, Devlin, that's not true. Of course I'm concerned with the bottom line. Show me a businessman who isn't and I'll show you a failure. I made Taggert Industries what it is today by looking at the bottom line, but by God, I've never produced a product or built a factory that was harmful to anyone."

"Then how do you explain Hemotolin? When Dr. Malroux was field-testing the drug he discovered it was having adverse effects. He expressed his concerns to Biehl and your two chemists, but they were reluctant to admit that the drug might be flawed. Instead, they told him to increase the dosage. By the time they finally realized that the drug was destroying the patient's immune system, it was too late. He died."

A baffled Taggert turned to Gloria. "Will you tell me what the hell he's talking about?"

Devlin slammed his hand on Taggert's highly polished desk. "Are you telling me you don't know?"

The veins stood out on Taggert's temples. "That's exactly what I'm saying."

Devlin saw the look of genuine puzzlement and indignation on Taggert's face and suddenly he understood. Taggert was telling the truth. He didn't know. The coverup had all been Gloria's doing.

Devlin turned to the woman who for the past three weeks had pulled his strings like a puppet. "So you engineered this whole thing yourself."

"Engineered what?" a frustrated Taggert bellowed.

Devlin fixed Gloria with hardened steel-gray eyes. "How well did you know Kurt Biehl?"

"You're out of line," Gloria snapped. "I don't owe you any—"

"How well did you know him!" Devlin shouted.

"We worked on several projects together. I told you that."

"Did you know him personally?"

"No."

He tossed the photograph of her and Biehl on Taggert's desk. "Exactly which project was this?"

Gloria glanced down at the photo, but she didn't pick it up.

Taggert snapped up the photo and studied it. "What the hell is going on?"

"Your 'right-hand woman' used her . . . interpersonal skills to talk Kurt Biehl into field-testing a drug that they both knew was unsafe. Then, when the patient died, she directed him to destroy all references to the drug and consolidate all the records under another name."

Bewildered, Taggert turned to Gloria. "Is this true?"

Gloria glared at Devlin. "You cops have such vivid imaginations."

He returned her stare. "I couldn't make this up." He threw copies of the deleted memos on Taggert's desk. "It's all there."

A look of uncertainty crept into her face. "How . . . how is that possible? You said yourself, Biehl destroyed the files."

Devlin shrugged. "He deleted them. We undeleted them."

"But there was no way you could find . . . " The words slipped out before she could stop herself.

Devlin grinned. "I'll have Marie explain it to you. She's in the C&C room at the other end of the floor."

Taggert, who'd been glancing through the memos, looked up at Gloria. "Tadvid?" he whispered incredulously.

"What's that?" Devlin asked.

"An experimental leukemia drug that we've been working on for years. A year ago it looked promising, but the lab test results were still too erratic. Gloria proposed we field-test it anyway, but I vetoed the idea. I said I wouldn't let a drug with my name on it go out to the public, even under experimental conditions, unless we were one-hundred-percent sure that it was safe." He ran his fingers through his hair in exasperation. "Gloria, how could you do this?"

Until now, Gloria had been carefully listening to Devlin's every word, trying to decide how much he actually knew and how much was a bluff. There seemed to be no point, though, in denying it any longer.

"How could I?" she said in response to Taggert's question. "Because it had to be done. We're not the only ones working on a drug, JT. Why shouldn't we be the first to bring it out?"

"One minor reason," Taggert said, biting off his words. "The matter of inconsistent lab results."

"That's what the field-testing is for," she said. "There are always going to be glitches—"

"Glitches? Someone died, for chrissake. Who was it?" he asked Devlin.

"George Elgin's son."

Taggert fell back in his chair, stunned by the realization that a madman was trying to kill him because of something Gloria had done.

Gloria continued her rationalization in the smooth, confident tone that had always worked for her in the past. "The boy was the only one to die. It was probably an anomaly. If we'd continued testing I'm confident that we would have found that to be the case."

"We're talking human lives, Gloria," Taggert said in disgust, "not lab mice."

"JT, you've lost your edge," she said scornfully. "You've let your instincts for the deal be subverted by this ridiculous lusting after political office. Someone had to make the hard decisions."

"If the drug is approved by the FDA, what will it be worth to the company?" Devlin asked.

"If we're first, we dominate the market," she said

with obvious pride. "You can't even put a price tag on that."

"And what was in it for you?"

Gloria, recognizing the loaded nature of the question, altered her expression from one of arrogance to one of modesty. "The sheer joy of beating our competitors to the market," she said blandly.

"Is that all?" Devlin said in a mocking tone. "Seems to me that if you pulled this off, the board of directors would be very grateful. I would imagine they'd want to reward you in some way. Maybe a promotion?"

"I'm well compensated for my work."

"The only promotion left is CEO," Taggert said in a flat tone. He was beginning to understand her plan. "I know you've been working the board, Gloria. How many are in your corner? Enough to unseat me?"

"Yes," Gloria said defiantly. "The success of Hemotolin would guarantee it."

Devlin gathered up the memos and the photo from Taggert's desk. "Now that we all understand each other, it's time to call the police."

Gloria jumped up, visibly distressed for the first time. "JT, you can't let him go to the police."

"Why the hell not?"

"Think of the publicity—"

"I don't give a damn about the publicity," Taggert growled.

"You care about money, don't you? Think of the exposure. We tested Hemotolin on one hundred and twenty-five subjects. What if more of them die?"

"You should have thought about that before."

"JT," she said in a more reasonable tone, "let's continue the testing. I know we can get the glitches out. With the revenues Hemotolin will earn when it hits the commercial market, we can easily underwrite whatever wrongful death lawsuits come out of it. The cost benefits are in our favor."

Taggert looked at her as if seeing her for the first time. "Gloria, you have no conscience."

"Don't be a fool," she snapped. "Do you think we'd be the first to put a less-than-perfect product on the market? For years Detroit fought building safety features into cars. What about the Pinto? The GMC pickup truck? What about Dalkon shields? This isn't a perfect world, JT. You and I don't make the rules, we just play the game, and whoever plays the hardest, wins."

Devlin had heard enough. Listening to Gloria's pathetic attempts to justify her behavior made him realize that she was a sociopath, incapable of understanding, or living by, the rules of society. "Taggert, I'm going down to my office and—"

"JT, back me on this." She was almost begging. "You and I hold all the cards. I'll go over the databases with a fine-tooth comb. Believe me, this time, I'll make sure that no records are left. It's his word against ours."

Taggert stood up slowly and shook his head. "Gloria, you're fired. I *want* Devlin to go ahead with this. Let the chips fall where they may. Perhaps you're right. Maybe it is time for me to step down. But by God, I'm glad that you won't be the one who succeeds me."

Gloria opened her purse and pulled out a small automatic pistol. "Then you leave me no choice."

"What are you going to do?" a wide-eyed Taggert asked.

She turned to Devlin and smiled. "I'll bet our clever security director knows what I'm going to do."

Devlin recognized the gun: a 9mm Beretta with a 12-round clip. "I got two guys down the hall," he said, slowly inching toward her. "You going to kill them too?"

"No need," Gloria replied coolly. "I shoot you both. Then, when they rush in, I tell them it was Elgin and he ran out that door," she said, pointing to an exit that led to the screening room. "They'll search, but he'll have gotten away. He does have a track record."

Devlin remembered talking to a hostage negotiator once who'd told him that a gunman rarely kills someone while they're talking. It was one of those weird etiquette things—the bad guy always waits for a lull in the conversation. Devlin figured it was worth a try.

"Before you pull the trigger," he said quickly, "maybe you could answer a question that's been bothering the hell out of me. Why did you choose me for the security director's job?"

She smiled scornfully. "I was wondering why that obvious question never occurred to you before. I interviewed dozens of intelligent ex-cops who were much more qualified than you. But they were too good. I couldn't take the chance that one of them might get to the bottom of the Hemotolin project. You, on the other hand, possessed the two qualities that I most needed. First, you were so apathetic you didn't even care if you got the job or not. Do you really think I would have purposely hired someone who would tell JT to his face that he's full of shit?" Her throaty, mocking laugh stung him. "When you said that, I knew you were the right man for the job."

"What was the second qualification?"

"I needed someone who'd be able to shoot a man who needed to be shot."

Devlin suddenly put it all together. "You couldn't afford to have the police catch Elgin because he would have exposed the Hemotolin project. You wanted him dead. And I was supposed to be the executioner."

"That's right."

Keep her talking. "Did you know about him all along?"

"Of course. Malroux called Biehl right after the kid died. He said he'd received a weird call from Elgin—that Elgin had threatened to find out why his son was dead. He promised to kill whoever was responsible. Naturally, I had to take precautions."

"*You* wrote the letter," Taggert said in wonderment.

"And it worked. I needed an excuse to hire my own security director."

While she'd been talking, Devlin had inched a little closer, but he was still ten feet away. If she fired a gun the way she did everything else, he didn't have much of a chance. But he also knew that shooting at a paper target was a hell of a lot different from shooting at a human being, especially one who's moving.

Elgin stopped the elevator one floor below the penthouse, donned his night-vision goggles, and slung the AK-47 strap around his neck. Then, as soon as his watch displayed 2:14 A.M., he shut off the lights in the elevator, turned on his night-vision goggles, and hit the up button.

Judging the distance between him and Gloria, Devlin tensed his body and waited for his chance. It came when she took her eyes off him and momentarily looked at Taggert.

As he lunged at her, the lights went out.

She fired wildly and Devlin felt a sharp biting pain in his right shoulder. Thrown off balance by the impact of the bullet, he crashed into a chair and fell to the floor. With the window shutters blocking the outside light, the room was suddenly pitch-black.

"Get down," he shouted to Taggert.

Gloria fired twice toward the sound of his voice and the bullets lodged in the seat cushion next to his head. Devlin counted the bullets: two at him; two into the chair. She had eight left.

Wincing in pain, he crawled behind a massive credenza and propped himself against the wall. Then he stuffed a handkerchief inside his shirt to staunch the flow of blood. As he drew his automatic from his shoulder holster, a blinding pain shot down his arm and the weapon fell to the floor. Groping with his left hand, he found it. He tried gripping it with his right hand, but there was no feeling in his fingers. He'd often practiced firing with his left hand and he was adequate, but under these circumstances—a darkened room with someone trying to kill him—adequate might not be enough.

"Gloria—"

She fired three rounds at the sound of his voice.

He'd wanted to tell her to give up but, apparently,

she was bent on killing them both. From the muzzle flash, he knew she was near the windows. He could have returned accurate fire, but he didn't know where Taggert was and Taggert was also armed. Under these circumstances, Devlin's gun was useless.

She's got five left, he said to himself, adjusting the blood-soaked handkerchief. Then, as he rested his sweat-soaked head against the wall, the meaning of the light failure suddenly hit him: Elgin was in the building!

Marie had been in the C&C center at the opposite end of the penthouse floor running diagnostics on the computer to determine the cause of the radio static, but she'd found nothing. She tried to call Royal on the tenth floor, but got no answer. Tired of waiting, she decided to go back down to see what he'd found. As she was walking down the hall toward the elevator, the lights went out. "Oh, no, Otis," she said, grabbing onto the walls. "What did you do?"

Groping her way back to the C&C room, she was relieved to see a soft glowing light coming from the computer monitor screen. She wasn't sure if the backup generator had been hooked up. The lights might be out, but at least the security computer was still operational.

She quickly typed in her password and for a moment stared unbelievingly at the dispassionate words on her screen: ACCESS DENIED. She tried again, and then, realizing what was happening, slowly sank into her chair. Elgin had taken over the system.

✴   ✴   ✴

When the lights went out on the penthouse floor, the two cops had sprung to their feet and immediately drawn their weapons.

"What the hell's going on?" Tony said, holding on to the wall for orientation. "I think I heard shots."

"I don't know, but we'd better get to Taggert."

"Wait," Tony said. "I hear the elevator. It's coming up."

Both cops, peering vainly into the impenetrable darkness, dropped into combat stances and pointed their weapons in the general direction of the elevator.

Manually operating the elevator, Elgin stopped it six feet above the landing and opened the doors. From his elevated position he peered down at the two cops. Through his night-vision goggles, he saw them crouched with their weapons drawn. They'd heard the doors open, but from their nervous, blank-eyed expressions it was clear that they had no idea who, if anyone, was in the elevator.

Silently, he aimed the AK-47 and fired a short burst into the face of the man on the left. His head exploded in a scarlet mist. With his back against the wall, the other cop slid to the floor, firing wildly into the elevator at his unseen assailant. But he was firing too low. Elgin sighted his weapon on the cop's chest and squeezed off a short burst, killing him instantly.

Elgin smiled. *Like shooting fish in a barrel.*

STILL HIDING BEHIND THE CREDENZA in Taggert's office, Devlin gingerly touched his shoulder. The handkerchief was saturated. His left hand gripped his pistol even tighter as sounds of automatic gunfire came from the direction of the elevator. *Shit. Elgin is in the penthouse and I only have one good hand.*

"Gloria," he called out. "Hear that? Elgin—"

She fired again and the round splintered a cabinet six feet away. *Four rounds left.* After a couple of minutes, he yelled, "Goddamn it, listen to me. We all have to stick together."

Terrified, Gloria crouched under the conference table and tried to think. She knew what the gunfire meant. Elgin would be coming after Taggert and anyone who stood in his way would be killed. He wanted Taggert, but there was no way JT would go out there voluntarily. To save her own life she would have to deliver JT.

She whispered, "JT, where are you?"

"Over here," he said in a shaky voice.

She started crawling toward the sound of his voice. "What do you think we should do?"

"Stick together like Devlin says."

She paused to listen. In the dark it was difficult to determine direction, but it sounded like he was somewhere near his desk. She started moving again. "JT, I'm really sorry about what happened. When this is over, we have to talk about it."

Devlin was intently listening to the sound of her voice and realized that she was moving closer to Taggert. Suddenly it occurred to him: *She was stalking him.* "Taggert," he called out. "Don't say another word."

"Why—"

Furious that Devlin had ruined her plan, Gloria fired wildly in the direction of Taggert's voice.

Devlin heard the dull thumping sound of a body falling or diving onto the floor and whispered, "Taggert, not another word. No matter what."

He didn't know if the CEO had been hit or not, but neither did Gloria. One thing was certain: She'd fired three rounds. That meant she had only one bullet left. He had to find a way to get her to waste that last round quickly. He didn't need Elgin *and* her trying to kill him—especially in the dark and especially with a useless right hand.

He groped the top of the table he was hiding under and found a heavy glass ashtray. Just as he was about to fling it across the room, a voice outside in the corridor called out, "Hey in there. What's all the shooting about?"

Devlin froze. Elgin had found them. He'd followed the sound of the gunfire to Taggert's office.

"Hello? Anybody home?"

Devlin held his breath, praying that Taggert, if he was still alive, would keep his mouth shut. Elgin was using a standard recon tactic: draw the enemy out; find out how many people are in the room and where they are.

Devlin was wondering how much more he owed Taggert when his stomach knotted: *Oh, God, no . . . Marie! Where is she?*

"Hey, lady in the nice red dress," Elgin called out. "I know you're in there. Why don't you come on out before you get hurt?"

Think, woman, think! Gloria chided herself. *There must be a way to cut a deal with this guy.*

"I'm . . . I'm afraid you'll hurt me," she said in a small, defenseless voice.

"I don't want to hurt you. My business is with Jason Taggert."

"He's . . . he's right here in this room," she said quickly.

Knowing Taggert's temper, she was surprised that he didn't say something. Maybe he was dead. But there was no way to find out. "I'm just a . . . friend," she continued. "I don't know what this is all about."

"Okay, I believe you. Come on out."

"How . . . how do I know that you won't hurt me, Mr. Elgin?" Gloria bit her lip, infuriated with the slip.

In the dark Devlin rolled his eyes. *The pressure was really getting to her,* he thought. The Gloria he knew would never be that stupid.

Elgin's easy, coaxing tone became a flat monotone. "How'd you know my name?"

"I . . . I don't know," Gloria said, trying to think of an appropriate answer. "I guess I heard Mr. Taggert say it."

"You're lying, bitch. Friend, my ass. You work for Taggert."

She heard the cold, murderous tone in his voice and fought a rising tide of panic. *Think*, she screamed at herself again. This wasn't about a merger or the price of the company's stock. This was about her *life*.

It occurred to her that, in spite of her predicament, she was still in a good bargaining position. Apparently Elgin didn't know who she was, and she could use that to her advantage.

She dropped the little girl act. "Listen," she called out, "I know something you should know. So here's the deal. I give you the information, you let me go."

"Let's hear it."

"I'll tell you when I'm sure that I'm safe," she said forcefully. "When I'm in the elevator."

Devlin shook his head. Gloria had no idea how out of her depth she was.

"I'm calling the shots, lady." Elgin's tone was flat and threatening. "What's your information?"

In frustration, Gloria silently pounded her fists on the carpet. What was she supposed to do? Without leverage, how could she negotiate?

"There's another man in this room," she blurted out. "His name is Mike Devlin. He's an ex-cop and he's armed."

Elgin snorted. "Hell, I know that. I saw him on the TV monitor when I was on the tenth floor overriding your security system. You're gonna need something better than that."

Gloria bit her lip. What else could she give him? Then she remembered what he'd just said: *I was on the tenth floor overriding the security system.*

"All right, I do have something better."

"Let's hear it."

"You'll let me go?"

Devlin heard the panic in her voice. The steely businesswoman, Taggert's "right-hand woman," the woman who thought she was tough enough to run all of Taggert Industries, was almost hysterical, and it was clouding her judgment. If she'd been thinking clearly she would know that Elgin had no intention of letting anyone off this floor alive.

"That depends on the information. Come on," Elgin barked. "I don't have all day."

She bit her lip anxiously. *How to play it so that you get what you want?*

"There's someone else on this floor," she said finally. "A woman named Marie."

In a cold fury, Devlin raised his gun toward the sound of her voice and started to squeeze the trigger. She was offering up Marie to save her own life. At that moment, if he'd known for certain where she was hiding, he would have gladly emptied the clip into her black heart. He eased his finger off the trigger. It took all his will not to yell to her to shut up, but he couldn't give his position away. Elgin knew he was in here, but he didn't know exactly where, and Devlin had no intention of giving up that information.

"She's in a computer room on the other end of the floor," Gloria continued. "I can show you where. She's a computer expert and she'll be able to undo whatever it is that you've done."

"She can't do much without electricity."

"The security system has a backup generator."

Elgin tensed, angry at himself for not having thought of that possibility. Until now, he'd been enjoying toying with her. Plus, he'd been curious when he heard someone, probably Devlin, say something about them "sticking together." Who was firing at who? The question had bothered him. The possibility of another shooter on the premises introduced a wild-card element, and he didn't like surprises. Right now, though, he had a pretty good idea who was firing at who. This bitch didn't care how many body bags she left behind, so long as she got her ass out safe.

If what she said was true, then there was no more time for fun and games. He'd thought the tall black man had been the architect of the system. But if this bitch was telling the truth, he had to find the computer expert and stop her.

Elgin closed his eyes. He pictured the penthouse floor plan in his mind's eye and concluded the woman had to be in one of those rooms on the northern side of the floor.

Time to shift priorities. Taggert and Devlin could wait. After all, there was no way off the floor. He'd booby-trapped the emergency doors. If anything, the slight delay would make the hunt more interesting.

He dropped into a prone position and leveled his AK-47 at the office door opening. "Okay, that's good information," he said. "But I don't have all night. If you want to get out of here, you'd better come now."

"All right, I'm coming."

Gloria stood up and cautiously groped her way toward the door, holding the gun in front of her, prepared to pull the trigger if either Devlin or Taggert tried to stop her.

From his prone position in the hallway, Elgin saw her through the grainy green glow of his goggles. Slowly, she groped her way through the doorway with one hand outstretched hesitantly and the other holding the small automatic. "Do you have a gun?" he called out.

"No," she lied.

When she was about twenty-five feet away, he tossed a roll of masking tape at her chest. Screaming in fright, she pulled the trigger and her remaining round splintered the ceiling molding. In her panic, she kept clicking on an empty chamber, swinging the gun in a wide arc.

Elgin stood up and silently moved in front of her as she came down the corridor toward him, cautiously sliding one foot in front of the other. When she was directly in front of him, he whispered softly, "You lied to me."

The unexpected sound of his voice, so close, startled her, and as she stepped back, she tripped over her ankle-length gown. Crawling on her hands and knees, she bumped into his knees and recoiled. Disoriented, she staggered to her feet and crashed into the wall.

Elgin spun her around and slammed her against the wall. As she bounced off, he smacked her face hard. "You lied to me," he hissed. "How do I know you're not lying about the other woman and the generator?"

"I swear . . . I'm telling you the truth. . . . She's the one who put this system together. . . . There *is* a generator. . . . I'm telling you the truth."

Elgin saw the wide-eyed terror in her eyes and believed her. Now that he knew she was telling the truth, she was disposable. He grabbed her by the hair and threw her against the opposite wall. "Follow this wall to the elevator," he said. "The key is in the control panel. Turn it and it'll take you to the lobby."

Elgin watched with silent amusement as Gloria, moving her hands up and down the wall, groped her way toward the elevator. Finally, she came to an opening and her hand probed the empty space. *She'd found the elevator! Freedom!* Uttering a sigh of relief, she stepped into the void. Her one long scream, reverberating in the elevator shaft, tapered off into silence as she plunged the forty floors to her death.

Elgin chuckled. "Watch that first step, it's a bitch." He snatched up his AK-47 and set out for the north side of the penthouse floor.

While Gloria was negotiating for her life, a puzzled Devlin had been trying to figure out why Elgin had let his presence be known. Why would he surrender surprise and stealth, the two most important components of an assassin's plan? How could he be so complacent? Why would he toy with them this way?

Suddenly, he knew the answer. Elgin had to be wearing a night-vision device. The darkness was in his favor. Devlin didn't have goggles, but there was something he could do to neutralize that advantage.

After Devlin was sure that Gloria had left the office, he painfully crawled toward the door leading from the office to the screening room. Once inside, he ran his hand across the back of each seat in the last row, carefully keeping count. When he came to number eleven, he felt around under the plush cushioned seat where he'd taped a flashbang grenade.

SWAT teams used these grenades, which were capable of producing a shattering noise and more than a two-million-candlepower flash, to distract their target, but this device would serve an even better purpose. Devlin knew that the dazzling flash would disable Elgin's goggles instantaneously by burning out the phosphorescent screen. Then Elgin would be as blind as he was.

He crawled to the door leading out to the corridor. As he opened it slowly, he heard Elgin whisper something about a key in the control panel. Moments later, he heard Gloria's sickening scream echoing in the elevator shaft and the sound of Elgin's maniacal laughter reverberating in the corridor.

For a moment he was immobolized with fear and doubt. *How was he going to stop this madman—in the dark, with a useless shooting hand?* Then he heard the sound of Elgin's footsteps coming toward him, and the momentary panic faded as he forced himself to concentrate on what he must do next. He pulled the pin and, when he judged that Elgin was close enough, rolled the grenade out into the corridor. He ducked his head back inside the room and covered his eyes.

The deafening report and blinding flash caught Elgin by surprise. Instinctively, he threw himself to the ground and, rolling over and over again, fired short bursts from his submachine gun.

Holding his breath and listening intently for the sound of an attack, it took him a second to realize that he was staring wide-eyed into utter blackness. In disgust he ripped the useless goggles off and threw them aside. Devlin had taken away his advantage, but even blind men can get around in the dark. Taking a deep breath to control his rage, he closed his eyes and pictured the penthouse floor plan as clearly as though he were still standing in front of that paint-chipped wall in the Bowery flophouse.

He knew Devlin had to be somewhere in front of him, so he couldn't go that way. He closed his eyes and mentally envisioned an alternate route. *The dining room.* That's the way to go. Slowly, he backed down the corridor, holding his weapon in front of him with one hand and feeling for the dining room door with the other. He came to the end of the corridor, stopped, and cocked his head in puzzlement. He should have found the dining room door by now. Retracing his steps, he moved forward again very slowly.

Devlin felt a surge of elation when he heard Elgin's muttered curse, knowing that he'd rendered the goggles useless. Holding his breath and cocking his head, he strained to hear the sound of Elgin's movement, but there was only silence. After waiting a while longer, he decided it was time to move.

The next thing he had to do was to retrieve the submachine gun he'd locked in a closet next to the elevator. Then he had to get to the other side of the building and find Marie before Elgin did. But first, he had to get to the elevator in the dark. Fortunately, he'd spent so much time walking these corridors with the building contractor that he still had a very good recollection of the layout.

He began to crawl, but with only one useful hand, it wasn't practical. Feeling totally exposed, and violating every rule of close combat, he stood up. It was an eerie feeling, walking down a corridor, fully erect, wondering if he was going to suddenly bump into Elgin.

o   o   o

When Marie had seen the ACCESS DENIED message on her screen, she knew that Elgin was in the building. Then, when she'd heard the gunfire out by the elevators, followed by a very loud explosion, she knew she was in imminent danger.

Elgin might be right outside the C&C door, but she couldn't think of that now. What was important was to break into the system and override Elgin's program. She tried a few routine approaches, but they didn't work. Then she remembered that Elgin's wife had said he was a genius with computers. She pushed the hair out of her eyes and hunched over the keyboard. *Let's see who the genius really is.*

Five minutes after Ray Towne called 911, two cops, looking like a modern version of Laurel and Hardy, sauntered into the lobby. Pushing his cap to the back of his head, the fat one said, "What's the problem?"

After Towne explained the disappearance of Tommy Nolen, the radio static, the stopped elevators, and his inability to contact anyone on the penthouse floor, the skinny cop, chewing on a thick wad of gum, said to his partner, "You take the report, I'll take a look downstairs. If you ask me," he whispered to his partner, "I think the guy went for coffee."

The young cop took the stairs down to the basement garage. He pushed open the steel door leading into the vestibule, stopped abruptly, and promptly swallowed his gum. "Holy Mother of God," he muttered, viewing the butchered remains of Nolen and Armond. He fumbled for his portable radio with shaky fingers. "Central," he said in a quaking voice, "this is Sector Charlie. I have a double homicide in

the garage at the Taggert Tower. I need the ME and
the squad." Then he remembered what the security
guard had said about the unexplained loss of contact
with the penthouse. "And send the Emergency Service
forthwith," he added.

In the darkness it seemed to take forever, but Devlin
was almost at the elevator. Suddenly, he tripped over
something and went down hard. Holding his gun out
in front of him, he held his breath, praying that Elgin
hadn't heard him. After a few seconds of silence, he
reached out to feel what he'd tripped over. The carpet was wet and sticky, then he felt a body and wet
clothing. *It was one of his TAC cops*.

Feeling along the walls, he found the elevator
door opening.

The utility closet was just beyond the elevator. As
quietly as he could, he opened the door, ran his
hands along the top shelf and with a feeling of pro-
found relief felt the cold, hard metal of the K&P submachine gun.

Elgin, too disciplined to scream out, stood in the
middle of a room working his jaw muscles in frustration and rage. He'd finally found the dining room and
had passed through another door that should have
taken him into the kitchen, but he was dead-ended in
a storage room.

He'd spent all those hours memorizing the floor
plan and now none of the doors were where they
were supposed to be. There was only one explanation. Devlin had reconfigured the room layout. In a

blinding rage he pictured Devlin in his mind's eye. *I'm going to find a* special *way to kill you. Right after I take care of Taggert.*

Elgin squatted on the floor and forced himself to think. He didn't know whether Devlin had committed the new layout to memory, but it didn't much matter. In the dark, man against man, with only his ability to stay stone-quiet to protect him, Elgin had proven himself the best. The dark was his friend. No ex-cop was going to stop him from completing his mission.

Slowly, as if in a trance, his body rising up specter-like from the floor, Elgin felt around the room, looking for the door opening. Even the beating of his heart seemed to still, so silent were his movements.

Two detectives were escorting an ashen-faced Ray Towne out to their squad car as the lieutenant in charge of the Emergency Service cops burst through the revolving doors with four of his men.

"Who was that?" the lieutenant asked a patrol sergeant who was standing by the lobby guard station.

"Building security. The poor bastard just IDed his boss and some other guy who works for the company. What a mess. One of the DOAs is missing a hand."

Lieutenant Finn took off his hat and ran his hand through his bushy red hair. "Thank God I don't have to handle that crap anymore. Are the elevators still out?"

The sergeant pointed at the terminal monitor. "See for yourself, Loo. They're all off-line except one. But the guard couldn't get it to come down to the lobby."

"I understand the lights are off in the fire stairway. Anybody try to turn them back on?"

"The building engineer tried but he couldn't do it.

Something about the lights being hooked up to a computer."

"How many people in the penthouse?"

"According to the guard, Jason Taggert, another executive, the company security director, and a couple of people who are working on the computer systems."

"Could they have caused this screw-up with the lights and elevators?"

"The building engineer said they're in the process of installing a new security system that ties all this stuff together. They're working late tonight to get the bugs out. Could be."

The lieutenant shook his head in disgust. He was going to have to climb forty flights of stairs because some asshole pushed the wrong button. "Does this have anything to do with the two DOAs in the basement?" he asked.

"The squad doesn't think so. They figure it's the work of some whacko. So whaddaya gonna do, Loo?"

The lieutenant looked down at the static terminal screen and put his hat back on. "We got people stuck up there. We gotta go get 'em."

The sergeant's face broke out in a wide smile. "Better you than me."

The trim lieutenant looked down at the sergeant's bulging belly. "Yeah, I guess so," he deadpanned. "I got enough trouble without giving CPR to cops."

He turned to his four-man team, each of whom was carrying the ropes, crowbars, and tools necessary to get through locked doors and elevators. "Okay, let's go."

The cops looked at each other. "Go where, Loo?"

The lieutenant pointed toward the ceiling. "The penthouse."

"How many floors?"

"Forty."

Amidst a chorus of groans and whistles, the five men headed for the fire emergency stairs.

Devlin moved cautiously from room to room, wondering who he might encounter. At this moment he didn't know where Taggert was—or if he was even alive. Unlike Elgin, he couldn't afford to shoot indiscriminately. He had to worry about Marie, and possibly Taggert, getting in the line of fire. He touched his throbbing shoulder and moved on.

As he slowly groped his way through the maze of rooms, making a concerted effort to be as silent as possible, he almost regretted the convoluted passage his reconstruction had created. But he consoled himself with the thought that Elgin confronted the same problem—without benefit of a floor plan.

As he moved along, Elgin was getting better at orienting himself. The trick, he'd discovered, was to always keep a northerly direction in his mind. No matter how many detours or corridors there were, he kept all of his movements in his head and constantly veered north. Just like he'd done on night patrols in Vietnam, every sixty seconds he stopped, squatted, and listened. For most soldiers night patrols in enemy territory are a nerve-racking experience, but Elgin had thoroughly enjoyed them.

According to his best reckoning, he was almost at the other end of the building. Then it was just a matter of checking each spare room until he found her.

* ◦ ◦

Devlin had developed his own technique for moving through the darkened penthouse. First, he removed his shoes. Then, every time he came to a room he opened the door, paused, and listened. Only when he was certain he heard nothing did he go in. As he did, he quickly stepped to the side, unwilling to remain framed in a doorway, even in this utter darkness. It was a slow, tedious way to move, but under the circumstances it was the only safe way to go.

What made the time seem to extend interminably was his concern for Marie. Maybe she'd left the floor before the electricity went out. But if she hadn't and Elgin got to her first . . .

He couldn't let himself think that way. What he was counting on was that Elgin had no idea which specific room he was looking for. The room housing the recently installed C&C center had been arbitrarily selected and was not on the original floor plans. And even if he *had* known the original direct route, there were at least two layout alterations along the way that would confuse him.

Carefully, Devlin opened the door to what he knew was a huge unfinished room at least fifty feet square. The future plan was to turn it into a media center, but for now the room had become a storeroom for excess furniture and equipment. He listened quietly. When he heard nothing, he sidestepped into the room and squatted. He knew there was a door on the other side of the room that led out to the hallway. Down that hall was the C&C room.

He was about halfway across the room when he froze and cocked his head. It wasn't that he'd heard anything. It was more subtle than that. It was almost as if the density of the room had suddenly changed. There was something almost detectable in the quality of the air. A smell. The scent of sweat?

Noiselessly he sunk to the floor.

Crouched at the other end of the room, Elgin also sensed a presence. He swept the muzzle of his AK-47 in a wide arc and peered into the opaque blackness, look-ing—*feeling*—for some indication of where the unseen presence was. Barely breathing, he waited, muscles tensed and poised, for Devlin to give himself away.

But it was a standoff. Men with more fragile nerves might have been spooked into firing, but not Devlin or Elgin. Both men, standing less than forty feet apart, knew of the other's presence, but under these conditions they both knew that the first one to fire had better be right, because if he wasn't, he was a dead man. They were both eager to start the fire-fight, anything to end the maddening tension. But in the darkness, neither one could be sure of a killing shot.

After a while Elgin remembered an alternative way to go and slowly backed out of the room. A minute later Devlin, not having heard Elgin leave but sensing he'd gone, moved toward the other door. Stunned that Elgin had gotten there that fast in the dark, he felt the urgent need to quicken his pace.

He came out of the room and continued along the corridor. As he remembered it, the corridor made a sharp left turn no more than twenty-five yards ahead and the C&C room was one of six doors along that corridor.

As he felt his way along the wall, he kept an image of the floor plan in his mind and mentally tracked Elgin's progress. He guessed that Elgin would approach from the opposite direction and come straight down the corridor. Devlin calculated he'd get there a few precious moments before Elgin, giving him time to search for Marie.

As he approached the turn in the corridor, he was feeling confident that he would get to her first. Then he envisioned what Elgin would see from his viewpoint, and a dismaying thought occurred to him: If Marie was there working on the computer, there would be light. In this absolute blackness that light, even if it was coming from under a closed door, would shine like a beacon. Not caring that Elgin could be ten feet away from him, he shouted, "Marie, the light! Turn off the computer!"

Marie was hunched over the console intent on typing in a series of commands, none of which were working, when she heard Devlin's shouted warning. Immediately comprehending the danger, she punched the master cutoff switch, plunging the room into darkness.

As Elgin was creeping down the corridor, he'd seen the dim light in the distance and knew he'd found the computer room. Now that he had a little light to guide him, he picked up the pace. In just a minute he'd—

His thoughts were interrupted by Devlin's shouted warning. Then the lights went out and the

corridor that had been made three-dimensional by
the dim light became once again a dimensionless
black void. Muttering an oath, Elgin put his shoulder
against the wall for orientation and, moving blindly,
continued down the corridor at a much slower pace.

By the time Devlin got to the turn in the corridor,
Marie had turned off the lights. When he peeked
around the corner he saw only darkness. *Had she
heard his warning? Was she even there?* It was frustrating not knowing one way or the other, but he consoled himself with the thought that neither did Elgin.

It suddenly occurred to him that this might be his
only opportunity to get a shot at Elgin. If he'd calculated correctly, Elgin had to be coming toward him
from the opposite end of the corridor. He shook his
head to clear the numbing pain and light-headedness
that were beginning to impair his thinking. He would
have only one chance to do this and it was essential
that he get it right the first time. He peered into the
darkness beyond, trying to imagine how Elgin would
approach, and decided that Elgin would do it the
same way he would: hugging the wall for orientation.

But which wall? Was he right- or left-handed? If
he was right-handed, he knew he'd hug the left wall,
so his right arm would be free.

There was no time to think about it. Going with
the percentages, he decided to try a tactic they'd
practiced at the police range. The common wisdom
was that a bullet fired at a wall ricocheted off it, but
someone had discovered that if you fired a bullet at a
shallow angle, the bullet ran along, and parallel to,
the wall.

Devlin placed the muzzle of his weapon at waist
height alongside the wall that he assumed Elgin was

up against. Making sure he maintained a shallow angle, he squeezed off a burst and immediately dove to the floor.

Elgin, coming the other way, was sliding along the wall when he saw the muzzle flash ahead of him. But before he could react, a round tore into his thigh and another one into his side. The impact spun him around as he fired off a burst in the direction of the muzzle flash. He rolled over and, ignoring the sharp, searing pain in his side and leg, prepared for an attack. But other than his labored breathing, there was only silence in the darkened corridor. When he was certain Devlin wasn't going to launch an attack, he painfully retreated back the way he'd come.

At the other end of the corridor, Devlin lay on the floor, his weapon poised for a counterattack. He heard Elgin's faint, labored breathing receding and realized that he was gone. He wanted to call out to Marie, to make sure she was all right, to find out, indeed, if she were there. But he couldn't do that. If she answered, she'd give away both their positions.

He rose to his feet and, cautiously making his way forward to where Elgin had been, ran his hand up and down the wall. He felt something sticky and wet. He knelt down, ran his hand over the rug, and felt more wet puddles. He smiled grimly. Elgin had been hit. Now the match was a little more even.

Satisfied that he'd wounded Elgin and that Marie wasn't there, he started to think about Jason Taggert, who was still, he hoped, holed up in his darkened office. In the mood Devlin had been in when he'd read one incriminating memo after another in the

EDP center, he would have gladly left the fate of the
CEO in Elgin's hands, but that was before he'd discovered that Taggert had had nothing to do with
Hemotolin and Robby Elgin's death. Taggert deserved
his help.

Slowly and painfully, Devlin began to make his
way to the other side of the building toward Taggert's
office. He'd been hired to protect the feisty CEO and
that was what he was going to do.

After repeated attempts to override Elgin's tampering
had failed, Marie had looked for a hiding place. But it
was a small room and there was no place to hide. Then
she'd looked up at the ceiling and had an idea. Using a
chair, she climbed on top of a filing cabinet and
pushed the ceiling tiles aside. She saw pipes running
above the false ceiling. If necessary, she could grab
those pipes and haul herself up. She left the chair in
place and the ceiling opening exposed in case she
needed a quick getaway. Then she returned to her
console.

When she heard Devlin's shouted warning, she
killed the power to the terminal, climbed up on the
chair, and hoisted her small frame up into the drop
ceiling. Once safely inside the false ceiling, she slid
the tiles back in place.

From her hiding spot she heard the exchange of
gunfire and waited through the maddening silence
for over ten minutes. When she heard nothing, she
dropped back down into the room and turned on the
computer, once again illuminating the room. Just
before the interruption, she'd hit on a promising
approach and was anxious to get back to it. The

quicker the system was restored, the quicker help would arrive.

She sat back down at the terminal and resumed her task of cracking Elgin's system. As she was intently studying the information crawling across her screen, she suddenly became aware of a presence in the room with her. She spun around and screamed as Elgin's bloody hand closed on her throat.

Devlin was working his way back to the southeast corner of the floor toward Taggert's office when he heard Marie's scream. Instinctively, he spun around and, forgetting about the darkness and need for stealth, started running blindly back toward the C&C room. Then he stopped and dropped to his knees in frustration. *Don't just run into his field of fire,* Devlin chided himself. *That's what he wants.*

Still breathing heavily from his sudden sprint, he forced himself to remain motionless as he thought about his next step.

Elgin's having found Marie left two possibilities. Refusing to let his mind even consider the worst-case scenario, he pondered the alternative: Elgin was going to use her to flush him and Taggert out of hiding.

In the darkness on his knees the question gnawed at him: *Should I go after them?*

"Not a sound and I'll let you breathe," Elgin whispered in a raspy voice. His fingers closed tighter around her windpipe, sending her to the edge of asphyxiation. "Understand?"

When Marie's eyes communicated a desperate

"Yes," he let her go. She immediately began gasping for air, feeling light-headed.

He grabbed her by the hair and yanked her over to the console. Keeping one eye on her as he studied the series of commands she was using to break into his program, he said, "Interesting approach, but no cigar. What you need is the password."

"I don't . . . don't need your goddamn password," Marie gasped, still fighting for breath. "All I needed was a little more time."

He shoved her into a chair and, as his opaque eyes glazed over, rested the AK-47's muzzle on her forehead. "You're fresh out of time."

Feeling as if she were going to faint, Marie closed her eyes and said a quick prayer, regretting all the things she'd never get a chance to do with her boys.

Elgin suddenly lowered the weapon. "On second thought, maybe you're more valuable to me alive. I've been asking myself: Why would Devlin abandon Taggert and come all the way over to this side of the building to save you? Now that I see you, I know why. He must have the hots for you."

Marie hadn't thought about it, but even in her terrified state she felt a slight stirring of pleasure at that thought. Defiantly, she said, "Not for nuthin', Cupid, but I already got a boyfriend."

Elgin backhanded her across the face and Marie felt the salty taste of blood in her mouth. "Don't smart-talk me, bitch," he hissed. "I don't need you that much."

Marie said nothing, but she'd learned an important lesson. This guy had a short fuse and it wasn't a good idea to antagonize him.

He yanked her out of the chair. "Come on, we're gonna go look for your boyfriend."

Dragging her by the collar and holding her in front of him like a shield, he stepped outside into the corridor and bellowed, "*Devlin!* Can you hear me?"

Devlin, still on his knees in the corridor, held his breath and listened.

"I have the woman," Elgin called out. "You'd better remember that the next time you start shooting."

Devlin exhaled sharply. At least Marie was alive. And it appeared that Elgin was heading back to the other side of the building. For a moment he considered trying to ambush him along the way, but he quickly dismissed the idea. There were too many routes back to Taggert's office. If they passed each other, he'd be at one end of the building and Elgin, Marie, and Taggert would be at the other end.

Hunched over, Devlin pounded on the carpeted floor in frustration. It was like playing chess in the dark and not knowing where your opponent's—or your own—pieces were. He sat up abruptly. The chess analogy gave him an idea. In a chess match you defeat your opponent by blocking his options, forcing him into narrow pathways of your choosing. Why couldn't he do that to Elgin?

After a careful mental review of the floor plan, Devlin determined that there were only three possible routes back to Taggert's office. The easiest route involved a portion of a corridor. The other two were more complex, requiring Elgin to pass through several rooms. It could be done, he decided. Seal off the other routes and force Elgin to use the corridor.

As he started out for the first of the two rooms that he had to seal off, he began to formulate a plan

of action once he'd funneled Elgin into the narrow
confines of the corridor.

He wasn't quite sure what he was going to do, but
one thing he did know: If he erred, Marie would die.

32

WHEN DEVLIN ARRIVED AT THE first of the two rooms
that he planned to block, he closed and locked the
door. That, in and of itself, might do the trick. He
didn't think that Elgin would risk giving away his position by knocking a door down. But just to be on the
safe side, he slid a heavy credenza and a couple of
chairs in front of the door. Then he groped his way to
the second room and did the same. Now that the two
alternate routes were shut off, it left only one way for
Elgin to proceed. The corridor.

Knowing he had little time to waste, he went for-
aging for the materials he'd need for his ambush.
He'd never felt more tense. He'd been in some
pretty hairy situations, stared down the muzzle of
more than one gun. And, always, he'd pissed ice
water. So why was his heart racing?

Suddenly his mind flashed on a horrible image.
He was in a Brooklyn funeral parlor, dimly lit, a
tapestry of flowers lining the walls. All of the chairs,
straight-backed, wooden things, were empty except

for two. He looked more closely and saw Marie's boys staring at him, their eyes beseeching him, appealing for some explanation. He tried to speak, but the words wouldn't come.

He shook off the image. There was no time for such thoughts.

With methodical efficiency, he made his way to the kitchen and retrieved a flashbang grenade that he'd taped behind the refrigerator. Once more, he was grateful for his foresight. In the pantry he groped through closets and drawers looking for rope. He didn't find any, but he did find a twenty-five-foot extension cord. It would do.

Next he went back to the gym and ran his hands over the wall until he found the first-aid kit. He emptied its contents and stuffed a roll of gauze and a roll of adhesive tape into his pocket.

He had everything he needed. It was time to set the trap.

With the woman in front of him, it was slow going, but traveling as a twosome had its compensations. Elgin knew Devlin would hang back, unwilling to risk a shot.

Elgin came to a door that he was sure he'd used earlier, but it was locked. He put his shoulder to it and tried to force it, but it wouldn't give. The physical effort reopened his wound, sending a piercing pain into his side. He grabbed Marie by the collar and yanked her around. "Come on," he muttered. "We'll find another way."

◇　　◇　　◇

Devlin knotted the electrical cord about twelve inches up the leg of a conference table. Then he backed out of the room, crawled across the hall and into another room where he secured the other end of the cord to the leg of a desk. His trip wire—strung across the corridor almost a foot off the ground—was in place.

Moving farther down the corridor, he used adhesive tape to secure the flashbang grenade to a doorknob. Then he tied the gauze to the grenade's ring-pin and eased it out slightly so that it would come away with a minimal tug. Being careful not to pull the pin, he continued down the hallway, unraveling the roll of gauze as he went.

The plan was simple enough. Unless Elgin had found another way past him, he had to come down this corridor. He and Marie would trip over the electrical cord. Then, while Elgin was still confused and disoriented, Devlin would yank the grenade's pin, detonating the flash grenade. In the chaos he hoped—prayed—that Marie would get away. To distract Elgin further, Devlin, shielding his eyes from the light, would fire a few bursts from his automatic weapon into the ceiling.

He regretted that aspect of the plan. The narrow, confined corridor was the perfect killing zone. Under other conditions he would rake it with automatic fire, but he couldn't do that and take the chance of hitting Marie.

There was another alternative, one that didn't involve gunfire. He could position himself closer to the trip wire and jump Elgin when the grenade went off. But with one useless arm, hand-to-hand combat was out of the question.

He had to admit, it wasn't the best plan, but he was counting on Elgin's wounds, which he fervently hoped were as painful as his, Marie's reflexes, and a lot of luck.

After several dead ends, Elgin finally found a way to move south. By now he realized that Devlin had locked the doors and he was in a rage. The only thing that pacified him was the thought that with the woman as bait, he would eventually snare Devlin. The thought of what he would do to Devlin sustained him, helping him ignore the throbbing pain in his thigh and side.

They came out of a room and turned south into a corridor. To alert Devlin to their presence, Marie had purposely been talking to Elgin. But every time she said something, he smashed the back of her head with the butt of his AK-47. After the blood began trickling down the back of her neck, she changed her tactics. Looking for an excuse to cry out, she purposely veered into walls so that she could yelp in pain and surprise. Sometimes there was a blow from the rifle, sometimes not.

As they started down the corridor, she realized that it had been a while since she'd said anything. Faking a stumble and falling against the wall, she said, "Ow . . ."

Elgin smashed the butt against the back of her head and she saw stars. *You bastard!* She forced herself not to strike back at him. It would only invite a harder blow. *If I get the chance to—*

Before she could finish the thought, she really tripped over something and fell hard to the floor.

Elgin reached for her. "You stupid—" He caught his ankle on the electrical cord and fell over her. Suddenly there was a deafening explosion—magnified tenfold in the confined space—accompanied by an intense bright light.

"Ahhhh! . . . " Elgin threw a hand up to his eyes to shield them from the painful, illuminated brilliance and fired a burst down the hallway.

He'd been in total darkness for so long that his pupils had dilated to the maximum. Now, the sudden, unexpected two-million-candlepower flash burned into his exposed retinas, feeling like hot needles in his eyes. To protect themselves, his pupils contracted and his tear ducts spilled copious tears.

Blinking furiously to clear his vision, he reached out to grab the woman, but she wasn't there. To his left he caught a blurry glimpse of something moving past him. He spun around, pointed his weapon at the moving smudge, and was about to squeeze the trigger when there was a burst of automatic fire to his front. Dropping to the ground and spinning to meet the new threat, he emptied his clip in the general direction of the gunfire.

Then he heard Devlin yell: "Marie, hide. Don't try to leave the floor."

Elgin instantly understood what had happened and savagely jammed a new clip into his weapon. He rolled over and emptied it in the direction of the fleeing woman.

The grenade fizzled out and in a second it was black and still again. Ignoring the pain in his side, Elgin held his breath and listened with every fiber in his body. If Devlin was going to attack, this was the time. Slowly, he swung the muzzle of his AK-47 in a wide arc, prepared to empty the clip at the slightest noise. But there was no sound.

Elgin stared, wide-eyed, into the darkness that he'd become so used to, but it wasn't quite the same. Instead of a uniform, comforting black void, a huge, distracting orange circle floated in front of him. Temporarily, at least, the flash had burned the image into his retinas, destroying his night vision. For the time being, he was truly blind.

Devlin was pleased with the outcome of his ambush. It appeared that Marie, Elgin's trump card, had gotten away. He didn't know where she'd gone, but it didn't matter. There were plenty of places to hide—too many for Elgin to go looking for her. But not all had gone well. In his haste to gather together the materials for the ambush, he'd lost his handgun. It was small comfort that he still had his submachine gun. Ruefully, he recalled the advice of an army colonel who'd trained him in SWAT team tactics: Two is one; one is none.

Still, in spite of losing his gun, the odds were shifting in his favor. Elgin had lost his night vision and his hostage. There was nothing left for him but to go after Taggert and finish the job that he had set out to do.

And time was against him. Soon, Tommy Nolen would realize what was going on and notify the police. Once reinforcements arrived, Elgin was finished. In the meantime Devlin's job was to protect Taggert until the police arrived. With grim determination, he turned and started back toward the CEO's office.

＊   ＊   ＊

When they'd tripped over the electrical cord and the corridor had suddenly become illuminated, Marie had seen her opportunity and taken it. She knew Elgin might shoot her in the back, but it was a risk she was willing to take—anything to get away from that man. Shielding her eyes from the bright light, she saw an open door ahead and ducked inside as a burst of gunfire shattered the door frame. She dove onto the floor and crawled under the protective canopy of a desk.

Barely breathing, she listened for the telltale sounds of movement. But she heard nothing. After the pandemonium of the explosion and the loud staccato of the automatic gunfire, the silence was almost overwhelming. She knew Elgin was nearby and it took all her willpower to resist the impulse to get up and run. She told herself over and over again that her best defense against Elgin was absolute silence.

As she lay on the floor with her cheek pressed against the carpet, she heard the sound of Elgin's labored breathing and her body tensed. He was coming down the corridor toward her! She bit her lip and held her breath as the breathing got closer and closer, exhaling only when she heard him pass by her door.

Too frightened to move, she lay there, experiencing in the total darkness a dreamlike sensation of being suspended in time and space that was almost comforting. How long had she been there? Five minutes? Five hours? She couldn't be sure. Was there another world outside her darkened world? She could hardly remember.

She shook her head and sat up. The darkness and

fear were turning her mind to mush. She had to stay alert. Cautiously, she got up and felt around the top of the desk. Then she opened the center drawer and felt inside and found what she was looking for. A metal letter opener. It wasn't much of a weapon, but it would have to do. She'd made up her mind: Elgin would never lay another hand on her without a fight.

Groping her way to the door, she came out into the corridor and turned in the direction of the C&C room. Earlier, Michael had shouted a warning to hide and that's exactly what she wanted to do, but she couldn't. Someone had to find a way to get the lights turned back on and she was the only one who could do that.

After Elgin had backed down the corridor, he'd considered looking for the woman; after all, she couldn't have gone very far. But he'd decided against it. This cat-and-mouse game was taking way too much time. He'd done a good job of sealing off the penthouse, but eventually someone from the outside would get in. *Complete the mission,* he told himself, and turned toward the direction of Taggert's office.

"Hey, Loo. What floor is this?" someone called out in the darkness.

"Thirty-seven," Lieutenant Finn said, stopping at the landing to get his breath. "Bobby, check the floor."

As they'd been doing at every floor, one of the cops opened the fire door and, looking up and down the lighted corridor, called out, "Hello! Anyone here?"

He turned back to the lieutenant. "No one, boss."

Having caught his breath again, the lieutenant started up the stairs. "Come on," he said over his shoulder, "we're almost there."

In an effort to save their breaths, the other cops had long since stopped joking and making wisecracks. In silence the five men plodded up the stairs, the only sound, the scraping of five pairs of shoes on the metal-capped steps.

Suddenly the pitch-black stairwell was illuminated by a violent explosion. The force of the blast threw the lieutenant backward onto the other men and they all tumbled down the stairs in a confusion of shouts and screams.

"What happened . . . ?"

"Holy shit . . . "

The lieutenant screamed. "My leg . . . my leg is gone!"

One of the cops, groping on the floor, found his flashlight and turned it on the lieutenant.

"Oh, Jesus . . . Loo . . ." The lieutenant's left leg had been torn away and the stump was spurting blood.

While two cops tended to the injured lieutenant, the others drew the guns and with the beams of their flashlights searched the stairwell for the cause of the explosion.

Another cop grabbed his portable radio. "Central, we've had an explosion on the thirty-eighth floor landing. . . . The lieutenant's hurt bad. Call an ambulance." The cop looked at his commanding officer, who was starting to go into spasms. Once more he keyed the radio mike. "Central, tell them to haul ass."

Clipping the radio back onto his belt, he shined his light up the stairs. In its illumination he saw a

cone-shaped pattern of powder-burn marks radiating
from the top step of the landing up the sides of the
walls. He knew instantly what that meant. "Central,"
he communicated again, "we also need the Bomb
Squad and the TAC unit."

He looked down at the lieutenant, who was slipping into shock. They'd tied a tourniquet but there was
no time to wait for the paramedics to climb up thirty-
eight floors. It would take four of them to carry him
down. Without a word, he and the others dropped
their ropes and crowbars, gently lifted the lieutenant,
and began the long, slow descent to the lobby.

Devlin was almost at Taggert's office when he heard
the muffled explosion. He dropped to his knees and
rested his forehead on the carpet. Who had set off the
explosion?

His mind raced, scrolling through the possibilities.
Elgin must have set a booby trap, and then someone—a security guard? a cop?—had walked into it.
One thing was certain: If help was on the way, it was
going to take a hell of a lot longer. They had to figure
there were more bombs, and department procedure
would require everyone to move a whole lot slower.

Elgin wasn't far behind Devlin when he, too, heard
the explosion. But his reaction was very different. He
was pleased that the device had done its job, but it
also told him that reinforcements were on the way.
The police were delayed, but they would not be
denied. With greater determination, he moved forward in the darkness.

33

As Devlin groped his way along the last stretch of corridor leading to Taggert's office, he focused his thoughts on the best way to let the CEO know he was there. There were a couple of options, none good. He could call out to him, but he didn't know how close Elgin was. He could quietly slip into the office, but that might be dangerous. If he startled Taggert and the CEO had his gun trained on the door, he'd open fire for sure. But all this deliberation could be for nothing, Devlin thought. Gloria's burst of fire earlier might have actually found its mark. Jason Taggert might be dead. Still, one way or the other, Devlin had to go in and find out.

Crouching down to make himself less of a target, he slipped through the narrow opening between the massive oak doors and into the office. Assuming Taggert would hide as far away from the door as possible, Devlin started to crawl awkwardly toward the opposite wall. Suddenly, he felt the barrel of a gun jammed into his ribs and heard the click as the hammer came down on an empty chamber.

Reacting instinctively, he whipped the butt of his submachine gun around and heard a thud as it connected with tissue and bone. He dove on top of the prostrate body and drove the muzzle of his weapon into spongy flesh. He was about to squeeze the trigger when Taggert yelled out, "You son of a bitch—"

Devlin slapped his hand over Taggert's mouth. "Shut up," he hissed. The quick movement had opened his shoulder wound and it started to bleed again. Grimacing in pain, he slid off Taggert.

"My God, I could have killed you," Taggert whispered in disbelief. "I don't know why the gun didn't go off."

Devlin was stunned. In that moment he realized he owed his life to Nick Mangi. The young cop had removed the bullet from the chamber of Taggert's automatic the day of the shareholders' meeting. If he hadn't, Taggert would have emptied the clip into his side.

"Gimme the gun," Devlin whispered. Awkwardly, he jacked a round into the chamber and gave it back to Taggert. Now it was ready to fire. Under other circumstances he would have taken the loaded gun away from the CEO, but with his right hand useless, he needed all the firepower he could get.

Recovering from his initial shock, Taggert said, "Where have you been? I'm worried about Marie. I almost went searching for her, but I figured I didn't stand a chance. Is she . . . ?"

"She's okay . . . I think. How're you? You hit?"

"No, thank God. I still can't believe . . ." He shook his head. "I keep thinking of Gloria falling down that elevator shaft— Christ, what a night. What do we do now?"

"Stay alive. Elgin's on his way back here and he knows he doesn't have a lot of time."

"So let's get out of here."

"There's no place to go. The elevator isn't working and I'm betting the emergency doors have been booby-trapped. Besides, he might be right outside the door for all I know and I have no intention of walking into him."

"So we wait here?" Taggert said disbelievingly.

"That's right."

"Are you crazy? You said yourself—"

"We have the advantage. There are two of us and only one of him. If he wants us, he has to come in and get us."

"But there are two doors."

"I know. You'll cover the one leading to the screening room. I'll cover the one from the corridor." Devlin gripped Taggert's shoulder and felt taut muscles under the custom-made shirt. In his younger days he had probably been a hell of a street fighter, but what they were facing was no barroom brawl. "Taggert, I'm counting on you. Can you do it?"

In the darkness he heard the CEO's constricted voice. "I'll try, Mike."

Jason Taggert was no longer the strident CEO of a powerful company, just a man in a dark room trying to survive.

Devlin positioned Taggert behind a massive cherry-wood credenza facing the door leading into the screening room and gave him his instructions. "Don't shoot unless you know Elgin is in front of you. He may fire off a couple of recon rounds to make you return fire and give your position away. And another thing. What ever happens, don't move from this spot."

"Why not?"

"Because in this darkness it's the only way we can control fields of fire. I can't return fire if I don't know where you are at all times. One more thing. No matter what, no talking."

"But what if I—"

"Not a word. If he hears you, he'll know where you are and you're a dead man."

Satisfied that Taggert knew what he had to do, Devlin crawled back to a position that had an unobstructed field of fire on the doors he'd come through earlier. As he sat, braced against the wall waiting for Elgin, he thought of the irony of the situation. As a TAC team member it had been his job to go in after barricaded targets. Now he was the target.

Marie finally made it back to the C&C room. It had taken her a long time because she had to use trial and error to find her way through the maze of rooms and because she was so jumpy that every time she heard a noise—real or imagined—she ducked into a room and refused to move until she was certain there was no danger.

This time she locked the door behind her and stuffed rolled-up newspapers under the door so the light wouldn't penetrate into the hallway. Then she turned on the computer and stared at the blank screen. Now that she was there, she had no idea what to do next.

Down in the tenth-floor C&C room Otis Royal had been lapsing in and out of consciousness since Elgin had left, sinking ever deeper into shock. He'd pretended he was unconscious when Elgin had been working on the computer, but with half-closed eyes he'd carefully watched what Elgin had been doing. He understood few of the strange commands that appeared and disappeared on the screen, but there was one thing that he did understand and he'd memorized it: the password. Since Elgin had left him for dead, he'd been saying it and over again. It was what had sustained him.

He stared at the keyboard in frustration. It was no more than a foot away, but with his wrists and ankles taped to the chair, it might as well have been a hundred miles.

Royal knew he was dying. He could feel himself getting weaker and weaker. If he didn't do something right then, it would be too late. Mustering all his energy, he threw his body forward and the chair slid forward an inch. He grimaced from the pain and did it again. The chair moved a little closer. After five more thrusts, he was close enough to lean his long torso over the console.

With tears of agony streaming down his face, he leaned over and put his mouth on a pencil. Using his lips and tongue, he worked the tip of the pencil into his mouth. Then, using the eraser end as a pointer, he leaned over the keyboard and pecked the letter *T*. He tried to strike the *A* key, but he hit the *S* instead. Blinking to clear his vision, he laboriously pressed the delete key, then the *A* key. As he struck the *R* key, he gagged and spat the pencil out. It rolled across the desk, coming to rest teetering on the edge.

Royal blinked to clear his vision, but the room was

becoming darker and his field of vision had narrowed
to a very small circle. He leaned forward, realizing
that if he didn't grab the pencil properly it would fall
to the floor. He winced at the excruciating pain, and
gently gripped the pencil in his mouth again. When
he looked down at the keyboard he could barely see
the letter *G*. Just as he tapped the letter, the small
cone of vision closed. The pencil fell to the floor and
Royal's head dropped forward.

It had been so quiet that Devlin, exhausted from tension and loss of blood, had been dozing off. Suddenly
there was a loud thumping sound and the two oak
doors crashed open. Devlin trained his weapon in the
general direction of the doors and held his breath,
anticipating an attack.

From the opposite end of the room Taggert
opened fire at the sound. Silently, Devlin cursed.
Elgin had thrown something against the doors to
draw fire and the inexperienced Taggert had reacted
to it. But Devlin couldn't really blame the CEO. His
was a rarefied world of impeccably furnished board-
rooms, corporate jets, and power lunches in four-star
restaurants. A world where *predators* and *prey* were
figures of speech, not reality. Nothing in his background had prepared him for this moment.

Devlin sized up their situation: Elgin now knew
they were in here. Worse, Devlin had counted
Taggert's shots. The CEO had only one round left.
Whatever advantage he and Taggert might have had
had disappeared.

As if things couldn't get worse, Devlin heard a
rustling sound and realized that Taggert was moving

out of his position. A few seconds passed. *Goddamn it!* Now he wasn't sure where the CEO was.

The discharge of gunfire in reaction to the thrown fire extinguisher had told Elgin what he wanted to know. Taggert was inside. Devlin was too disciplined to do anything that stupid. He didn't know where the ex-cop was, but it didn't really matter anymore. It was payback time. There was no tomorrow.

Crawling toward the doors, Elgin decided on his final strategy. It was too late for caution. He would move about the room until he flushed out Taggert. Then, in the dark, the CEO would pay for his acts. He gently patted the small sheath that hung from a clip on his belt, making sure the scalpel was still there.

Devlin heard the sound of a vase falling over and hitting the carpet. He swung his weapon in that direction and swore under his breath. Elgin was in the room.

Marie had been staring at the blank screen, cupping her chin in her hands, wondering what to do, when she saw the letter *T* appear on the screen. Then the letter S was deleted, replaced by the letter *A*. Then the letter *R* appeared. The typing stopped.

"Tar?" she said aloud, wondering if the word was the message or just the beginning of one. Almost fifteen seconds later the letter *G* appeared. The typing stopped again.

Staring at the screen, she realized it was Otis and tears welled up in her eyes. Since this madness had started she'd been wondering what had become of him. She'd hoped he'd been able to avoid Elgin, but now, seeing these letters haltingly appear on the screen, she feared the worst.

Puzzled, she stared at the letters on the screen: *T-A-R-G*. What could they mean? Suddenly, it hit her: Otis had given her the password!

She typed the letters at the DOS prompt, but nothing happened. She ran her fingers through her hair in exasperation. "Okay," she said, talking to the screen, "it can't be the whole password. Think. What could the rest of it be? What would Elgin use as a password?"

As she stared at the four letters on the screen, it suddenly came to her. "Of course!" With trembling fingers, she typed *T-A-R-G-E-T*, and after what seemed like an eternity, her familiar menu appeared on the screen.

With tears of joy, she quickly typed the commands that took her into the sysops file and one by one deleted all the commands that Elgin had added. Then she went into the setup file and, one by one, began to reverse all of Elgin's instructions.

Devlin heard a noise to his left. He turned his weapon in that direction and remained motionless. Then he heard the muffled sounds of someone bumping into furniture. Was it Taggert bumbling around in the dark again? Elgin getting careless? Or Elgin purposely trying to spook Taggert into giving his position away? Devlin, exhausted and weakened by loss of blood, was losing his sharpness and he didn't know how much longer he could go on with this cat-and-mouse game. What he wanted to do more than anything else in the world was to stand up and start blasting away. But he couldn't do that—not with Taggert somewhere in the room.

It suddenly occurred to him that if the sounds were made by Elgin, he was being outflanked. Could Elgin know his position? No. He hadn't made a sound. Still, it was time to relocate, but with Elgin maneuvering about in the same space, how could he be sure he wouldn't bump into him? Then a thought occurred to him: the middle of the room!

All night Devlin had been moving through rooms by hugging the walls because it was easier to orient himself. But there was another, more primal reason: a wall provided a greater sense of security. Even in total darkness, exposing himself in a wide-open space went against all his instincts. Assuming Elgin felt the same way, there was little chance of running into him in the middle of the room.

Painfully, Devlin got to his feet and, crouching, carefully started to move across the room. Just as he got to the center, he heard a strange, faint humming noise. He stopped and cocked his head. It was a familiar sound . . . like a motor. . . . An elevator! In that instant he realized two things: Marie had found a way to turn the power back on, and he was standing, exposed, in the middle of the room!

Before he could react, several things happened simultaneously. The room began to hum with the activating motors of fax machines and computers, which after hours of oppressive silence sounded unusually loud. The electric shutters, reactivating in the default mode, whirred and, one by one, began to open. Then, suddenly, the office was bathed in harsh bright light as the overhead fluorescent lights came on.

He dove for the cover of the conference table, but as he did, there was a burst of automatic fire from his left. A searing hot stab in his leg spun him around. He crashed into the side of Taggert's desk and the collision jarred his weapon out of his hand. Squinting through painful, watery eyes, he desperately clawed out for it, but a hand seized the back of his head and slammed his face into the carpet.

Elgin jammed the muzzle into the small of his back. "One move," he said, "and you're an instant paraplegic."

He kicked Devlin's weapon away and yanked him to a kneeling position. "Where's Taggert?" he asked, training the AK-47 on him.

Devlin, still squinting from the harsh overhead lights, gazed around the office. With overturned furniture everywhere and bullet holes in the walls and ceiling, it looked like a battleground. And he and Elgin looked like battle-hardened veterans. The front of Elgin's military fatigues was covered with coagulated blood. The right sleeve of his own shirt was saturated with blood, his hands were stained red, and a fresh bright-red stain was expanding across his pants leg.

Devlin shook his head, acting as though he were bewildered. It wasn't a stretch. He'd taken this job a little over three weeks ago because he thought it was going to be a breeze. *What a joke!* Despite his pain—and the certain knowledge that he was going to die—he grinned.

He looked up into Elgin's watery black eyes, which were now closed to mere slits. "Beats the shit out of me," he said. "I've been looking for him all night."

Elgin's kick to Devlin's chest slammed him against Taggert's desk. The ex-Phoenix assassin loomed over Devlin, glaring down at him with an all-consuming hatred. He wanted desperately to empty a clip into that smirking face, but he needed him. With the lights back on it was only a matter of minutes before reinforcements came flooding through those doors. He didn't have the time to look for Taggert. Devlin would have to tell him where he was.

He grabbed Devlin's collar and yanked him to his feet. "Where is he?"

"I don't know."

Elgin slammed the rifle butt into Devlin's wounded right shoulder, spinning him around. "Where is he?" he repeated.

Devlin, writhing in pain, held on to Taggert's desk for support and found himself looking straight down at the beaker of the new and improved acid that Taggert was so proud of. And there, on the floor just beyond the edge of the desk, he saw Taggert's custom-made Italian shoes sticking out. The CEO was literally under Elgin's nose.

Elgin yanked Devlin around and lowered the weapon to his crotch. His opaque eyes went flat. "Last chance, hero. Where is he?"

Devlin let his eyes flick to the mahogany doors that concealed Taggert's liquor cabinet and entertainment system.

Elgin, catching the furtive glance, smiled and backed away cautiously. "My guess is behind door number one," he said. As he started to turn, Devlin scooped up the beaker and smashed it against Elgin's head.

Elgin howled as the powerful acid began to eat into his face and eyes. In torment, he blindly fired a burst, chewing up the rug where Devlin had been standing.

But Devlin wasn't there. After he'd thrown the acid, he'd rolled across Taggert's desk, ducked down, and come face-to-face with the wide-eyed CEO.

From their protected position both men watched Elgin writhing in agony as the powerful acid ate through his flesh. Elgin cursed and stumbled about the room, randomly firing bursts from his weapon.

Suddenly, Devlin heard Marie call his name.

"Don't come in here," he yelled. "Don't—"

It was too late. She barged through the oak doors, froze at the horrifying sight of Elgin's destroyed face, and screamed.

Devlin saw it all happening in slow motion. Elgin, blind and driven half insane by the burning acid, heard the scream and spun around to face Marie. The muzzle of the AK-47 came up. Simultaneously, Devlin snatched the automatic pistol out of Taggert's hand and stood. "Elgin," he shouted. "I'm here!"

Hesitating for just an instant, Elgin turned the weapon toward his tormentor. As he did, the round from Devlin's gun impacted with the stock of the weapon and tore it out of his hands. Stumbling back, Elgin crashed into Marie and locked his arm around her.

Devlin dove across the desk and drove his left fist into Elgin's throat. Gagging for breath, Elgin let Marie go, but he blindly hurled himself onto Devlin.

The two men—barely recognizable as men, looking more like beasts covered with blood and singed flesh—rolled over and over, each trying to strangle the other. It was a contest Devlin couldn't win. His right arm hung limp and lifeless as Elgin's fingers wrapped around Devlin's neck, powered by an adrenal rage.

Taggert had just leaped over the desk to help when Devlin managed to plant both his feet in Elgin's midsection. As pin spots swirled before his eyes, Devlin leg-pressed violently forward. Off balance, Elgin lost his grip and tumbled backward. Behind him, a floor-to-ceiling window, already fragmented by gunfire, gave way, and for one fleeting instant Elgin hung suspended in space.

The next instant Elgin's body vanished, ripped downward by gravity, and a long, howling scream floated on the morning air.

Recalling what Elgin had said to Gloria, Devlin muttered, "You're right, Elgin. That first step is a bitch."

As he fell back to the floor amid a shower of broken glass, Marie rushed toward him. Her blood-stained clothes were torn and her short hair was matted from perspiration. Streaks of eyeliner traced the paths of her tears.

"Michael . . . oh, God . . . look at you." She bent over him. "Are you okay?"

Wearily, he tilted his head. "What the hell did you think you were doing, barging in here like that?"

She smiled. "Making sure you weren't dead, goddamn it." She wiped at her eyes. "I was so . . . so scared. I thought you were—"

He grabbed her hand, pressed tight. "Well, it was a stupid thing to do. The next time—"

Suddenly, Marie began to giggle. As her giggling turned into a full-throated laugh, she looked up at Taggert. "Did you hear that?" she said, still laughing. "The 'next time.'" She turned back to Devlin. "Michael, if you want me to wrestle psychos for a living, you're going to have to pay me a lot more than you do now."

"We'll work something out," he whispered, and his hand pressed tighter.

She put her finger to his lips. "It's a deal," she said softly.

As she tended to his wounds, a beam of light, reflecting off a building across the street, shone on Devlin's face. Wearily, he turned his head toward the windows. A new dawn was painting a soft, rosy glow on the glass-and-steel skyscraper across the street. Although it was hours until the real workday began, lights in dozens of offices were winking on as ambitious workers arrived to get an early start.

Suddenly there was a loud commotion and five fatigue-clad TAC team officers burst into the room, weapons at the ready. Nick Mangi spotted Devlin and pulled his ski mask off. "Jesus, Mike, are you okay?"

Devlin grinned. "Damn it, Mangi, you're out of position again. Look," he said, nodding toward the other TAC team members. "You're blocking everyone's field of fire."

Taggert chuckled. "Listen to him," he said to Mangi. He turned to Devlin, held his gaze. "The man knows what he's talking about."